BATMAN
OVERDRIVE

WRITTEN BY
Shea Fontana

ILLUSTRATED BY
Marcelo DiChiara

COLORED BY
Hilary Sycamore

LETTERED BY
Corey Breen

BATMAN CREATED BY
BOB KANE WITH BILL FINGER

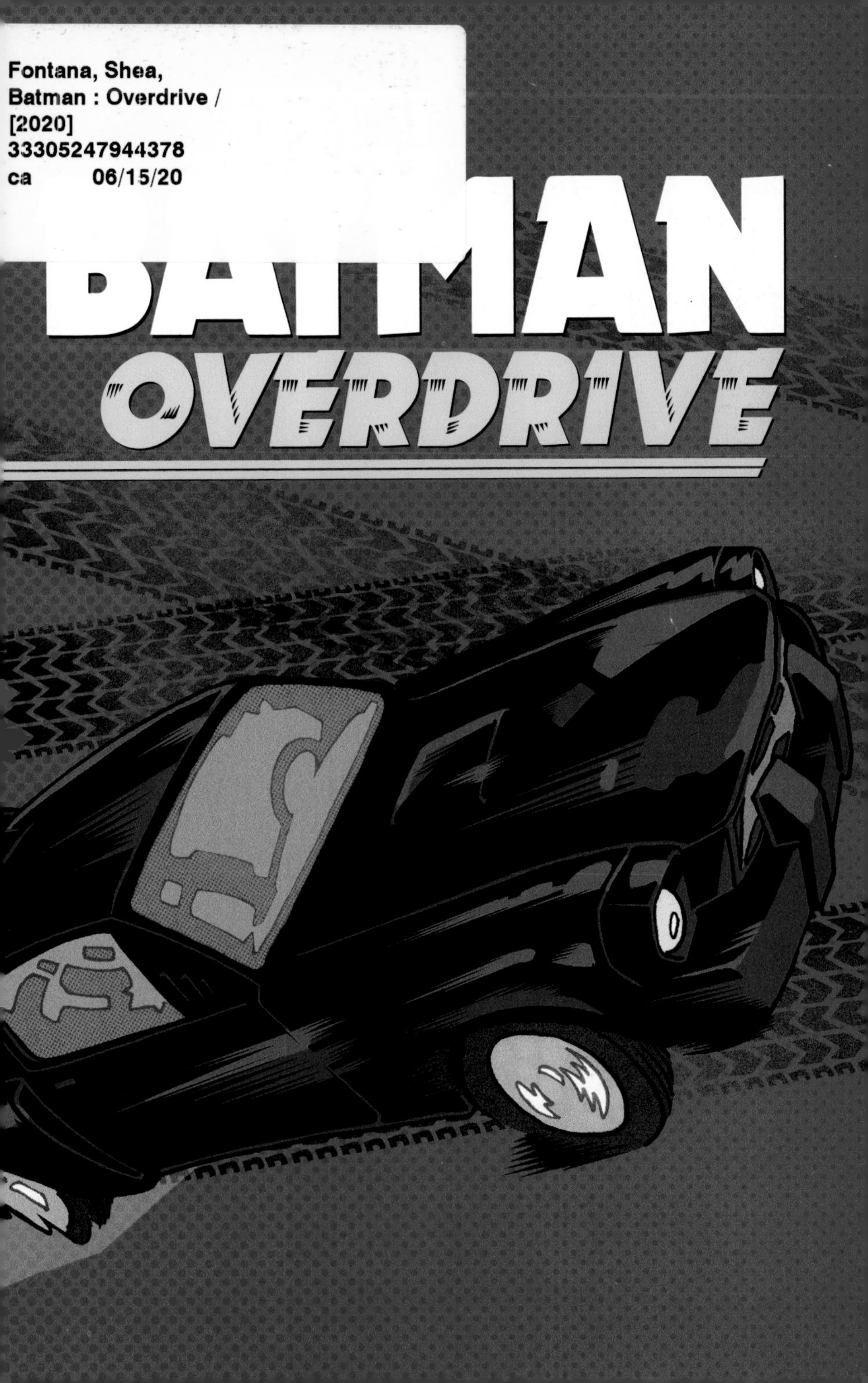
OVERDRIVE

LAUREN BISOM & JIM CHADWICK Editors

DIEGO LOPEZ Associate Editor

STEVE COOK Design Director – Books

AMIE BROCKWAY-METCALF Publication Design

BOB HARRAS Senior VP – Editor-in-Chief, DC Comics

MICHELE R. WELLS VP & Executive Editor, Young Reader

DAN DiDIO Publisher

JIM LEE Publisher & Chief Creative Officer

BOBBIE CHASE VP – New Publishing Initiatives & Talent Development

DON FALLETTI VP – Manufacturing Operations & Workflow Management

LAWRENCE GANEM VP – Talent Services

ALISON GILL Senior VP – Manufacturing & Operations

HANK KANALZ Senior VP – Publishing Strategy & Support Services

DAN MIRON VP – Publishing Operations

NICK J. NAPOLITANO VP – Manufacturing Administration & Design

NANCY SPEARS VP – Sales

BATMAN: OVERDRIVE

DC Comics, 2900 West Alameda Ave., Burbank, CA 91505
Printed by LSC Communications, Crawfordsville, IN, USA.
1/24/20.
First Printing.
ISBN: 978-1-4012-8356-8

Library of Congress Cataloging-in-Publication Data

Names: Fontana, Shea, author. | DiChiara, Marcelo, artist. | Sycamore,
Hilary, colourist. | Breen, Corey, letterer.
Title: Batman : overdrive / author, Shea Fontana ; artist, Marcelo DiChiara ;
colorist, Hilary Sycamore ; letterer, Corey Breen.
Description: Burbank, CA : DC Comics, [2020] | Audience: Ages 10-14 |
Audience: Grades 4-6 | Summary: Teenage loner, pre-Batman Bruce Wayne
hones his detective and combat skills as he scours the underbelly of
Gotham looking for clues, and begins building the Batmobile while still
processing the pain of his parents' death.
Identifiers: LCCN 2019041972 | ISBN 9781401283568 (paperback) | ISBN
9781779503664 (ebook)
Subjects: LCSH: Graphic novels. | CYAC: Graphic novels. | Mystery and
detective stories. | Grief--Fiction. | Self-actualization
(Psychology)--Fiction.
Classification: LCC PZ7.7.F656 Bat 2020 | DDC 741.5/973--dc23
LC record available at https://lccn.loc.gov/2019041972

PEFC Certified

This product is from
sustainably managed
forests and controlled
sources

PEFC

PEFC/29-31-337   www.pefc.org

Table of Contents

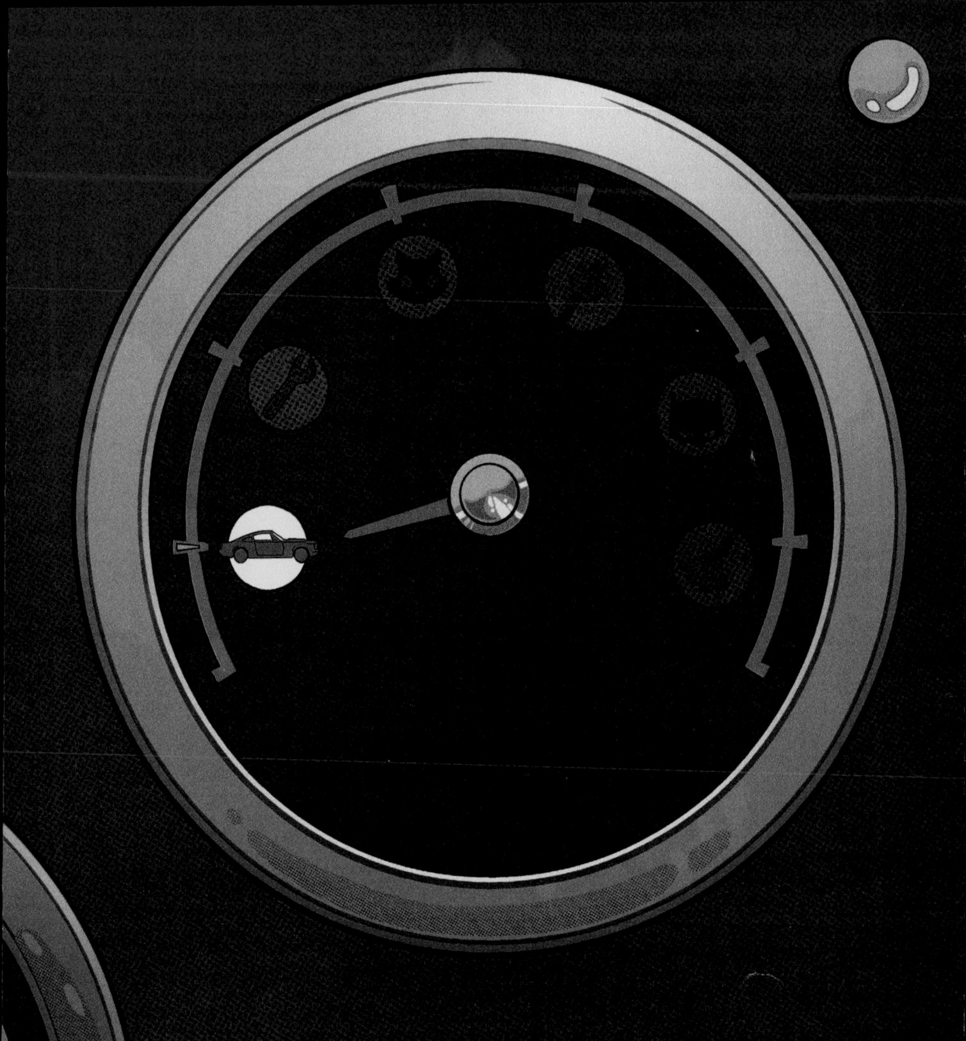

START YOUR ENGINES

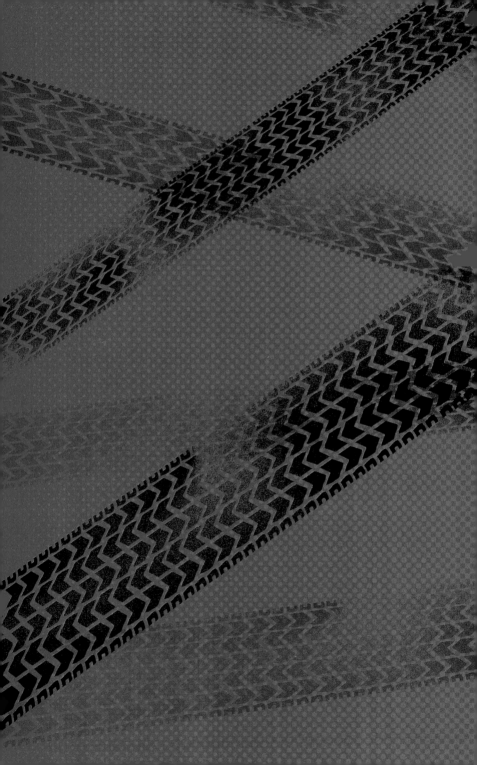

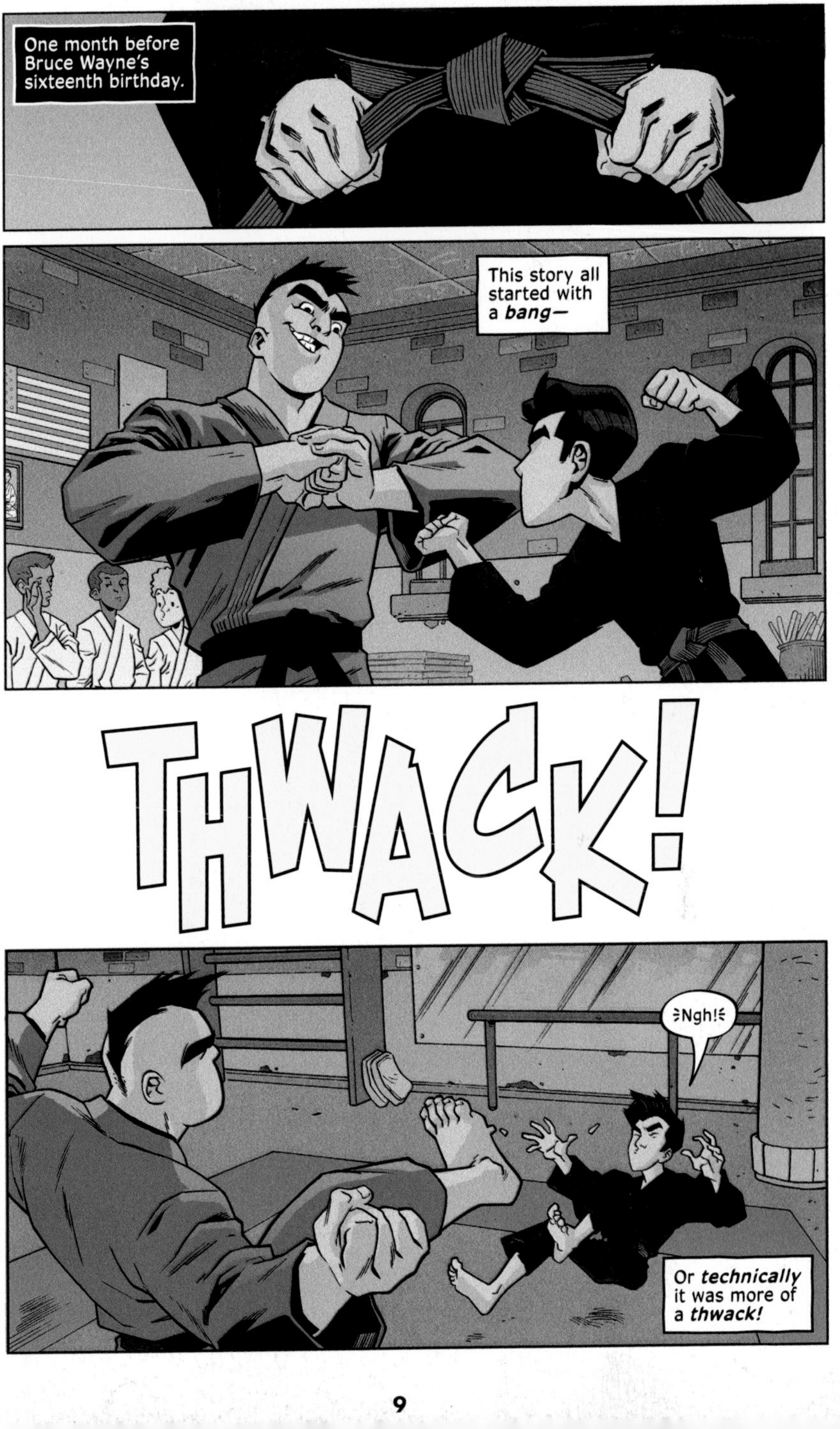
One month before Bruce Wayne's sixteenth birthday.
This story all started with a *bang*—
THWACK!
Ngh!
Or *technically* it was more of a *thwack!*

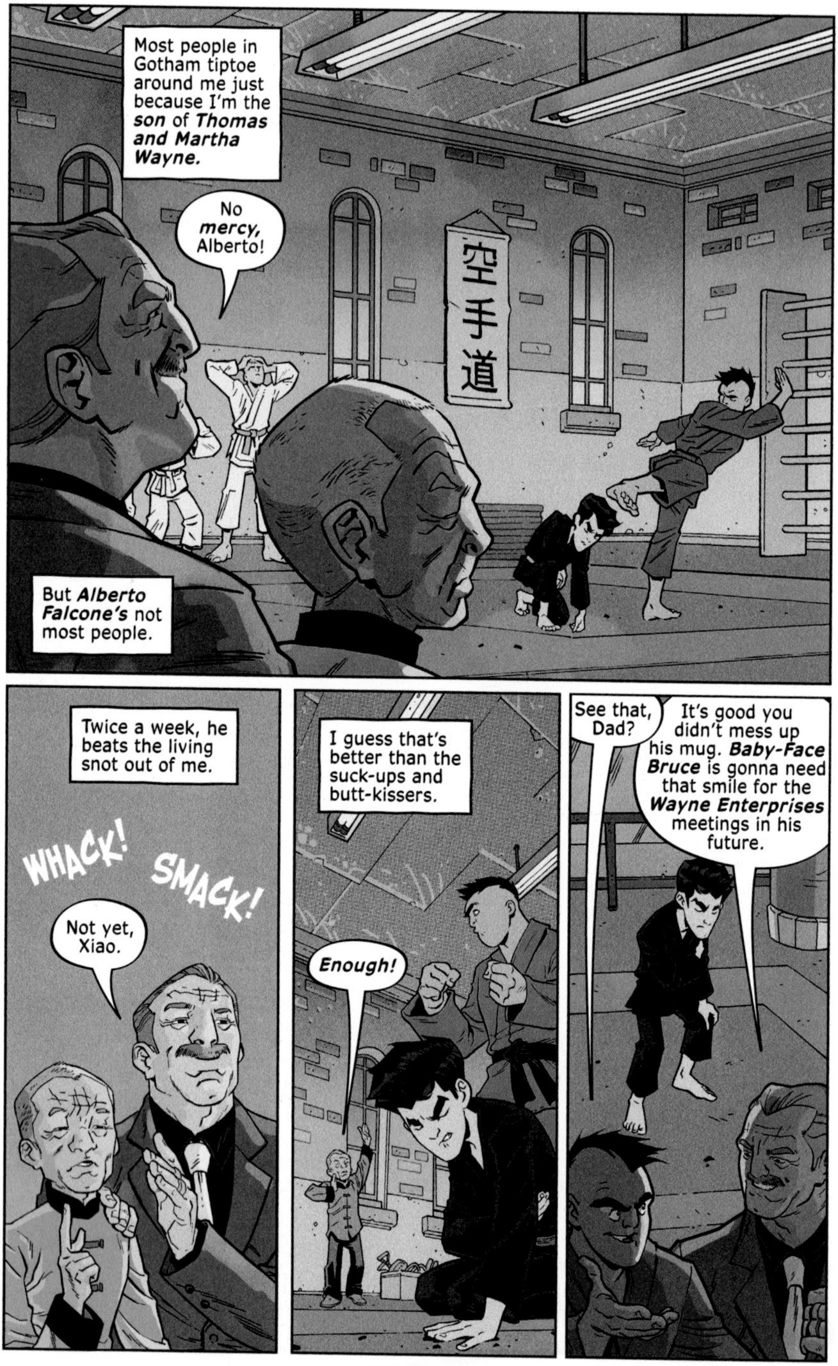
Most people in Gotham tiptoe around me just because I'm the *son* of *Thomas and Martha Wayne.*
No *mercy,* Alberto!
空手道
But *Alberto Falcone's* not most people.
Twice a week, he beats the living snot out of me.
WHACK!
SMACK!
Not yet, Xiao.
I guess that's better than the suck-ups and butt-kissers.
Enough!
See that, Dad?
It's good you didn't mess up his mug. *Baby-Face Bruce* is gonna need that smile for the *Wayne Enterprises* meetings in his future.

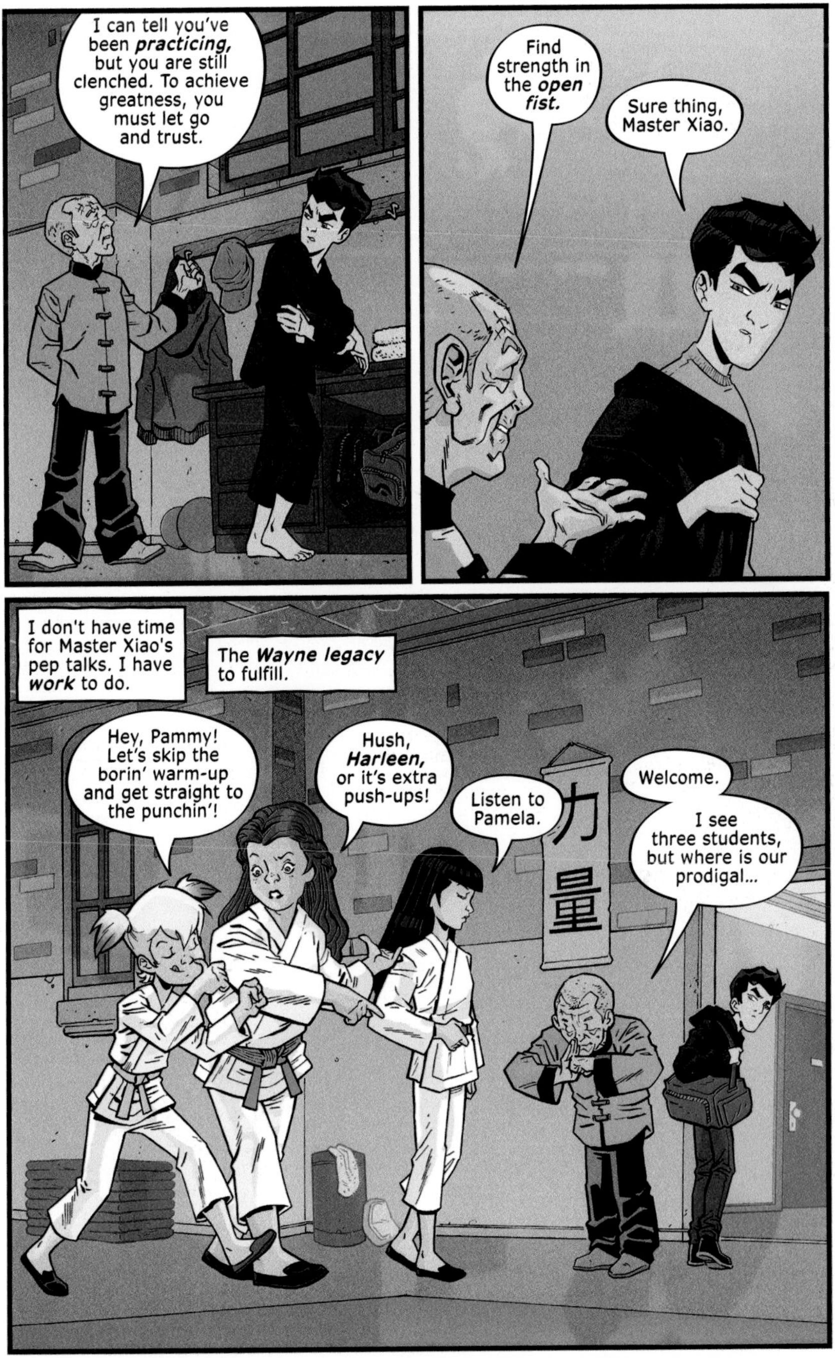
I can tell you've been *practicing,* but you are still clenched. To achieve greatness, you must let go and trust.
Find strength in the *open fist.*
Sure thing, Master Xiao.
I don't have time for Master Xiao's pep talks. I have *work* to do.
The *Wayne legacy* to fulfill.
Hey, Pammy! Let's skip the borin' warm-up and get straight to the punchin'!
Hush, *Harleen,* or it's extra push-ups!
Listen to Pamela.
Welcome.
I see three students, but where is our prodigal...
力量

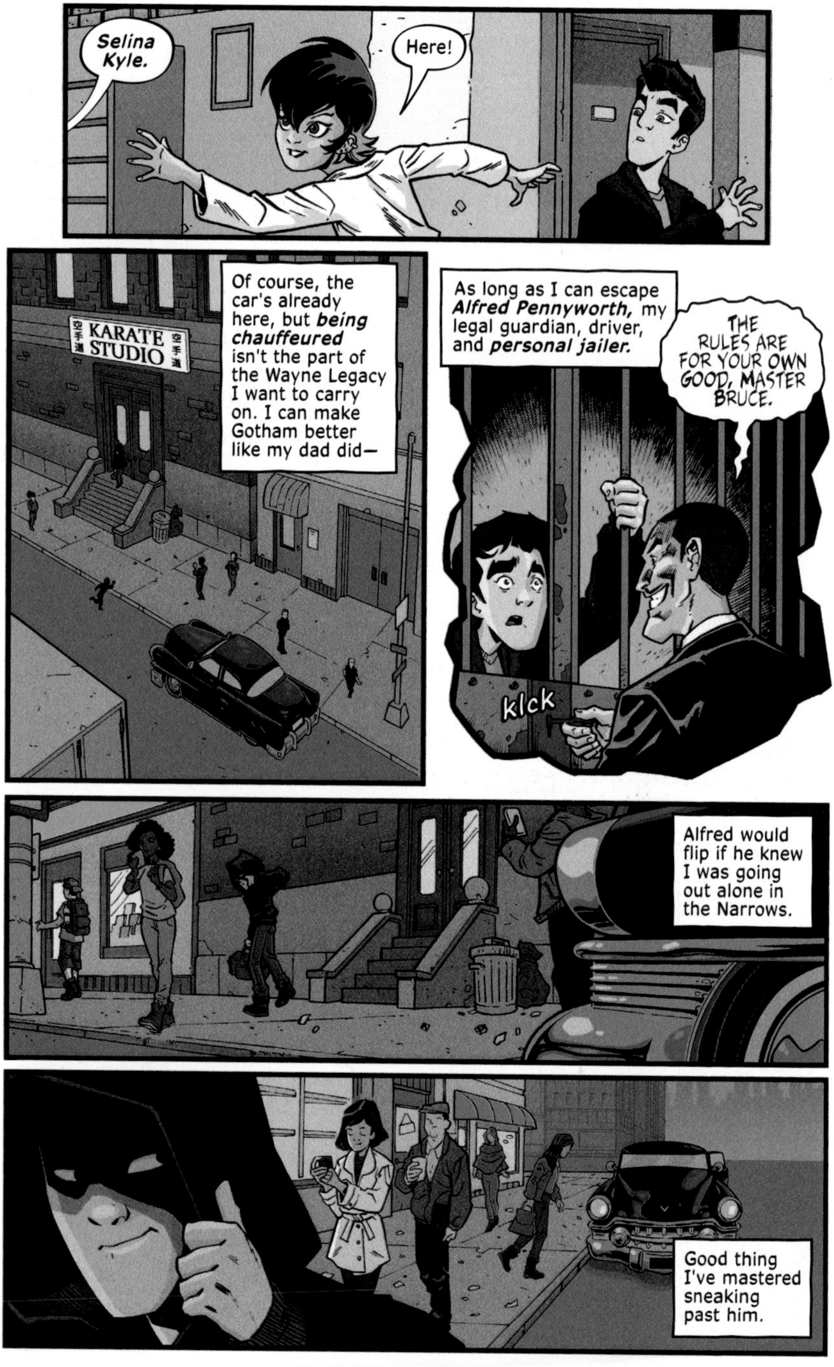
Selina Kyle.
Here!
Of course, the car's already here, but being chauffeured isn't the part of the Wayne Legacy I want to carry on. I can make Gotham better like my dad did—
KARATE STUDIO
As long as I can escape Alfred Pennyworth, my legal guardian, driver, and personal jailer.
THE RULES ARE FOR YOUR OWN GOOD, MASTER BRUCE.
klck
Alfred would flip if he knew I was going out alone in the Narrows.
Good thing I've mastered sneaking past him.

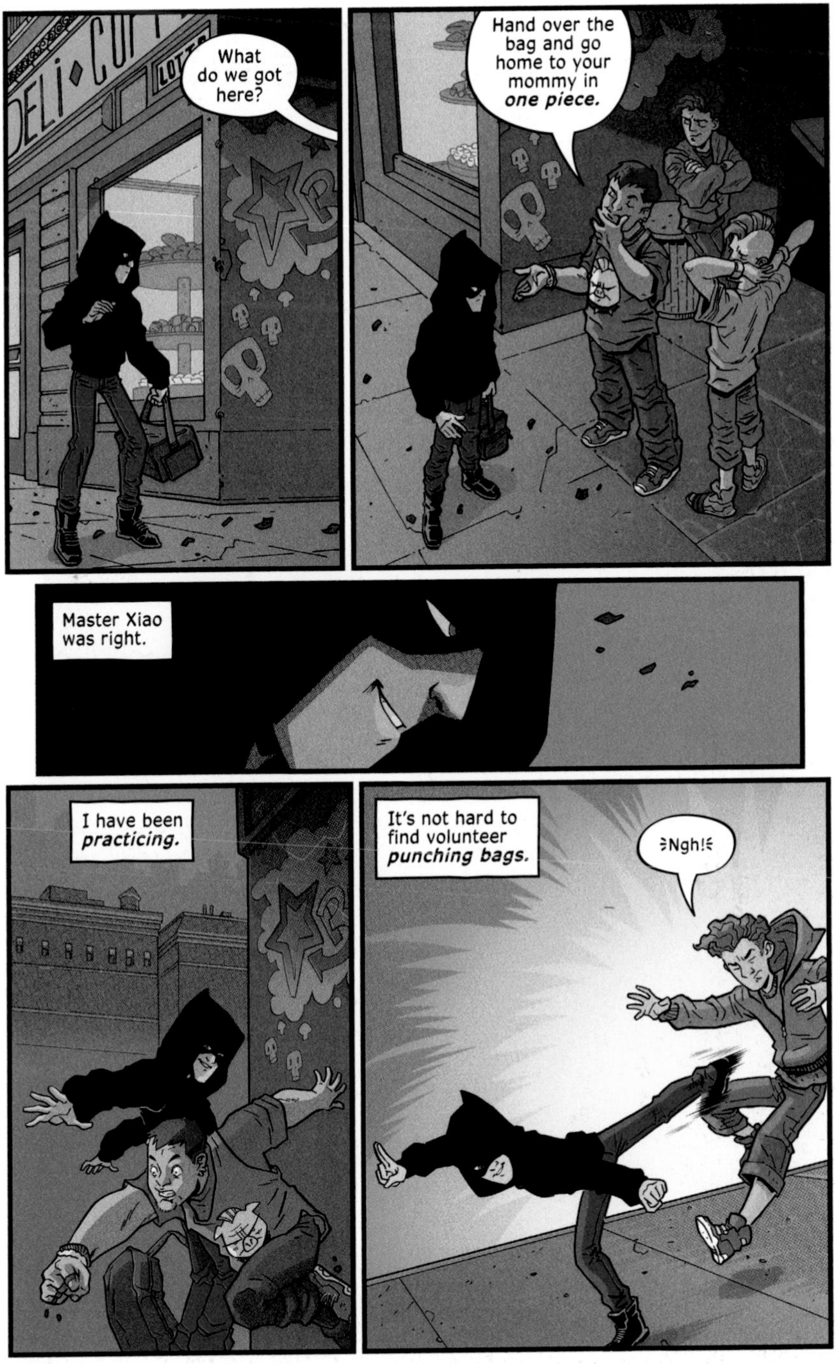
What do we got here?
Hand over the bag and go home to your mommy in *one piece.*
Master Xiao was right.
I have been *practicing.*
It's not hard to find volunteer *punching bags.*
Ngh!

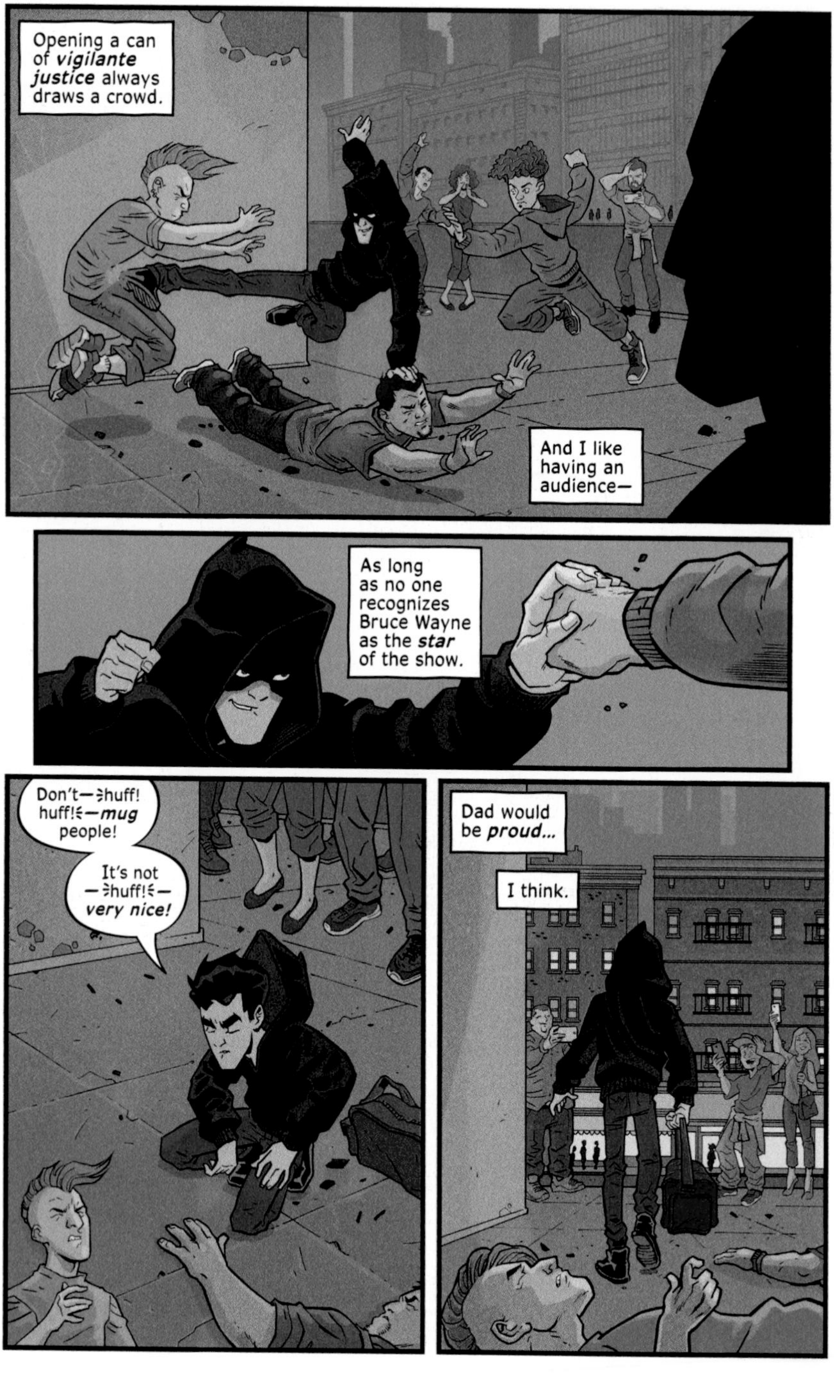
Opening a can of *vigilante justice* always draws a crowd.
And I like having an audience—
As long as no one recognizes Bruce Wayne as the *star* of the show.
Don't—huff! huff!—*mug* people!
It's not —huff!— *very nice!*
Dad would be *proud...*
I think.

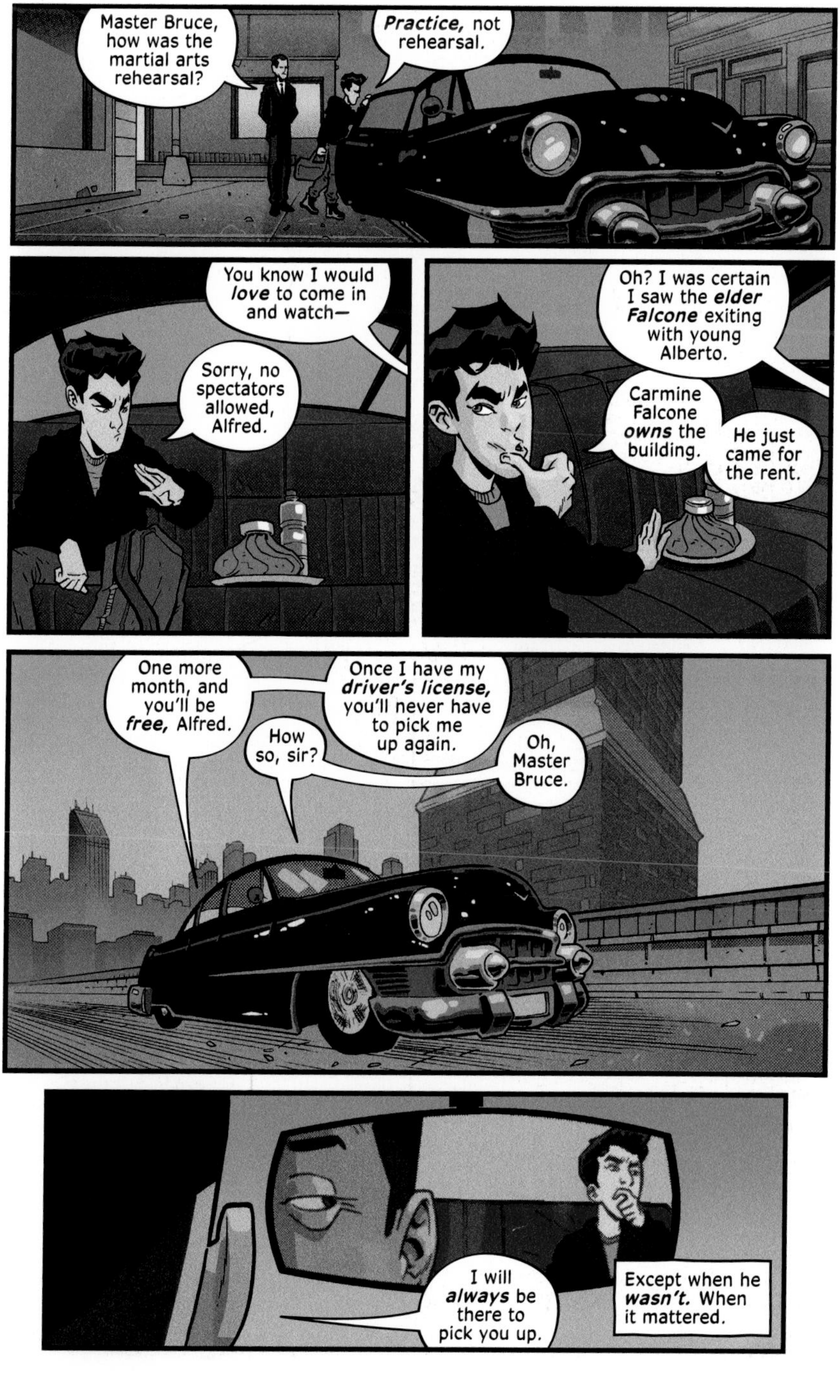
Master Bruce, how was the martial arts rehearsal?
Practice, not rehearsal.
You know I would *love* to come in and watch—
Sorry, no spectators allowed, Alfred.
Oh? I was certain I saw the *elder Falcone* exiting with young Alberto.
Carmine Falcone *owns* the building.
He just came for the rent.
One more month, and you'll be *free,* Alfred.
How so, sir?
Once I have my *driver's license,* you'll never have to pick me up again.
Oh, Master Bruce.
I will *always* be there to pick you up.
Except when he *wasn't.* When it mattered.

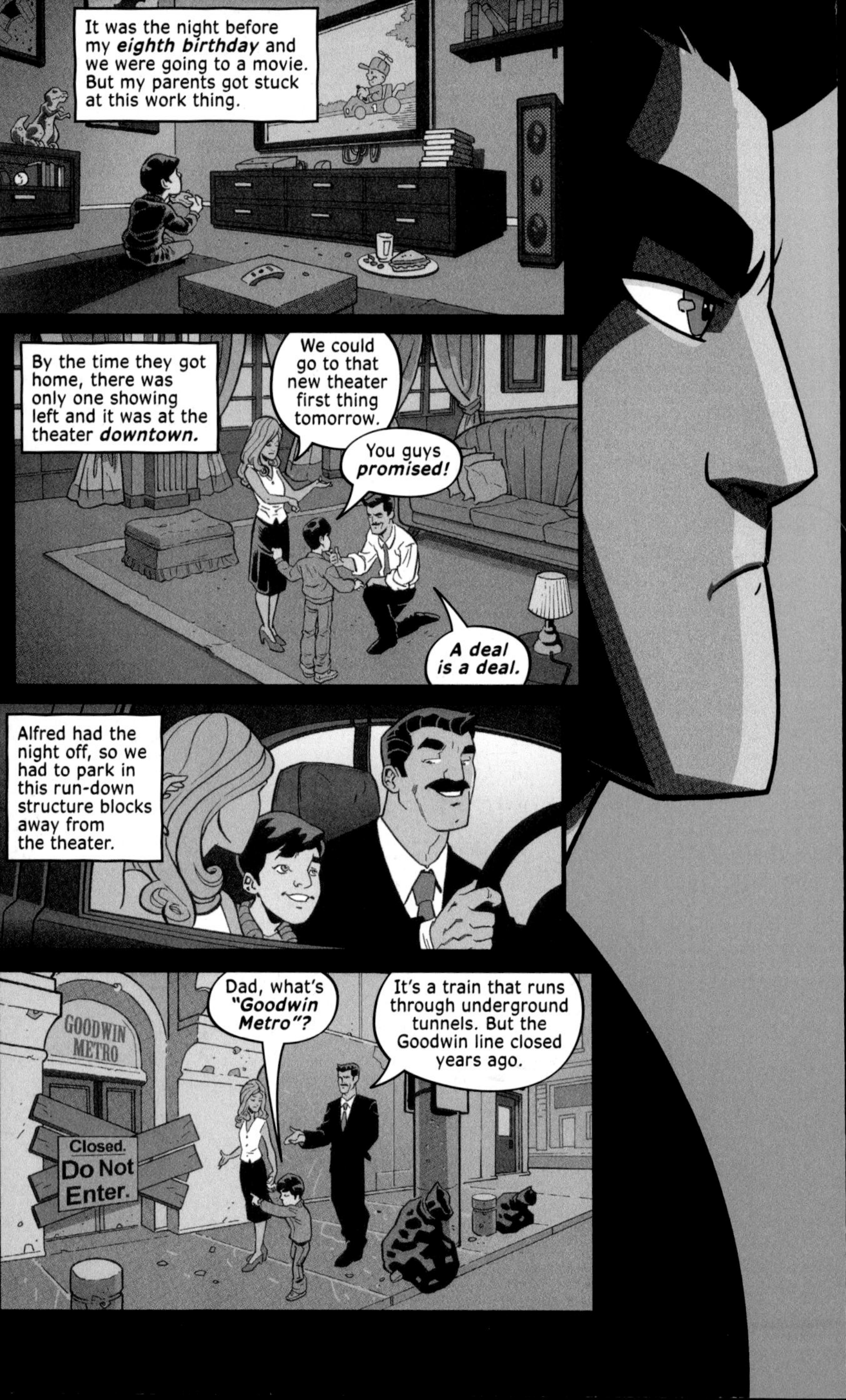
It was the night before my *eighth birthday* and we were going to a movie. But my parents got stuck at this work thing.
By the time they got home, there was only one showing left and it was at the theater *downtown.*
We could go to that new theater first thing tomorrow.
You guys *promised!*
A deal is a deal.
Alfred had the night off, so we had to park in this run-down structure blocks away from the theater.
GOODWIN METRO
Closed. Do Not Enter.
Dad, what's *"Goodwin Metro"?*
It's a train that runs through underground tunnels. But the Goodwin line closed years ago.

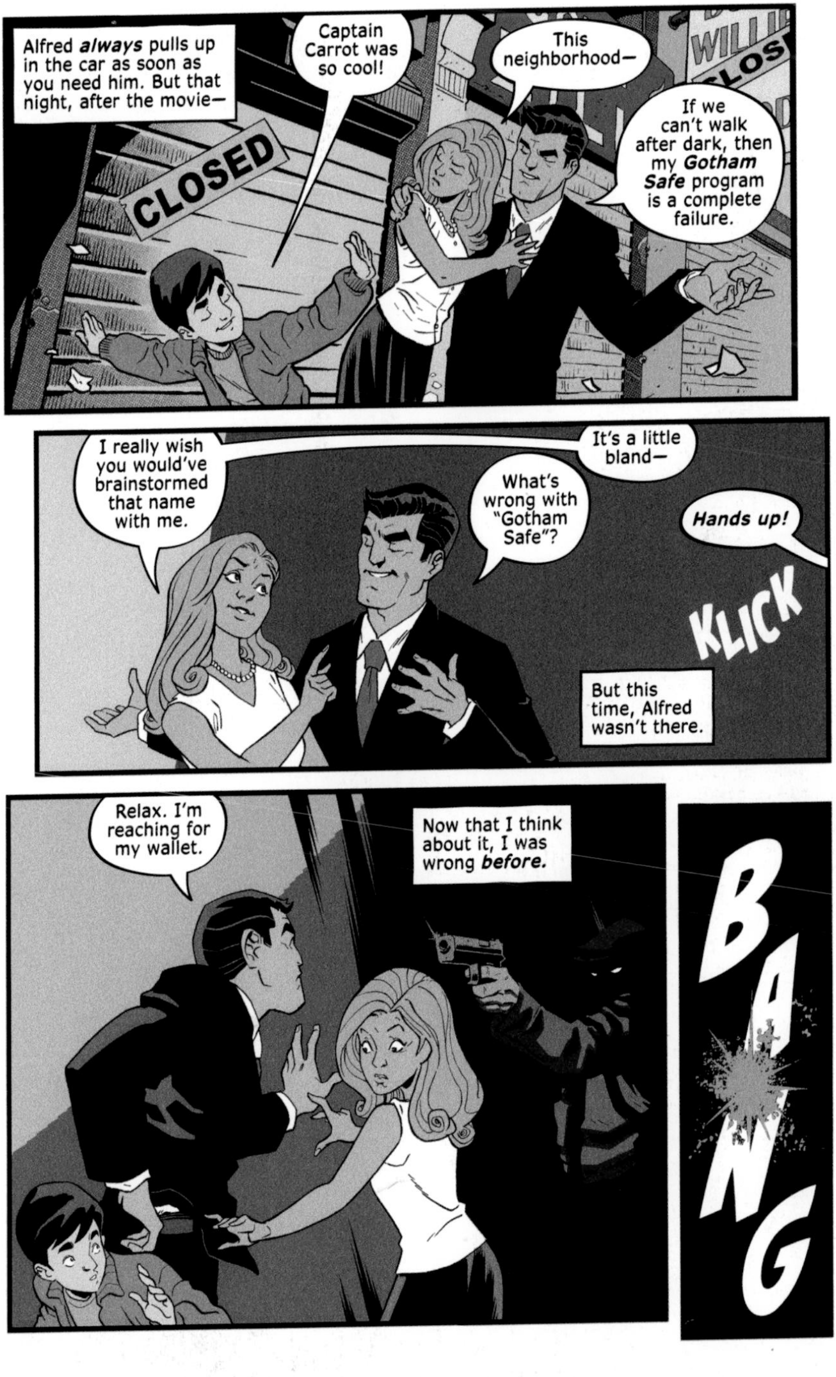

Alfred *always* pulls up in the car as soon as you need him. But that night, after the movie—
Captain Carrot was so cool!
CLOSED
This neighborhood—
If we can't walk after dark, then my *Gotham Safe* program is a complete failure.
It's a little bland—
I really wish you would've brainstormed that name with me.
What's wrong with "Gotham Safe"?
Hands up!
KLICK
But this time, Alfred wasn't there.
Relax. I'm reaching for my wallet.
Now that I think about it, I was wrong *before.*
BANG

Wayne Manor. Now.

That was the *BANG* that started my story.

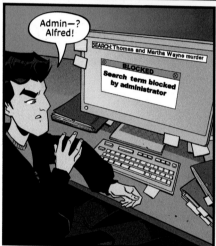

Admin—? Alfred!

SEARCH: Thomas and Martha Wayne murder

BLOCKED
Search term blocked by administrator

The cops claim that they got the guy who did it.

But no trial means this "killer" was never *proven guilty* in court.

Wayne T.

Suspect in custody.

JACK PERCY, SUSPECT IN WAYNE MURDER, DIES BEFORE TRIAL.

My dad was too cool to let some wimp like that Percy guy murder him.

There have to be more clues out there.

If I'm gonna make dad proud, *I* have to solve my parents' murders.

Master Bruce?

SEARCH: Thomas Wayne

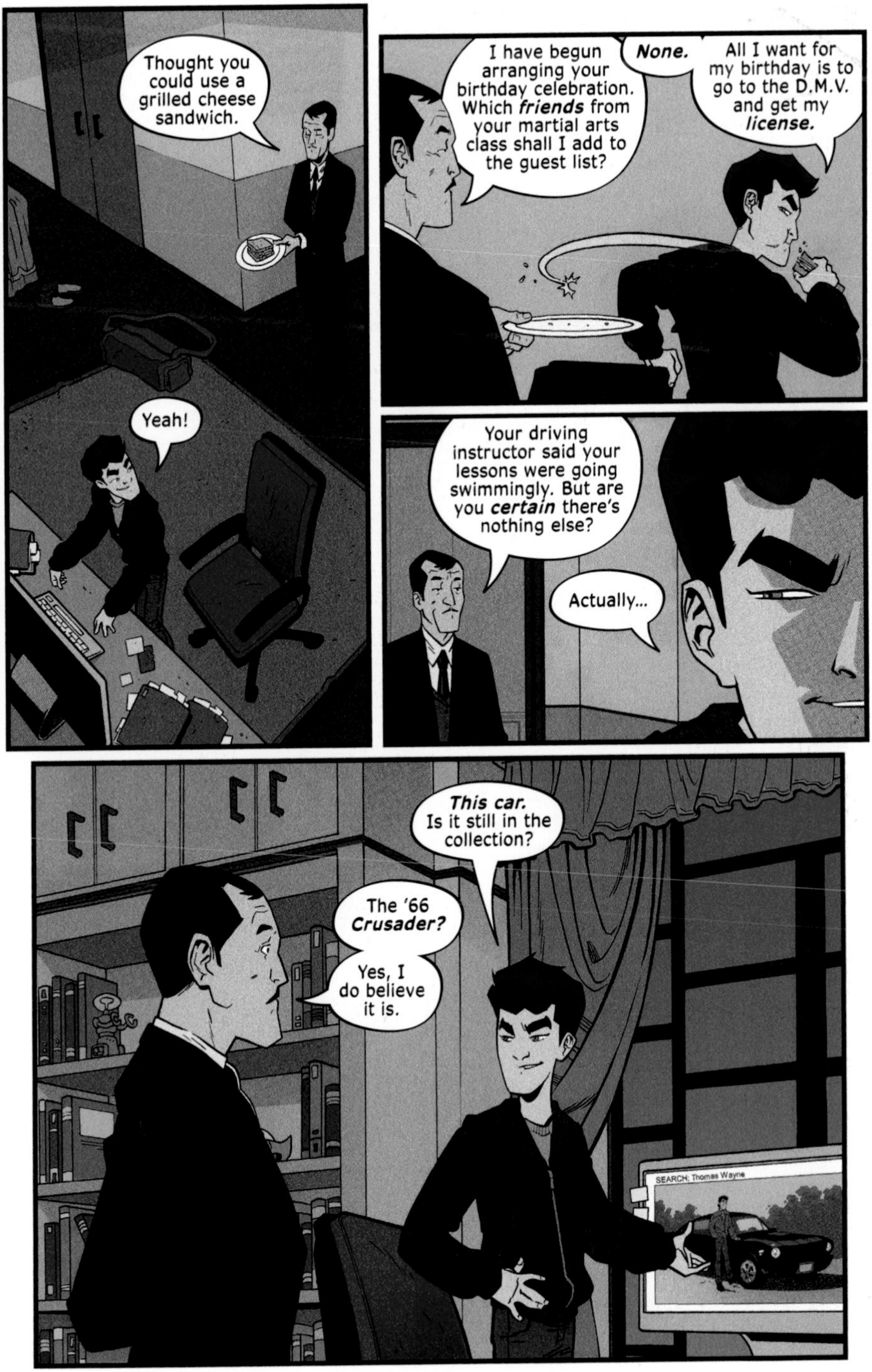
Thought you could use a grilled cheese sandwich.
Yeah!
I have begun arranging your birthday celebration. Which *friends* from your martial arts class shall I add to the guest list?
None.
All I want for my birthday is to go to the D.M.V. and get my *license.*
Your driving instructor said your lessons were going swimmingly. But are you *certain* there's nothing else?
Actually...
This car. Is it still in the collection?
The '66 *Crusader?*
Yes, I do believe it is.
SEARCH: Thomas Wayne

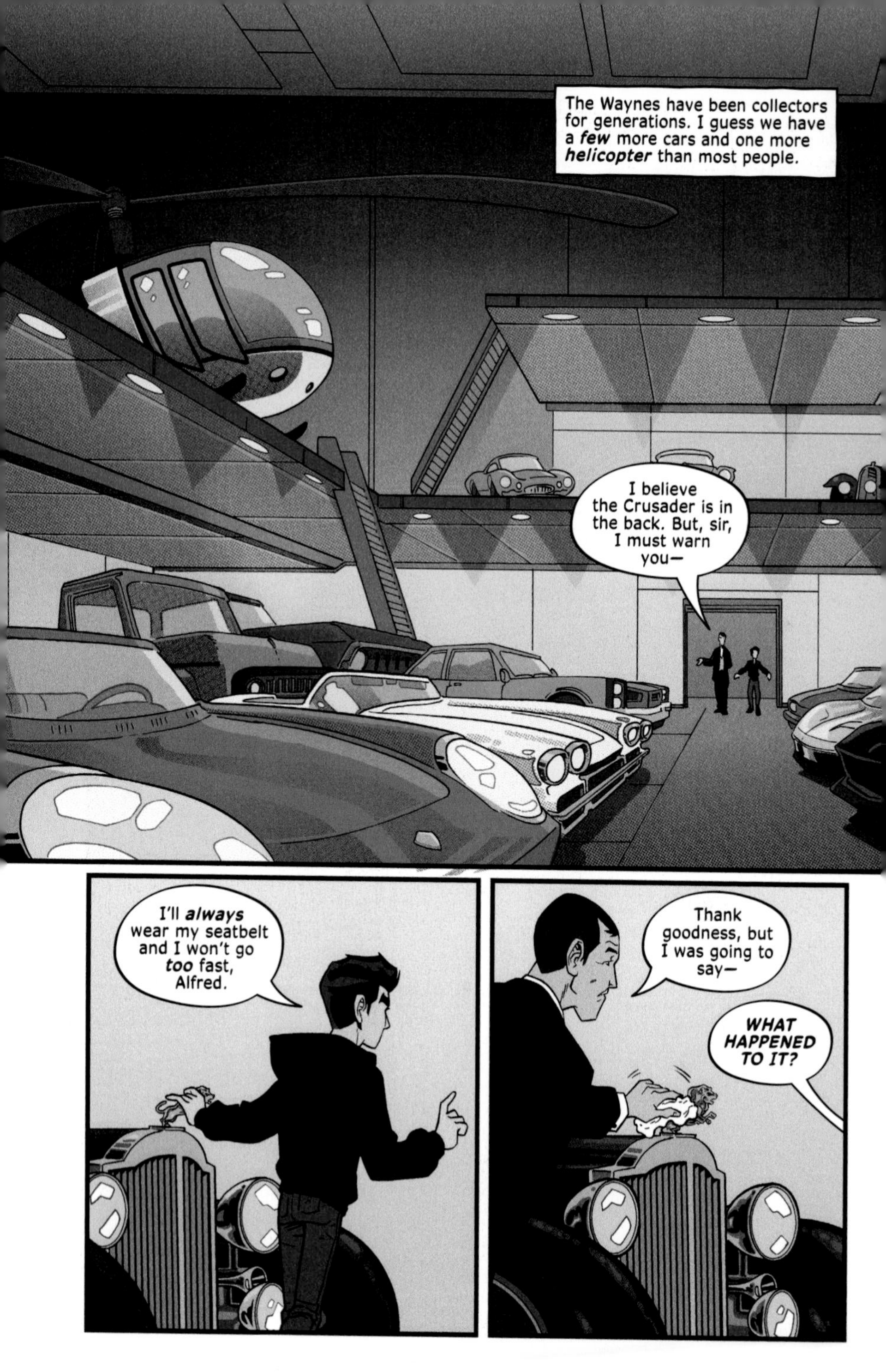

The Waynes have been collectors for generations. I guess we have a *few* more cars and one more *helicopter* than most people.
I believe the Crusader is in the back. But, sir, I must warn you—
I'll *always* wear my seatbelt and I won't go *too* fast, Alfred.
Thank goodness, but I was going to say—
WHAT HAPPENED TO IT?

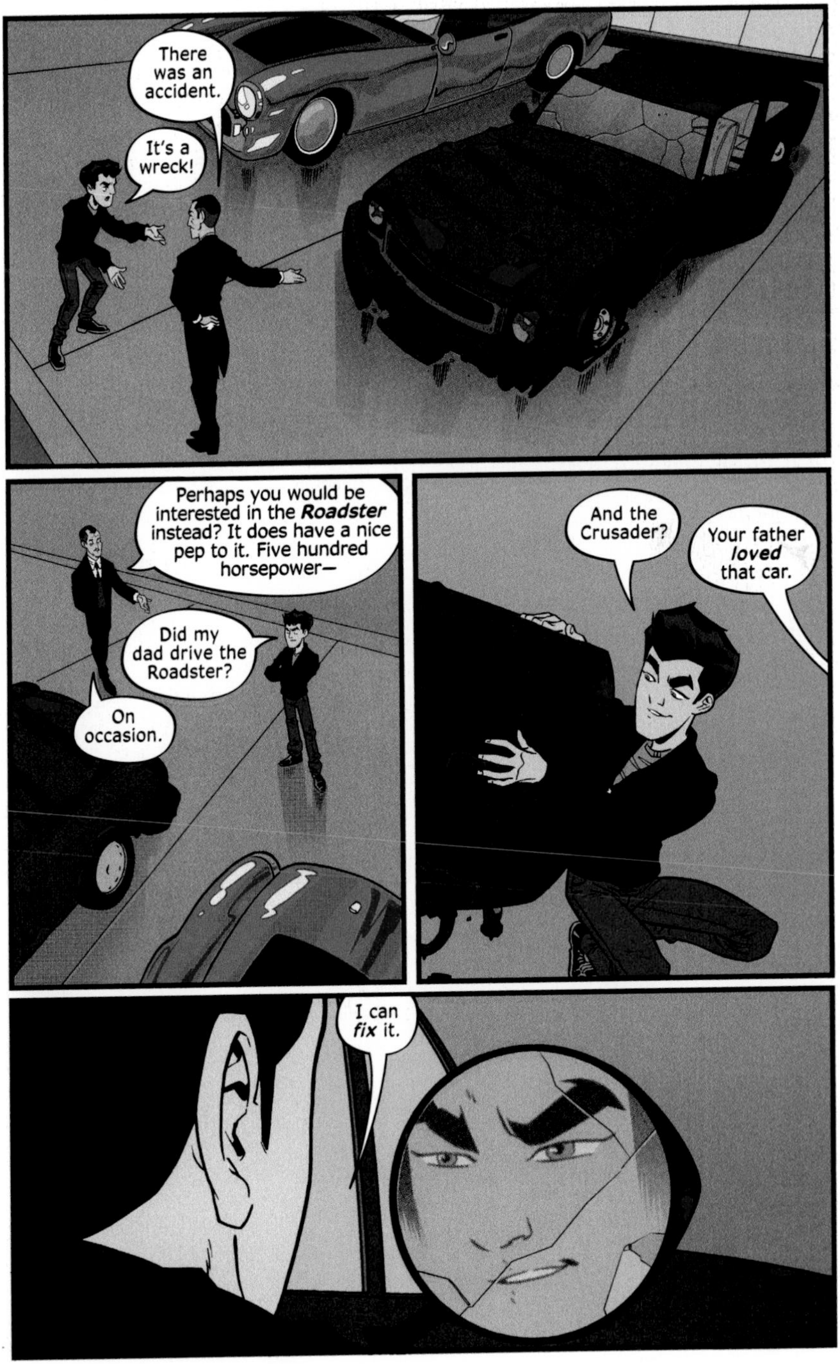

There was an accident.
It's a wreck!
Perhaps you would be interested in the *Roadster* instead? It does have a nice pep to it. Five hundred horsepower—
Did my dad drive the Roadster?
On occasion.
And the Crusader?
Your father *loved* that car.
I can *fix* it.

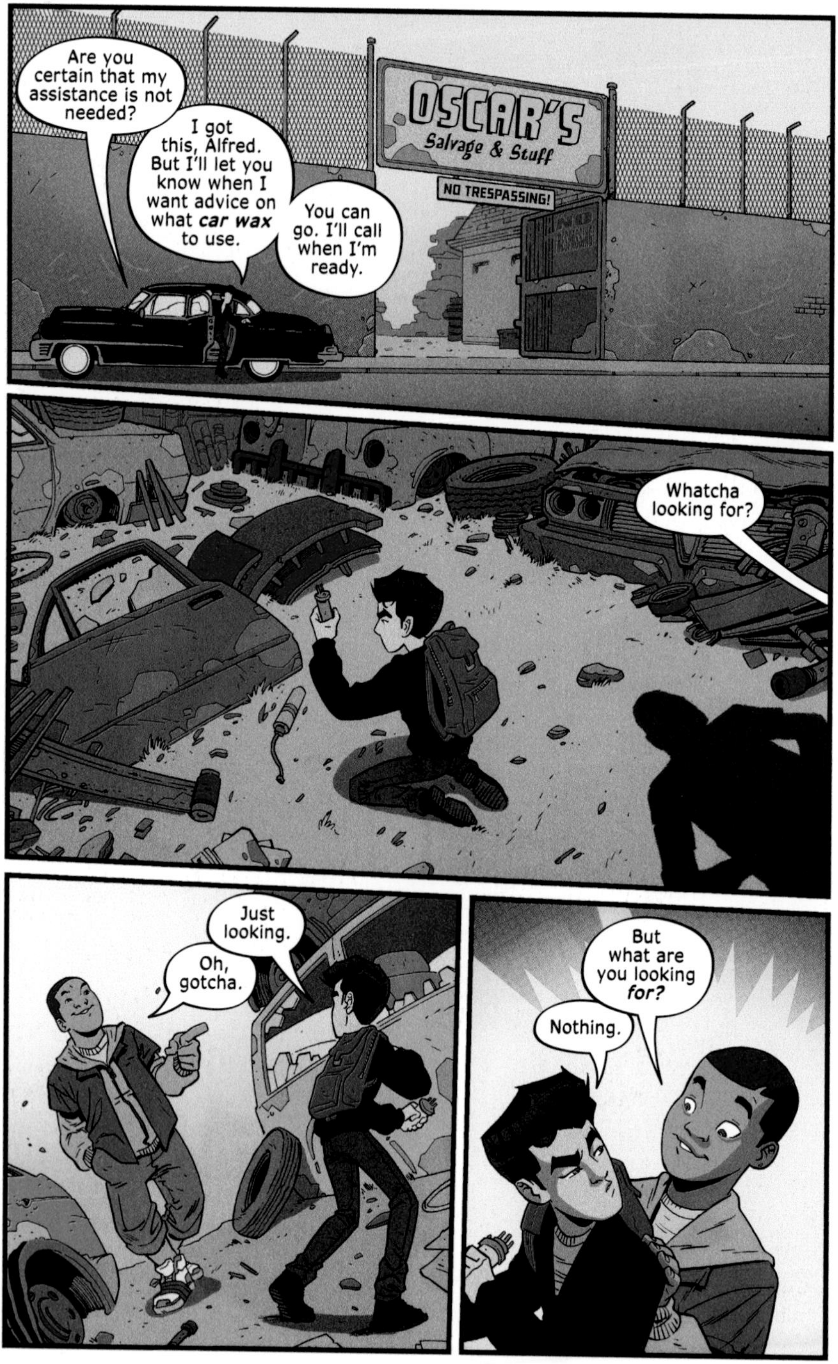

OSCAR'S
Salvage & Stuff
NO TRESPASSING!
Are you certain that my assistance is not needed?
I got this, Alfred. But I'll let you know when I want advice on what *car wax* to use.
You can go. I'll call when I'm ready.
Whatcha looking for?
Just looking.
Oh, gotcha.
But what are you looking *for?*
Nothing.

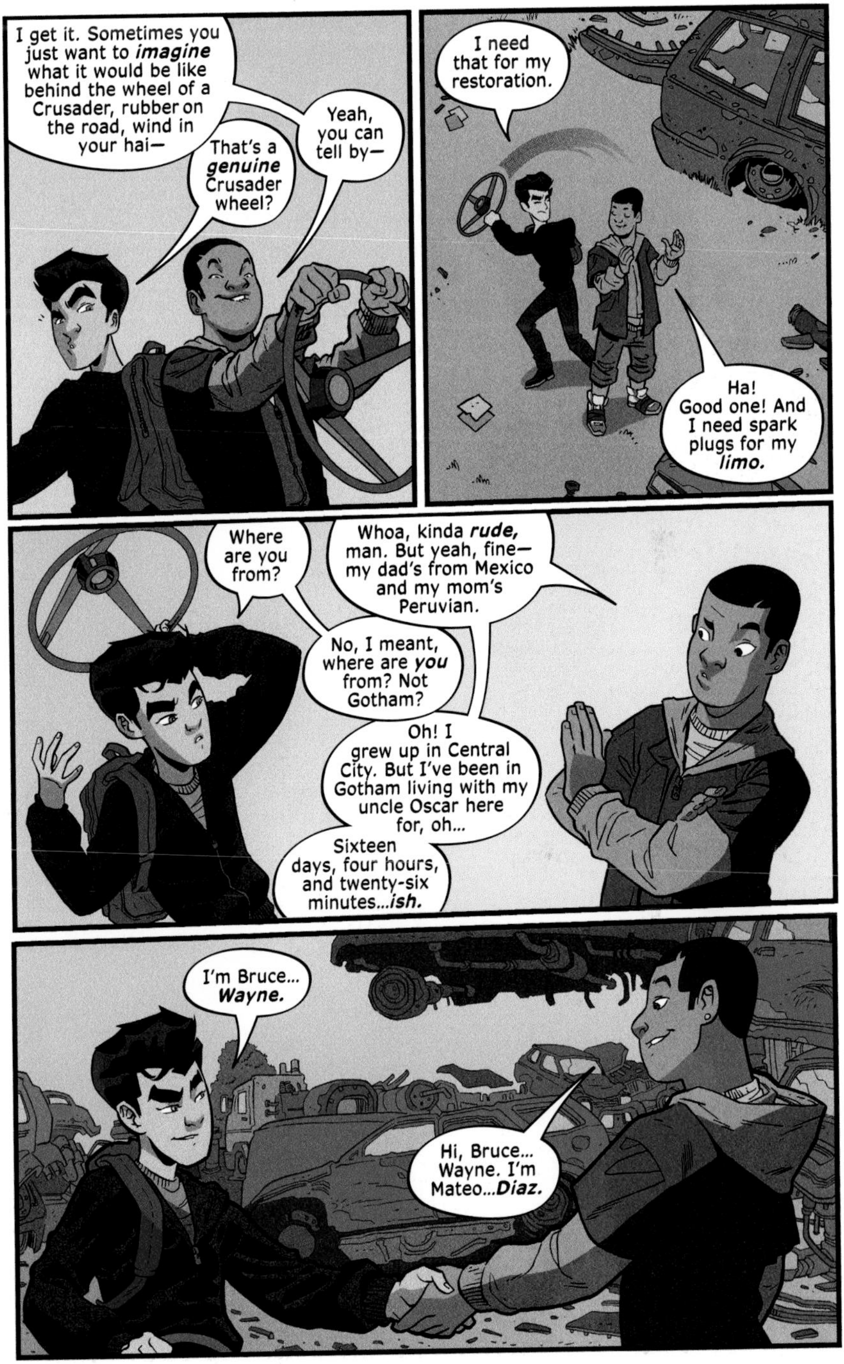
I get it. Sometimes you just want to *imagine* what it would be like behind the wheel of a Crusader, rubber on the road, wind in your hai—
That's a *genuine* Crusader wheel?
Yeah, you can tell by—
I need that for my restoration.
Ha! Good one! And I need spark plugs for my *limo.*
Where are you from?
Whoa, kinda *rude,* man. But yeah, fine— my dad's from Mexico and my mom's Peruvian.
No, I meant, where are *you* from? Not Gotham?
Oh! I grew up in Central City. But I've been in Gotham living with my uncle Oscar here for, oh...
Sixteen days, four hours, and twenty-six minutes...*ish.*
I'm Bruce... *Wayne.*
Hi, Bruce... Wayne. I'm Mateo...*Diaz.*

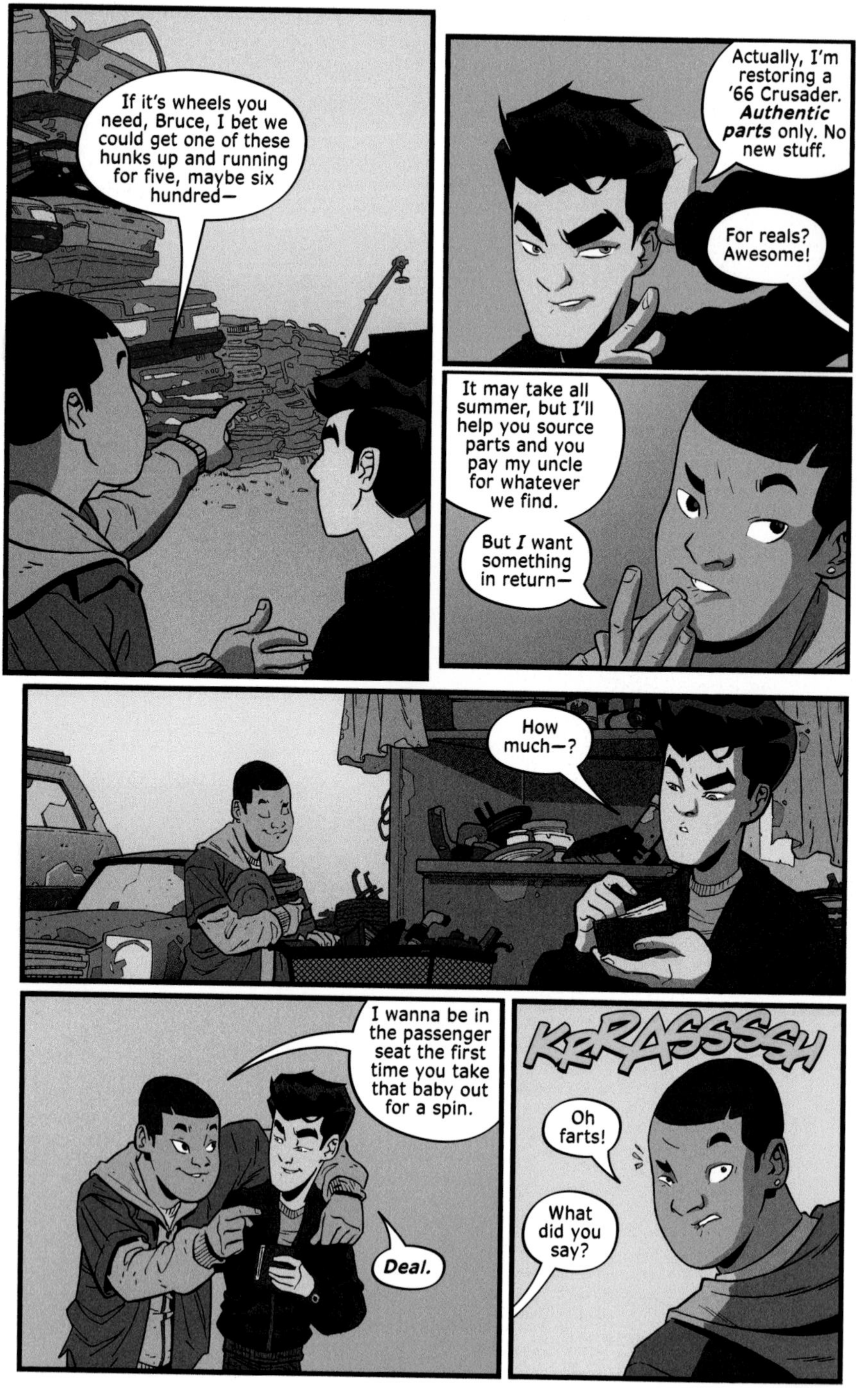
If it's wheels you need, Bruce, I bet we could get one of these hunks up and running for five, maybe six hundred—
Actually, I'm restoring a '66 Crusader. ***Authentic parts*** only. No new stuff.
For reals? Awesome!
It may take all summer, but I'll help you source parts and you pay my uncle for whatever we find.
But *I* want something in return—
How much—?
I wanna be in the passenger seat the first time you take that baby out for a spin.
Deal.
KRRASSSSH
Oh farts!
What did you say?

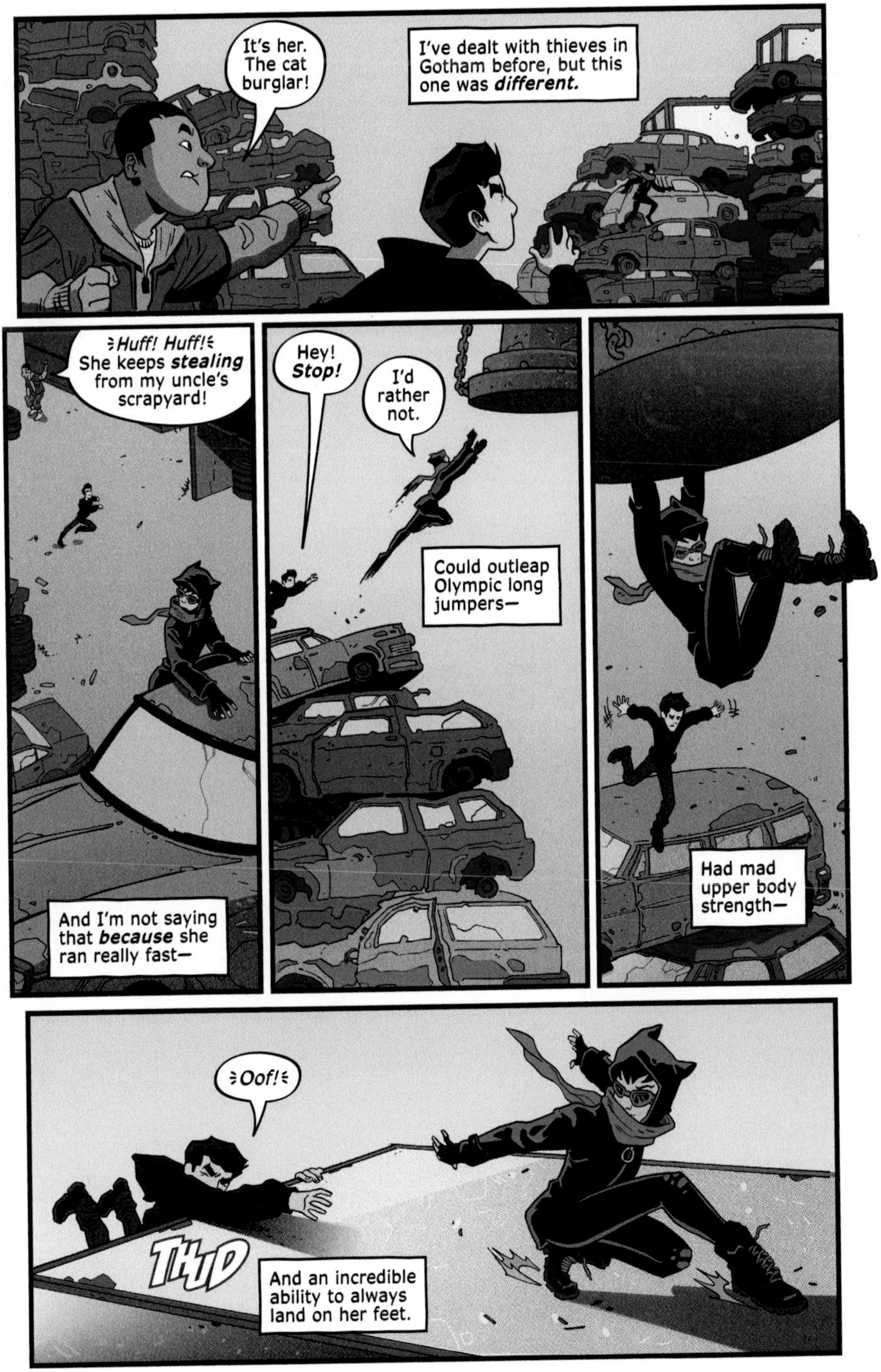
It's her. The cat burglar!
I've dealt with thieves in Gotham before, but this one was *different.*
Huff! Huff! She keeps *stealing* from my uncle's scrapyard!
And I'm not saying that *because* she ran really fast—
Hey! *Stop!*
I'd rather not.
Could outleap Olympic long jumpers—
Had mad upper body strength—
Oof!
THUD
And an incredible ability to always land on her feet.

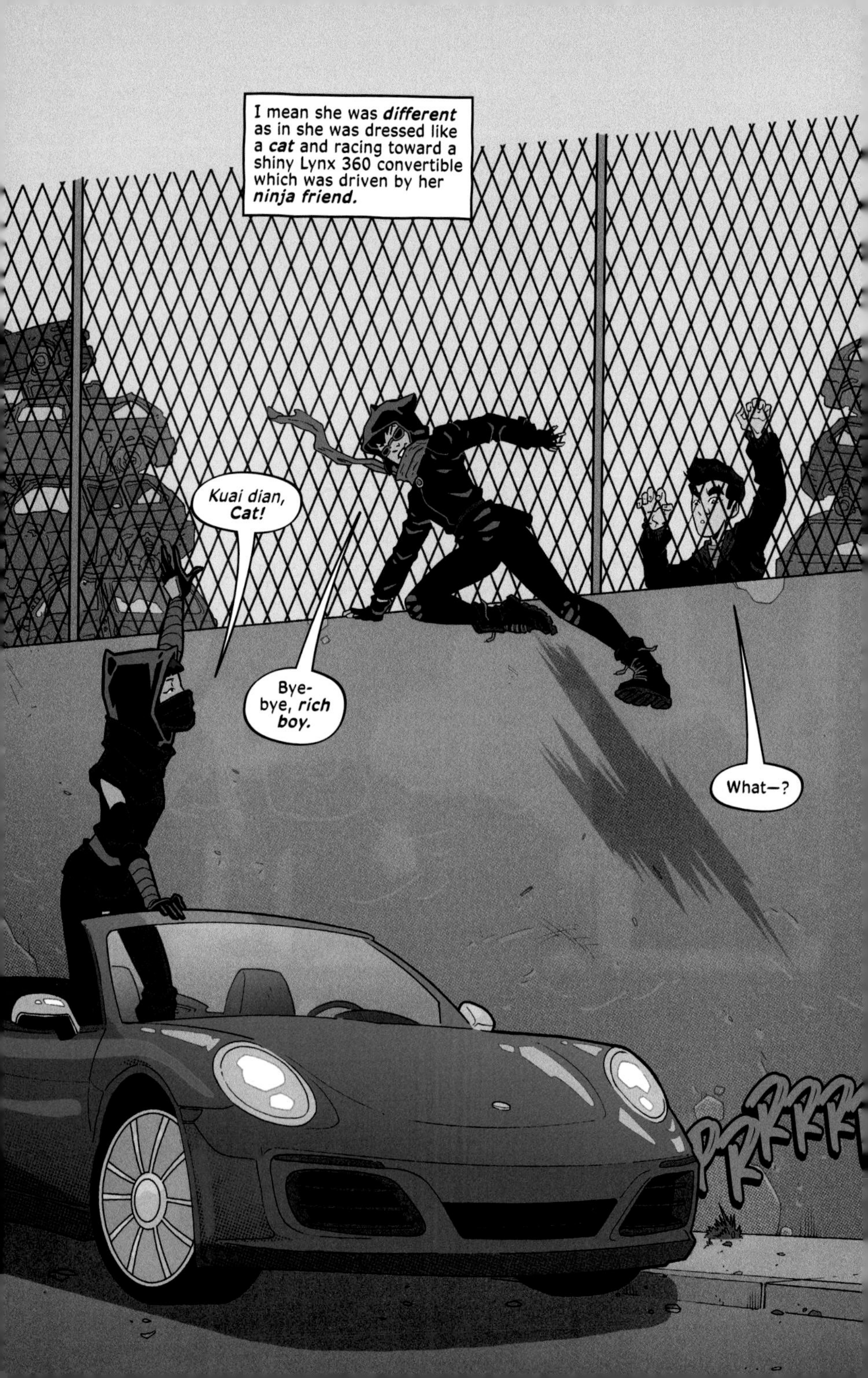
I mean she was *different* as in she was dressed like a *cat* and racing toward a shiny Lynx 360 convertible which was driven by her *ninja friend.*
Kuai dian, **Cat!**
Bye-bye, *rich boy.*
What—?
PRRRR

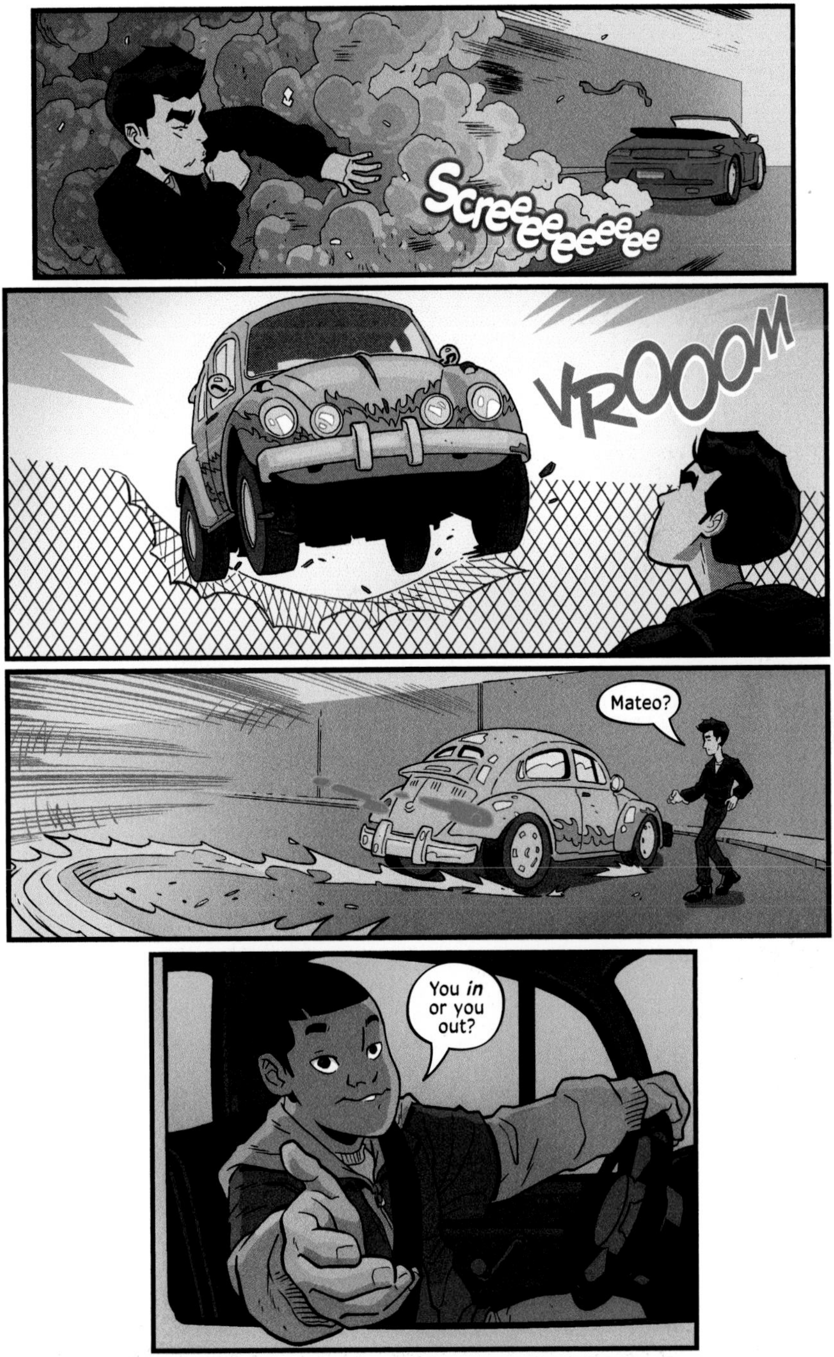
Screeeeeeeeee
VROOOM
Mateo?
You *in* or you out?

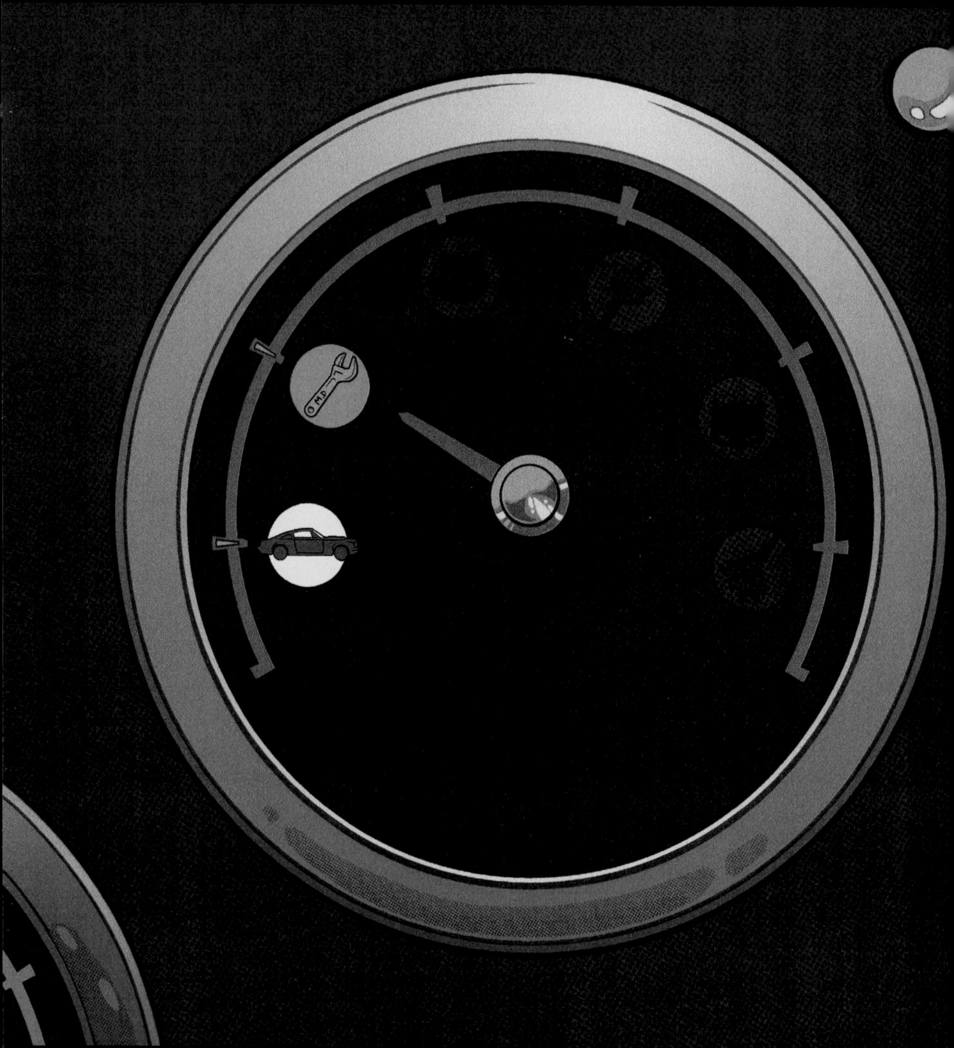

REV UP

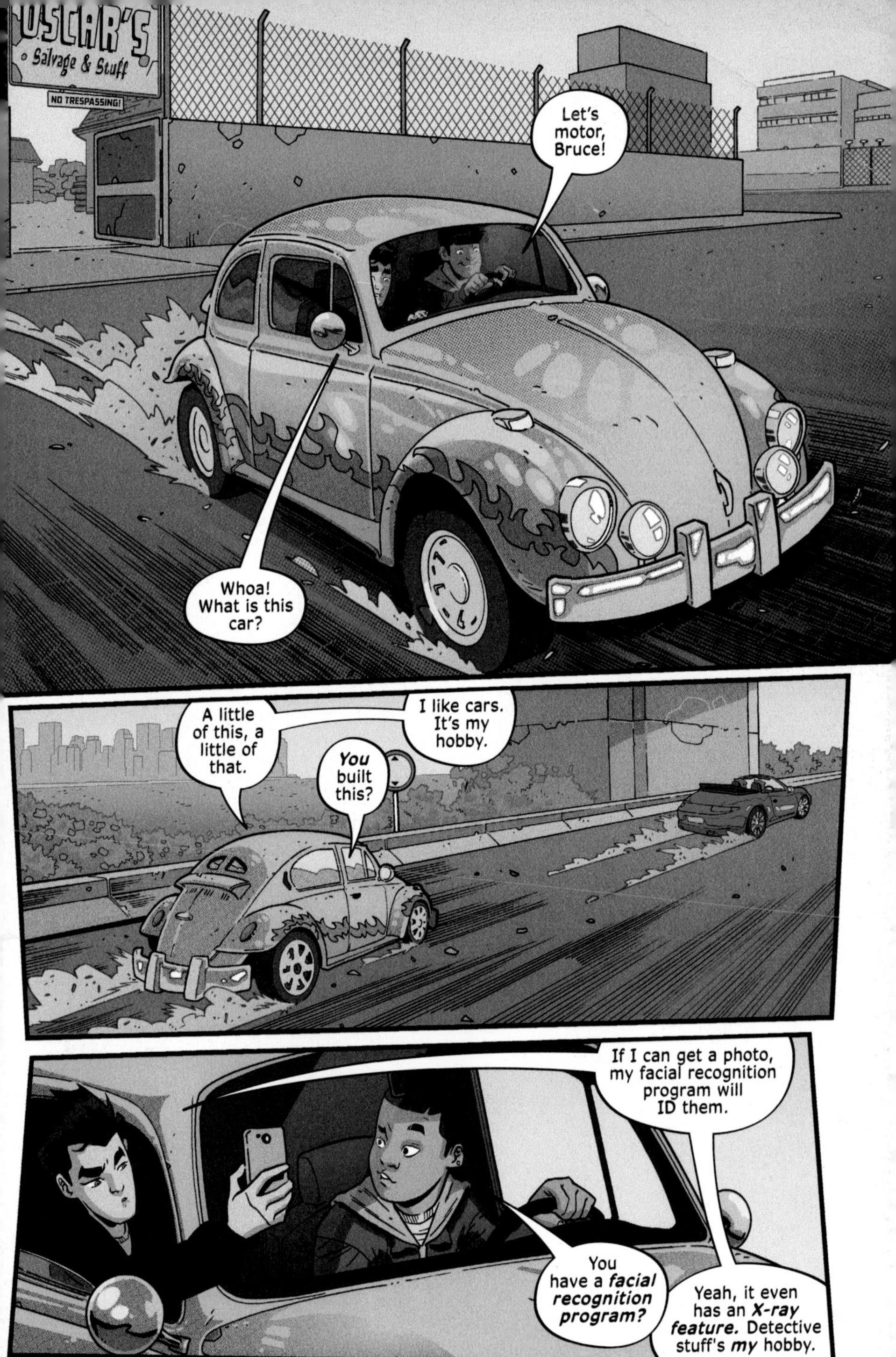
OSCAR'S
Salvage & Stuff
NO TRESPASSING!
Let's motor, Bruce!
Whoa! What is this car?
A little of this, a little of that.
I like cars. It's my hobby.
You built this?
If I can get a photo, my facial recognition program will ID them.
You have a ***facial recognition program?***
Yeah, it even has an ***X-ray feature.*** Detective stuff's ***my*** hobby.

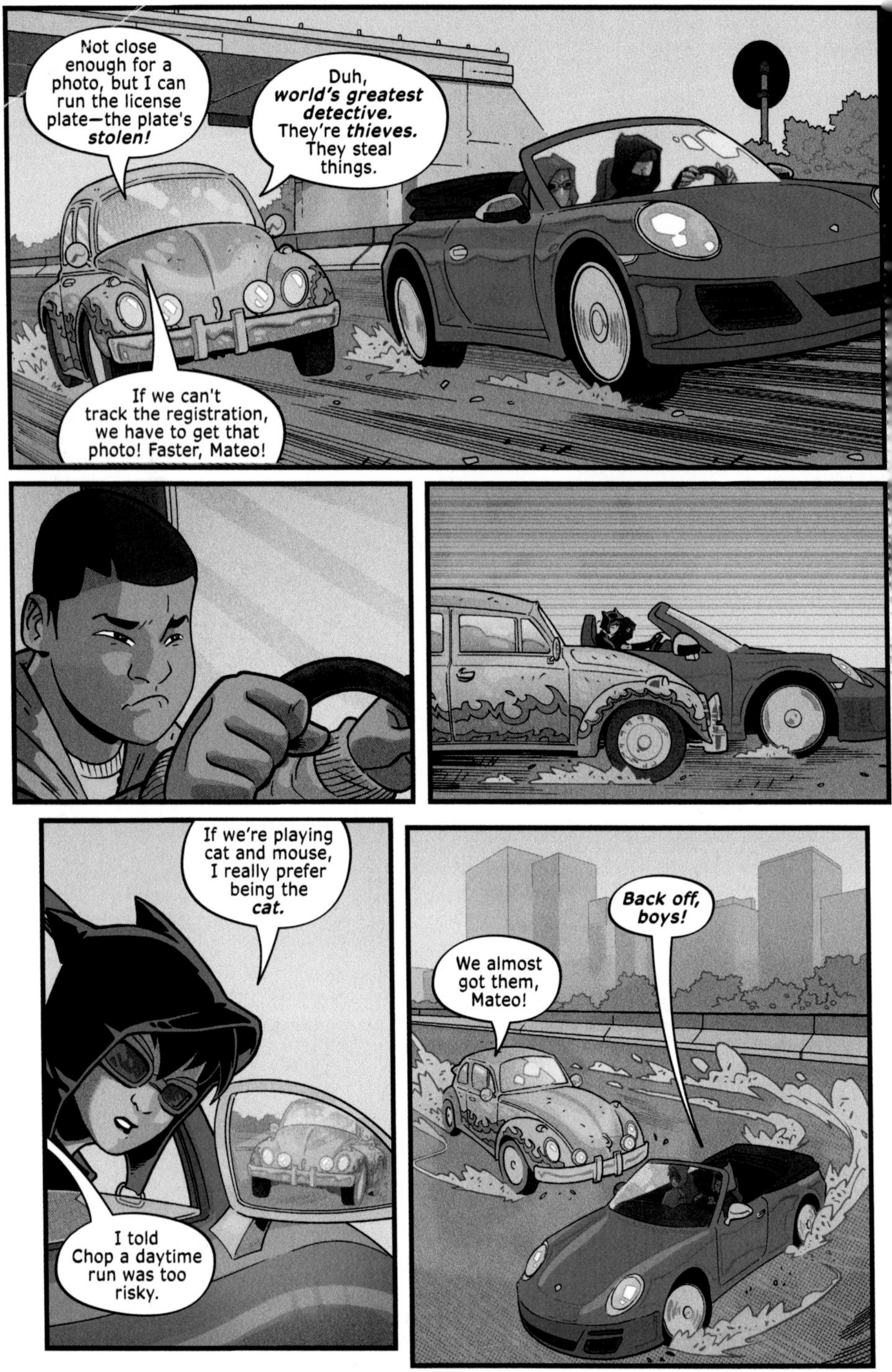
Not close enough for a photo, but I can run the license plate—the plate's *stolen!*
Duh, ***world's greatest detective.*** They're ***thieves.*** They steal things.
If we can't track the registration, we have to get that photo! Faster, Mateo!
If we're playing cat and mouse, I really prefer being the ***cat.***
I told Chop a daytime run was too risky.
We almost got them, Mateo!
Back off, boys!

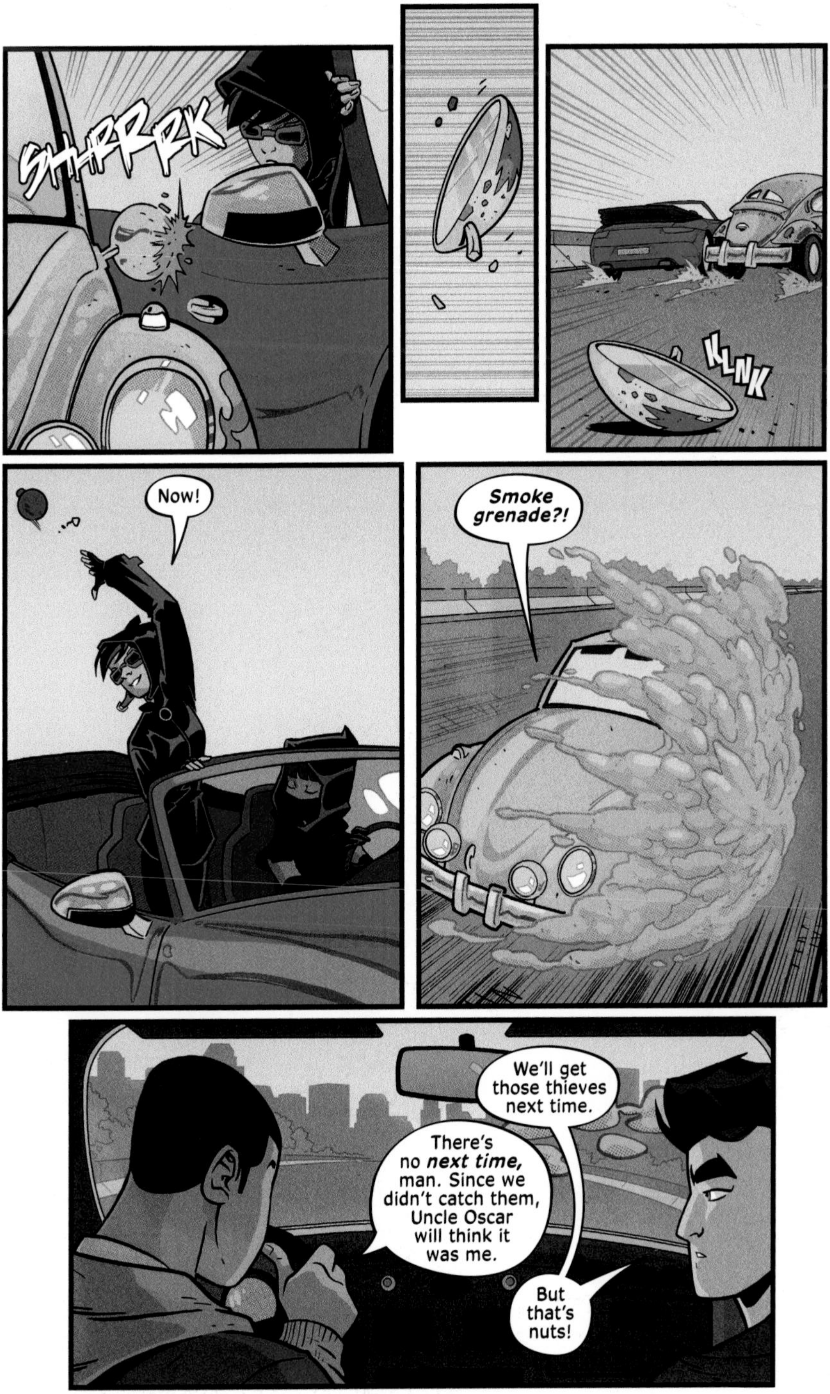
SHHRRRK
KLLNK
Now!
Smoke grenade?!
We'll get those thieves next time.
There's no *next time,* man. Since we didn't catch them, Uncle Oscar will think it was me.
But that's nuts!

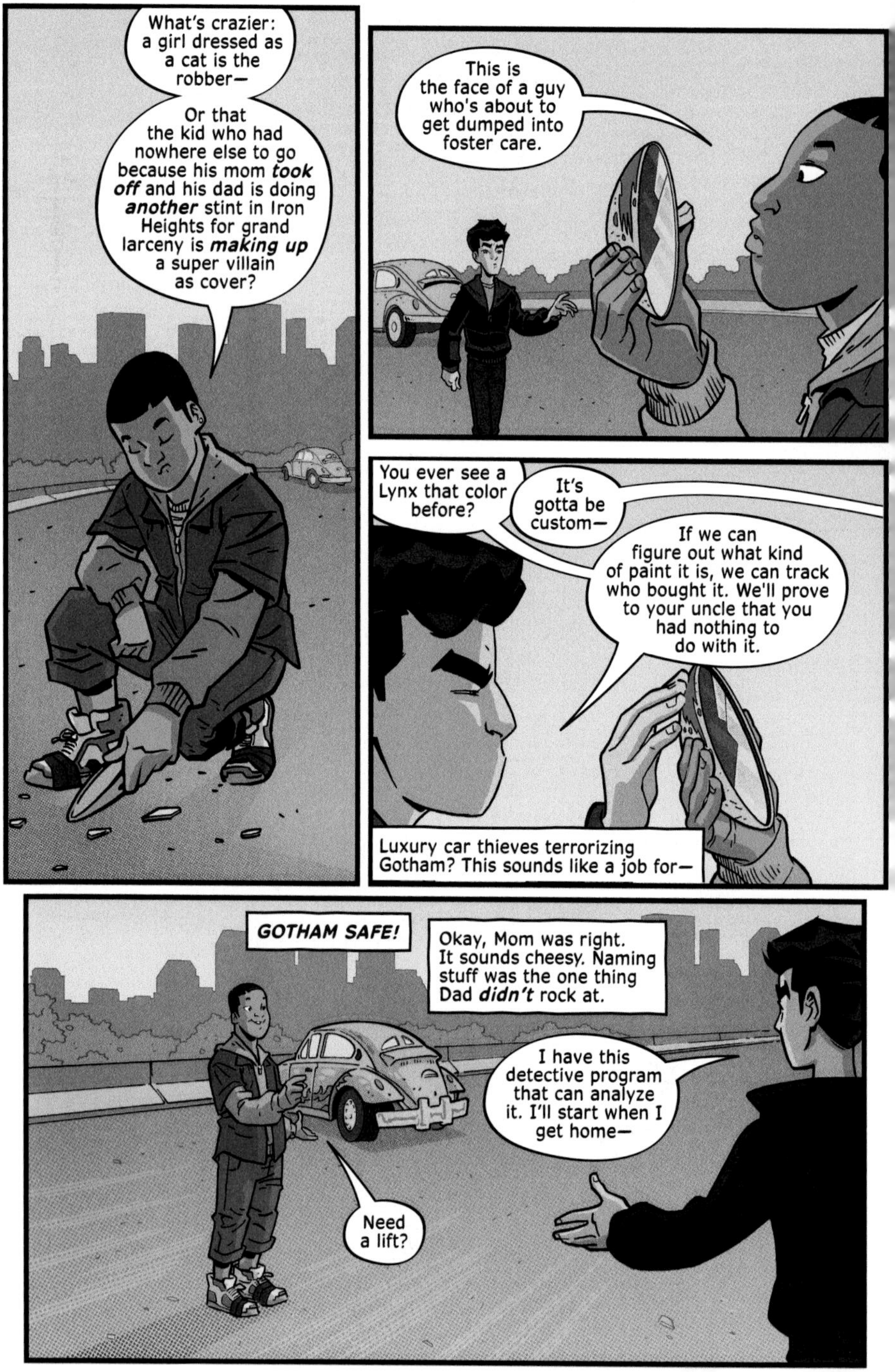
What's crazier: a girl dressed as a cat is the robber—
Or that the kid who had nowhere else to go because his mom took off and his dad is doing another stint in Iron Heights for grand larceny is making up a super villain as cover?
This is the face of a guy who's about to get dumped into foster care.
You ever see a Lynx that color before?
It's gotta be custom—
If we can figure out what kind of paint it is, we can track who bought it. We'll prove to your uncle that you had nothing to do with it.
Luxury car thieves terrorizing Gotham? This sounds like a job for—
GOTHAM SAFE!
Okay, Mom was right. It sounds cheesy. Naming stuff was the one thing Dad didn't rock at.
I have this detective program that can analyze it. I'll start when I get home—
Need a lift?

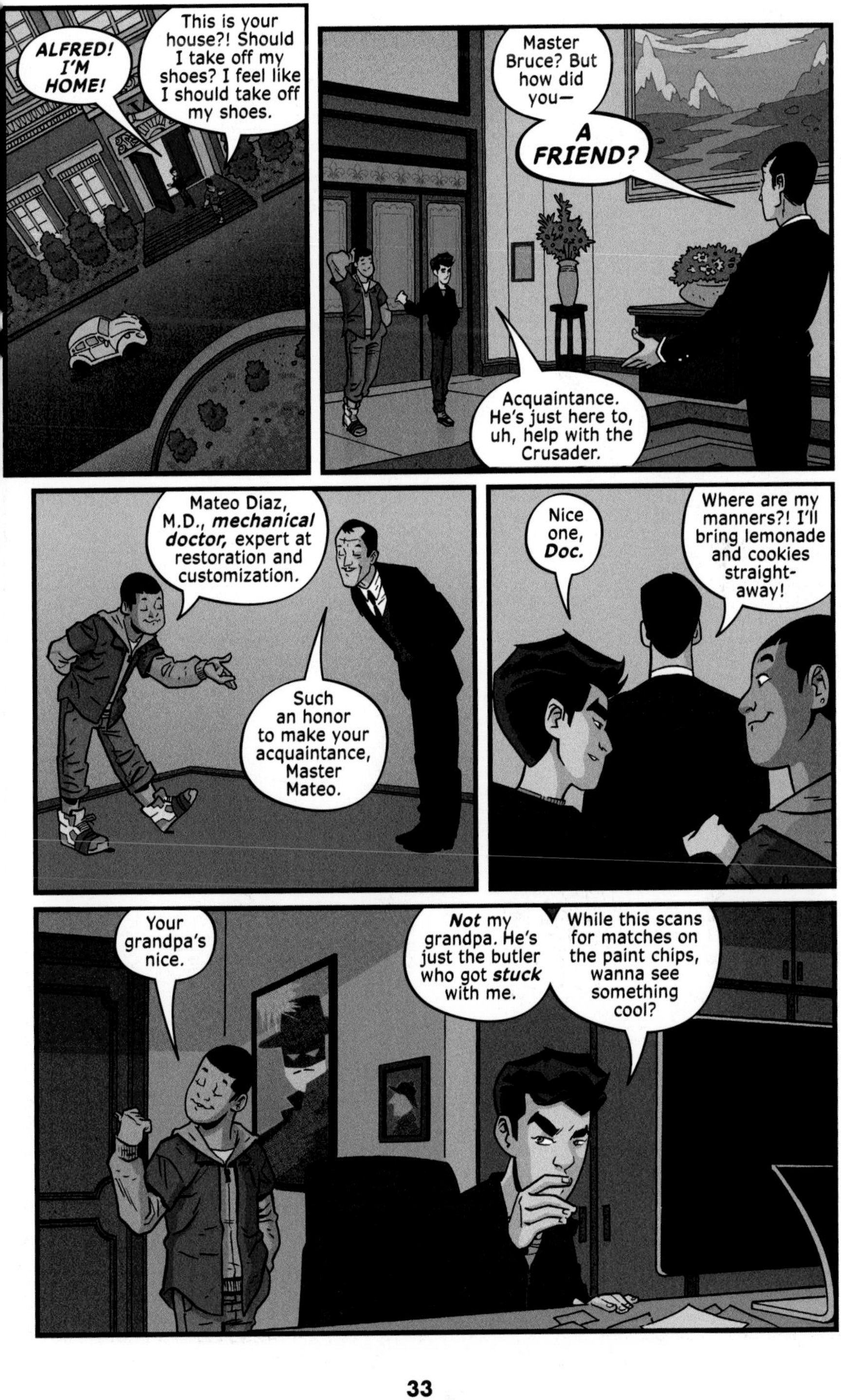
ALFRED! I'M HOME!
This is your house?! Should I take off my shoes? I feel like I should take off my shoes.
Master Bruce? But how did you—
A FRIEND?
Acquaintance. He's just here to, uh, help with the Crusader.
Mateo Diaz, M.D., *mechanical doctor,* expert at restoration and customization.
Such an honor to make your acquaintance, Master Mateo.
Nice one, *Doc.*
Where are my manners?! I'll bring lemonade and cookies straight-away!
Your grandpa's nice.
Not my grandpa. He's just the butler who got *stuck* with me.
While this scans for matches on the paint chips, wanna see something cool?

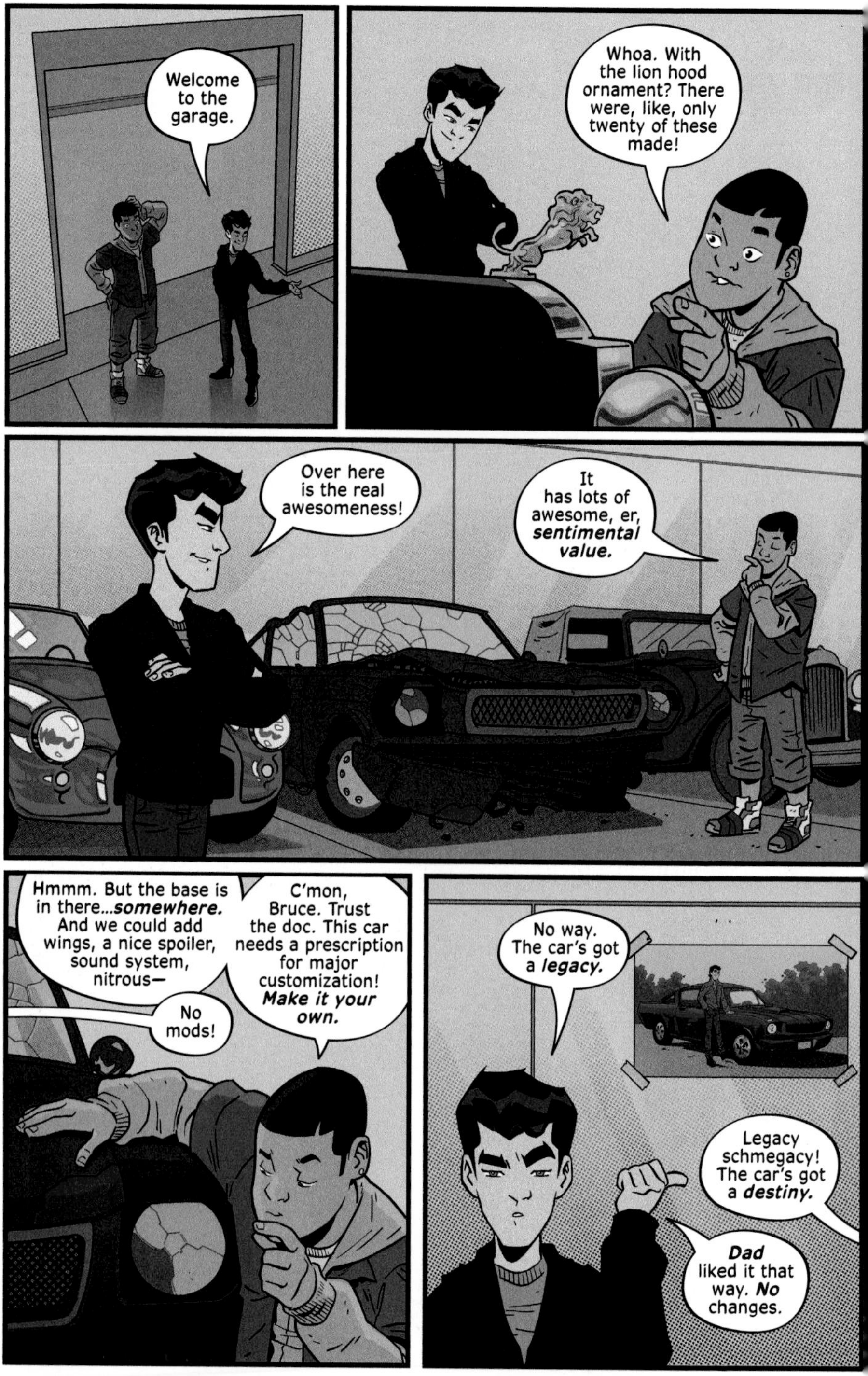
Welcome to the garage.
Whoa. With the lion hood ornament? There were, like, only twenty of these made!
Over here is the real awesomeness!
It has lots of awesome, er, *sentimental value.*
Hmmm. But the base is in there...*somewhere.* And we could add wings, a nice spoiler, sound system, nitrous—
No mods!
C'mon, Bruce. Trust the doc. This car needs a prescription for major customization! *Make it your own.*
No way. The car's got a *legacy.*
Legacy schmegacy! The car's got a *destiny.*
Dad liked it that way. *No* changes.

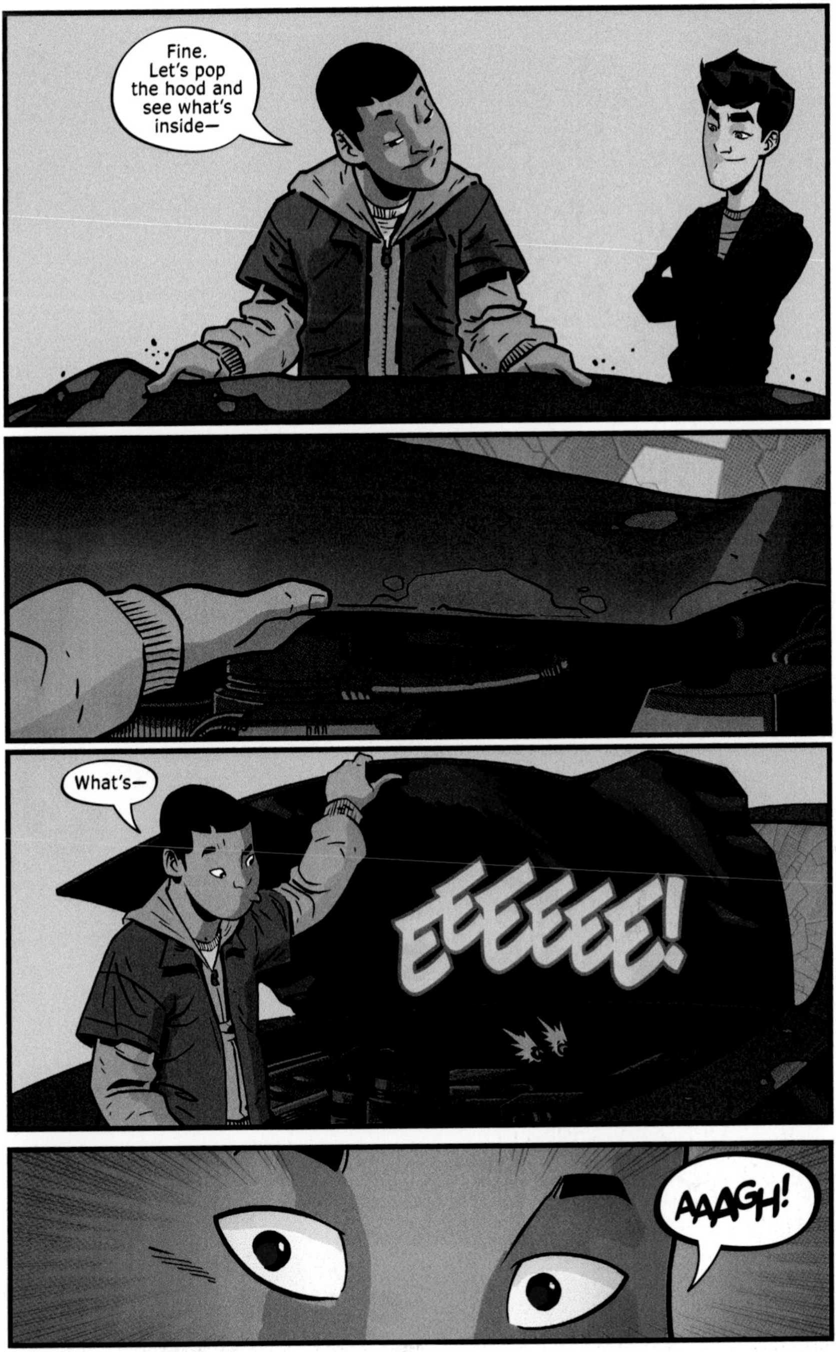
Fine. Let's pop the hood and see what's inside—
What's—
EEEEEE!
AAAGH!

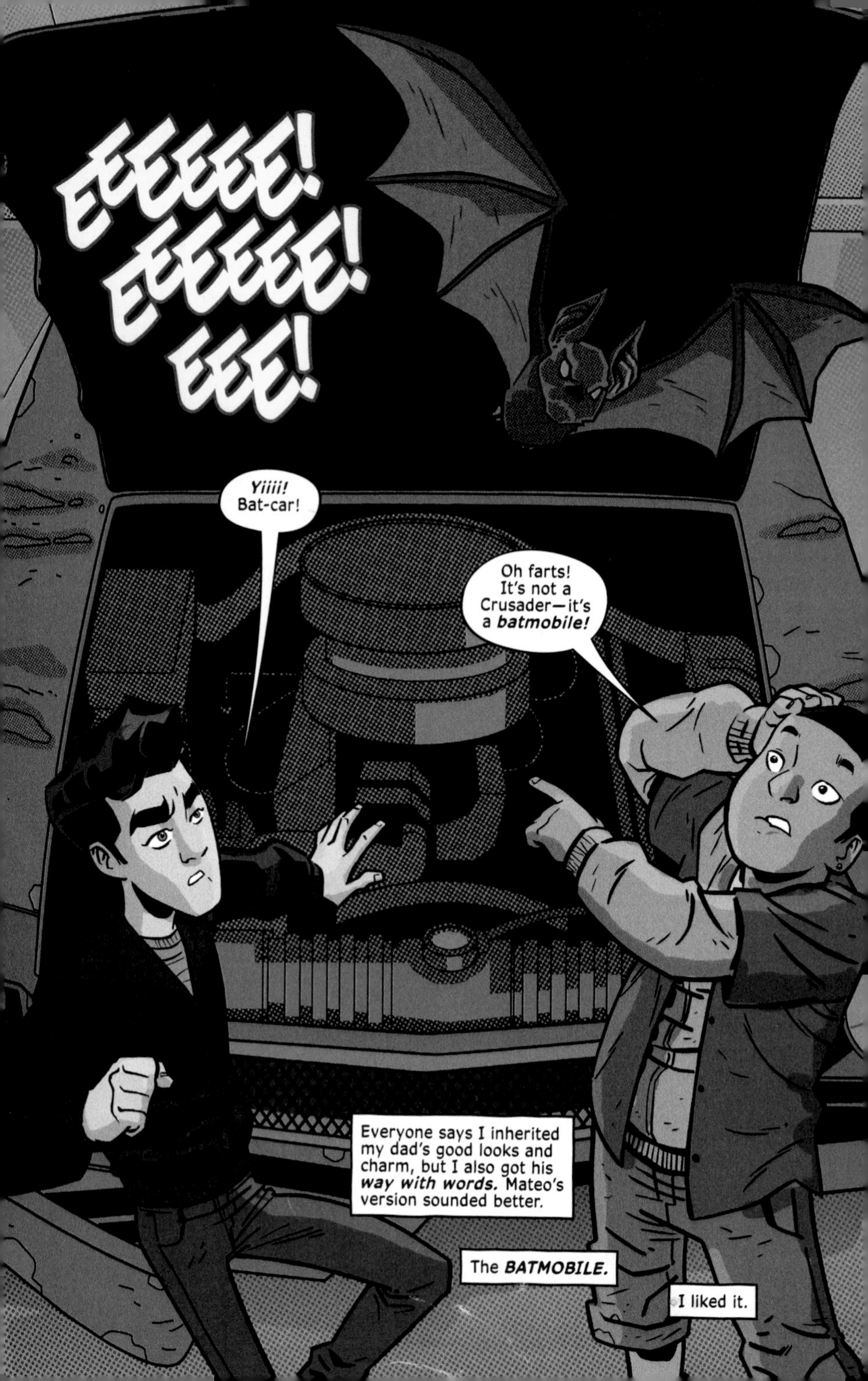
EEEEEE! EEEEEE! EEE!
Yiiii! Bat-car!
Oh farts! It's not a Crusader—it's a *batmobile!*
Everyone says I inherited my dad's good looks and charm, but I also got his ***way with words.*** Mateo's version sounded better.
The ***BATMOBILE.***
I liked it.

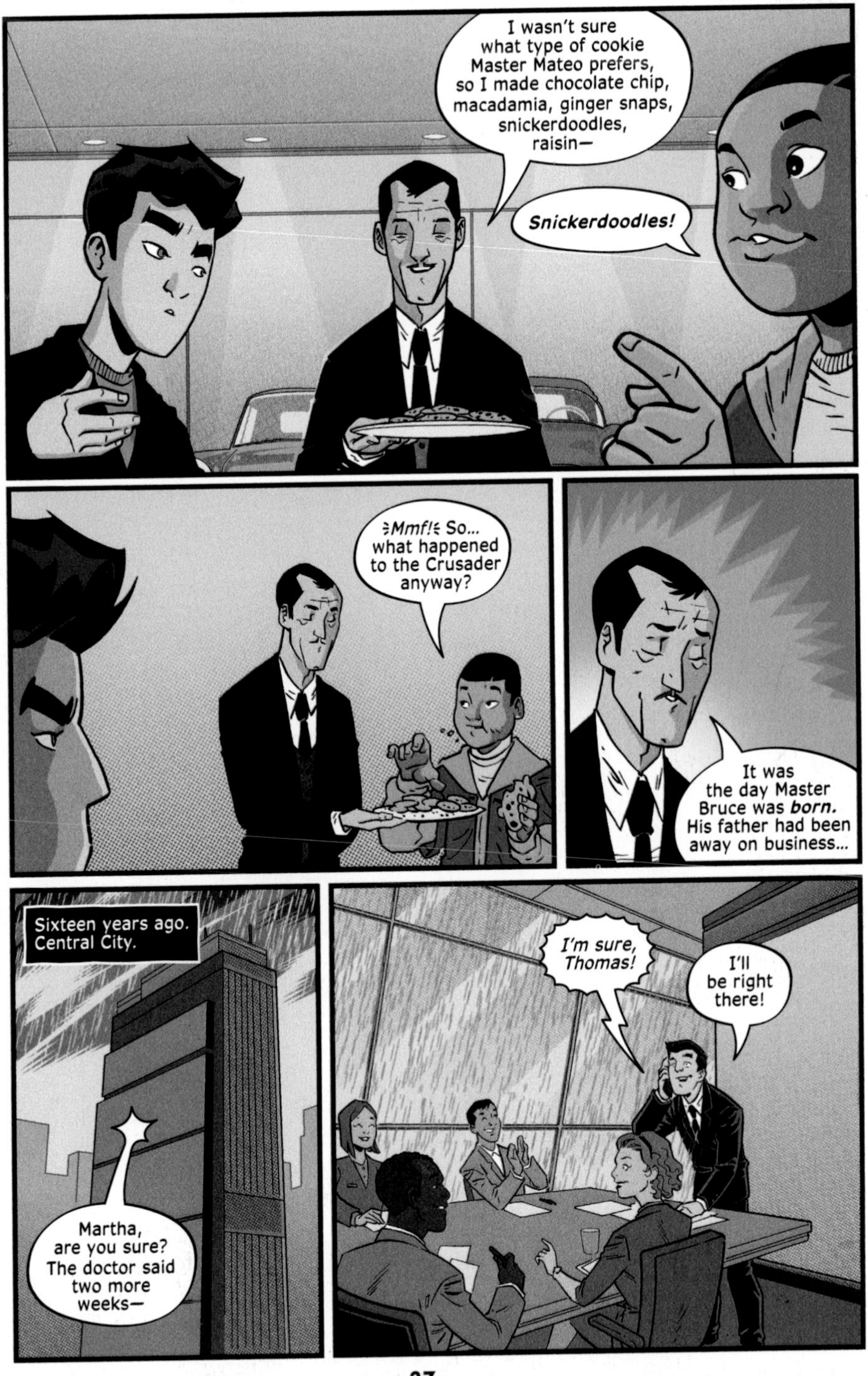
I wasn't sure what type of cookie Master Mateo prefers, so I made chocolate chip, macadamia, ginger snaps, snickerdoodles, raisin—
Snickerdoodles!
Mmf! So... what happened to the Crusader anyway?
It was the day Master Bruce was born. His father had been away on business...
Sixteen years ago. Central City.
Martha, are you sure? The doctor said two more weeks—
I'm sure, Thomas!
I'll be right there!

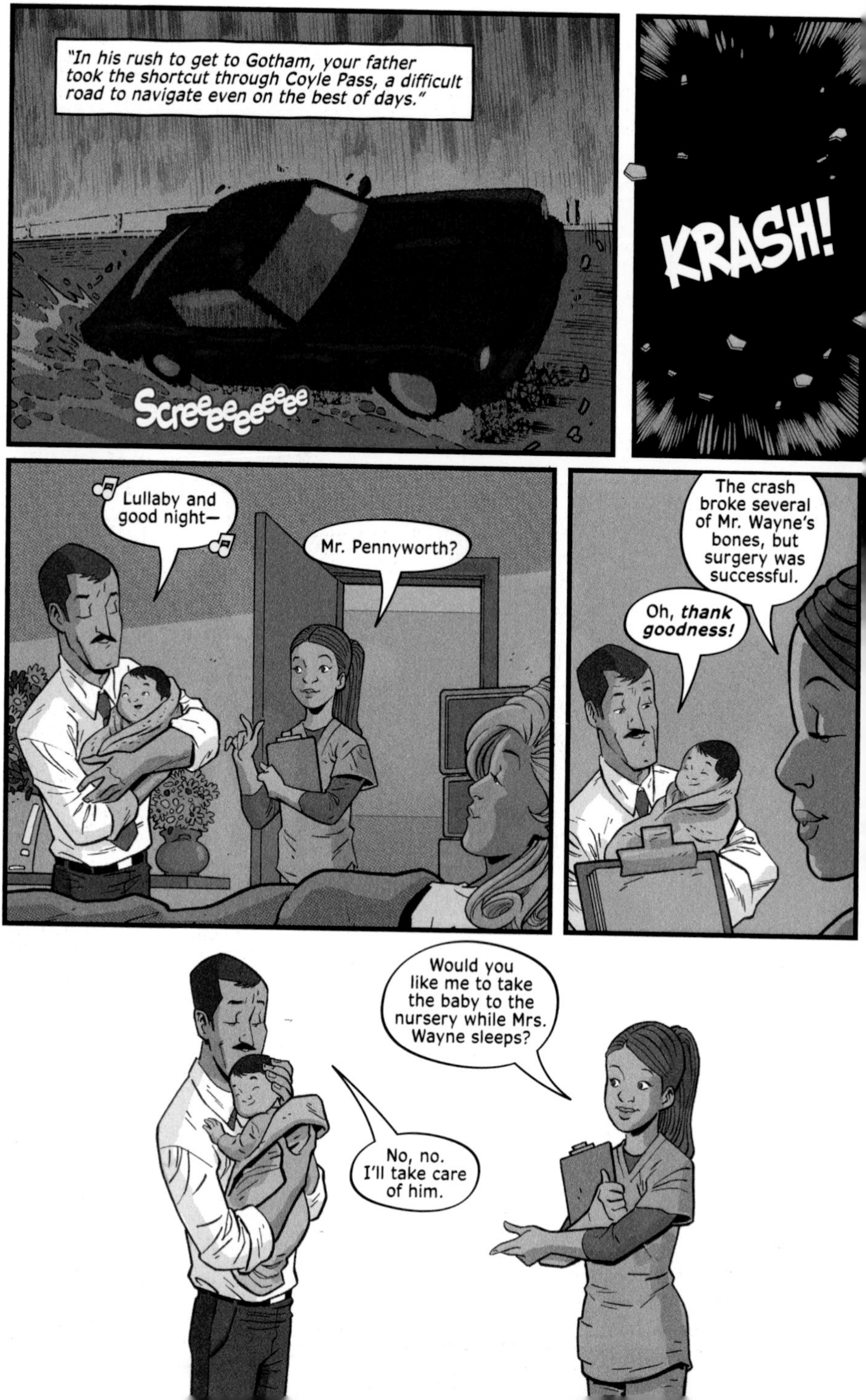
"In his rush to get to Gotham, your father took the shortcut through Coyle Pass, a difficult road to navigate even on the best of days."
Screeeeeeeee
KRASH!
Lullaby and good night—
Mr. Pennyworth?
The crash broke several of Mr. Wayne's bones, but surgery was successful.
Oh, *thank goodness!*
Would you like me to take the baby to the nursery while Mrs. Wayne sleeps?
No, no. I'll take care of him.

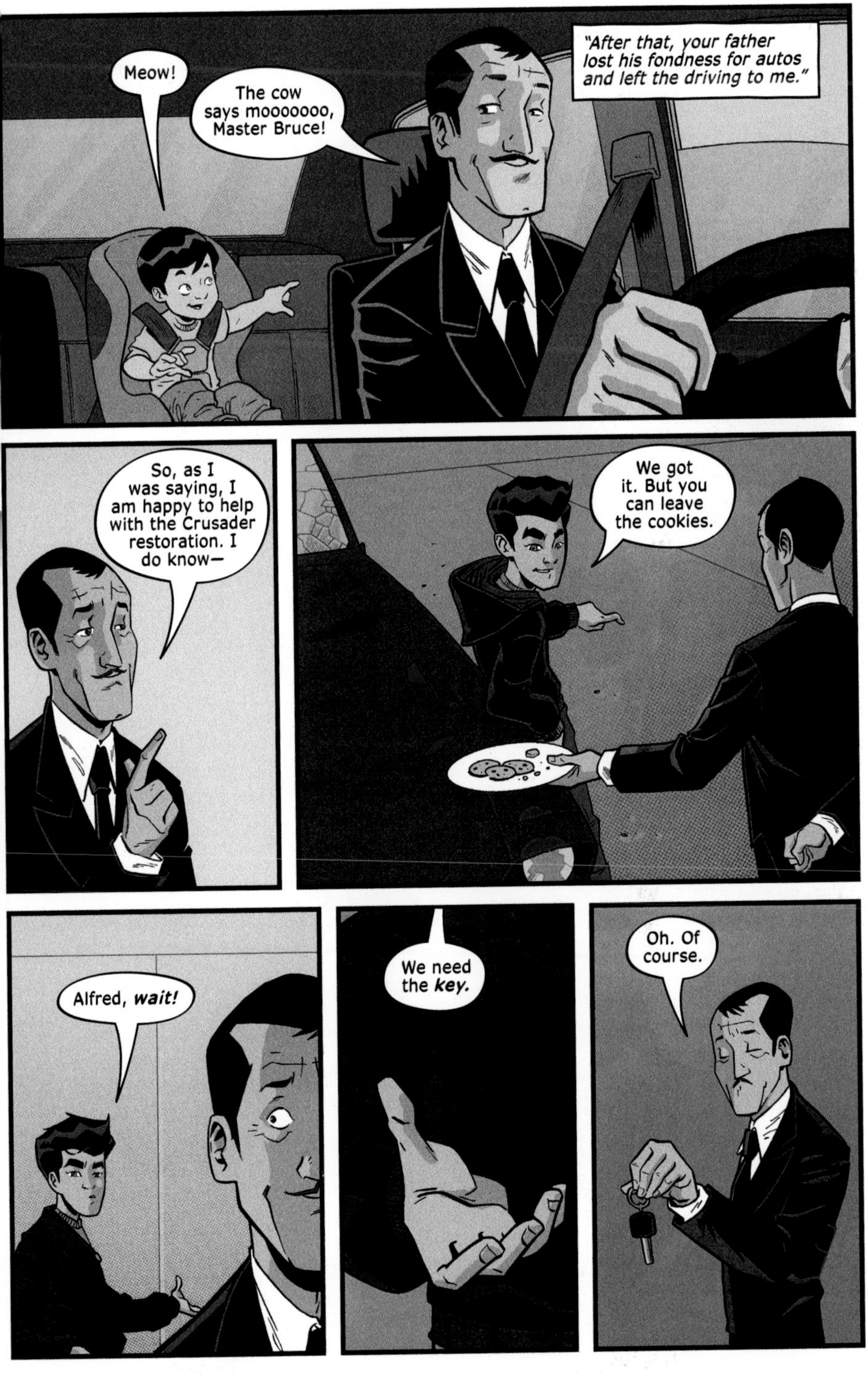
"After that, your father lost his fondness for autos and left the driving to me."
Meow!
The cow says mooooooo, Master Bruce!
So, as I was saying, I am happy to help with the Crusader restoration. I do know—
We got it. But you can leave the cookies.
Alfred, *wait!*
We need the *key.*
Oh. Of course.

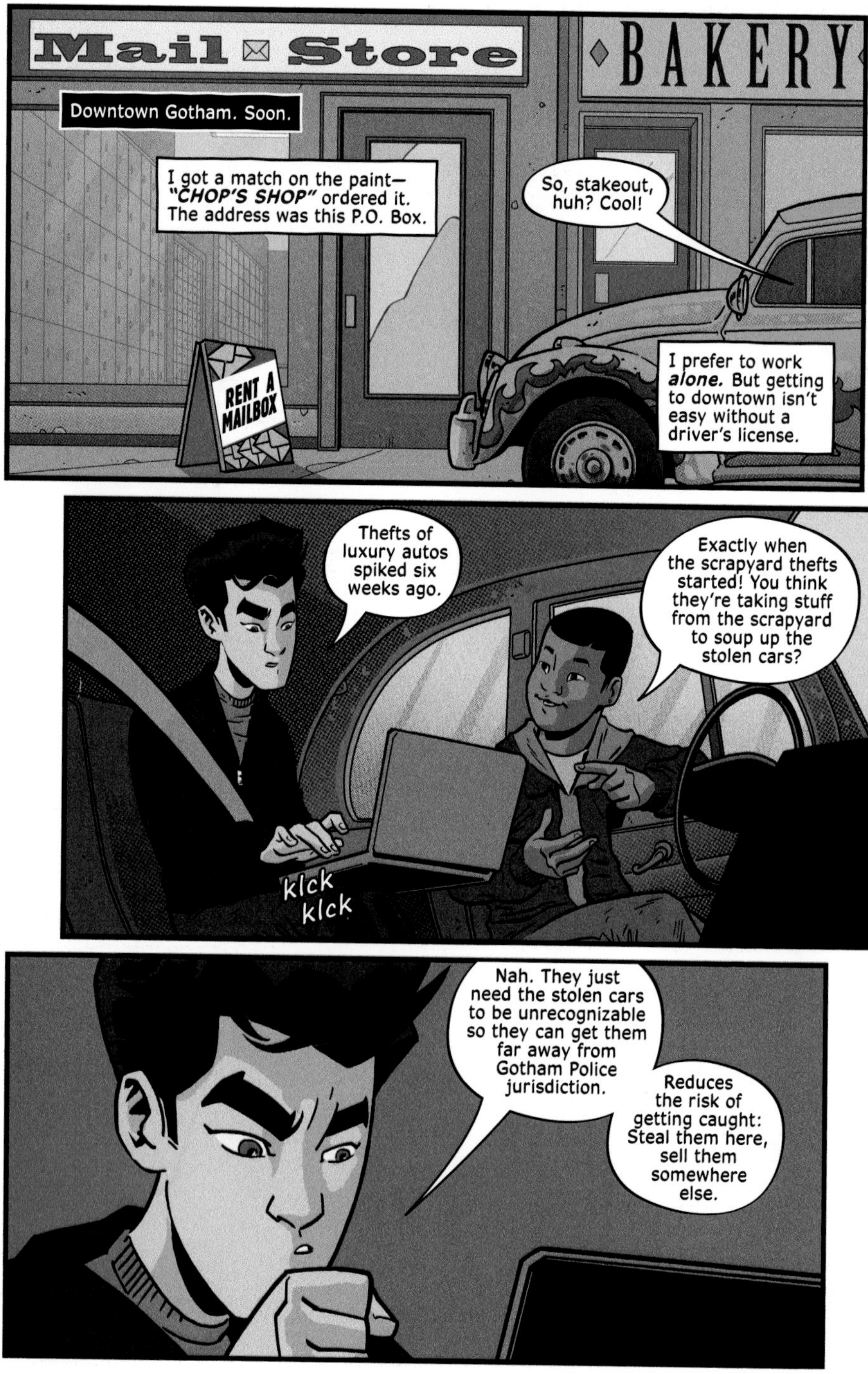
Mail Store
BAKERY
Downtown Gotham. Soon.
I got a match on the paint—**"CHOP'S SHOP"** ordered it. The address was this P.O. Box.
So, stakeout, huh? Cool!
RENT A MAILBOX
I prefer to work ***alone.*** But getting to downtown isn't easy without a driver's license.
Thefts of luxury autos spiked six weeks ago.
Exactly when the scrapyard thefts started! You think they're taking stuff from the scrapyard to soup up the stolen cars?
klck klck
Nah. They just need the stolen cars to be unrecognizable so they can get them far away from Gotham Police jurisdiction.
Reduces the risk of getting caught: Steal them here, sell them somewhere else.

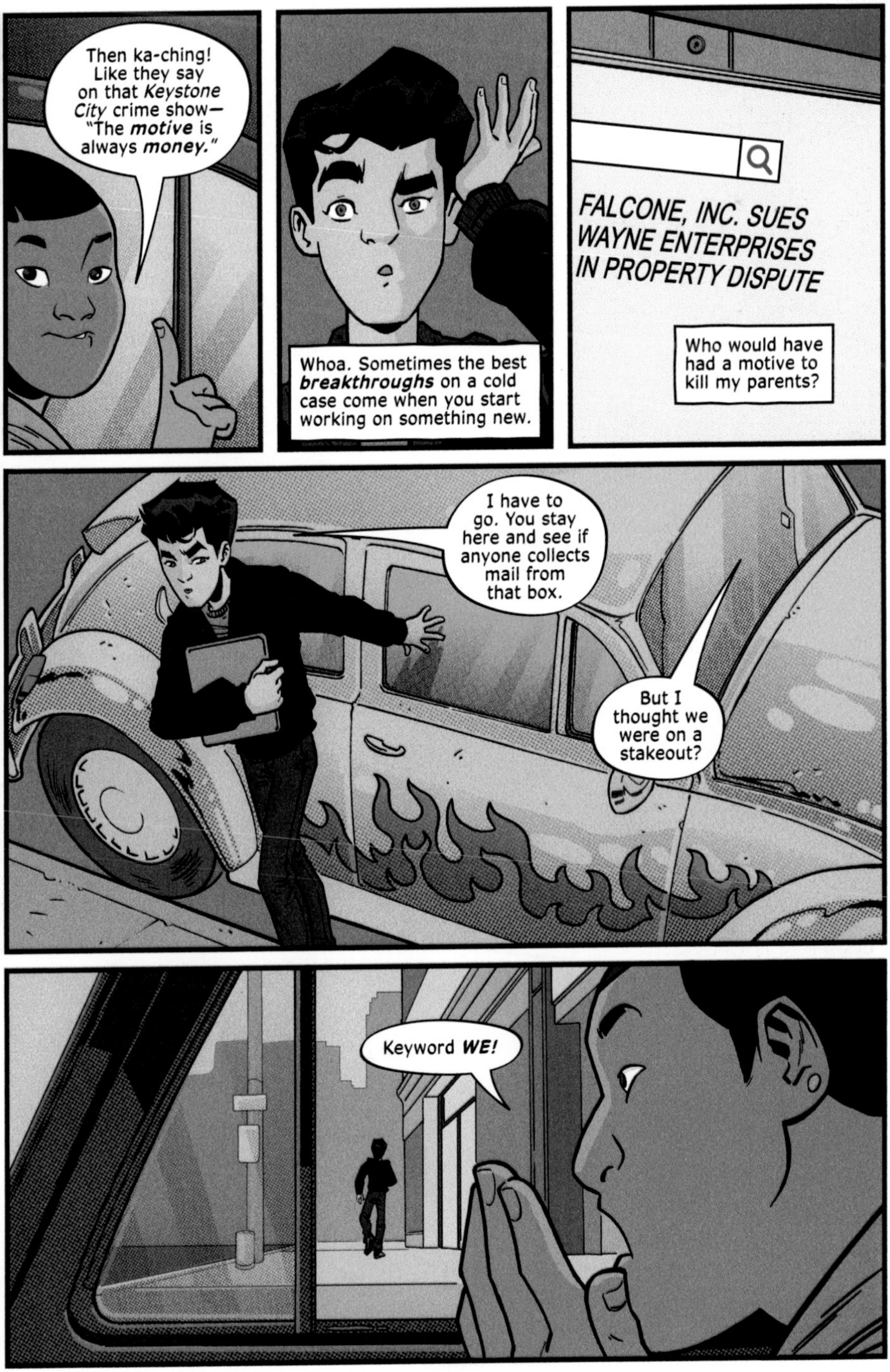
Then ka-ching! Like they say on that *Keystone City* crime show—"The ***motive*** is always ***money.***"
Whoa. Sometimes the best ***breakthroughs*** on a cold case come when you start working on something new.
FALCONE, INC. SUES WAYNE ENTERPRISES IN PROPERTY DISPUTE
Who would have had a motive to kill my parents?
I have to go. You stay here and see if anyone collects mail from that box.
But I thought we were on a stakeout?
Keyword ***WE!***

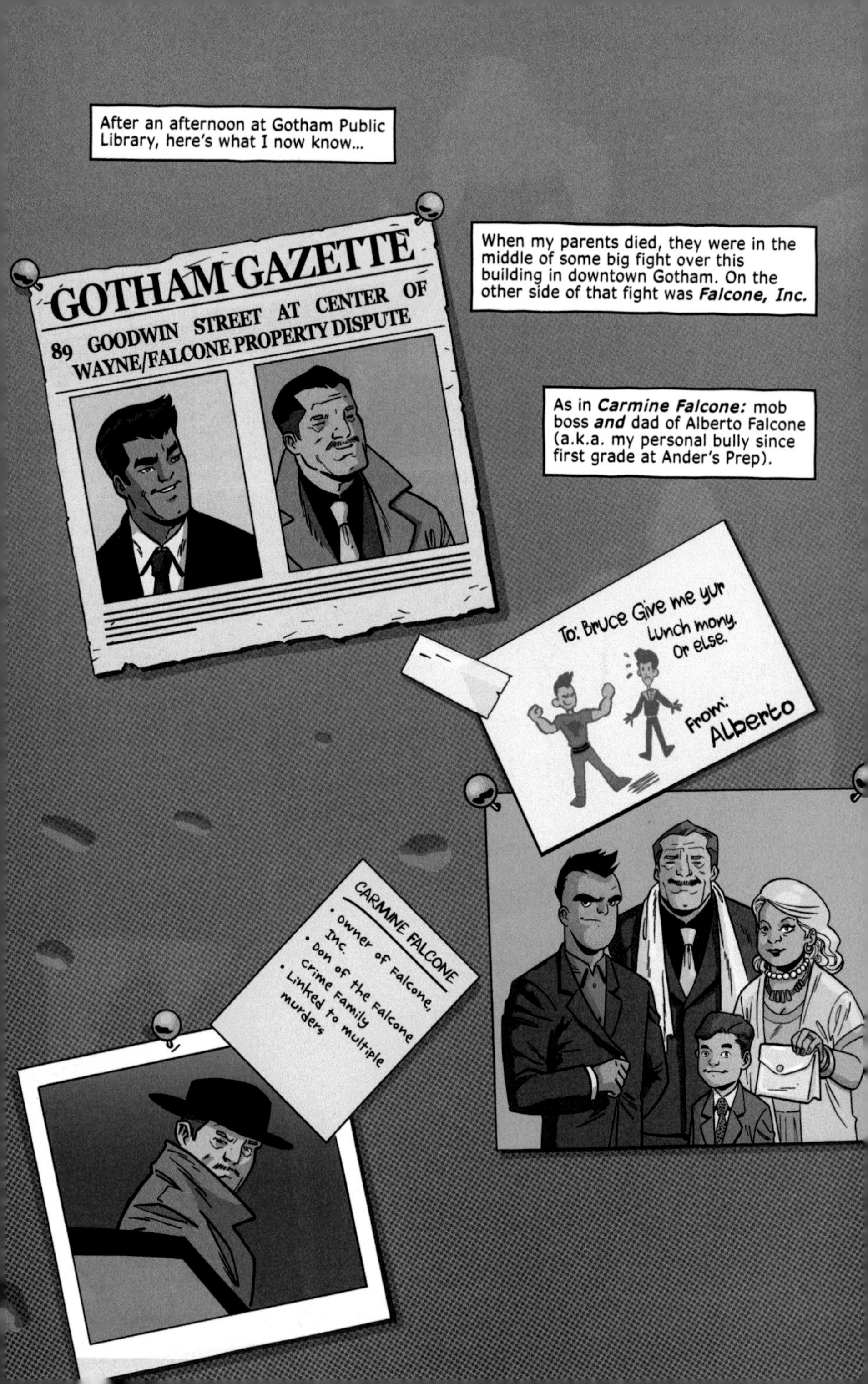
After an afternoon at Gotham Public Library, here's what I now know...
GOTHAM GAZETTE
89 GOODWIN STREET AT CENTER OF WAYNE/FALCONE PROPERTY DISPUTE
When my parents died, they were in the middle of some big fight over this building in downtown Gotham. On the other side of that fight was Falcone, Inc.
As in Carmine Falcone: mob boss and dad of Alberto Falcone (a.k.a. my personal bully since first grade at Ander's Prep).
To: Bruce Give me yur lunch mony. Or else.
From: Alberto
CARMINE FALCONE
• Owner of Falcone, Inc.
• Don of the Falcone crime family
• Linked to multiple murders

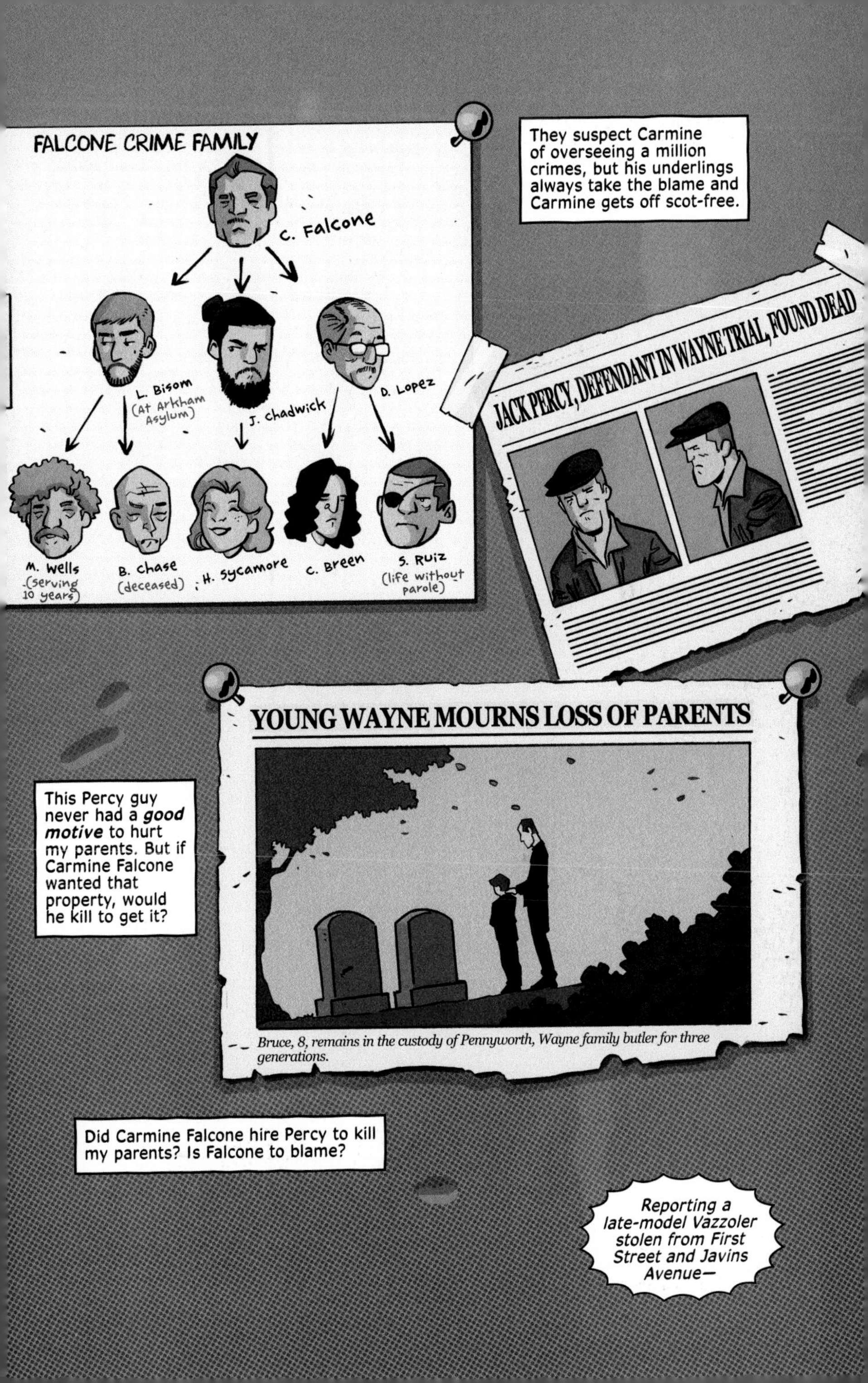

FALCONE CRIME FAMILY
C. Falcone
L. Bisom (At Arkham Asylum)
J. Chadwick
D. Lopez
M. Wells (serving 10 years)
B. Chase (deceased)
H. Sycamore
C. Breen
S. Ruiz (life without parole)
They suspect Carmine of overseeing a million crimes, but his underlings always take the blame and Carmine gets off scot-free.
JACK PERCY, DEFENDANT IN WAYNE TRIAL, FOUND DEAD
YOUNG WAYNE MOURNS LOSS OF PARENTS
Bruce, 8, remains in the custody of Pennyworth, Wayne family butler for three generations.
This Percy guy never had a good motive to hurt my parents. But if Carmine Falcone wanted that property, would he kill to get it?
Did Carmine Falcone hire Percy to kill my parents? Is Falcone to blame?
Reporting a late-model Vazzoler stolen from First Street and Javins Avenue—

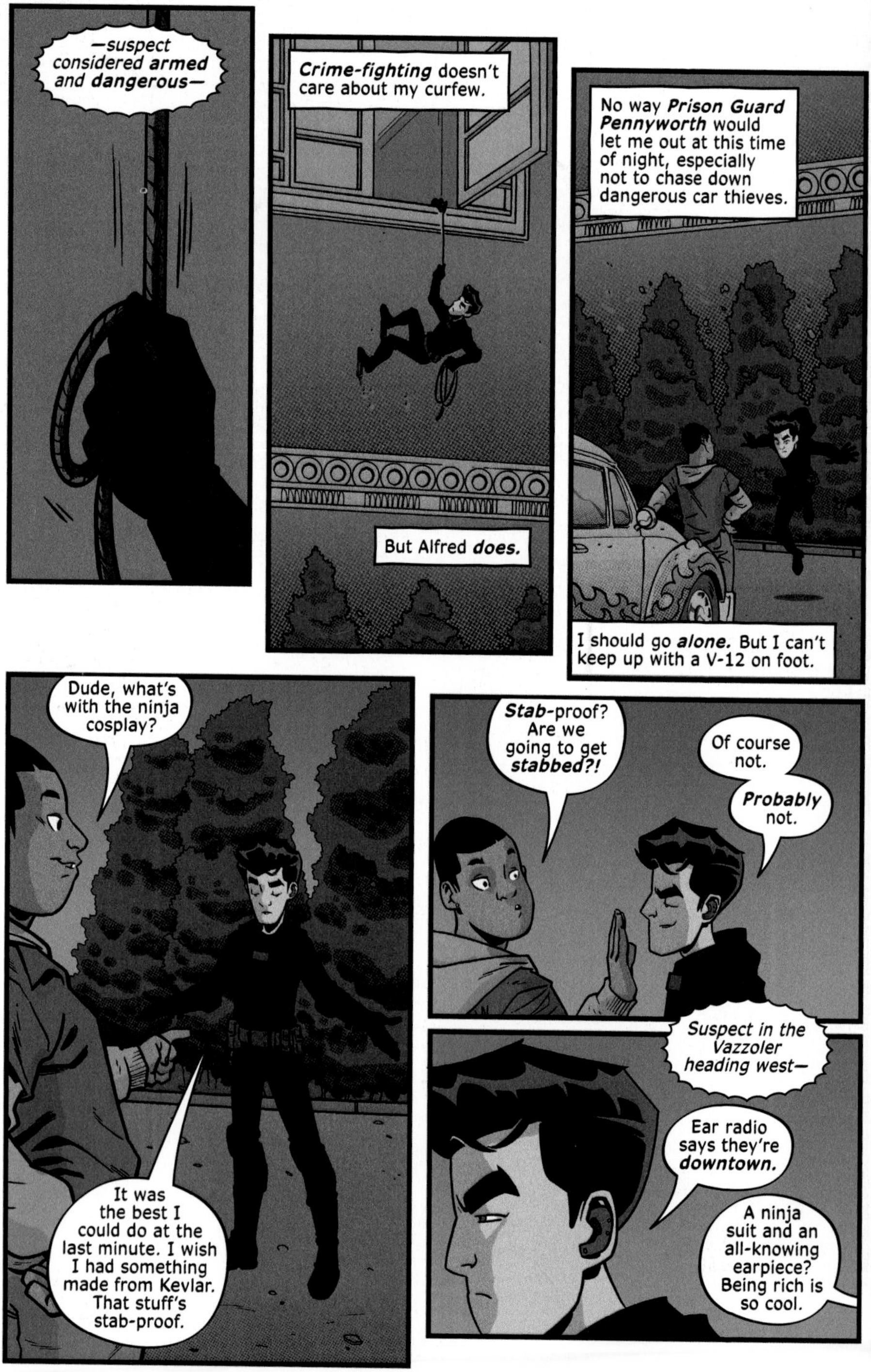
—suspect considered *armed* and *dangerous*—
Crime-fighting doesn't care about my curfew.
But Alfred *does.*
No way *Prison Guard Pennyworth* would let me out at this time of night, especially not to chase down dangerous car thieves.
I should go *alone.* But I can't keep up with a V-12 on foot.
Dude, what's with the ninja cosplay?
It was the best I could do at the last minute. I wish I had something made from Kevlar. That stuff's stab-proof.
Stab-proof? Are we going to get *stabbed?!*
Of course not.
Probably not.
Suspect in the Vazzoler heading west—
Ear radio says they're *downtown.*
A ninja suit and an all-knowing earpiece? Being rich is so cool.

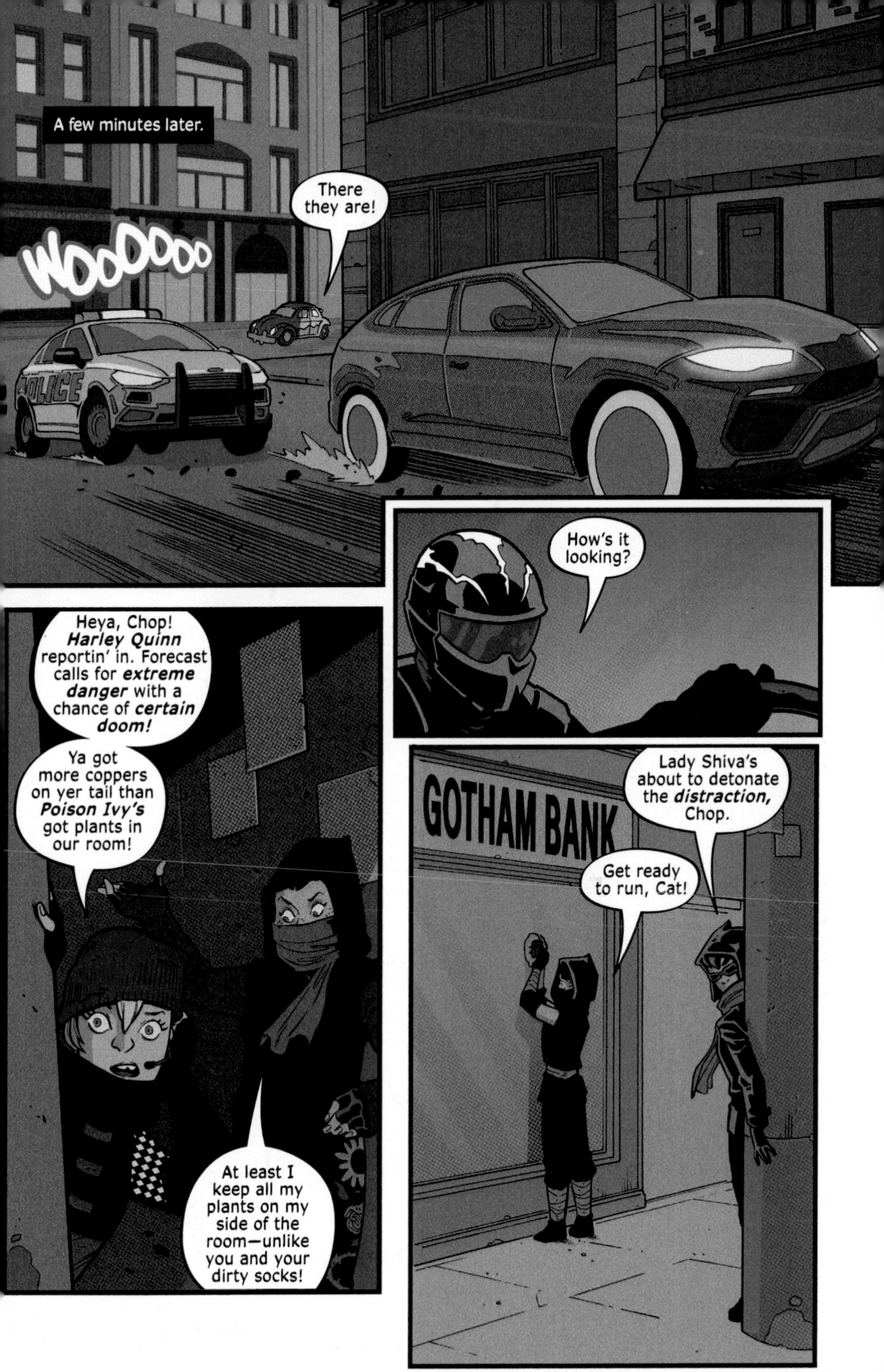
A few minutes later.
WOOOOOO
There they are!
POLICE
How's it looking?
Heya, Chop! Harley Quinn reportin' in. Forecast calls for extreme danger with a chance of certain doom!
Ya got more coppers on yer tail than Poison Ivy's got plants in our room!
At least I keep all my plants on my side of the room—unlike you and your dirty socks!
GOTHAM BANK
Lady Shiva's about to detonate the distraction, Chop.
Get ready to run, Cat!

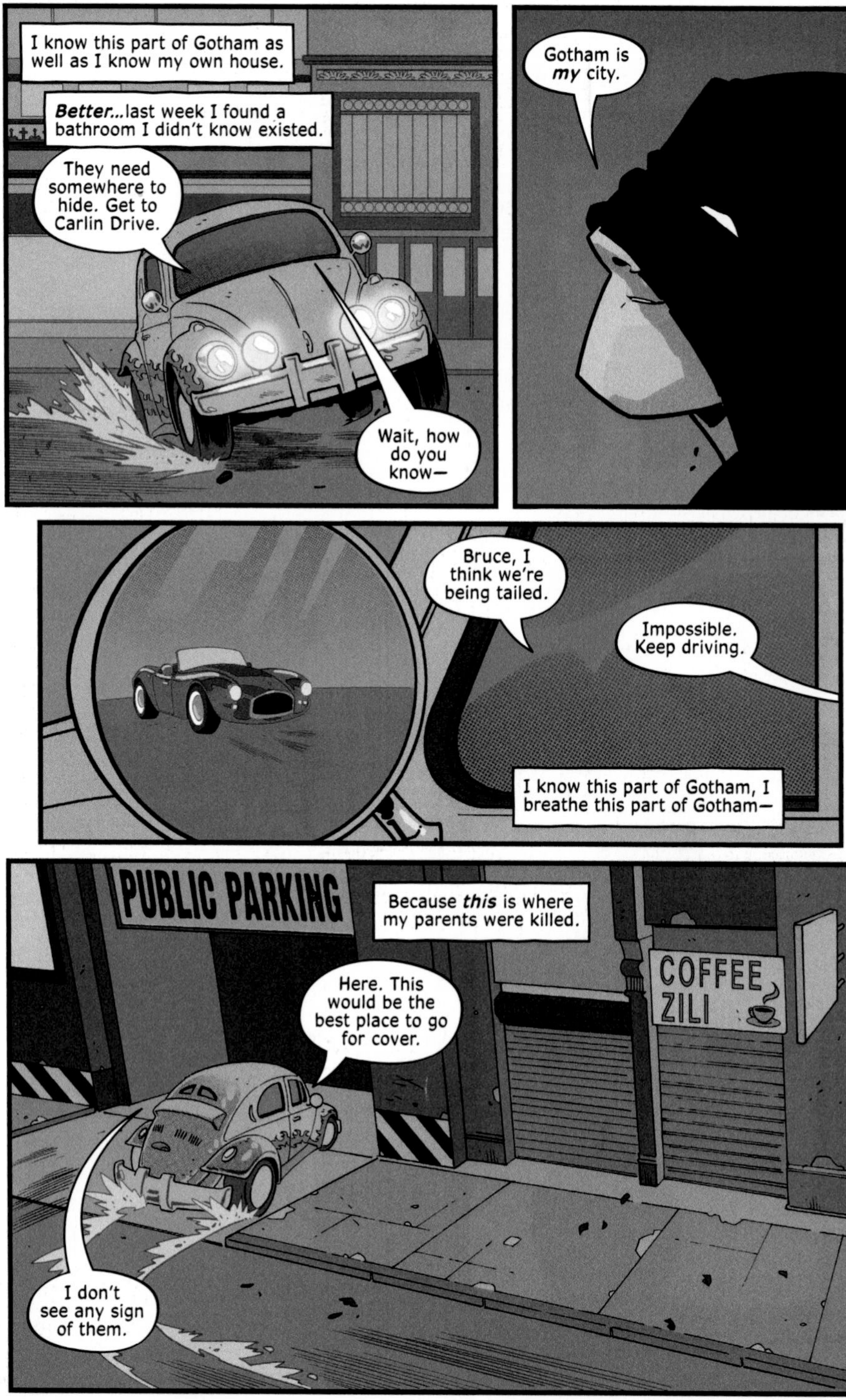
I know this part of Gotham as well as I know my own house.
Better...last week I found a bathroom I didn't know existed.
They need somewhere to hide. Get to Carlin Drive.
Wait, how do you know—
Gotham is my city.
Bruce, I think we're being tailed.
Impossible. Keep driving.
I know this part of Gotham, I breathe this part of Gotham—
PUBLIC PARKING
Because this is where my parents were killed.
COFFEE ZILI
Here. This would be the best place to go for cover.
I don't see any sign of them.

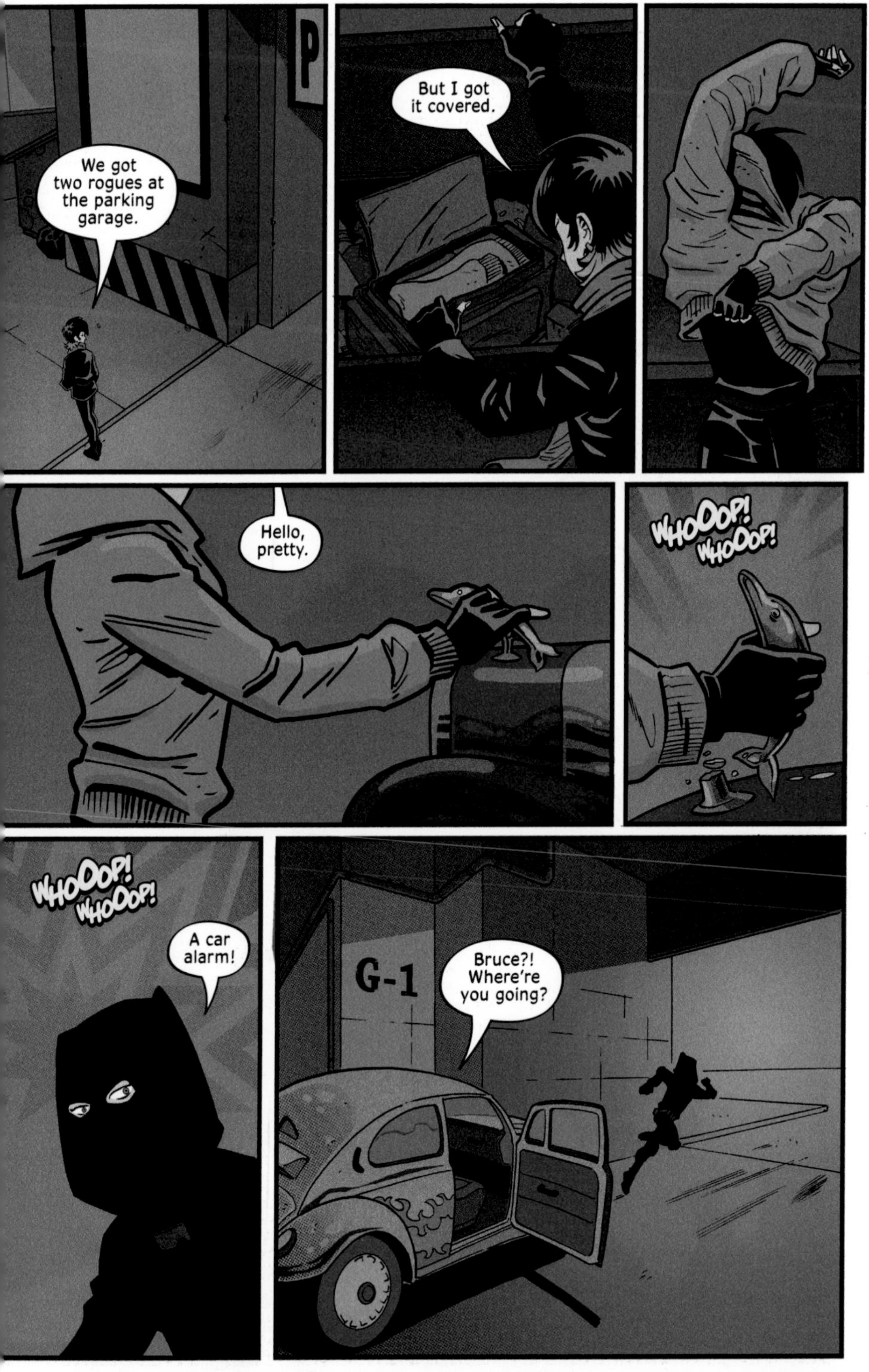
We got two rogues at the parking garage.
But I got it covered.
Hello, pretty.
WHOOOP! WHOOOP!
WHOOOP! WHOOOP!
A car alarm!
G-1
Bruce?! Where're you going?

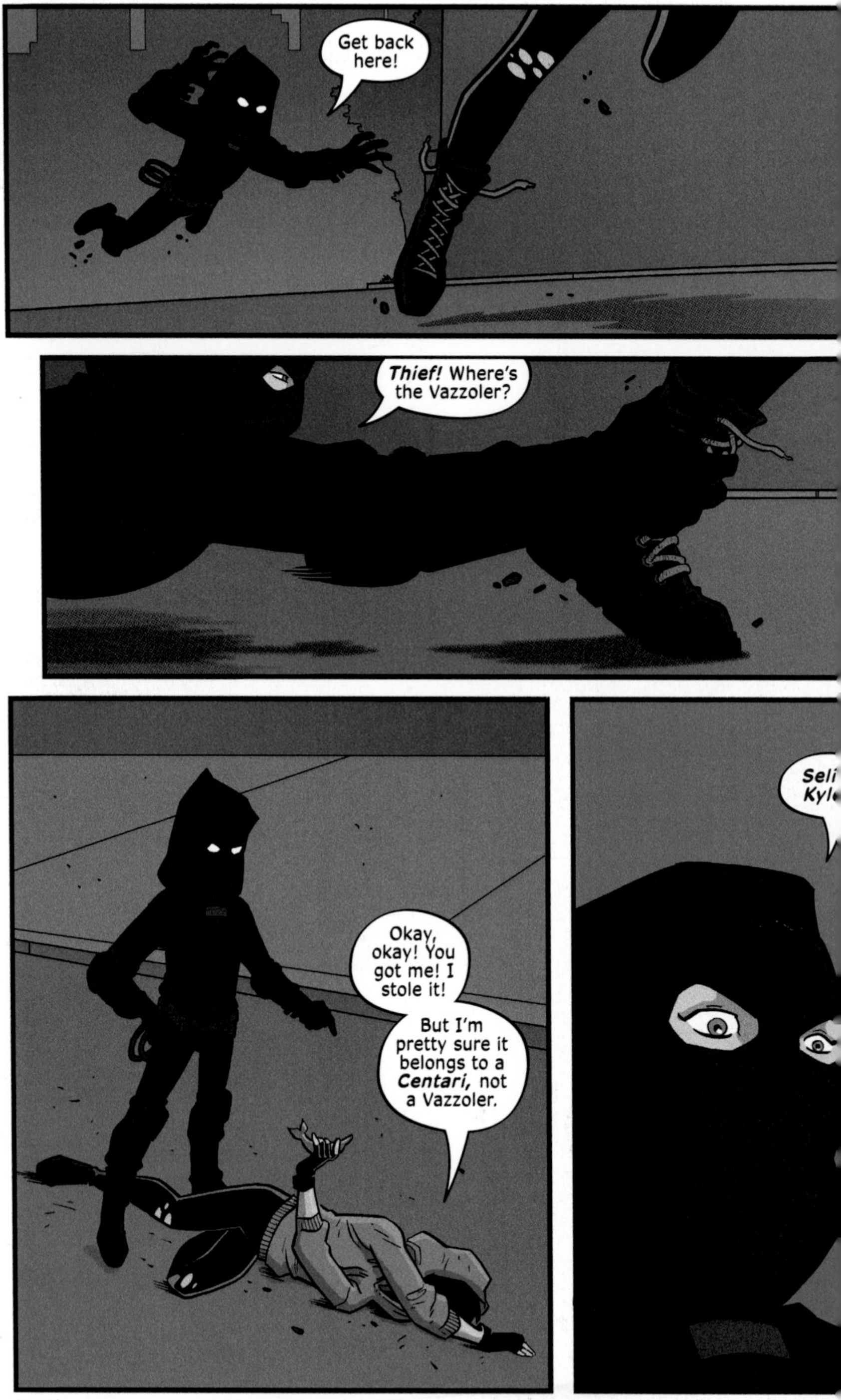
Get back here!
Thief! Where's the Vazzoler?
Okay, okay! You got me! I stole it!
But I'm pretty sure it belongs to a Centari, not a Vazzoler.

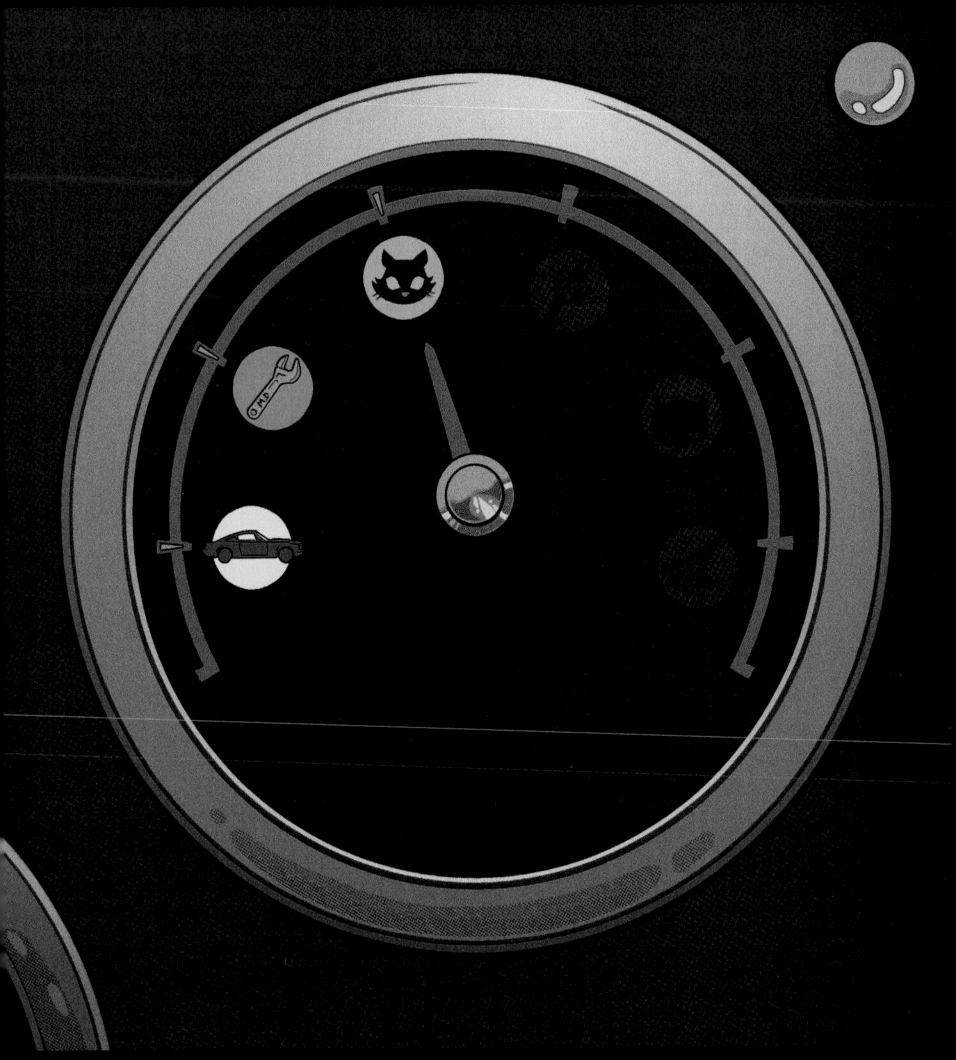

GET IN GEAR

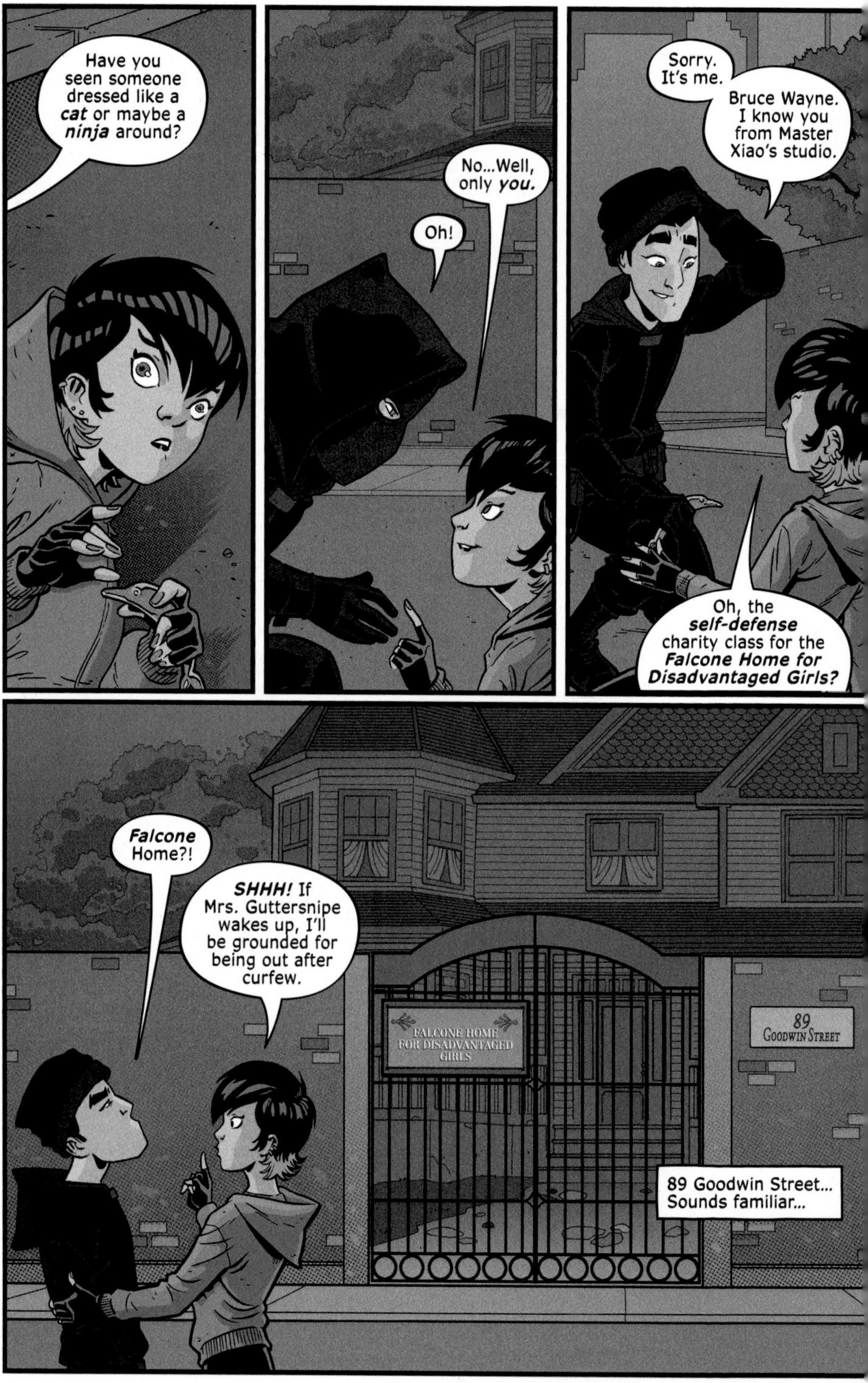

Have you seen someone dressed like a *cat* or maybe a *ninja* around?
No...Well, only *you.*
Oh!
Sorry. It's me.
Bruce Wayne. I know you from Master Xiao's studio.
Oh, the *self-defense* charity class for the *Falcone Home for Disadvantaged Girls?*
Falcone Home?!
SHHH! If Mrs. Guttersnipe wakes up, I'll be grounded for being out after curfew.
FALCONE HOME FOR DISADVANTAGED GIRLS
89 GOODWIN STREET
89 Goodwin Street... Sounds familiar...

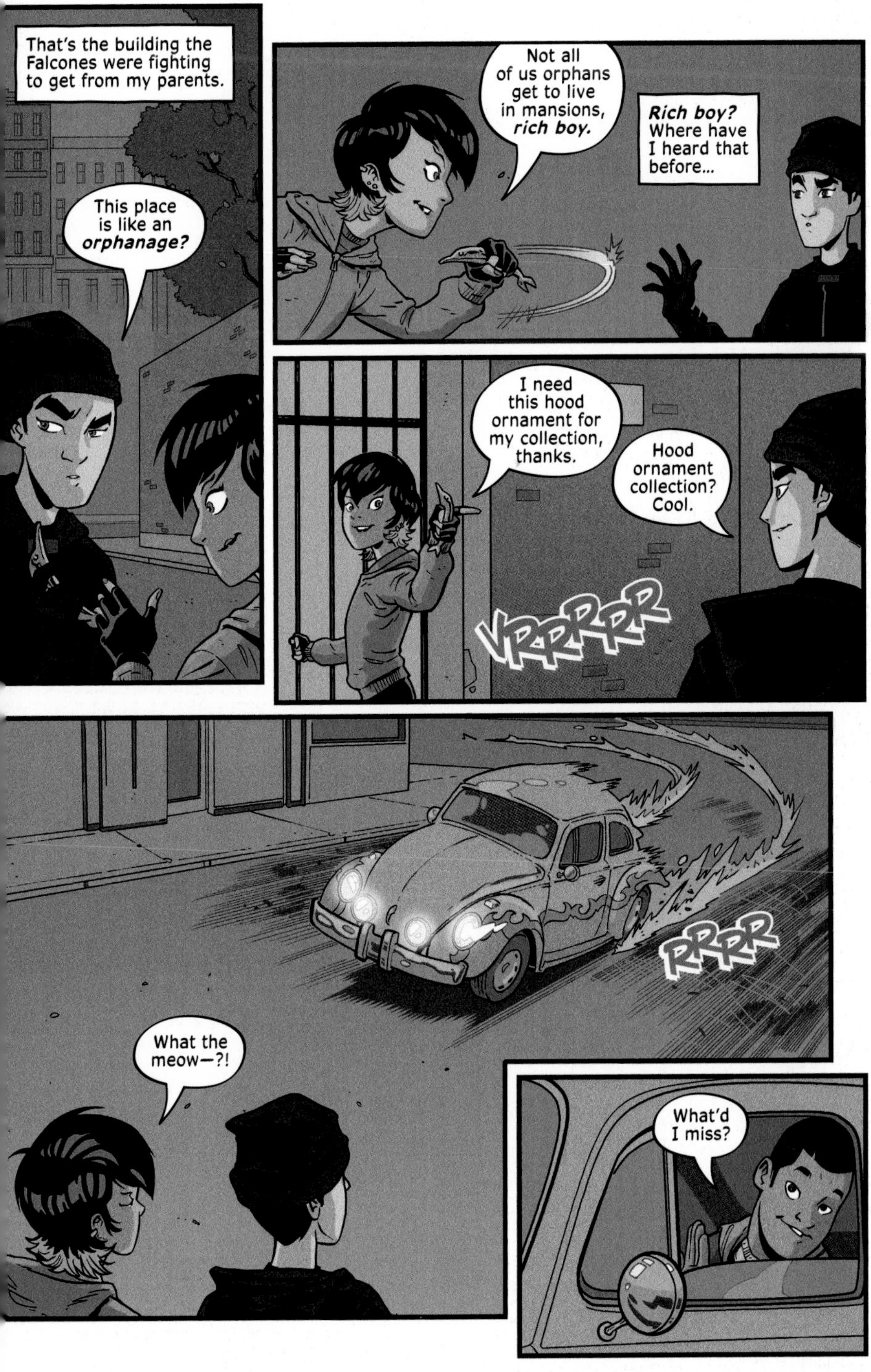
That's the building the Falcones were fighting to get from my parents.
This place is like an *orphanage?*
Not all of us orphans get to live in mansions, ***rich boy.***
Rich boy? Where have I heard that before...
I need this hood ornament for my collection, thanks.
Hood ornament collection? Cool.
VRRRRR
RRRR
What the meow—?!
What'd I miss?

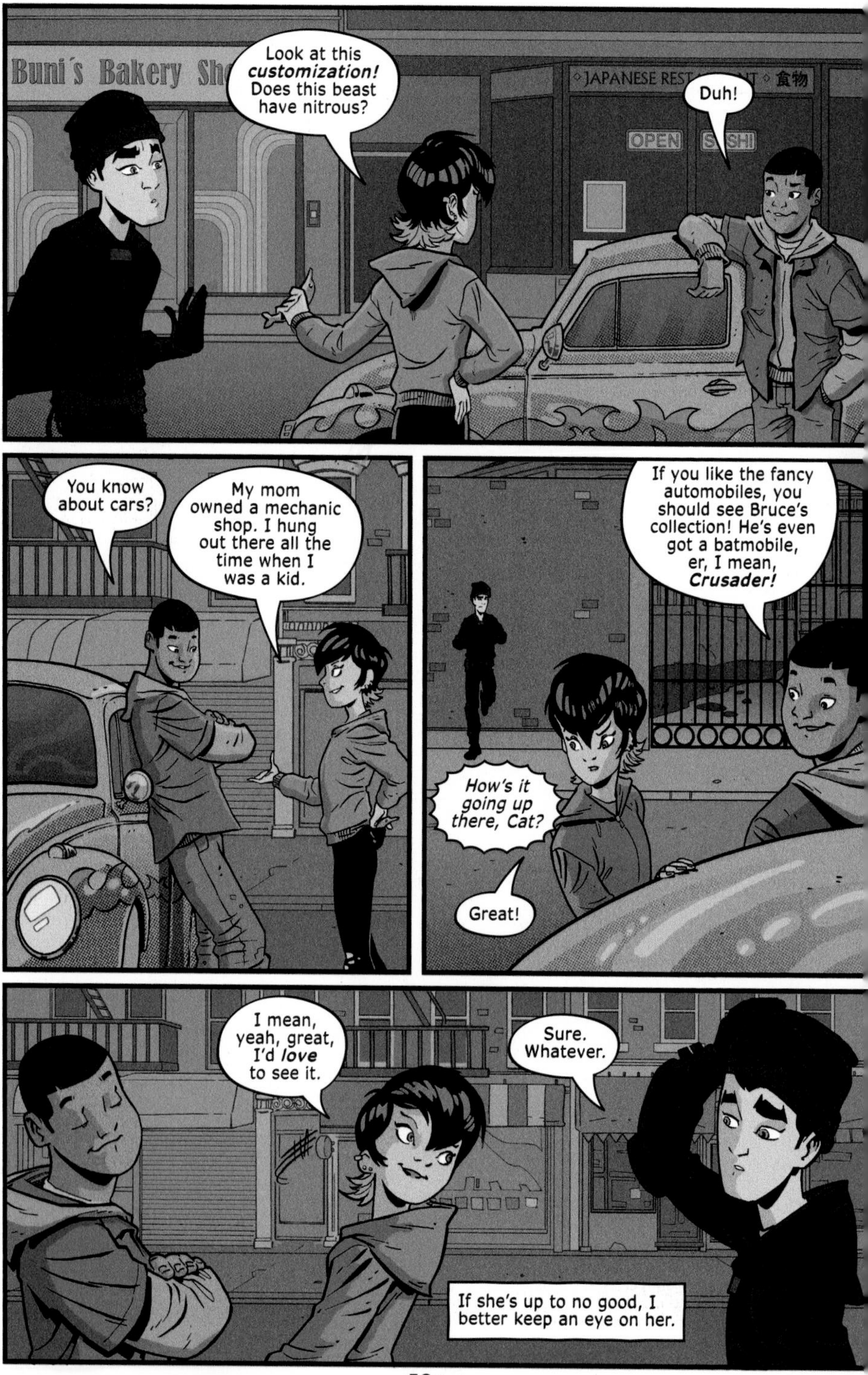
Buni's Bakery Sh
Look at this customization! Does this beast have nitrous?
JAPANESE REST
食物
Duh!
OPEN
You know about cars?
My mom owned a mechanic shop. I hung out there all the time when I was a kid.
If you like the fancy automobiles, you should see Bruce's collection! He's even got a batmobile, er, I mean, Crusader!
How's it going up there, Cat?
Great!
I mean, yeah, great, I'd love to see it.
Sure. Whatever.
If she's up to no good, I better keep an eye on her.

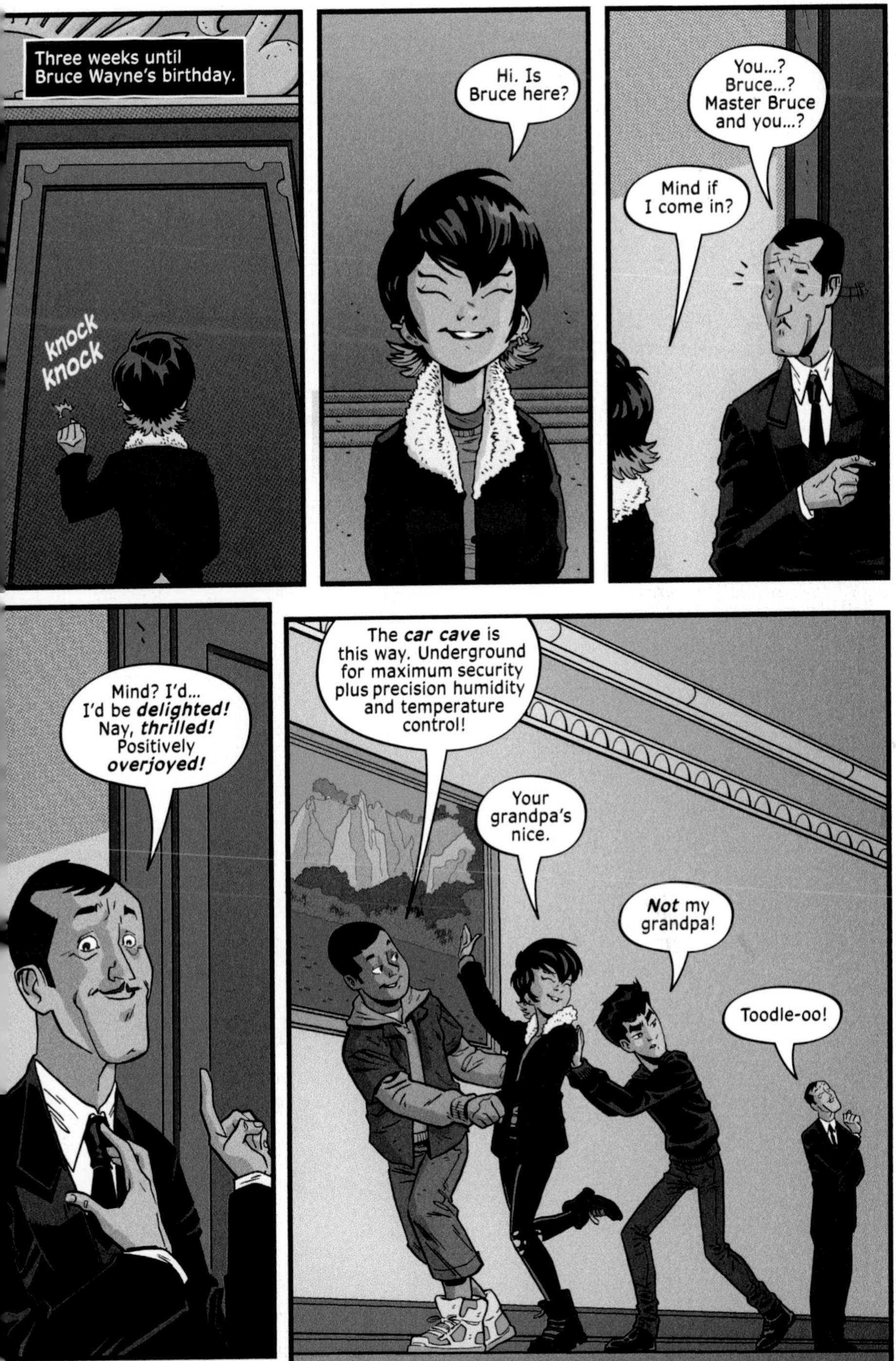

Three weeks until Bruce Wayne's birthday.
knock knock
Hi. Is Bruce here?
You...? Bruce...? Master Bruce and you...?
Mind if I come in?
Mind? I'd... I'd be *delighted!* Nay, *thrilled!* Positively *overjoyed!*
The *car cave* is this way. Underground for maximum security plus precision humidity and temperature control!
Your grandpa's nice.
Not my grandpa!
Toodle-oo!

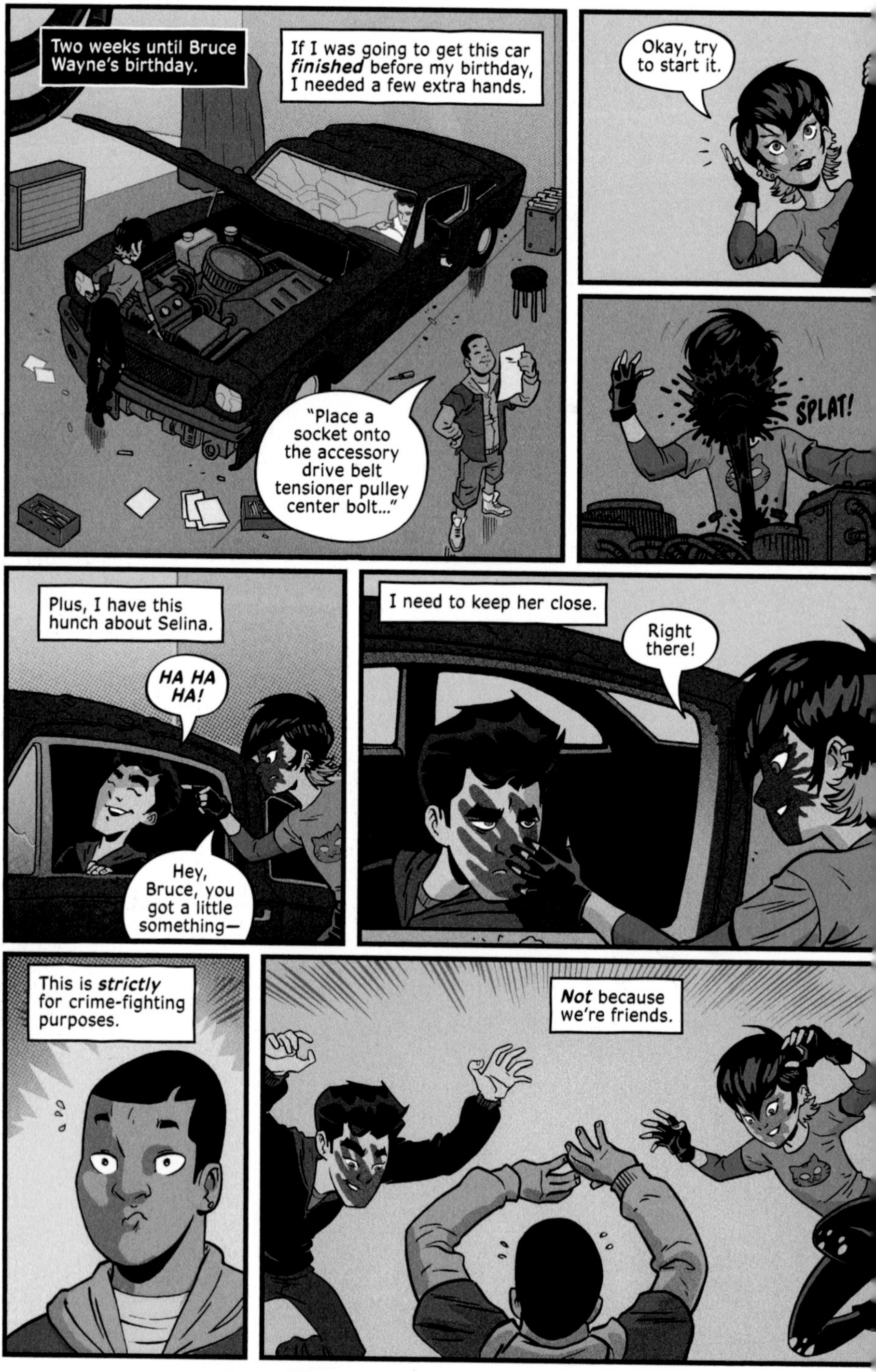
Two weeks until Bruce Wayne's birthday.
If I was going to get this car *finished* before my birthday, I needed a few extra hands.
"Place a socket onto the accessory drive belt tensioner pulley center bolt..."
Okay, try to start it.
SPLAT!
Plus, I have this hunch about Selina.
HA HA HA!
Hey, Bruce, you got a little something—
I need to keep her close.
Right there!
This is *strictly* for crime-fighting purposes.
Not because we're friends.

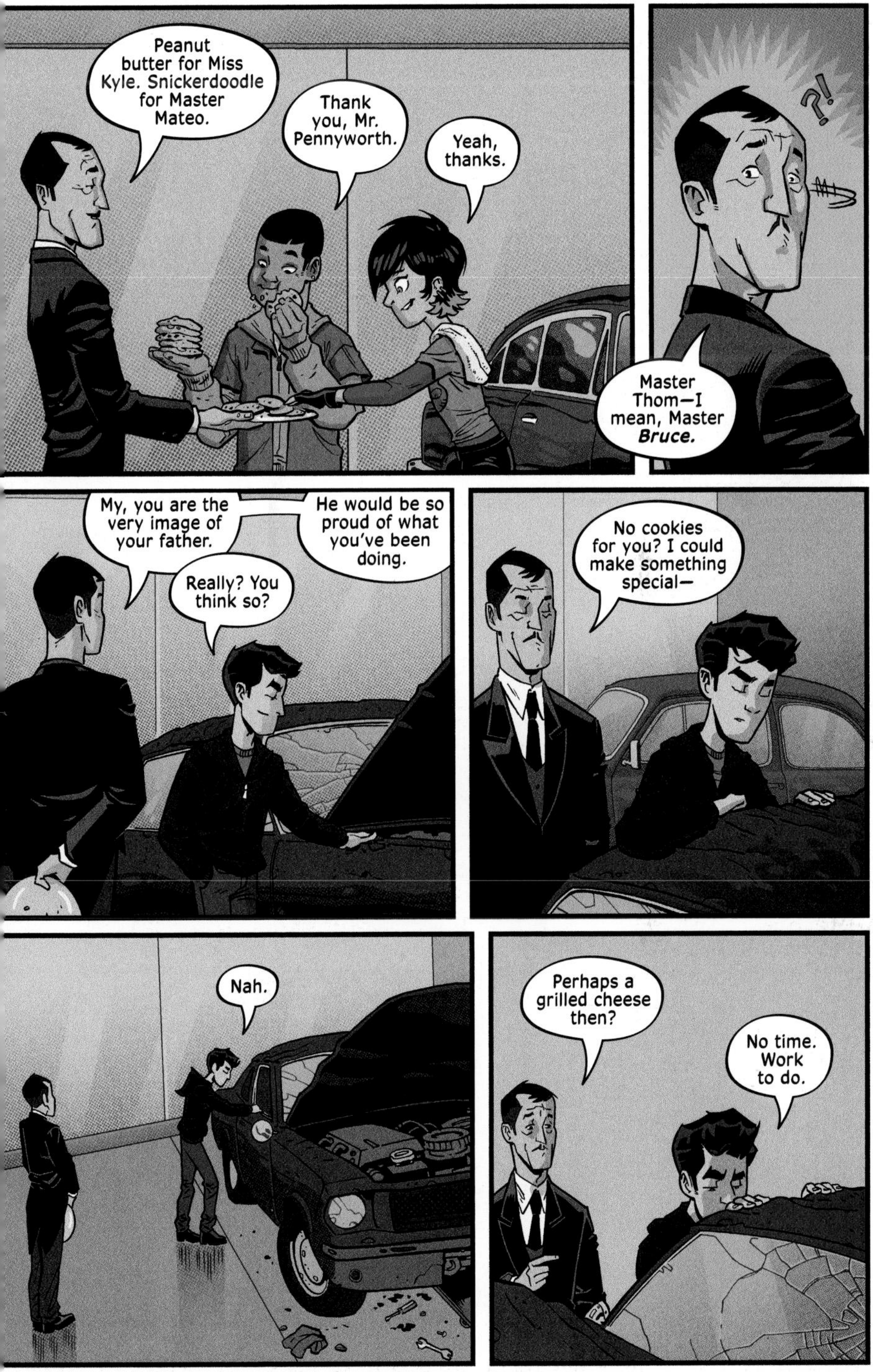
Peanut butter for Miss Kyle. Snickerdoodle for Master Mateo.
Thank you, Mr. Pennyworth.
Yeah, thanks.
?!
Master Thom—I mean, Master ***Bruce.***
My, you are the very image of your father.
He would be so proud of what you've been doing.
Really? You think so?
No cookies for you? I could make something special—
Nah.
Perhaps a grilled cheese then?
No time. Work to do.

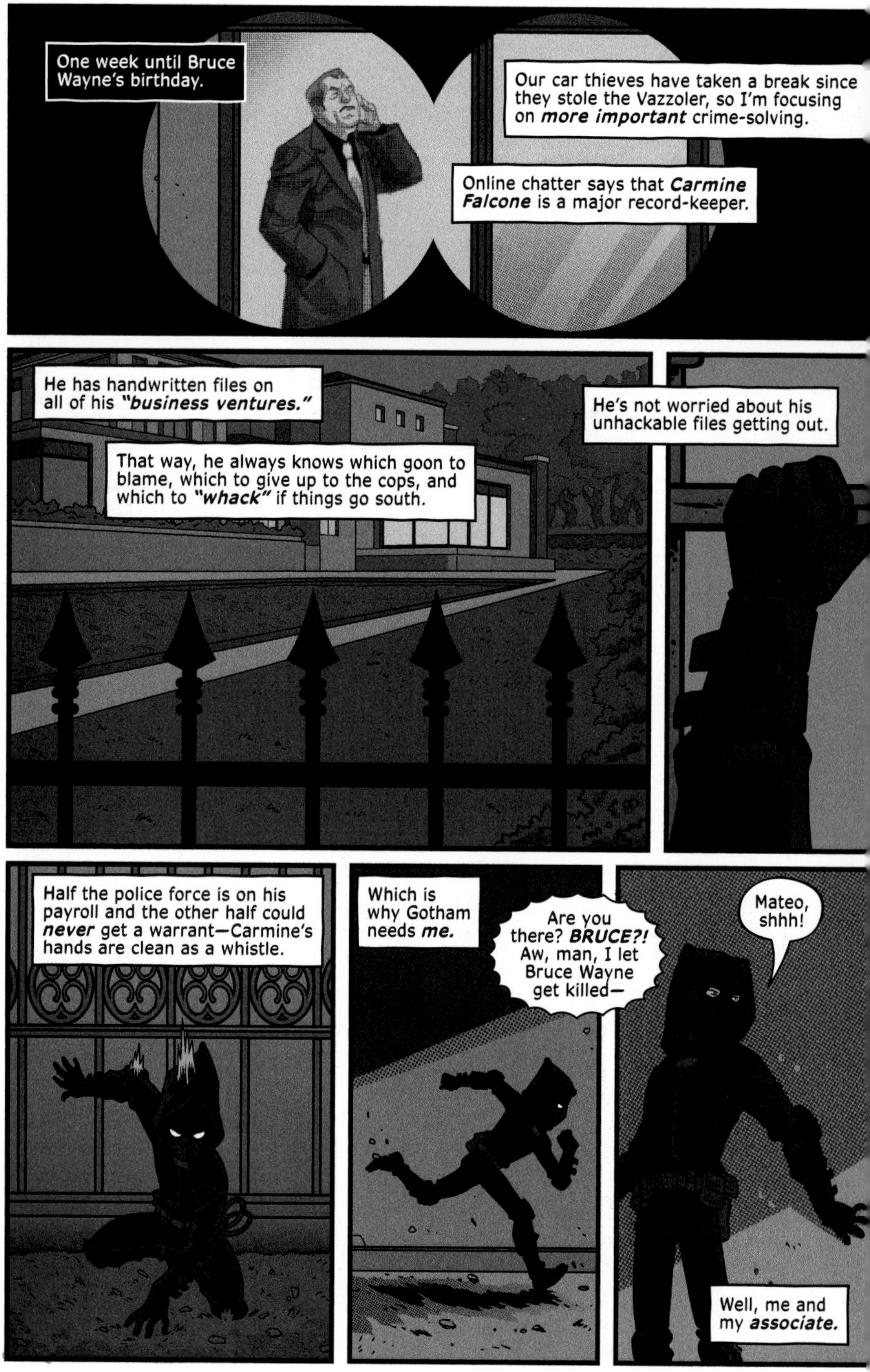
One week until Bruce Wayne's birthday.
Our car thieves have taken a break since they stole the Vazzoler, so I'm focusing on *more important* crime-solving.
Online chatter says that *Carmine Falcone* is a major record-keeper.
He has handwritten files on all of his *"business ventures."*
That way, he always knows which goon to blame, which to give up to the cops, and which to *"whack"* if things go south.
He's not worried about his unhackable files getting out.
Half the police force is on his payroll and the other half could *never* get a warrant—Carmine's hands are clean as a whistle.
Which is why Gotham needs *me.*
Are you there? *BRUCE?!* Aw, man, I let Bruce Wayne get killed—
Mateo, shhh!
Well, me and my *associate.*

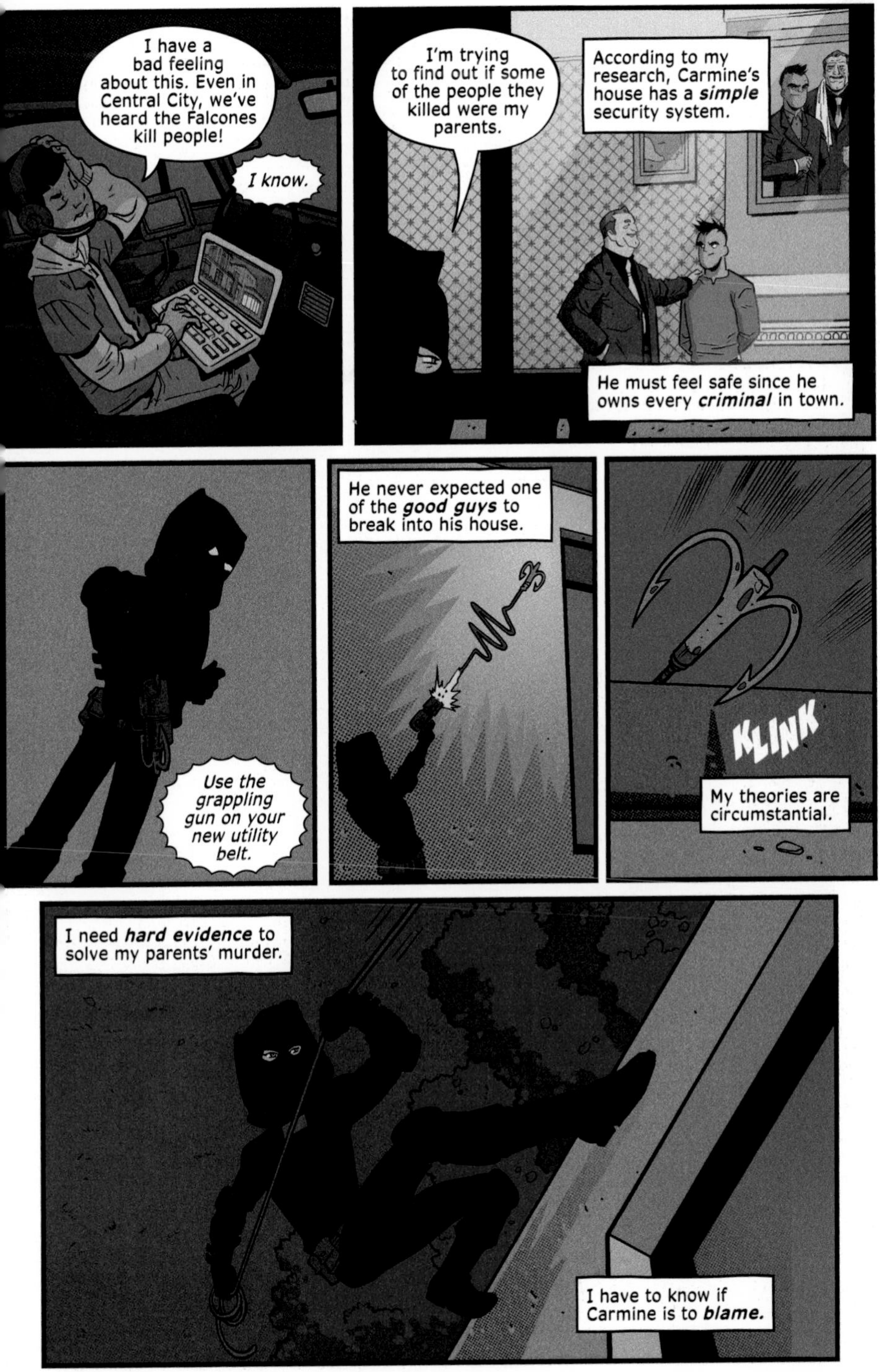
I have a bad feeling about this. Even in Central City, we've heard the Falcones kill people!
I know.
I'm trying to find out if some of the people they killed were my parents.
According to my research, Carmine's house has a simple security system.
He must feel safe since he owns every criminal in town.
Use the grappling gun on your new utility belt.
He never expected one of the good guys to break into his house.
KLINK
My theories are circumstantial.
I need hard evidence to solve my parents' murder.
I have to know if Carmine is to blame.

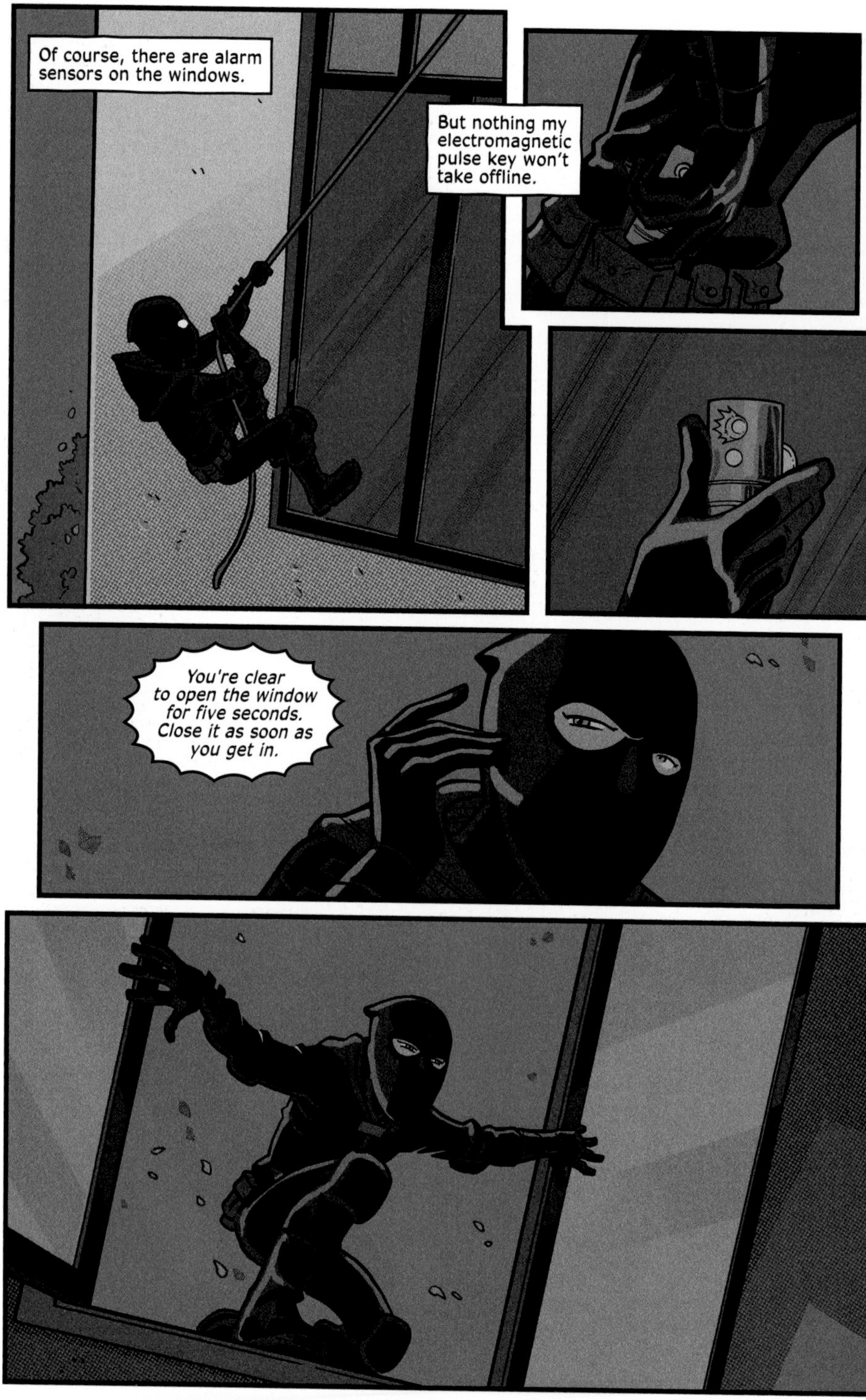
Of course, there are alarm sensors on the windows.
But nothing my electromagnetic pulse key won't take offline.
You're clear to open the window for five seconds. Close it as soon as you get in.

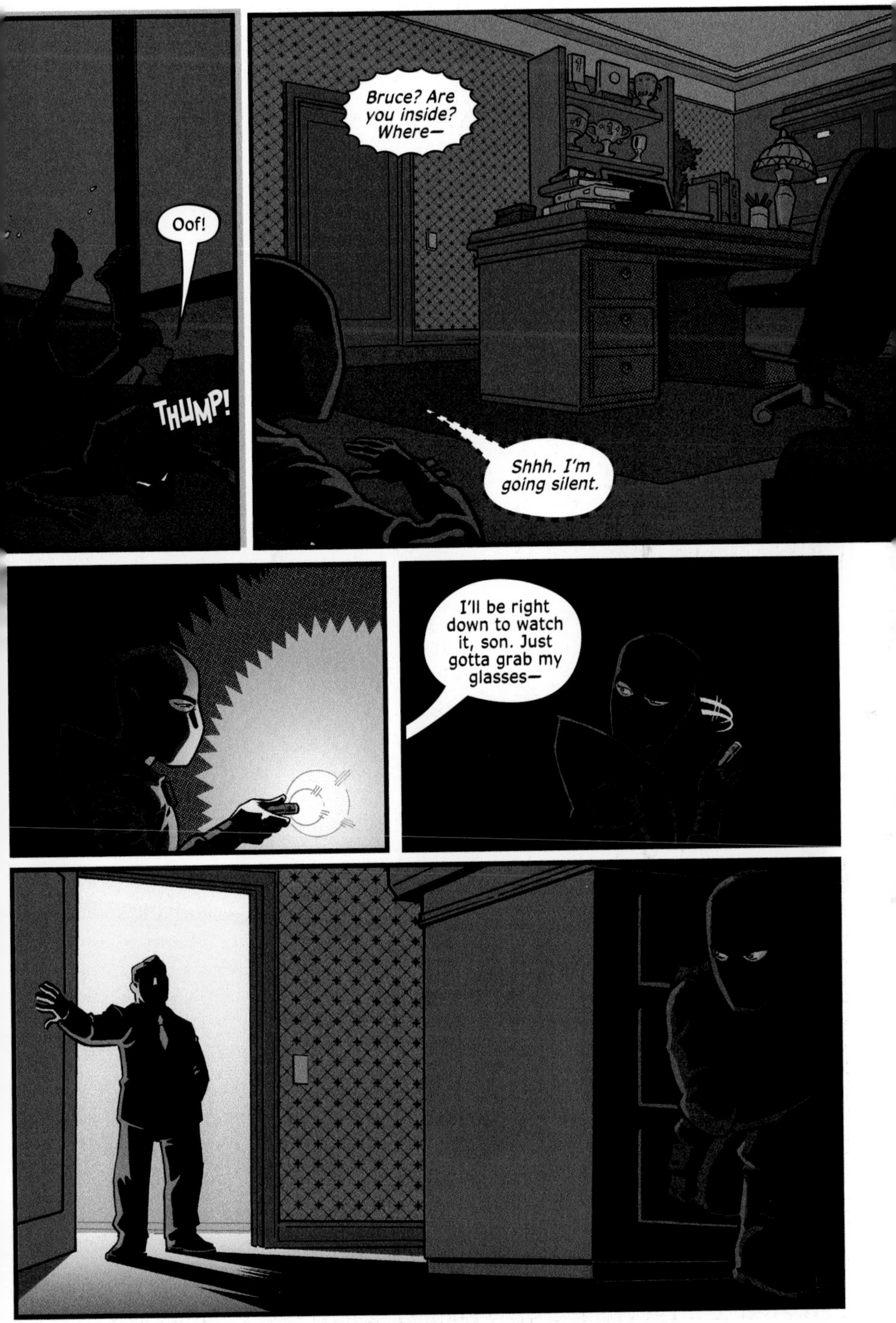
Oof!
THUMP!
Bruce? Are you inside? Where—
Shhh. I'm going silent.
I'll be right down to watch it, son. Just gotta grab my glasses—

Hiding, huh?!

Gotcha, sneaky glasses.

SLAM

All right, P's for Jack *Percy*.

A-D

E-J

K-P

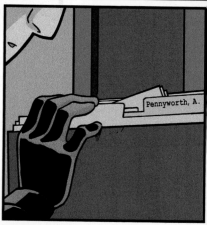

Pennyworth, A.

Alfred?

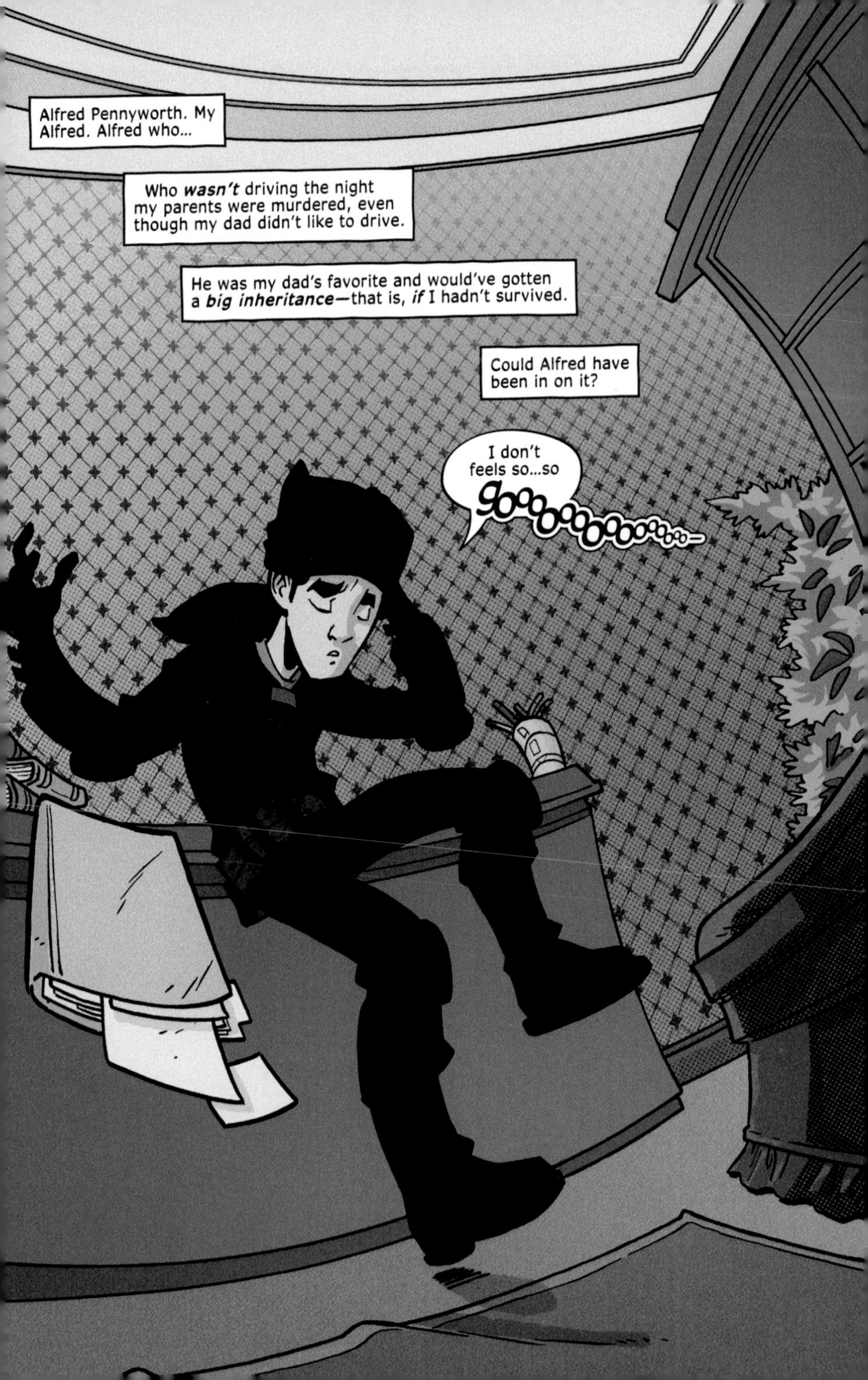
Alfred Pennyworth. My Alfred. Alfred who...
Who *wasn't* driving the night my parents were murdered, even though my dad didn't like to drive.
He was my dad's favorite and would've gotten a *big inheritance*—that is, *if* I hadn't survived.
Could Alfred have been in on it?
I don't feels so...so
gooooooooooooo—

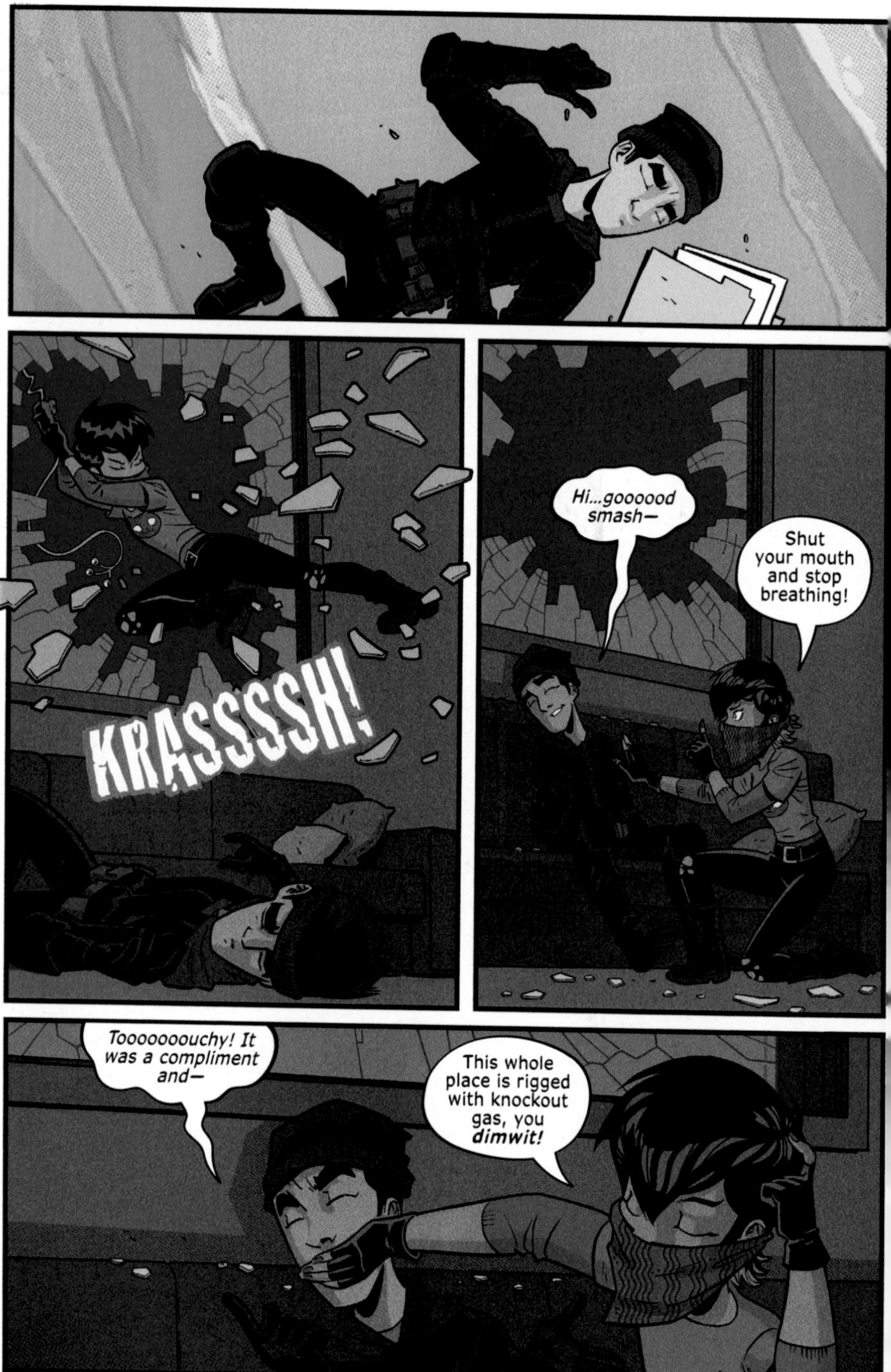
KRASSSSH!
Hi...goooood smash—
Shut your mouth and stop breathing!
Toooooooouchy! It was a compliment and—
This whole place is rigged with knockout gas, you *dimwit!*

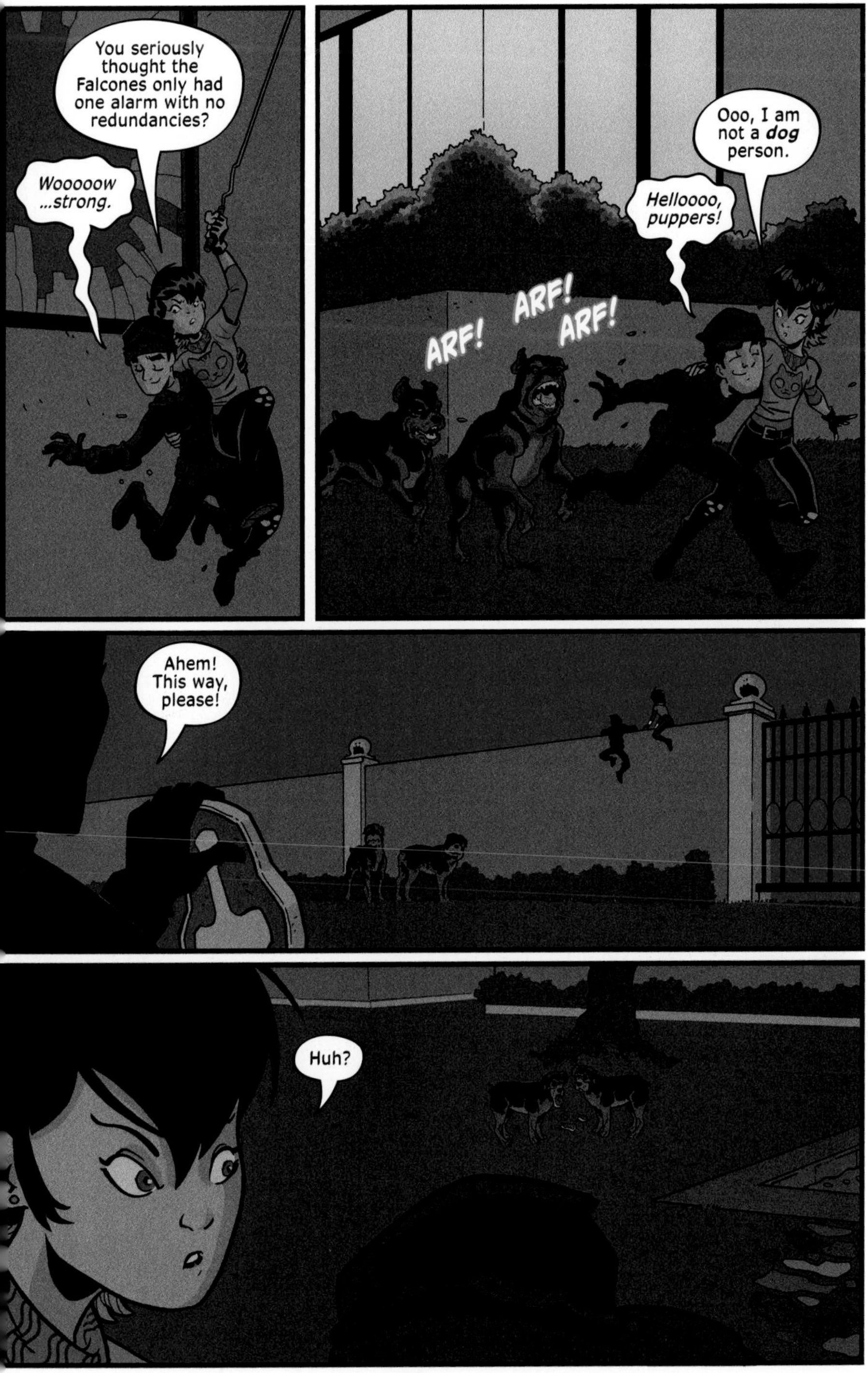
You seriously thought the Falcones only had one alarm with no redundancies?
Wooooow ...strong.
Ooo, I am not a *dog* person.
Helloooo, puppers!
ARF!
ARF!
ARF!
Ahem! This way, please!
Huh?

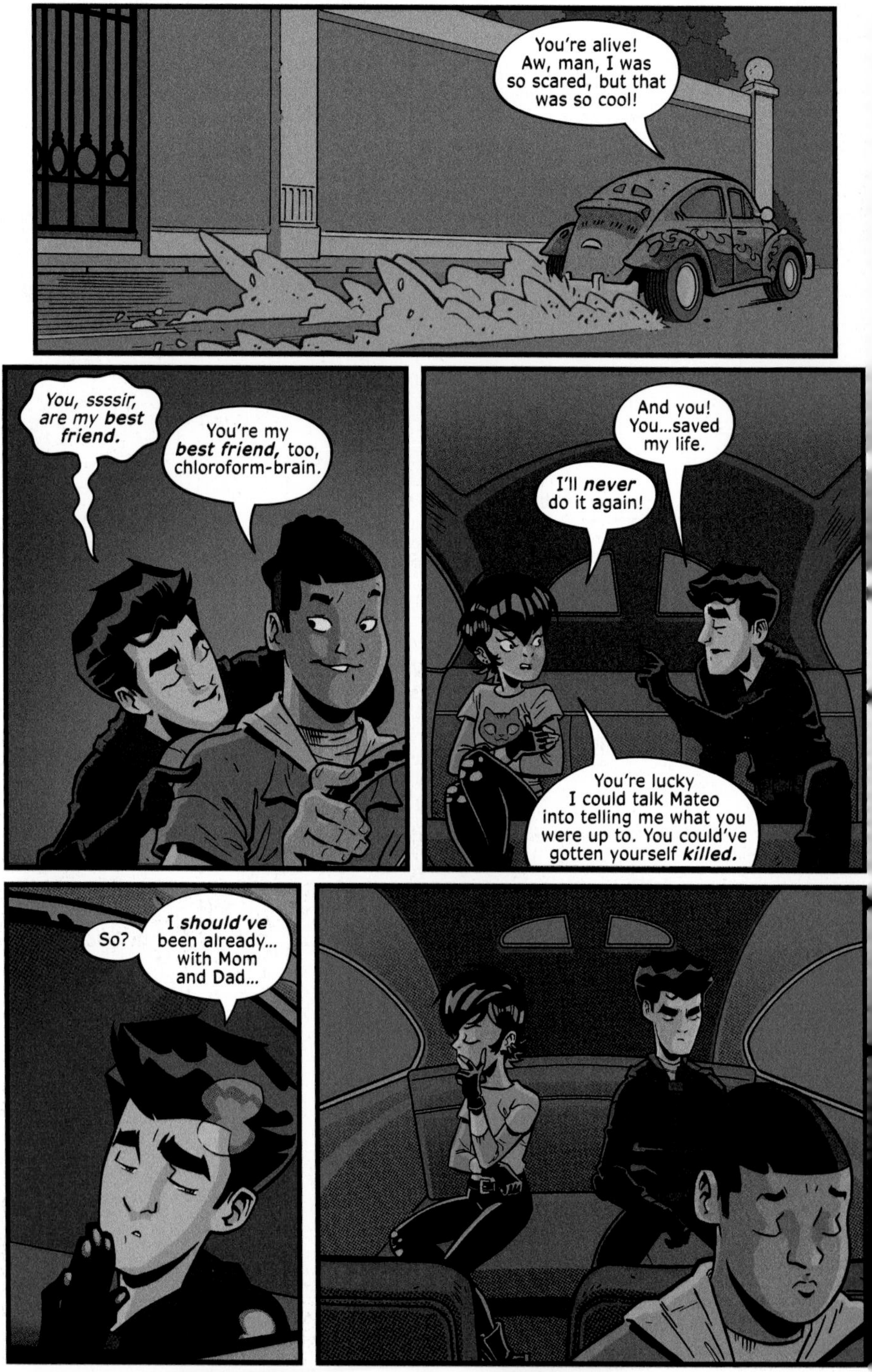
You're alive! Aw, man, I was so scared, but that was so cool!
You, ssssir, are my **best friend.**
You're my **best friend,** too, chloroform-brain.
And you! You...saved my life.
I'll **never** do it again!
You're lucky I could talk Mateo into telling me what you were up to. You could've gotten yourself **killed.**
So?
I **should've** been already... with Mom and Dad...

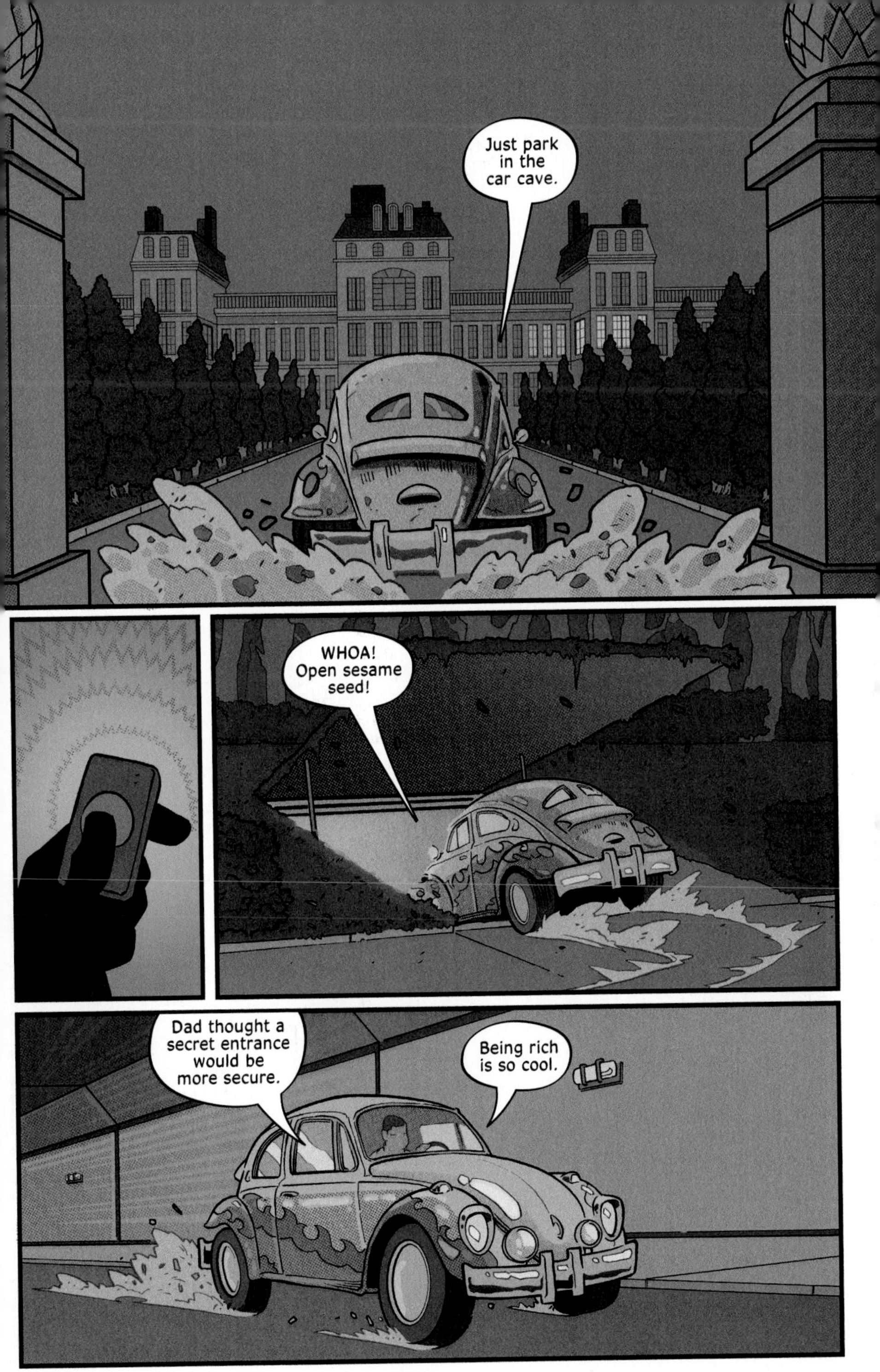
Just park in the car cave.
WHOA! Open sesame seed!
Dad thought a secret entrance would be more secure.
Being rich is so cool.

Keep it down, man. You'll wake Mr. Pennyworth.

Mr. Pennyworth?

KLANG!

It's Alfred's fault! He helped kill my parents!

C'mon, that's the knockout gas talking.

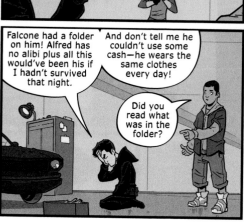

Falcone had a folder on him! Alfred has no alibi plus all this would've been his if I hadn't survived that night.

And don't tell me he couldn't use some cash—he wears the same clothes every day!

Did you read what was in the folder?

Didn't get the chance.

You don't *solve* a crime by *blaming* a guy, Sherlock. There's no *proof.*

I gotta go. I convinced my uncle to let me off the hook for the scrapyard thefts, but breaking curfew really gets to him.

66

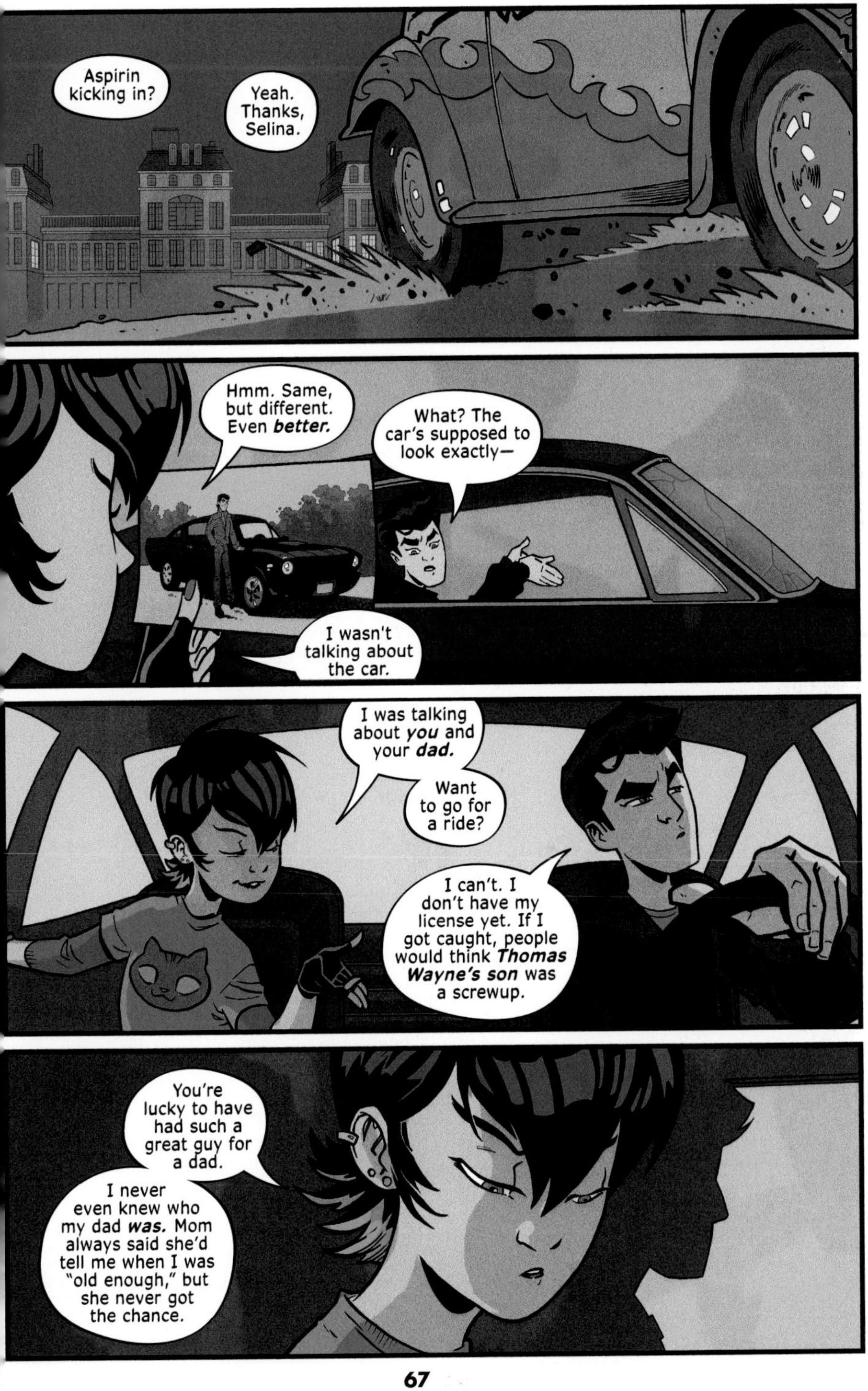
Aspirin kicking in?
Yeah. Thanks, Selina.
Hmm. Same, but different. Even *better.*
What? The car's supposed to look exactly—
I wasn't talking about the car.
I was talking about *you* and your *dad.*
Want to go for a ride?
I can't. I don't have my license yet. If I got caught, people would think *Thomas Wayne's son* was a screwup.
You're lucky to have had such a great guy for a dad.
I never even knew who my dad *was.* Mom always said she'd tell me when I was "old enough," but she never got the chance.

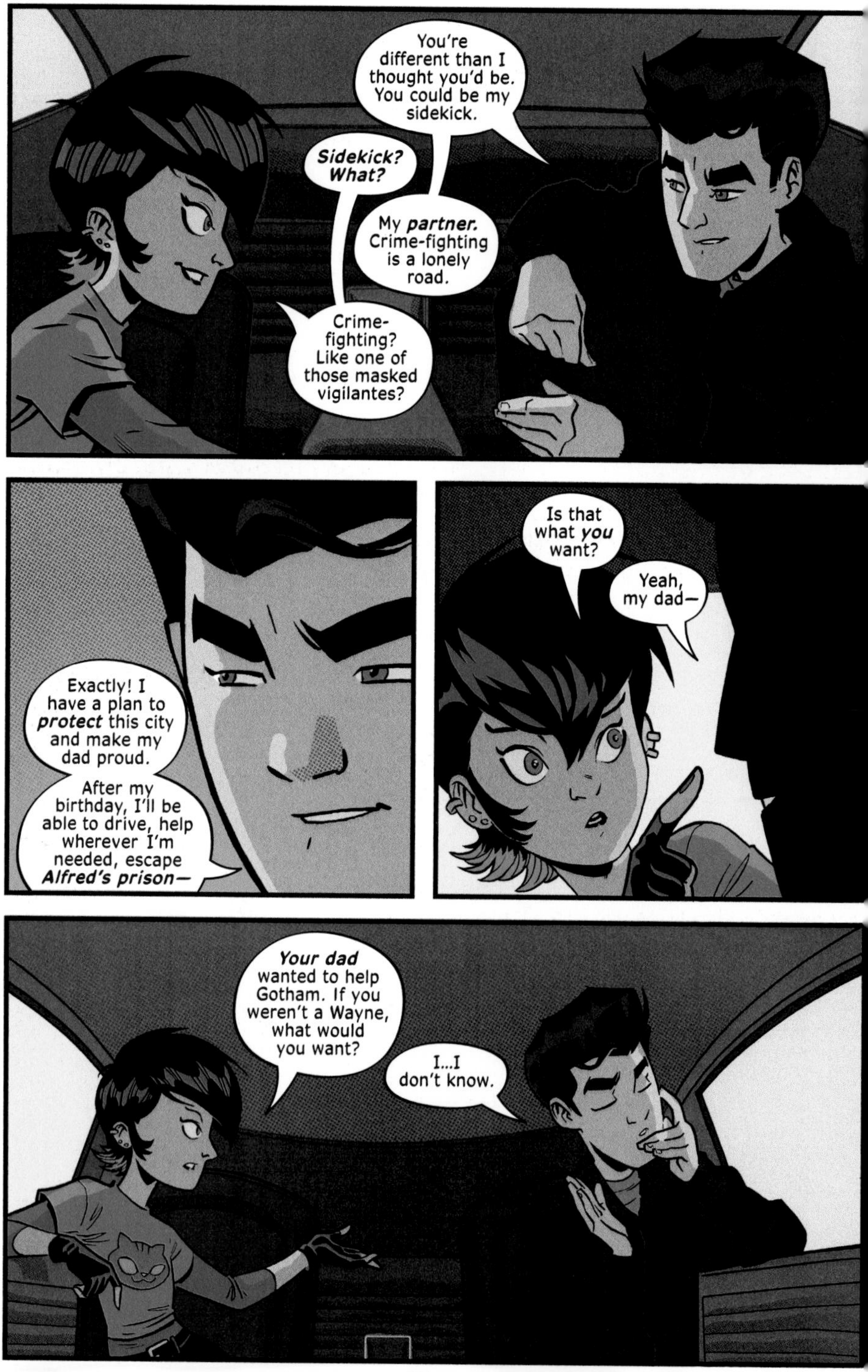
You're different than I thought you'd be. You could be my sidekick.
Sidekick? What?
My *partner.* Crime-fighting is a lonely road.
Crime-fighting? Like one of those masked vigilantes?
Exactly! I have a plan to *protect* this city and make my dad proud.
After my birthday, I'll be able to drive, help wherever I'm needed, escape *Alfred's prison*—
Is that what *you* want?
Yeah, my dad—
Your dad wanted to help Gotham. If you weren't a Wayne, what would you want?
I...I don't know.

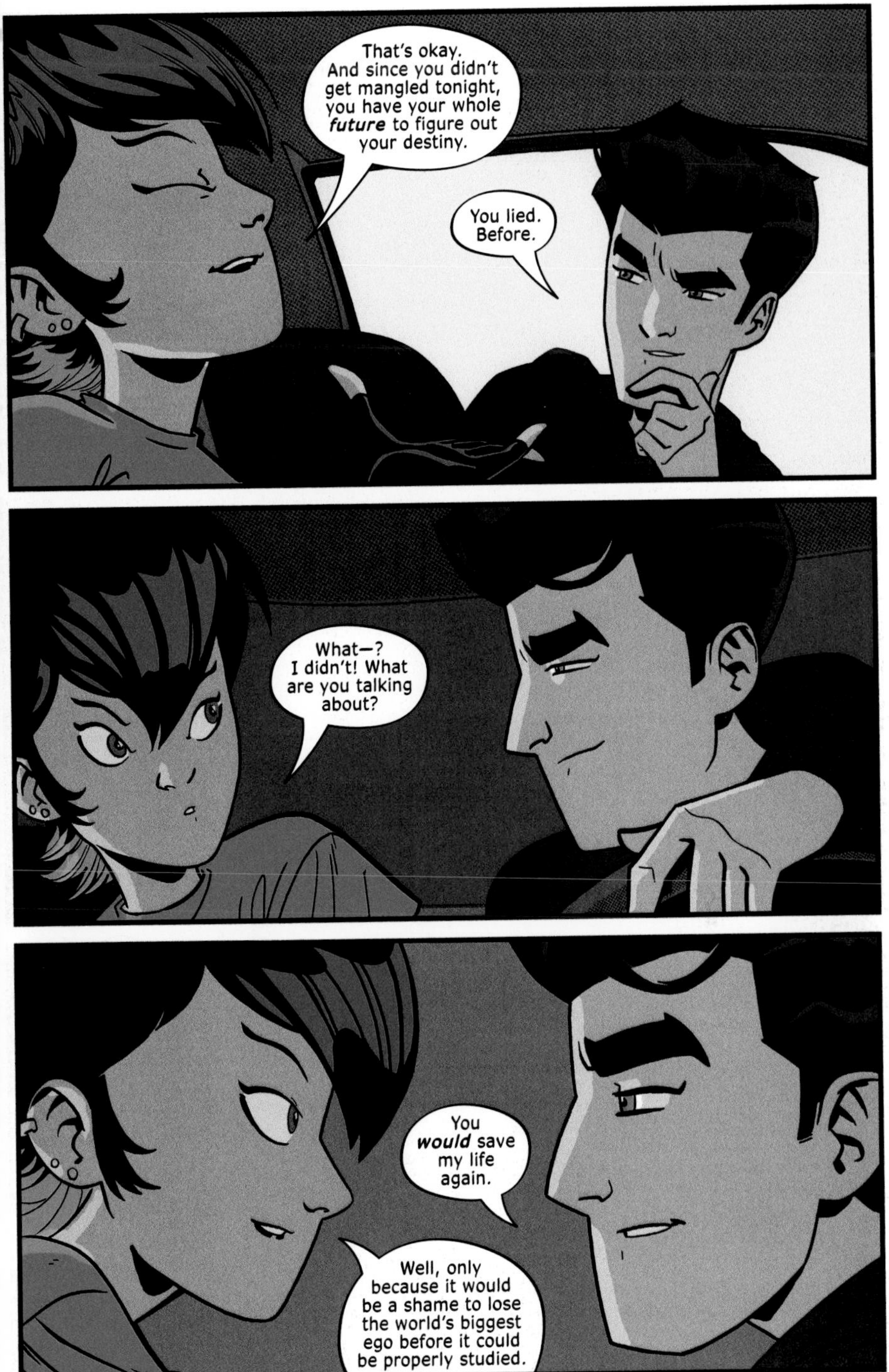
That's okay. And since you didn't get mangled tonight, you have your whole *future* to figure out your destiny.
You lied. Before.
What—? I didn't! What are you talking about?
You *would* save my life again.
Well, only because it would be a shame to lose the world's biggest ego before it could be properly studied.

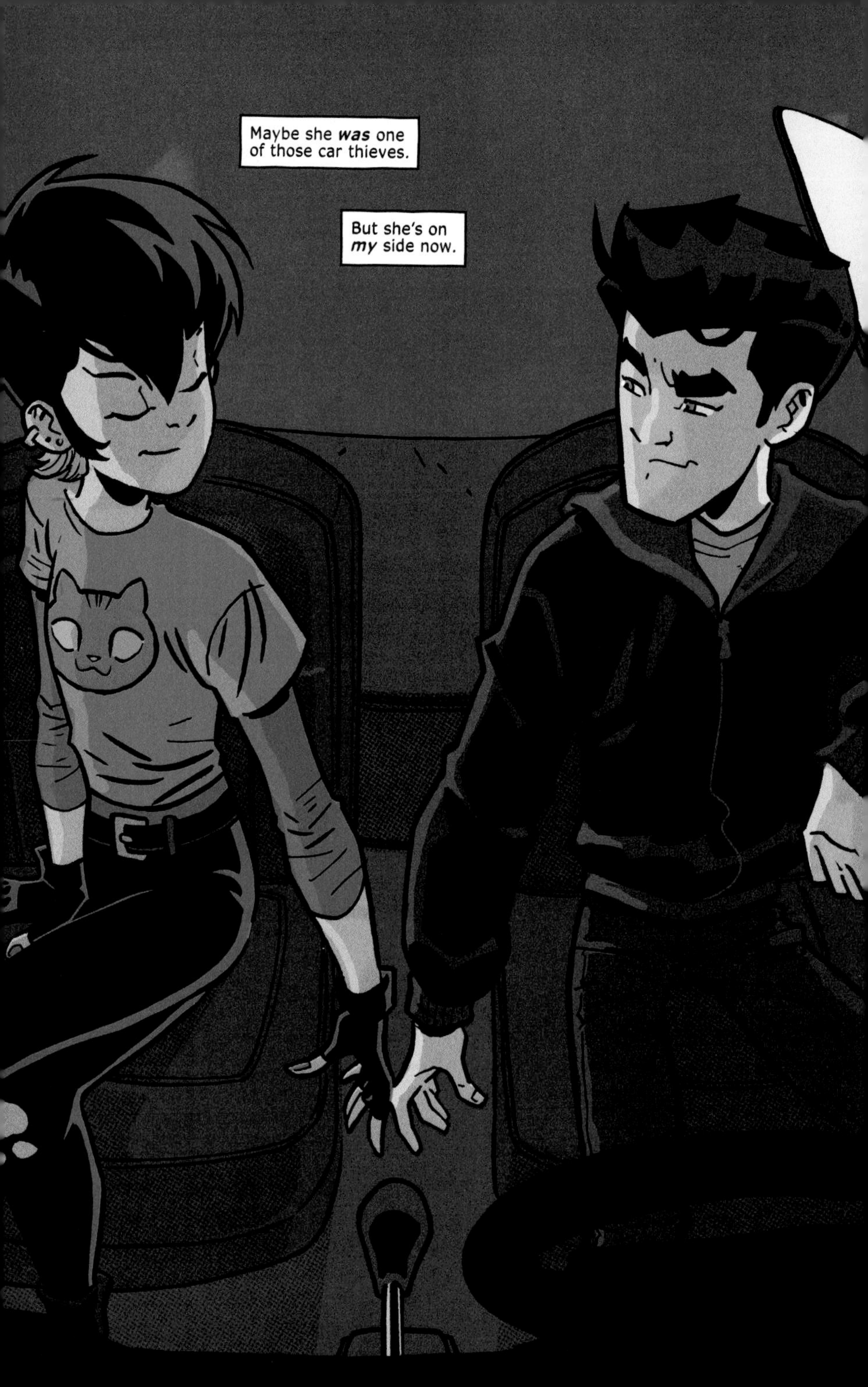
Maybe she *was* one of those car thieves.
But she's on *my* side now.

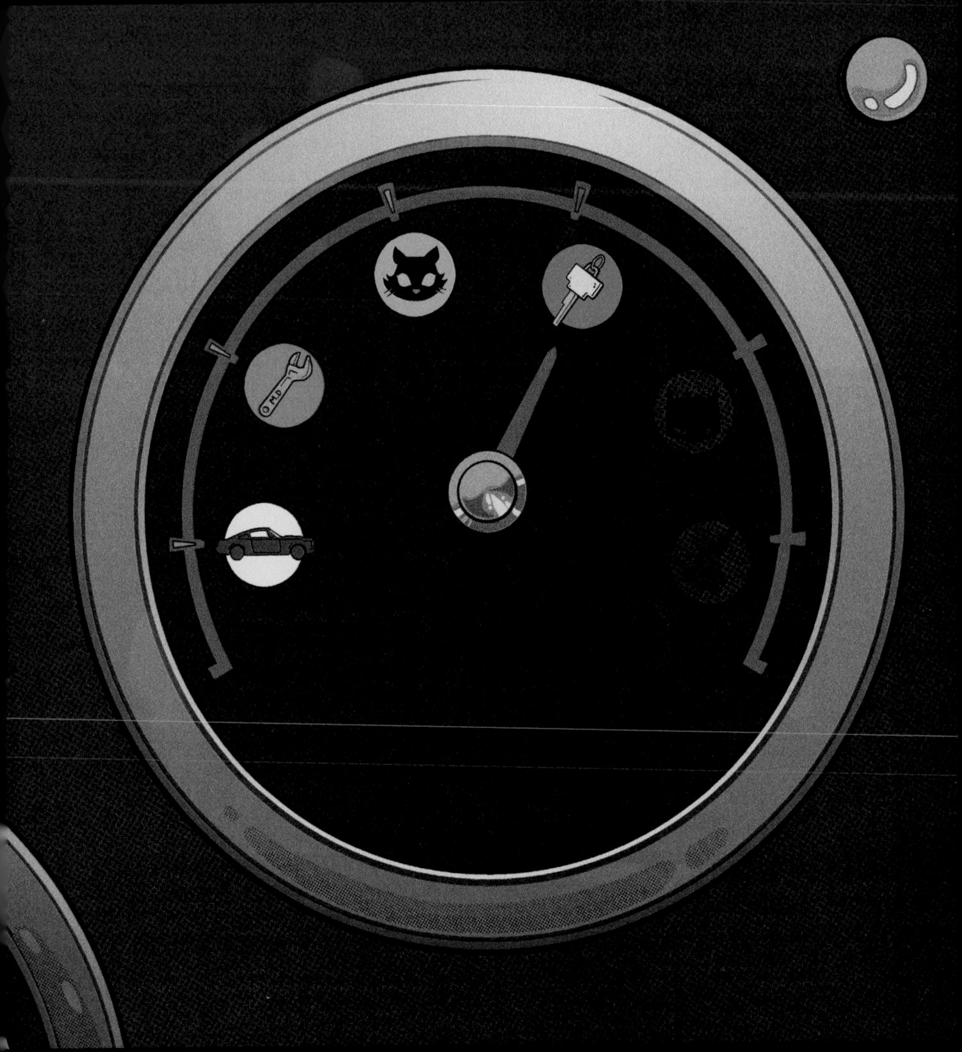
M.D

DRIVE ON

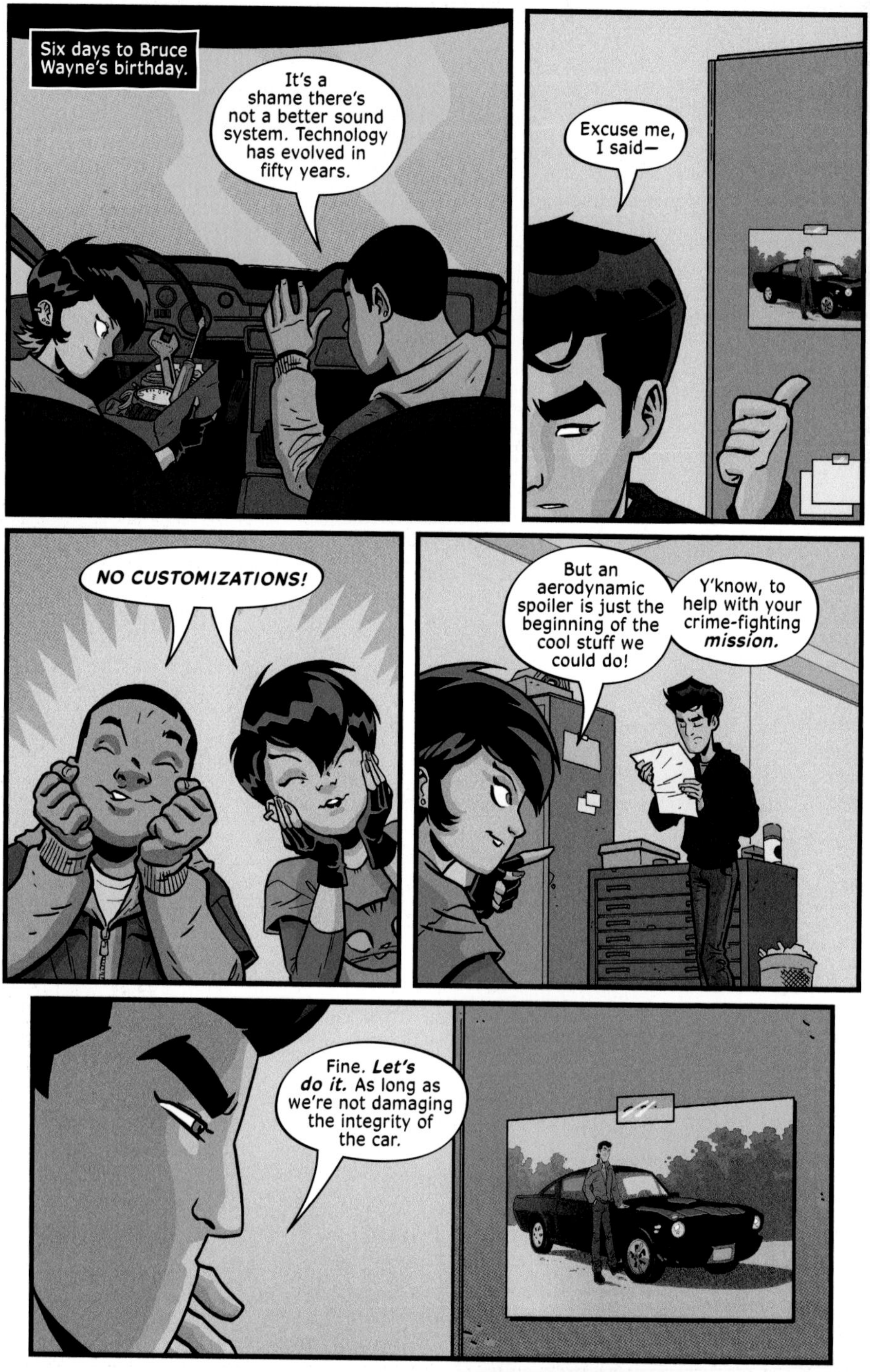
Six days to Bruce Wayne's birthday.
It's a shame there's not a better sound system. Technology has evolved in fifty years.
Excuse me, I said—
NO CUSTOMIZATIONS!
But an aerodynamic spoiler is just the beginning of the cool stuff we could do!
Y'know, to help with your crime-fighting *mission.*
Fine. *Let's do it.* As long as we're not damaging the integrity of the car.

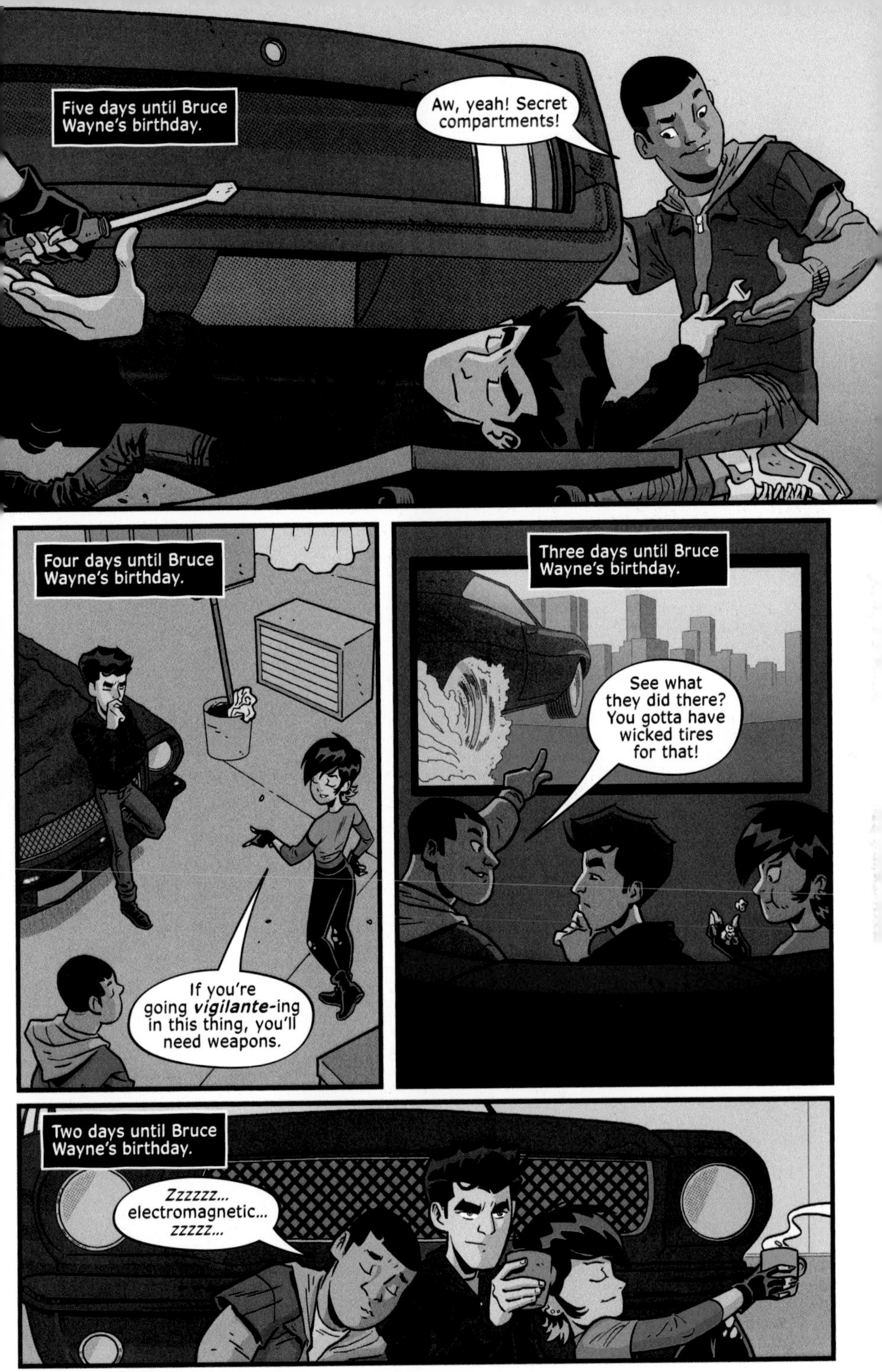
Five days until Bruce Wayne's birthday.
Aw, yeah! Secret compartments!
Four days until Bruce Wayne's birthday.
If you're going *vigilante*-ing in this thing, you'll need weapons.
Three days until Bruce Wayne's birthday.
See what they did there? You gotta have wicked tires for that!
Two days until Bruce Wayne's birthday.
Zzzzzz... electromagnetic... zzzzz...

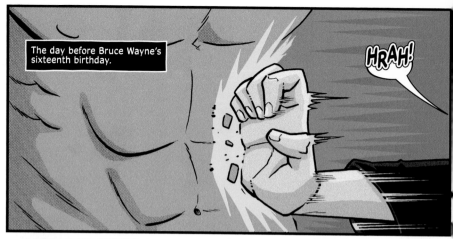

The day before Bruce Wayne's sixteenth birthday.

HRAH!

THWACK!

Hi-ya!

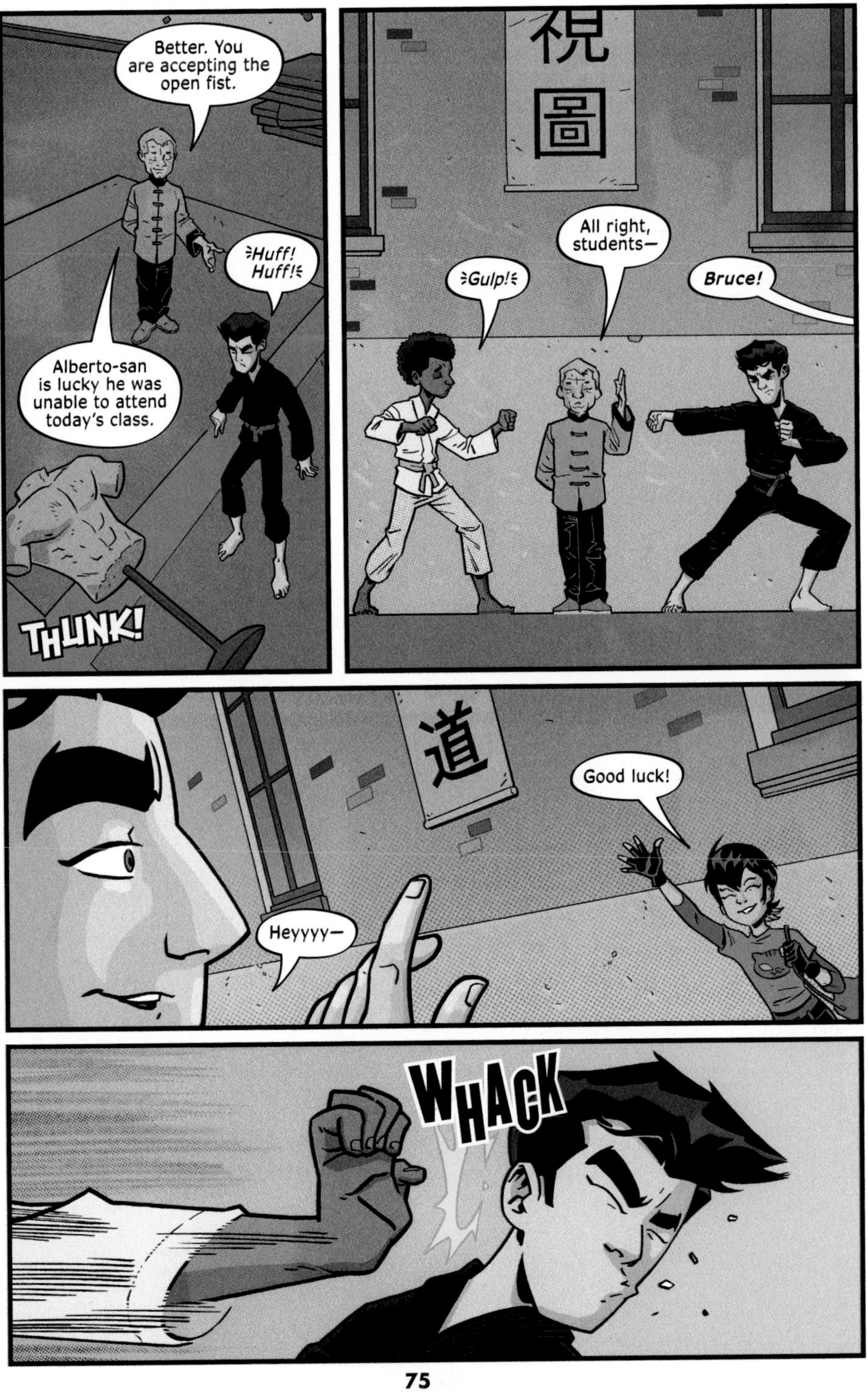

Better. You are accepting the open fist.
Huff! Huff!
Alberto-san is lucky he was unable to attend today's class.
THUNK!
視
圖
All right, students—
Gulp!
Bruce!
道
Good luck!
Heyyyy—
WHACK

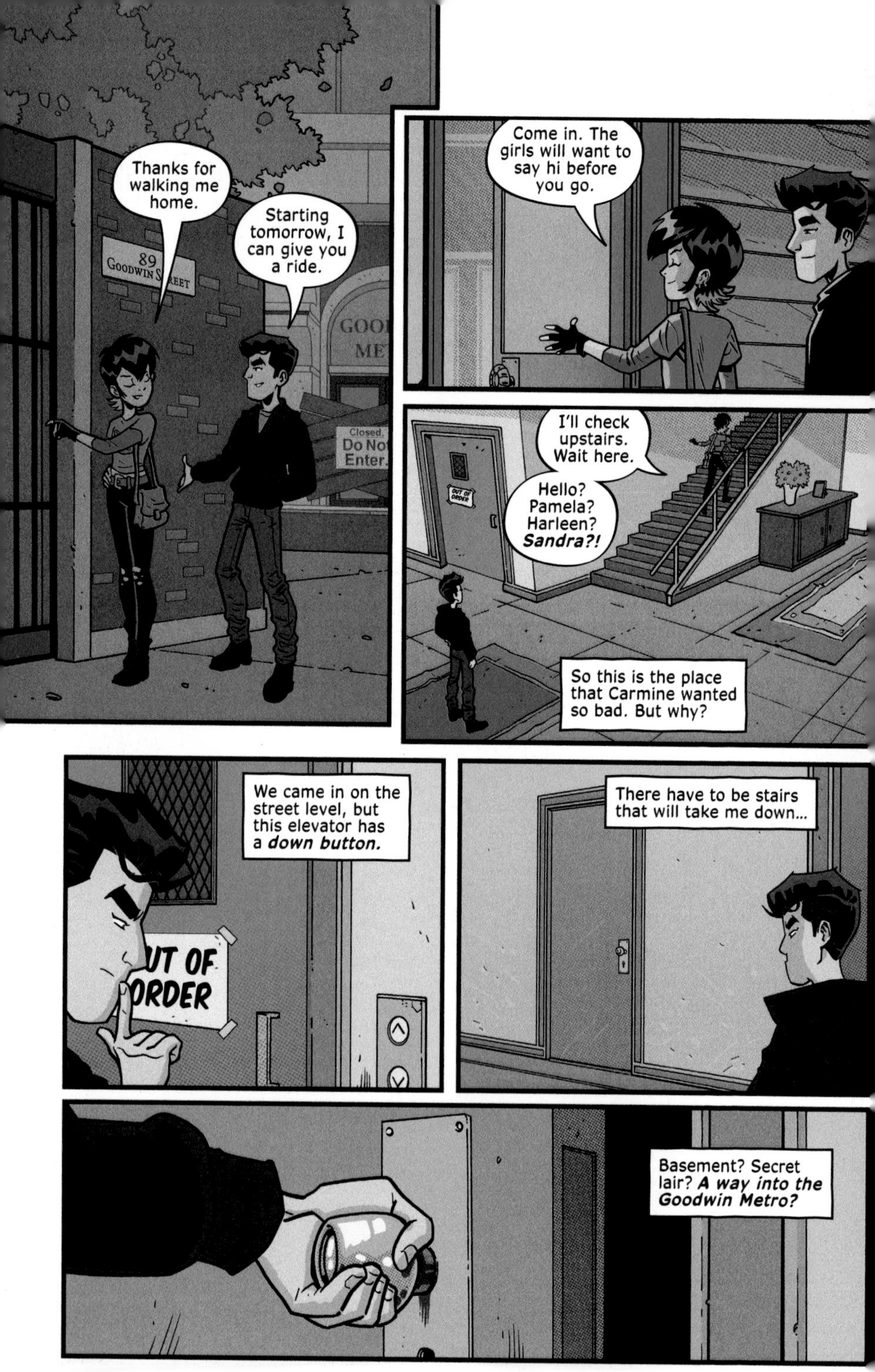
Thanks for walking me home.
89 Goodwin Street
Starting tomorrow, I can give you a ride.
Closed. Do Not Enter.
Come in. The girls will want to say hi before you go.
I'll check upstairs. Wait here.
Hello? Pamela? Harleen? ***Sandra?!***
OUT OF ORDER
So this is the place that Carmine wanted so bad. But why?
We came in on the street level, but this elevator has a ***down button.***
There have to be stairs that will take me down...
Basement? Secret lair? ***A way into the Goodwin Metro?***

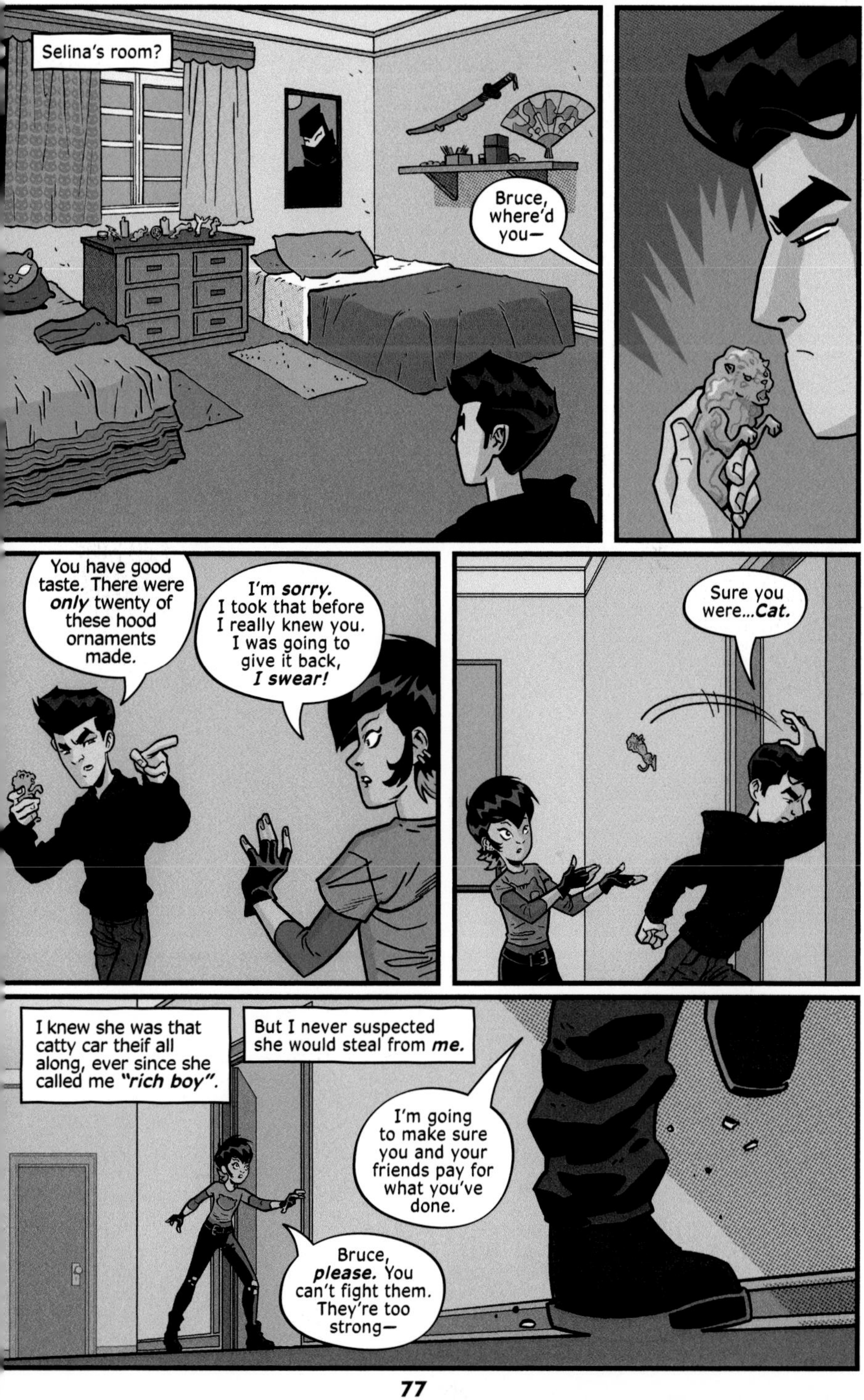

Selina's room?
Bruce, where'd you—
You have good taste. There were *only* twenty of these hood ornaments made.
I'm *sorry.* I took that before I really knew you. I was going to give it back, *I swear!*
Sure you were...*Cat.*
I knew she was that catty car theif all along, ever since she called me *"rich boy".*
But I never suspected she would steal from *me.*
I'm going to make sure you and your friends pay for what you've done.
Bruce, *please.* You can't fight them. They're too strong—

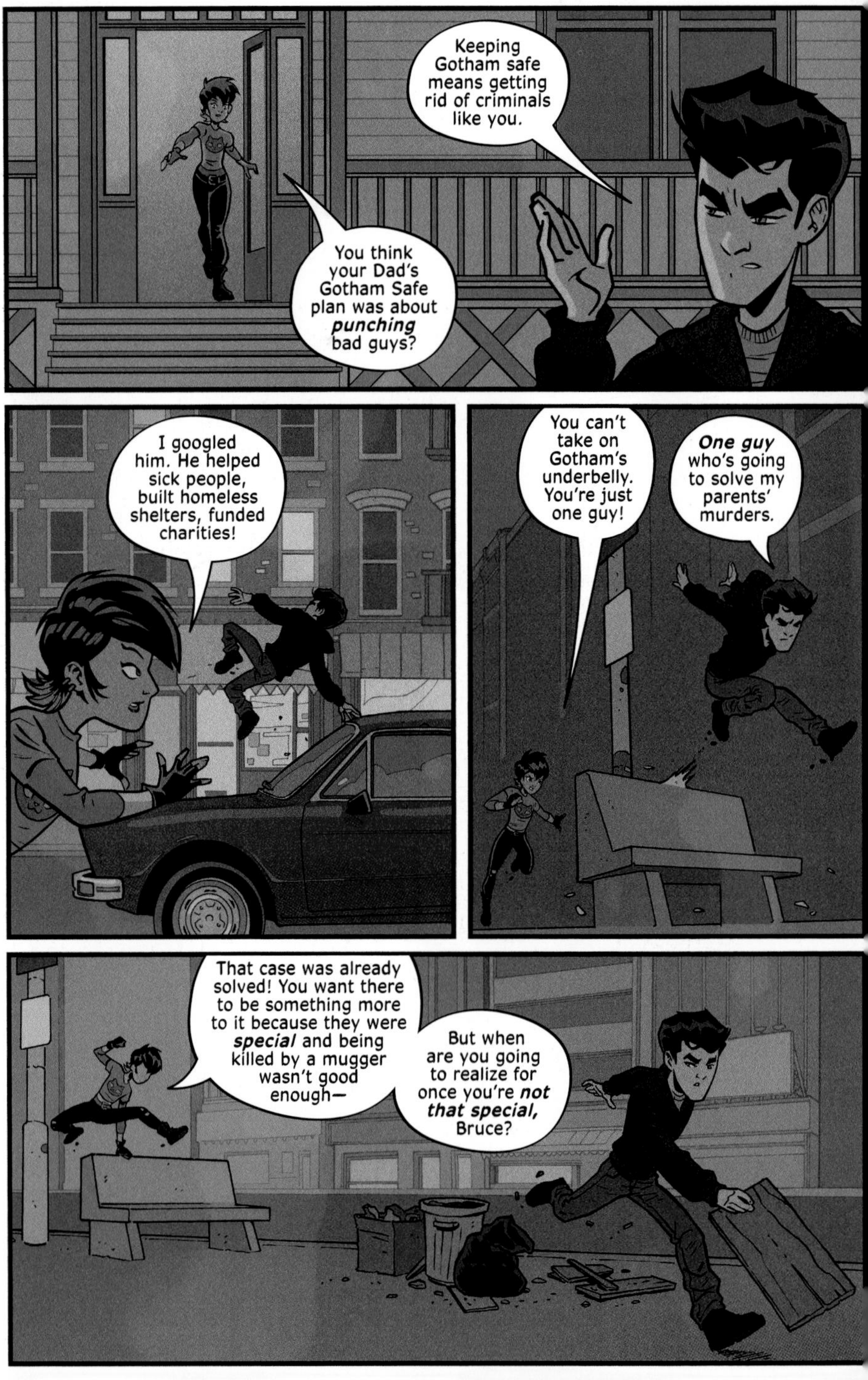
Keeping Gotham safe means getting rid of criminals like you.
You think your Dad's Gotham Safe plan was about *punching* bad guys?
I googled him. He helped sick people, built homeless shelters, funded charities!
You can't take on Gotham's underbelly. You're just one guy!
One guy who's going to solve my parents' murders.
That case was already solved! You want there to be something more to it because they were *special* and being killed by a mugger wasn't good enough—
But when are you going to realize for once you're *not that special,* Bruce?

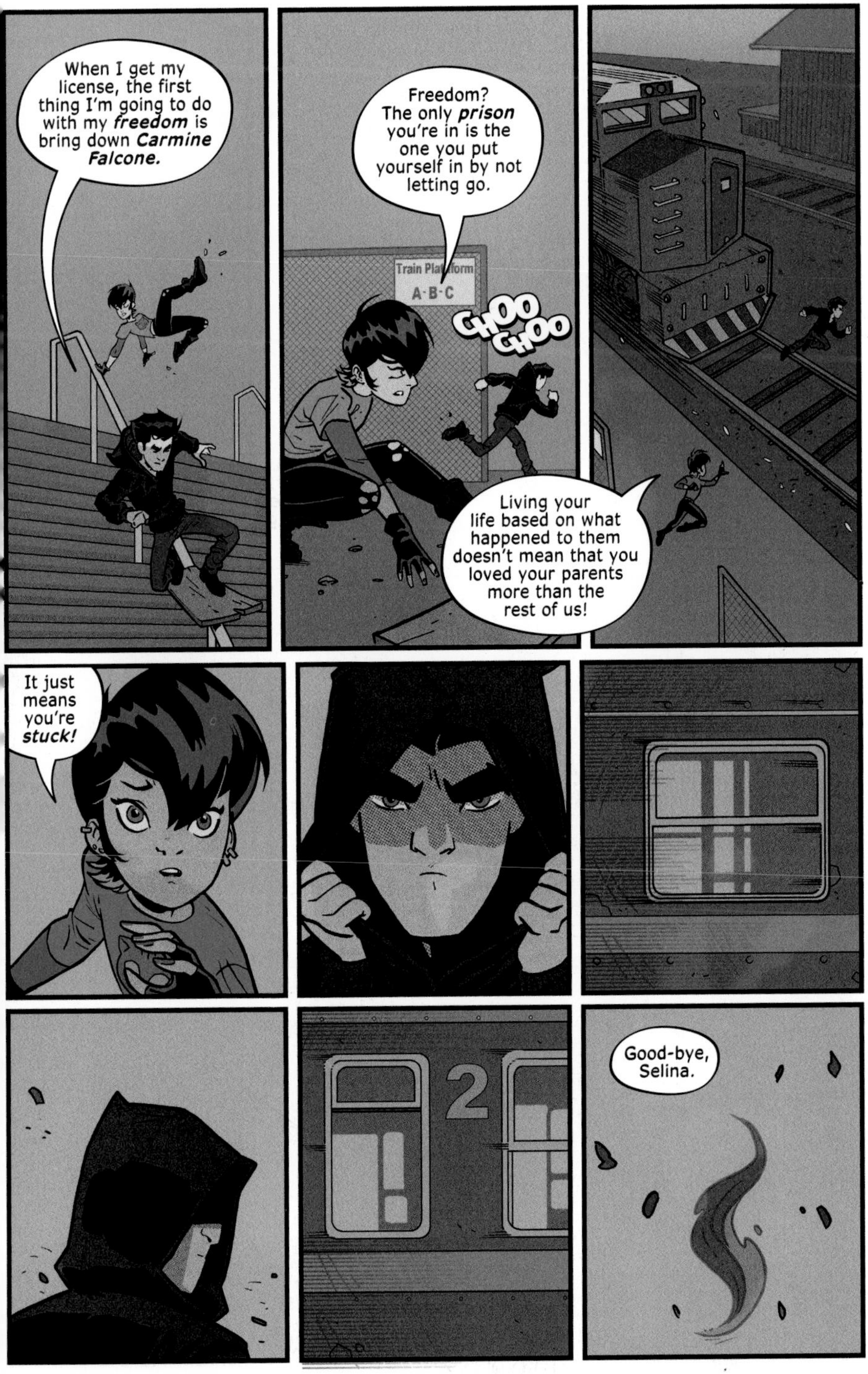
When I get my license, the first thing I'm going to do with my *freedom* is bring down *Carmine Falcone.*
Freedom? The only *prison* you're in is the one you put yourself in by not letting go.
Train Platform
A-B-C
CHOO CHOO
Living your life based on what happened to them doesn't mean that you loved your parents more than the rest of us!
It just means you're *stuck!*
2
Good-bye, Selina.

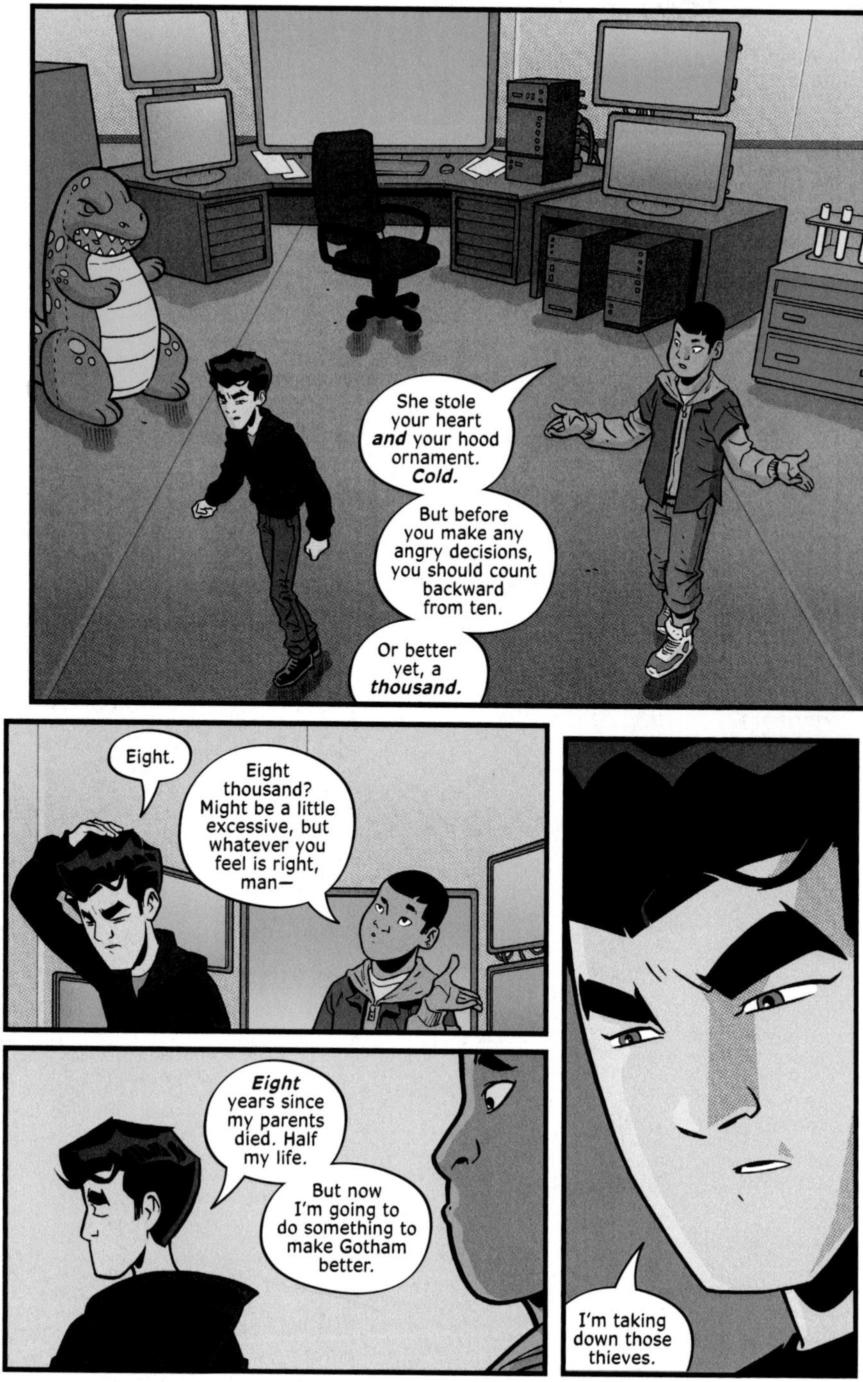
She stole your heart *and* your hood ornament. *Cold.*
But before you make any angry decisions, you should count backward from ten.
Or better yet, a *thousand.*
Eight.
Eight thousand? Might be a little excessive, but whatever you feel is right, man—
Eight years since my parents died. Half my life.
But now I'm going to do something to make Gotham better.
I'm taking down those thieves.

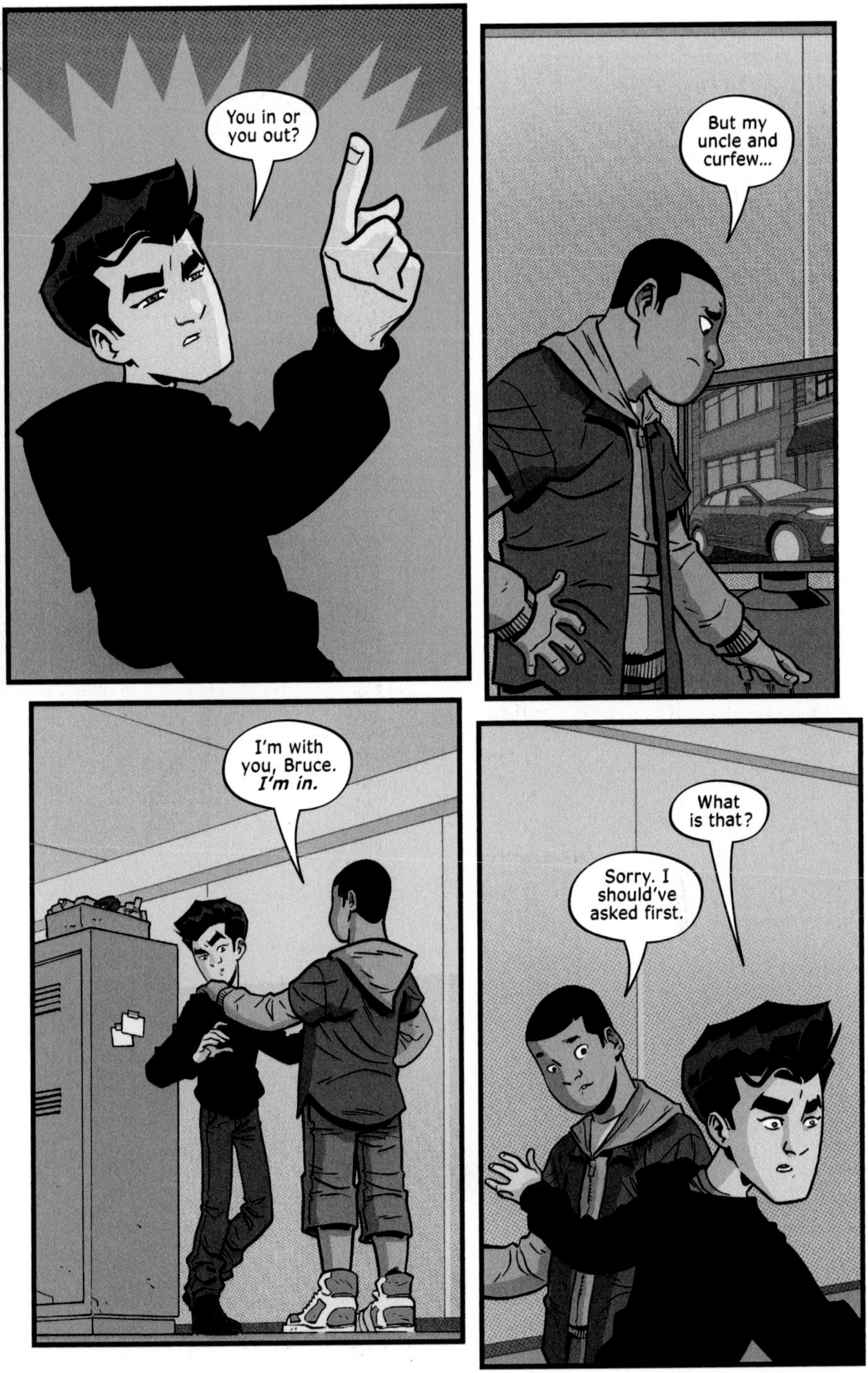
You in or you out?
But my uncle and curfew...
I'm with you, Bruce. *I'm in.*
What is that?
Sorry. I should've asked first.

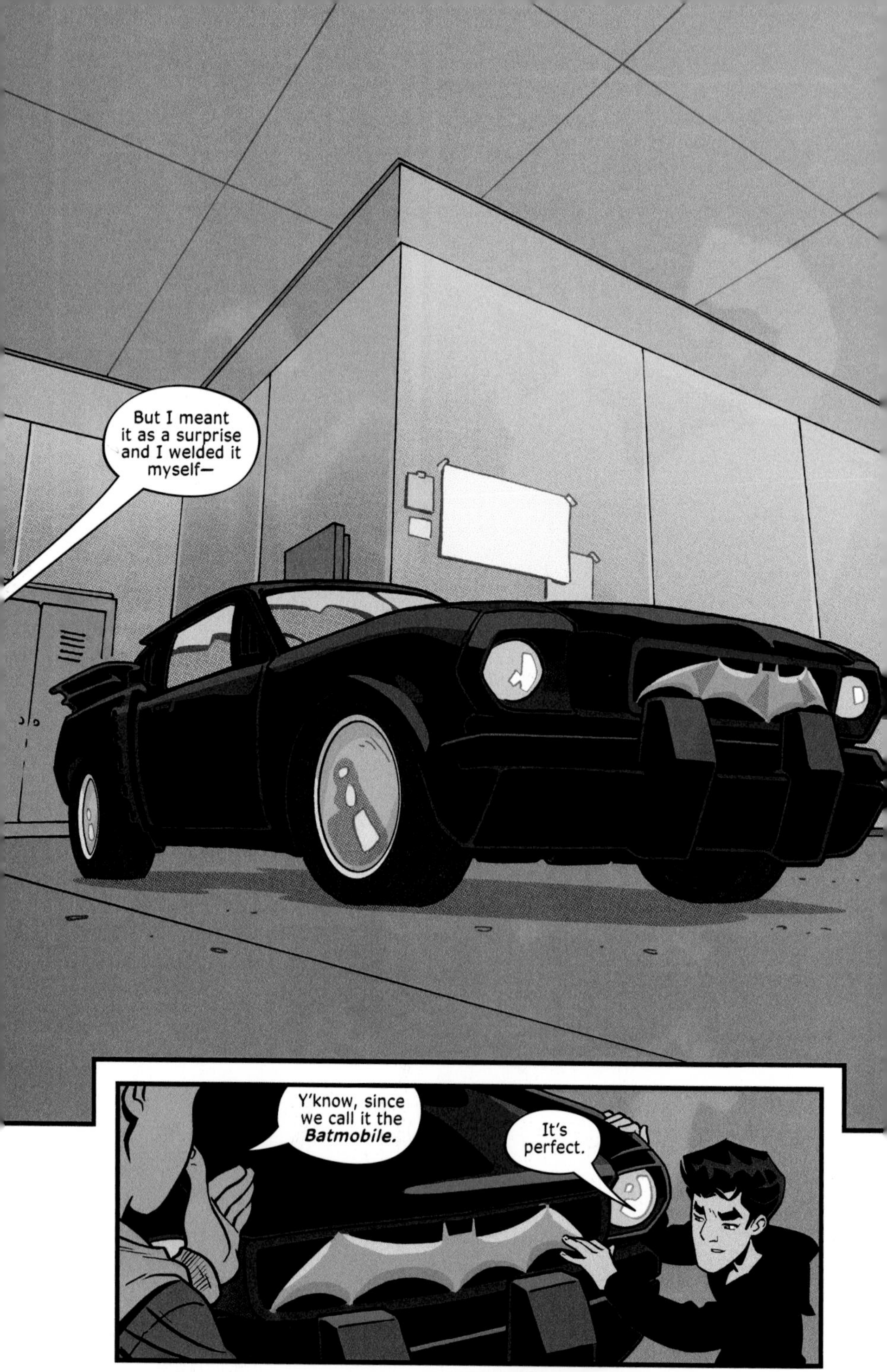
But I meant it as a surprise and I welded it myself—
Y'know, since we call it the *Batmobile.*
It's perfect.

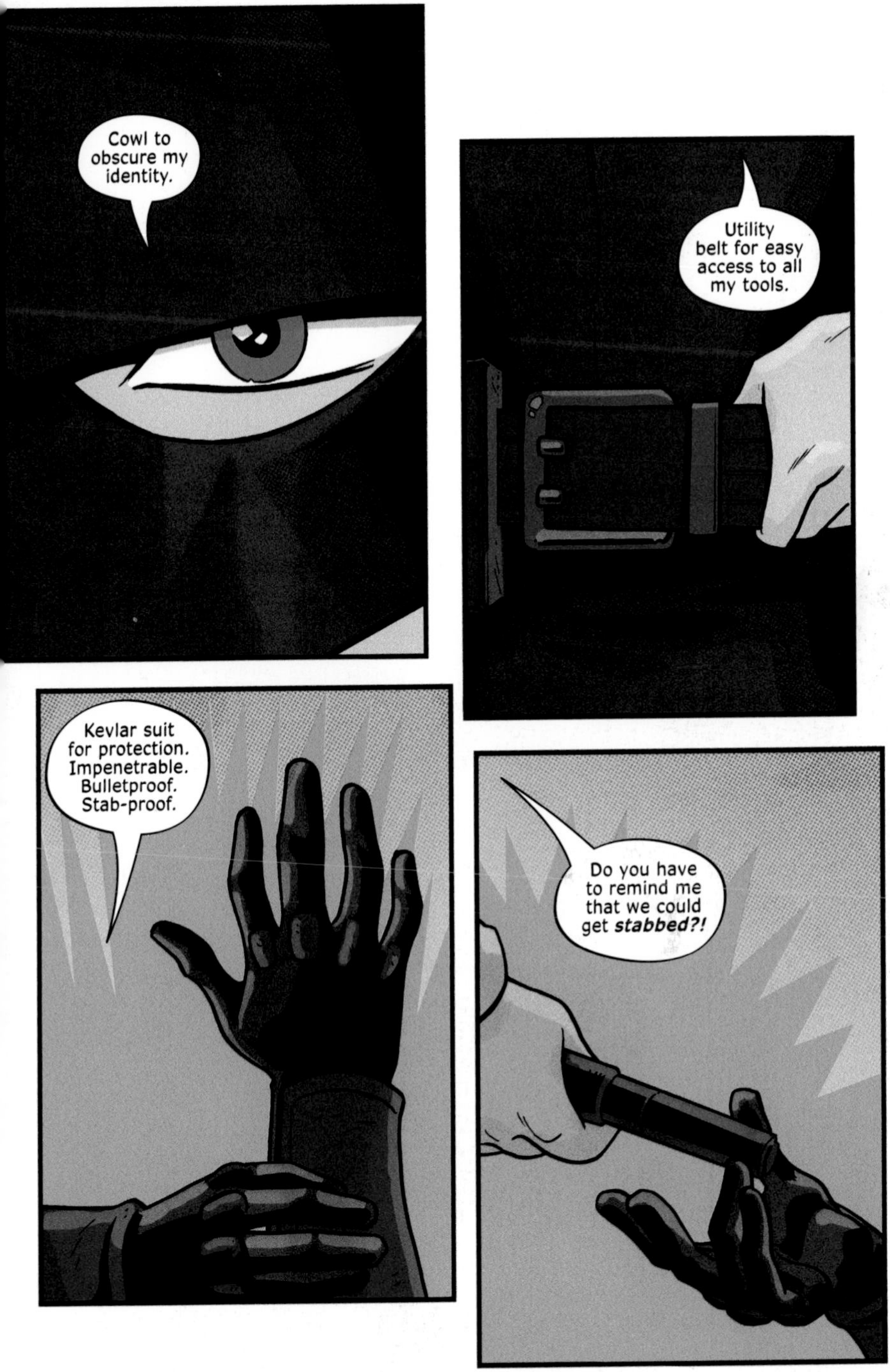
Cowl to obscure my identity.
Utility belt for easy access to all my tools.
Kevlar suit for protection. Impenetrable. Bulletproof. Stab-proof.
Do you have to remind me that we could get *stabbed?!*

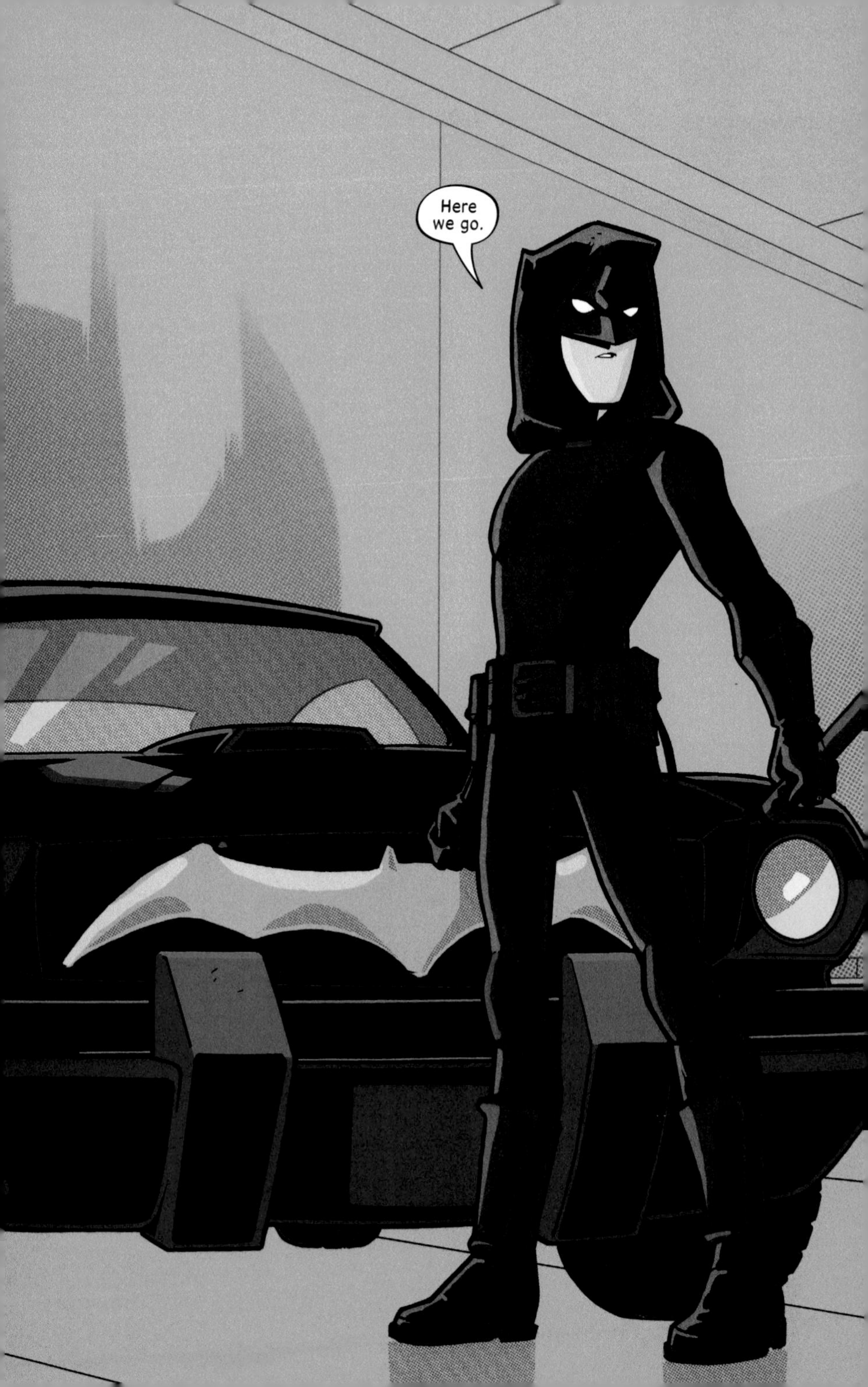
Here we go.

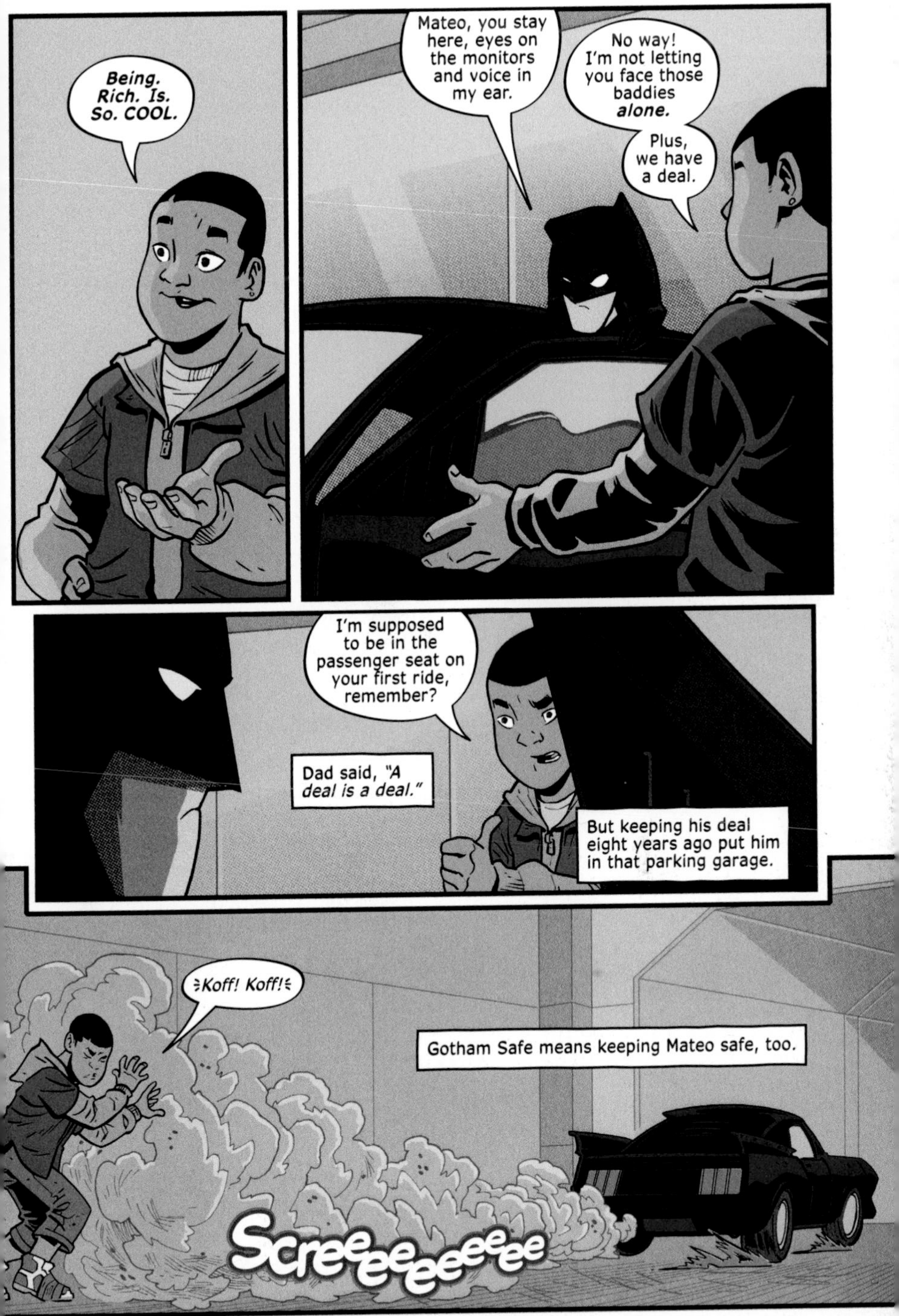
Being. Rich. Is. So. COOL.
Mateo, you stay here, eyes on the monitors and voice in my ear.
No way! I'm not letting you face those baddies *alone.*
Plus, we have a deal.
I'm supposed to be in the passenger seat on your first ride, remember?
Dad said, *"A deal is a deal."*
But keeping his deal eight years ago put him in that parking garage.
Koff! Koff!
Gotham Safe means keeping Mateo safe, too.
Screeeeeeeeee

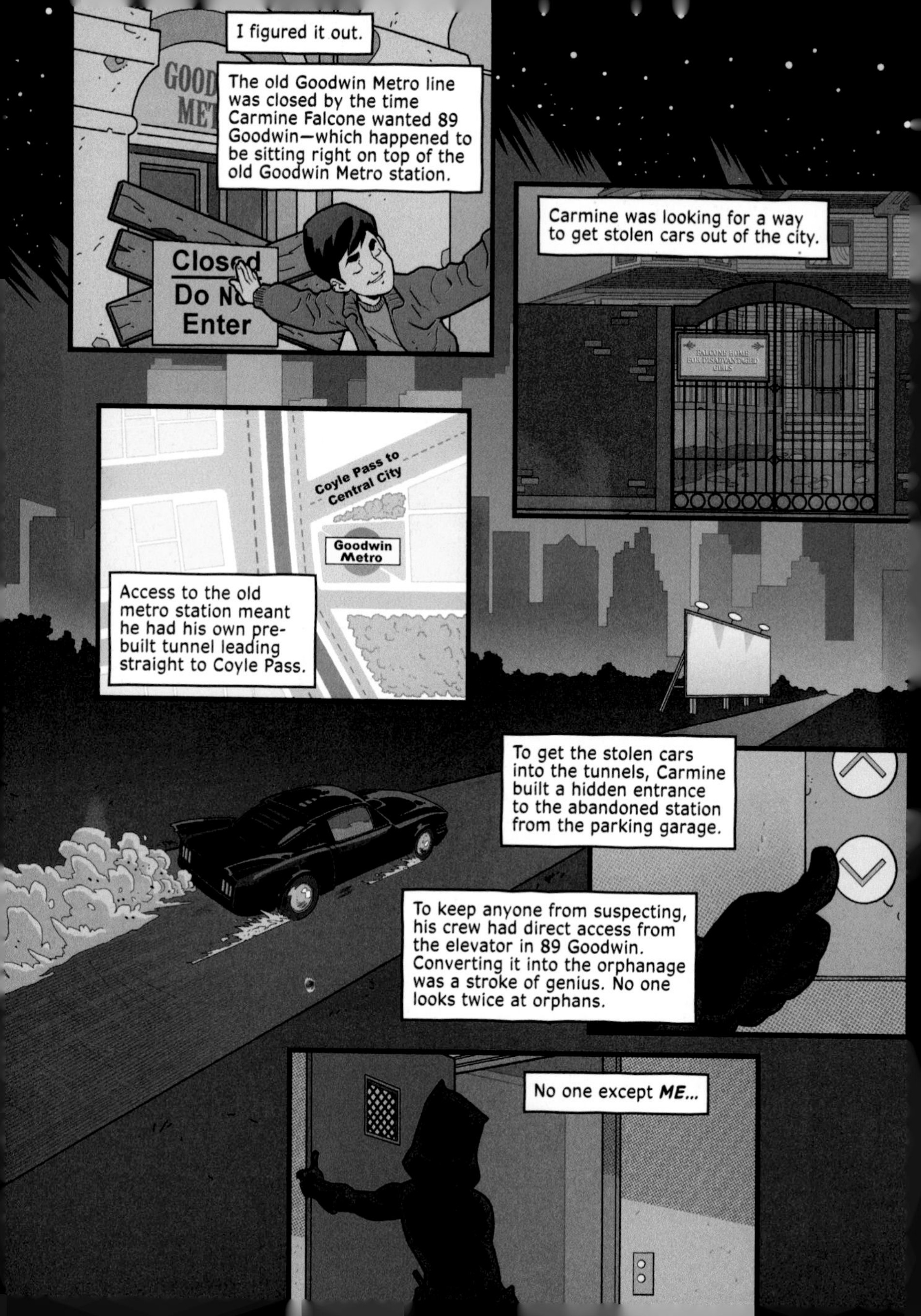
I figured it out.
The old Goodwin Metro line was closed by the time Carmine Falcone wanted 89 Goodwin—which happened to be sitting right on top of the old Goodwin Metro station.
Closed Do Not Enter
Carmine was looking for a way to get stolen cars out of the city.
Coyle Pass to Central City
Goodwin Metro
Access to the old metro station meant he had his own pre-built tunnel leading straight to Coyle Pass.
To get the stolen cars into the tunnels, Carmine built a hidden entrance to the abandoned station from the parking garage.
To keep anyone from suspecting, his crew had direct access from the elevator in 89 Goodwin. Converting it into the orphanage was a stroke of genius. No one looks twice at orphans.
No one except ***ME...***

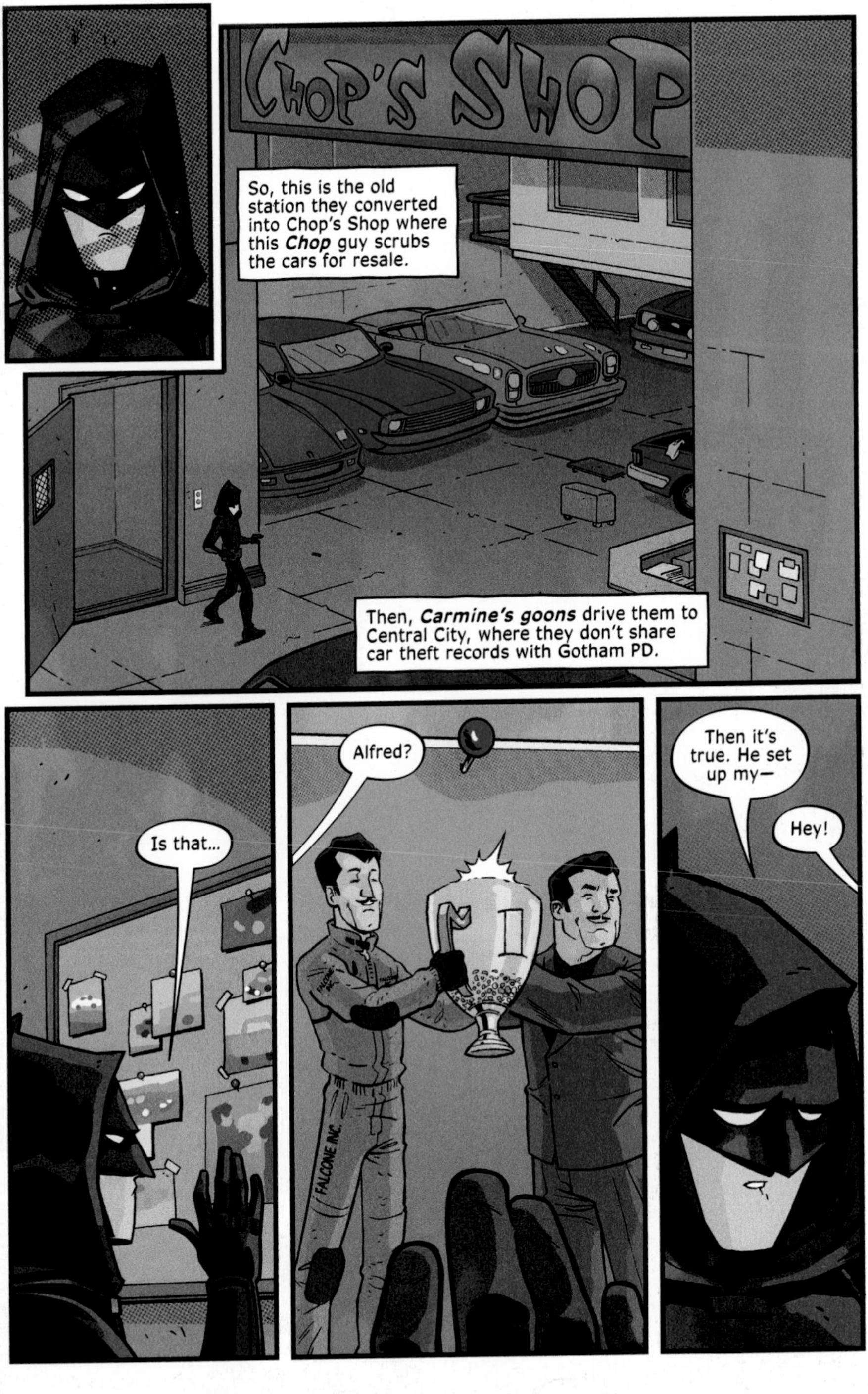
CHOP'S SHOP
So, this is the old station they converted into Chop's Shop where this *Chop* guy scrubs the cars for resale.
Then, *Carmine's goons* drive them to Central City, where they don't share car theft records with Gotham PD.
Is that...
Alfred?
FALCONE INC.
Then it's true. He set up my—
Hey!

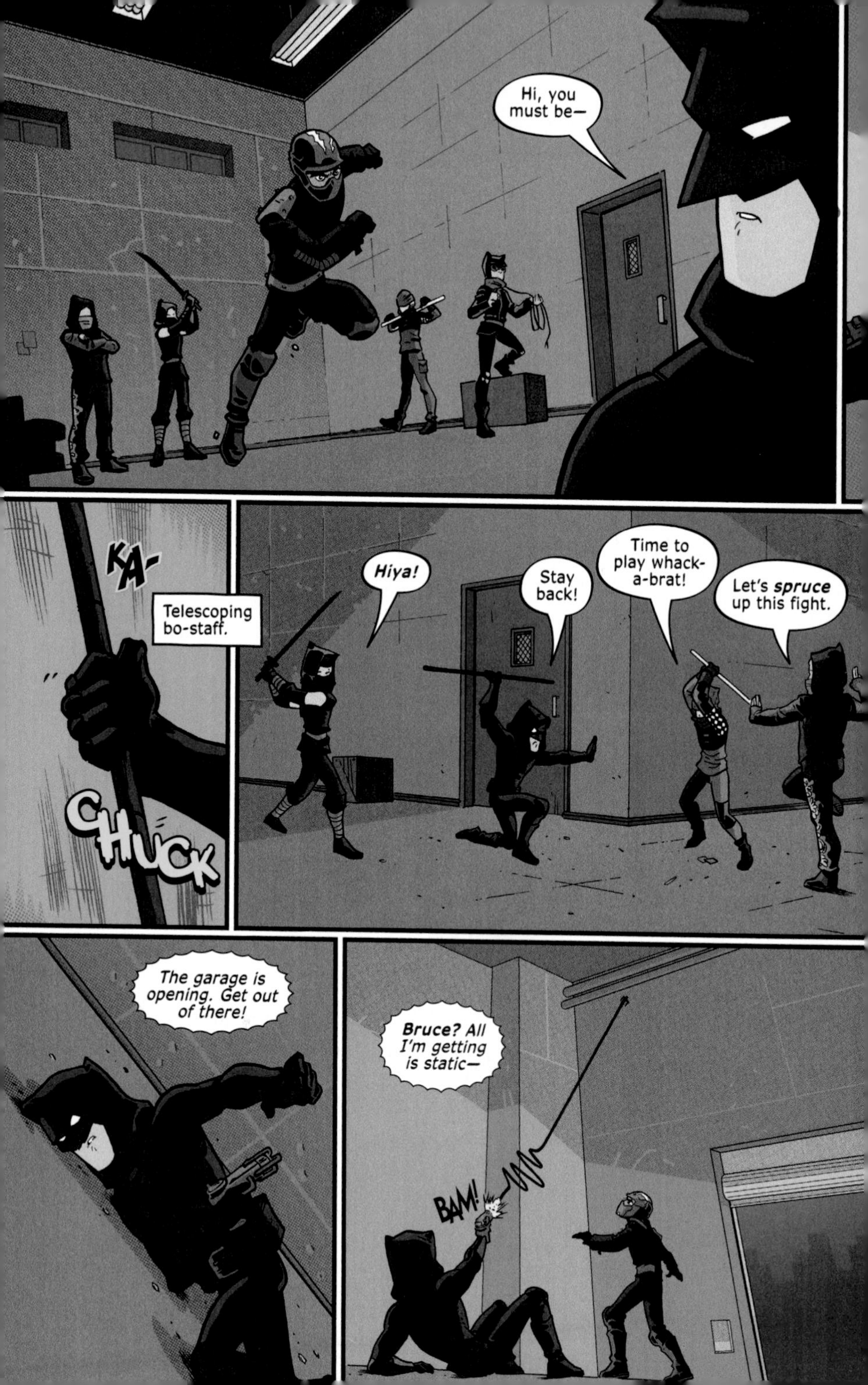
Hi, you must be—
KA-
Telescoping bo-staff.
CHUCK
Hiya!
Stay back!
Time to play whack-a-brat!
Let's *spruce* up this fight.
The garage is opening. Get out of there!
***Bruce?** All I'm getting is static—*
BAM!

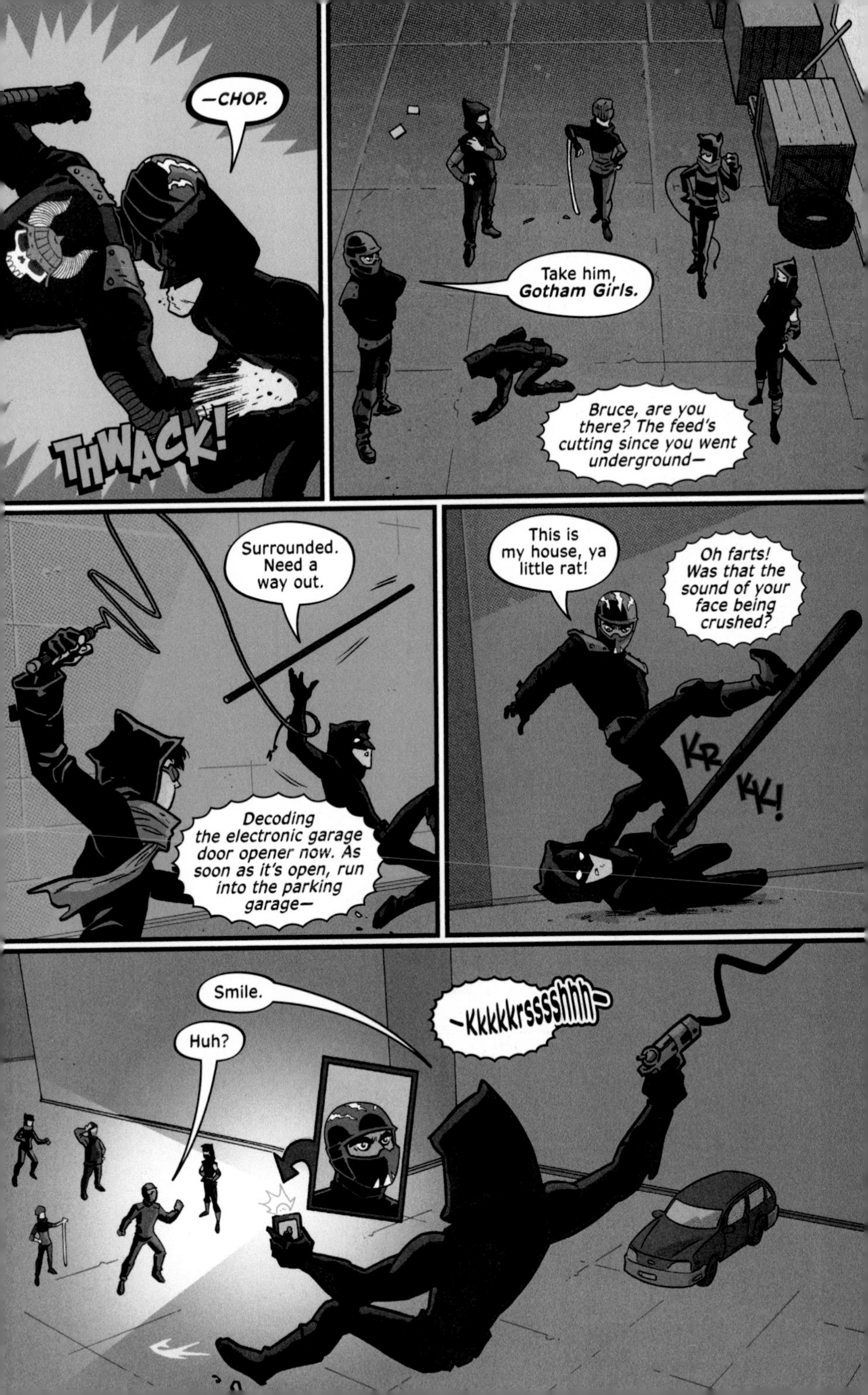

—CHOP.
THWACK!
Take him, *Gotham Girls.*
Bruce, are you there? The feed's cutting since you went underground—
Surrounded. Need a way out.
Decoding the electronic garage door opener now. As soon as it's open, run into the parking garage—
This is my house, ya little rat!
Oh farts! Was that the sound of your face being crushed?
KRKK!
Smile.
Huh?
-Kkkkkrsssshhh-

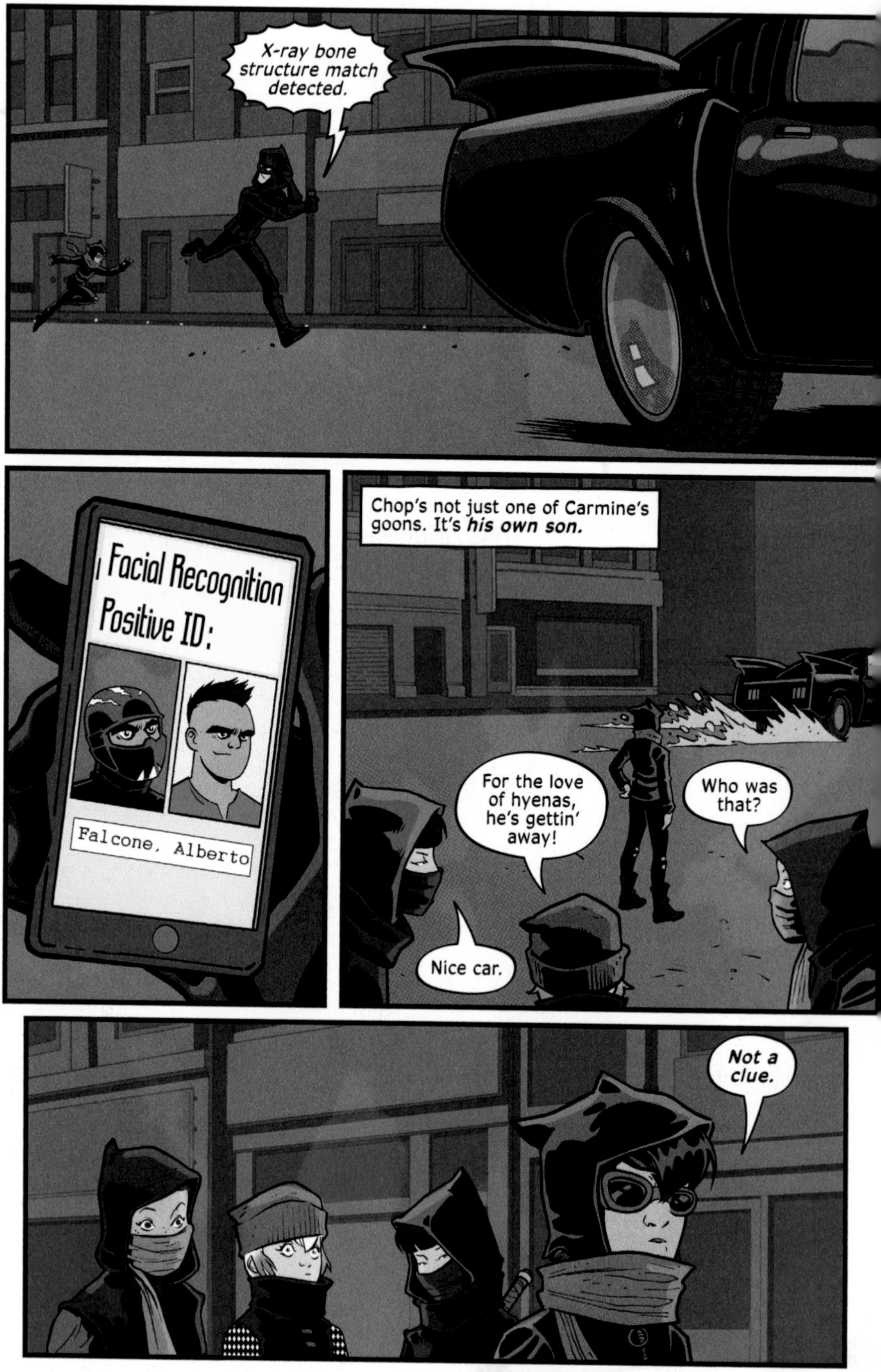
X-ray bone structure match detected.
Facial Recognition Positive ID:
Falcone, Alberto
Chop's not just one of Carmine's goons. It's ***his own son.***
For the love of hyenas, he's gettin' away!
Who was that?
Nice car.
Not a clue.

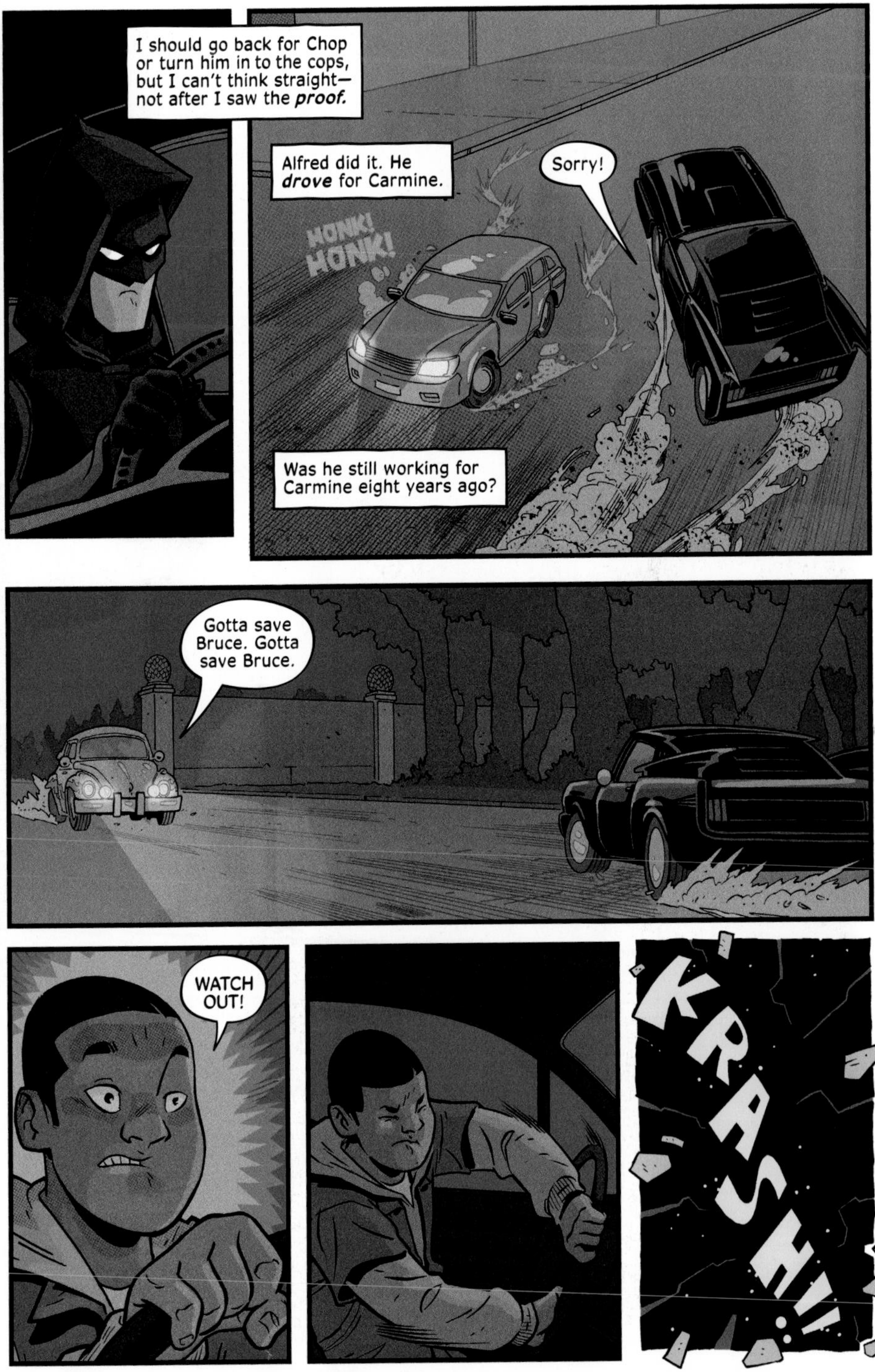
I should go back for Chop or turn him in to the cops, but I can't think straight—not after I saw the *proof.*
Alfred did it. He *drove* for Carmine.
HONK! HONK!
Sorry!
Was he still working for Carmine eight years ago?
Gotta save Bruce. Gotta save Bruce.
WATCH OUT!
KRASH!!

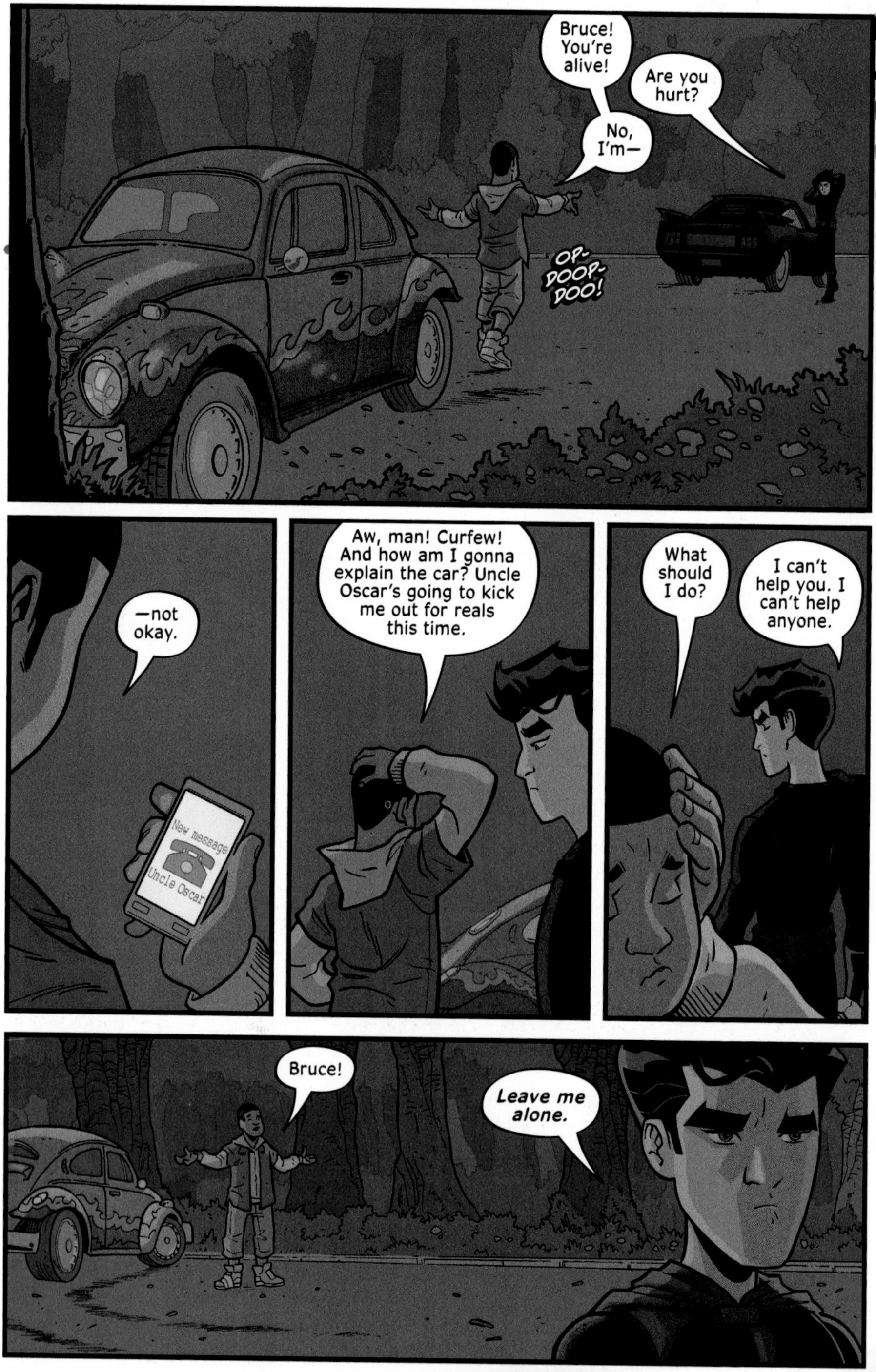
Bruce! You're alive!
Are you hurt?
No, I'm—
OP-DOOP-DOO!
—not okay.
New message
Uncle Oscar
Aw, man! Curfew! And how am I gonna explain the car? Uncle Oscar's going to kick me out for reals this time.
What should I do?
I can't help you. I can't help anyone.
Bruce!
Leave me alone.

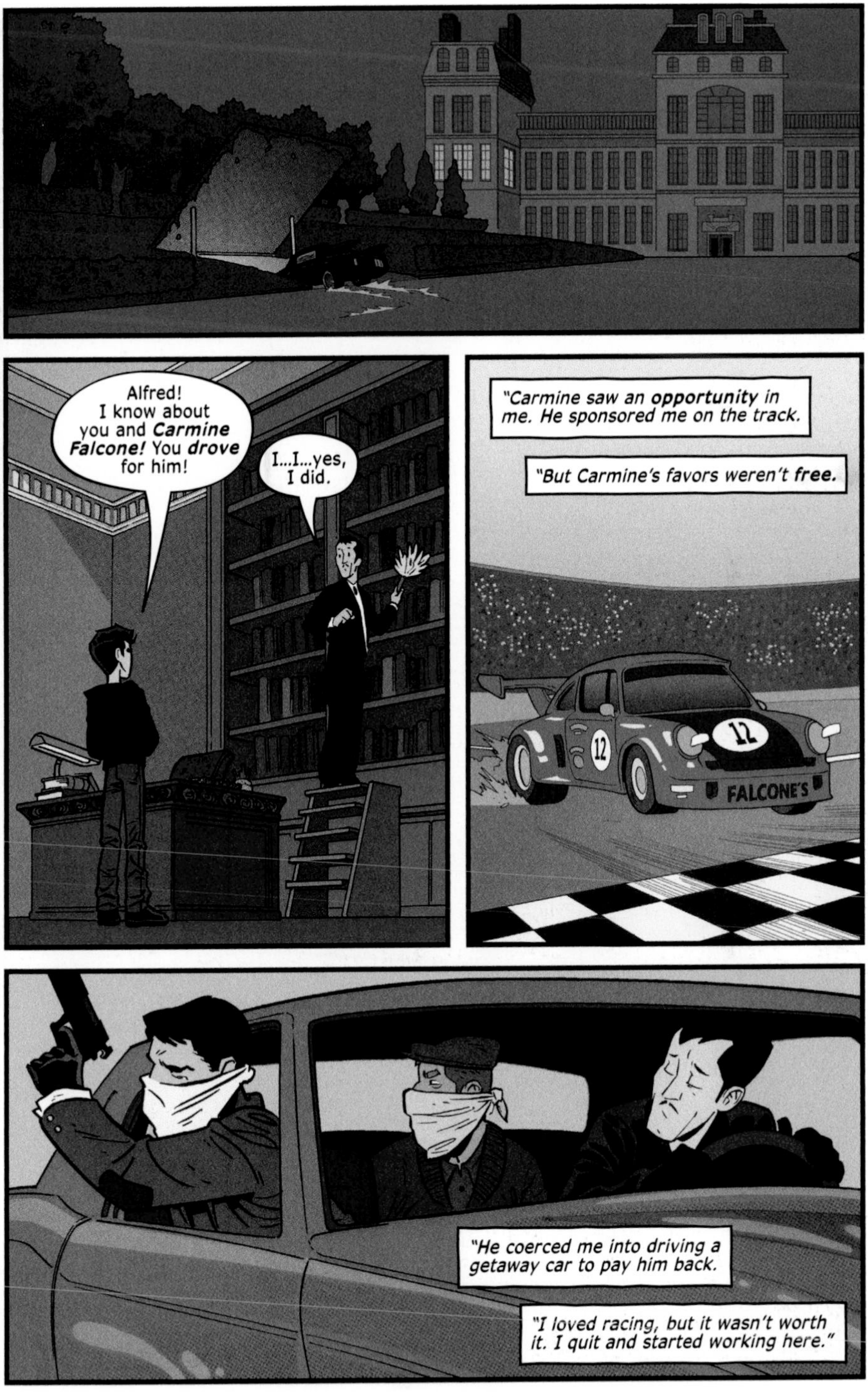
Alfred! I know about you and **Carmine Falcone!** You **drove** for him!
I...I...yes, I did.
"Carmine saw an **opportunity** in me. He sponsored me on the track.
"But Carmine's favors weren't **free.**
12
12
FALCONE'S
"He coerced me into driving a getaway car to pay him back.
"I loved racing, but it wasn't worth it. I quit and started working here."

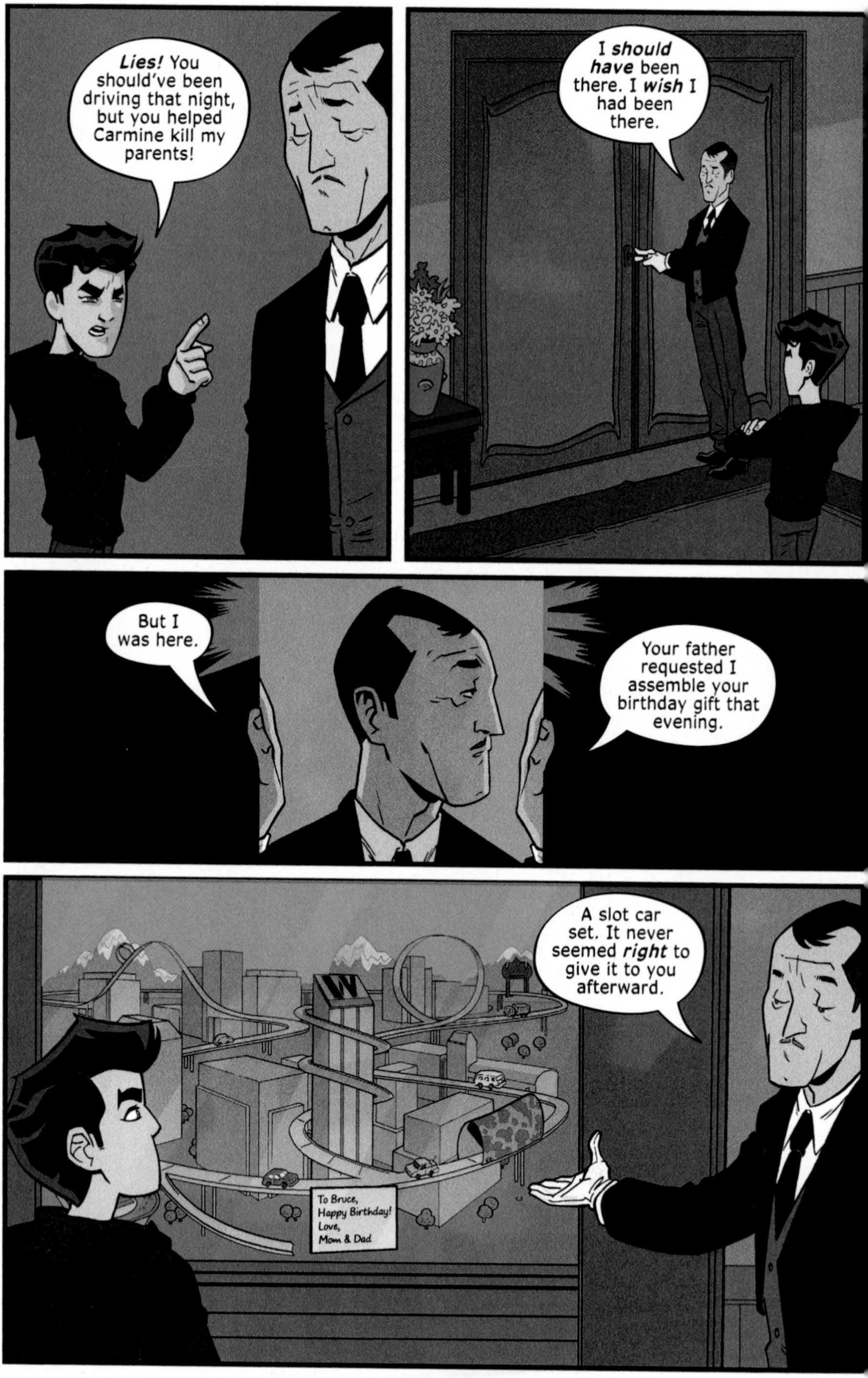
Lies! You should've been driving that night, but you helped Carmine kill my parents!
I should have been there. I wish I had been there.
But I was here.
Your father requested I assemble your birthday gift that evening.
A slot car set. It never seemed right to give it to you afterward.
To Bruce,
Happy Birthday!
Love,
Mom & Dad

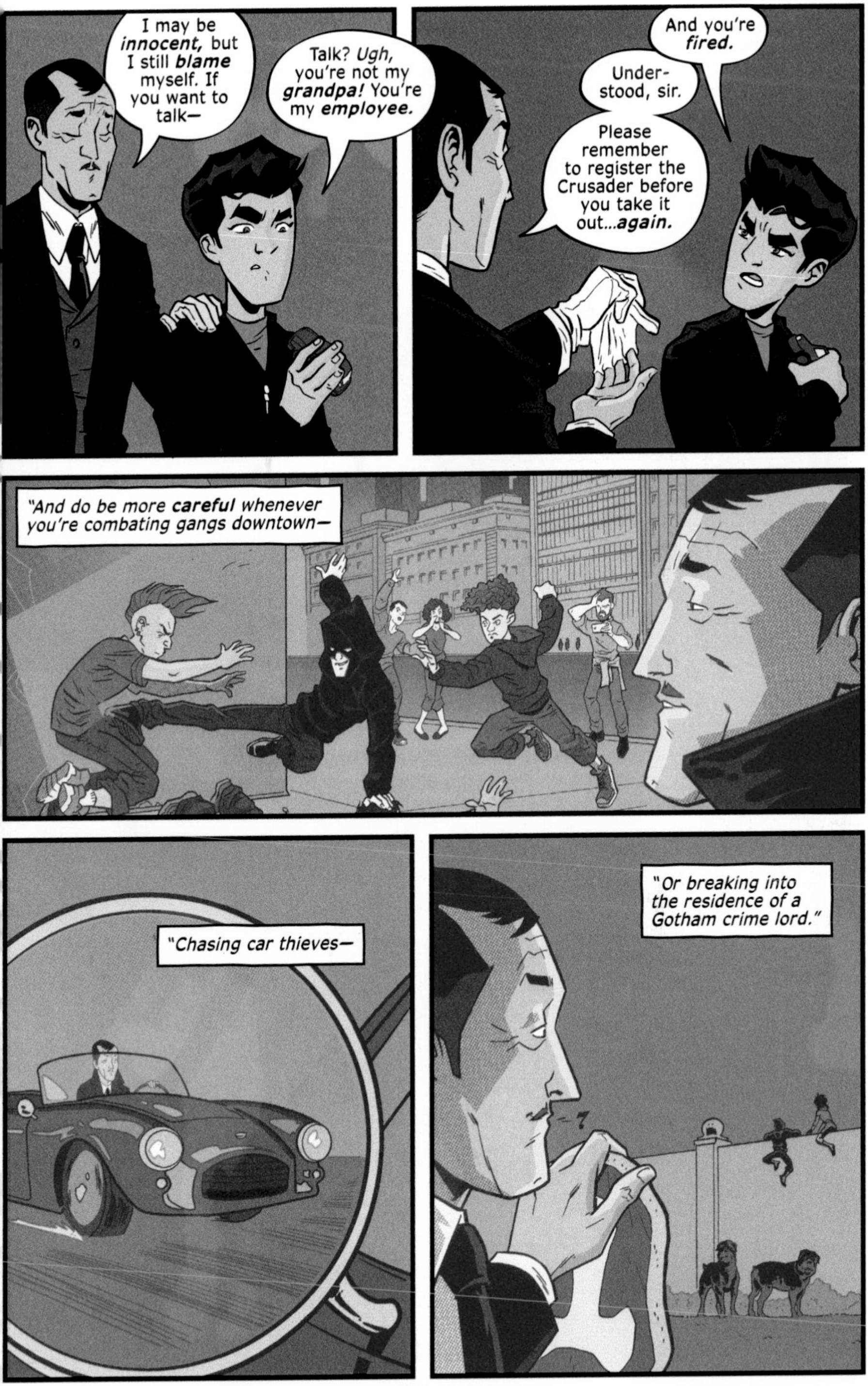
I may be *innocent,* but I still *blame* myself. If you want to talk—
Talk? *Ugh,* you're not my *grandpa!* You're my *employee.*
Under- stood, sir.
And you're *fired.*
Please remember to register the Crusader before you take it out...*again.*
"And do be more **careful** whenever you're combating gangs downtown—
"Chasing car thieves—
"Or breaking into the residence of a Gotham crime lord."

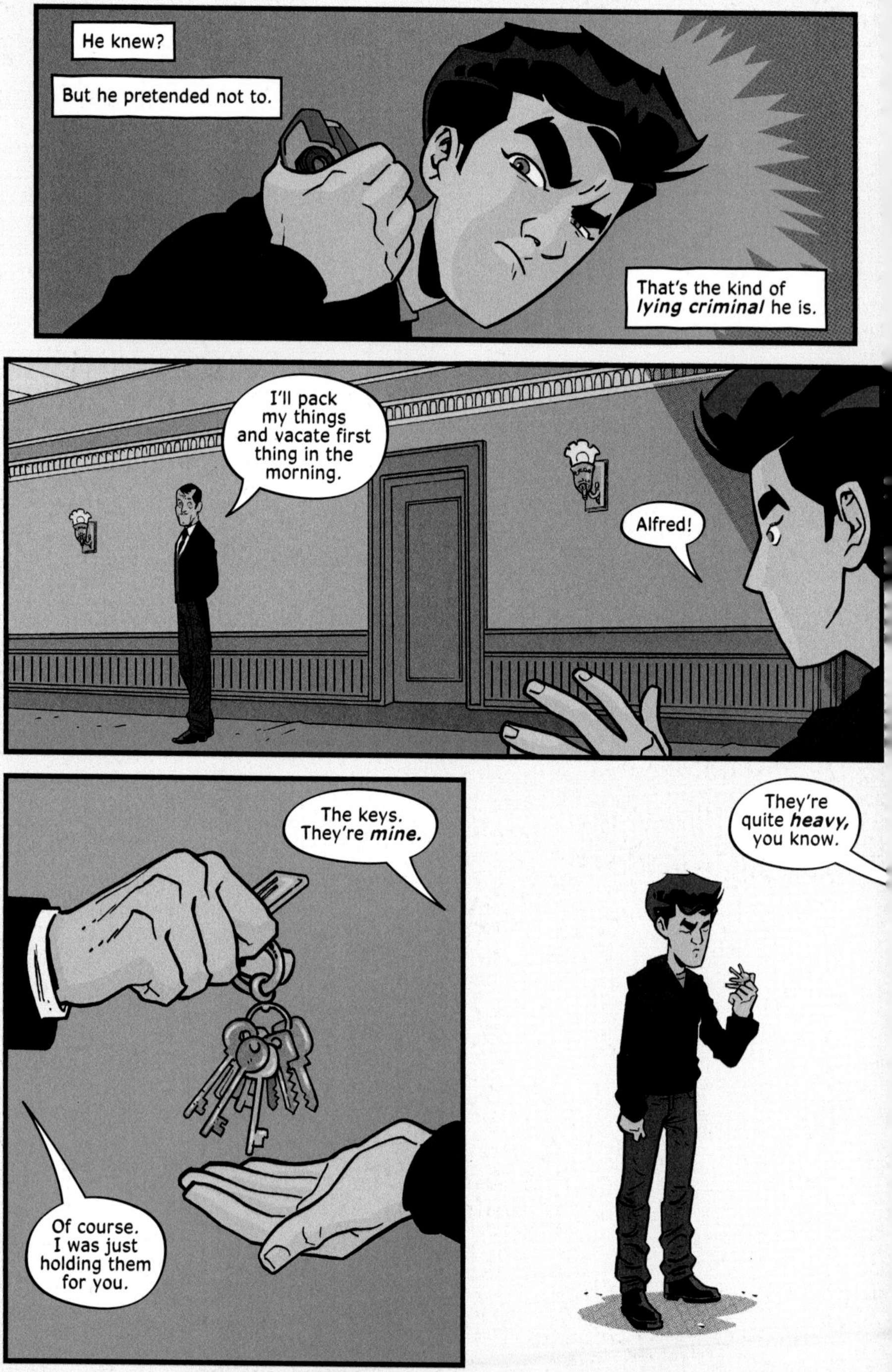
He knew?
But he pretended not to.
That's the kind of *lying criminal* he is.
I'll pack my things and vacate first thing in the morning.
Alfred!
The keys. They're *mine.*
Of course. I was just holding them for you.
They're quite *heavy,* you know.

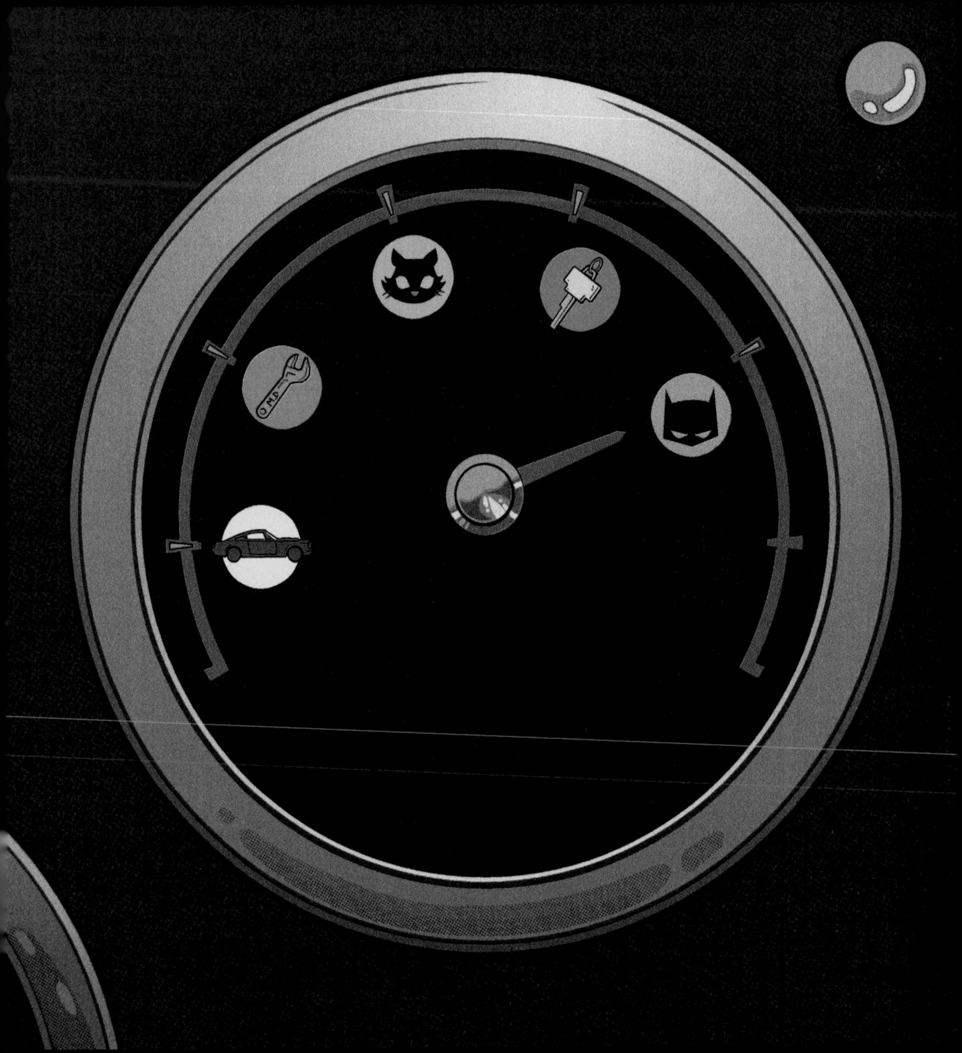

KICK IT UP

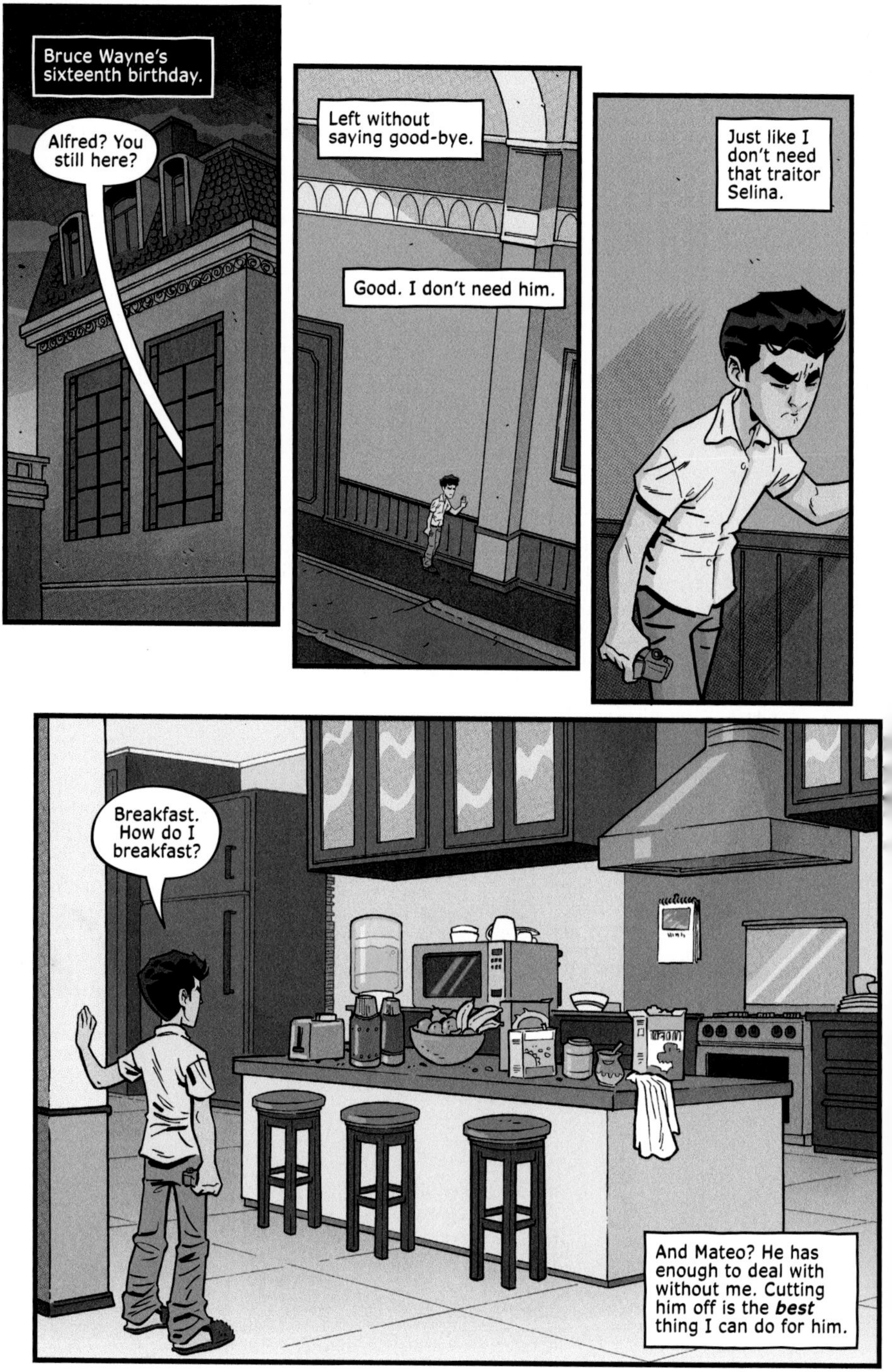

Bruce Wayne's sixteenth birthday.
Alfred? You still here?
Left without saying good-bye.
Good. I don't need him.
Just like I don't need that traitor Selina.
Breakfast. How do I breakfast?
And Mateo? He has enough to deal with without me. Cutting him off is the *best* thing I can do for him.

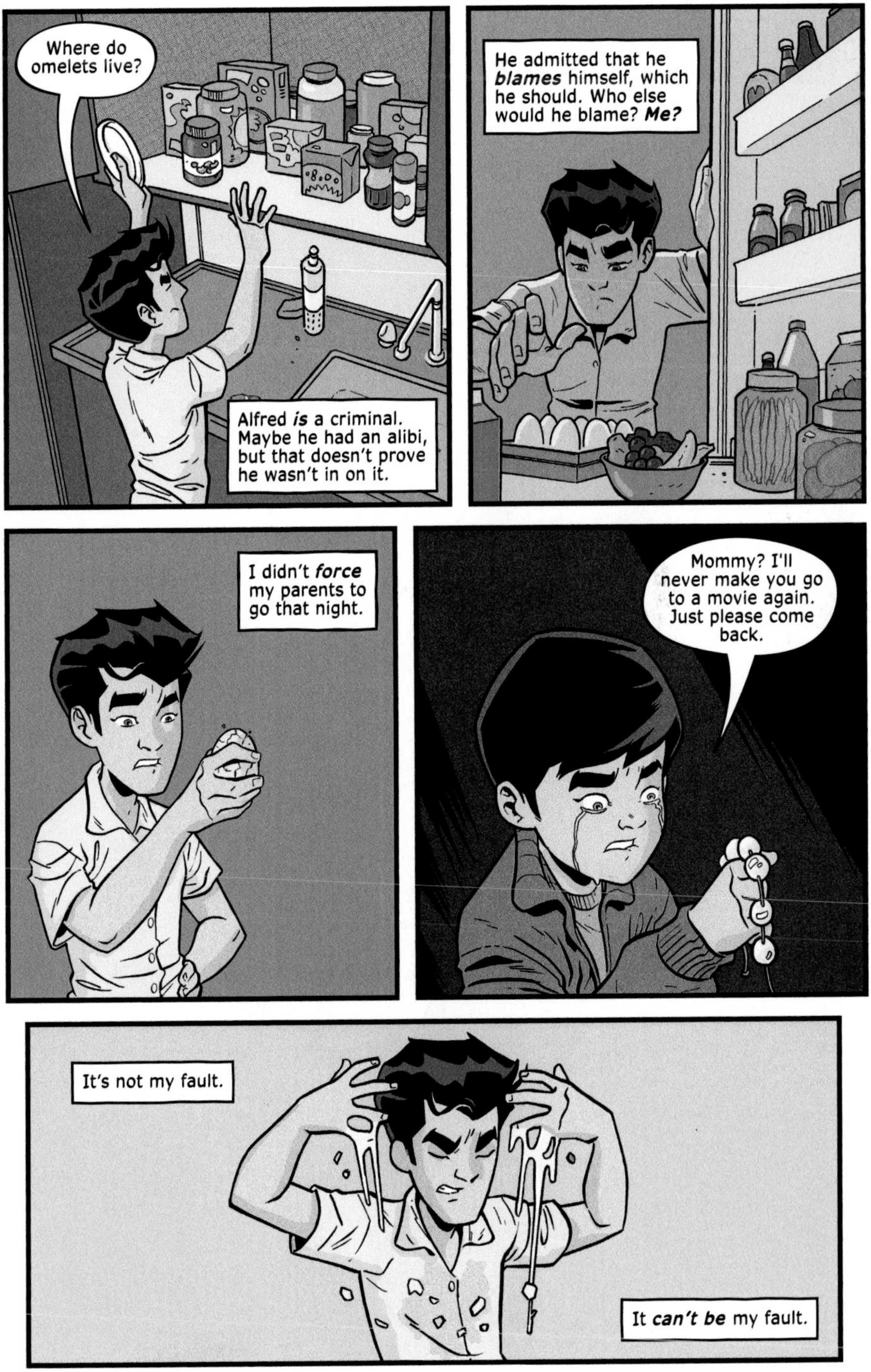
Where do omelets live?
Alfred *is* a criminal. Maybe he had an alibi, but that doesn't prove he wasn't in on it.
He admitted that he *blames* himself, which he should. Who else would he blame? *Me?*
I didn't *force* my parents to go that night.
Mommy? I'll never make you go to a movie again. Just please come back.
It's not my fault.
It *can't be* my fault.

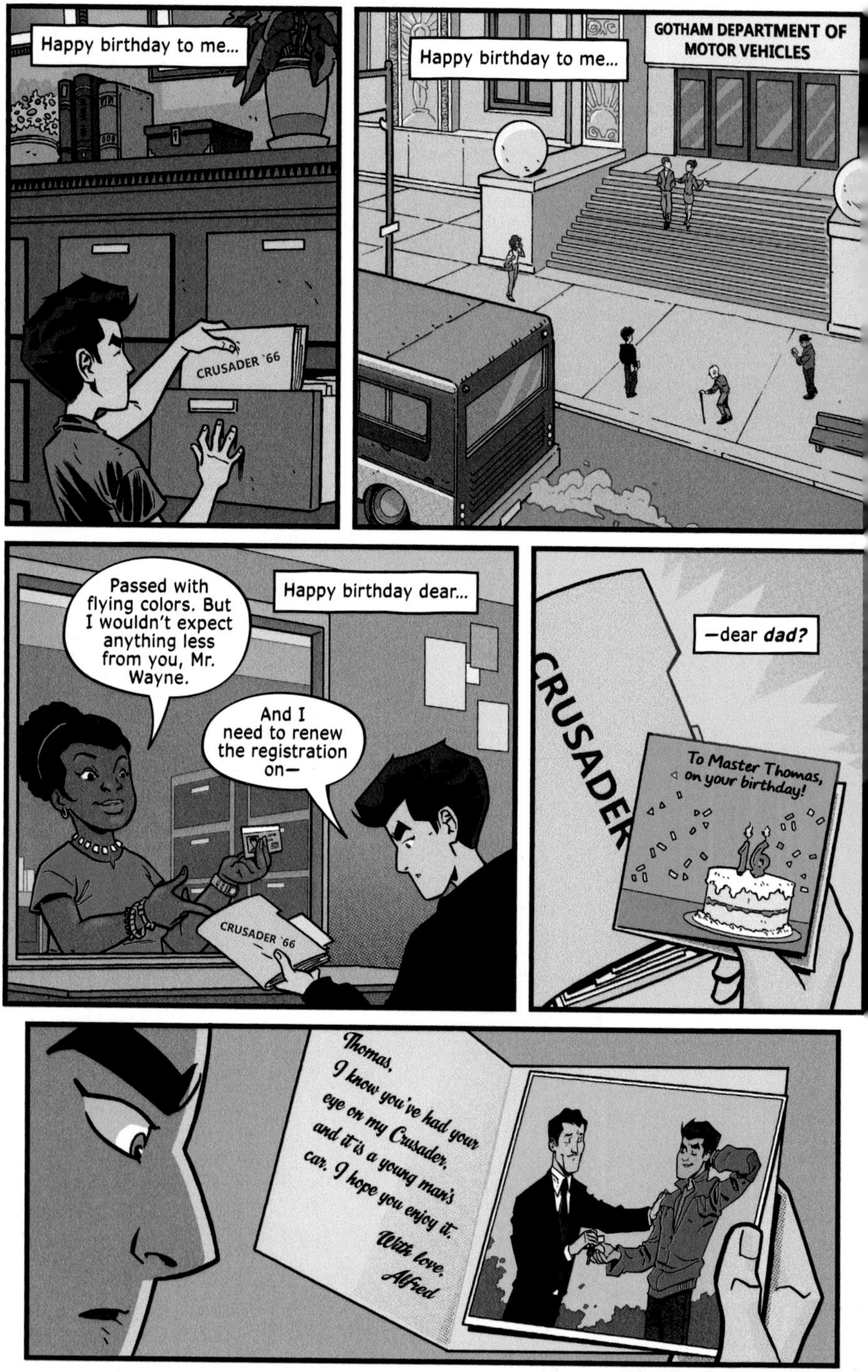
Happy birthday to me...
CRUSADER '66
GOTHAM DEPARTMENT OF MOTOR VEHICLES
Happy birthday to me...
Passed with flying colors. But I wouldn't expect anything less from you, Mr. Wayne.
Happy birthday dear...
And I need to renew the registration on—
CRUSADER '66
—dear *dad?*
CRUSADER
To Master Thomas, on your birthday!
Thomas,
I know you've had your eye on my Crusader, and it is a young man's car. I hope you enjoy it.
With love,
Alfred

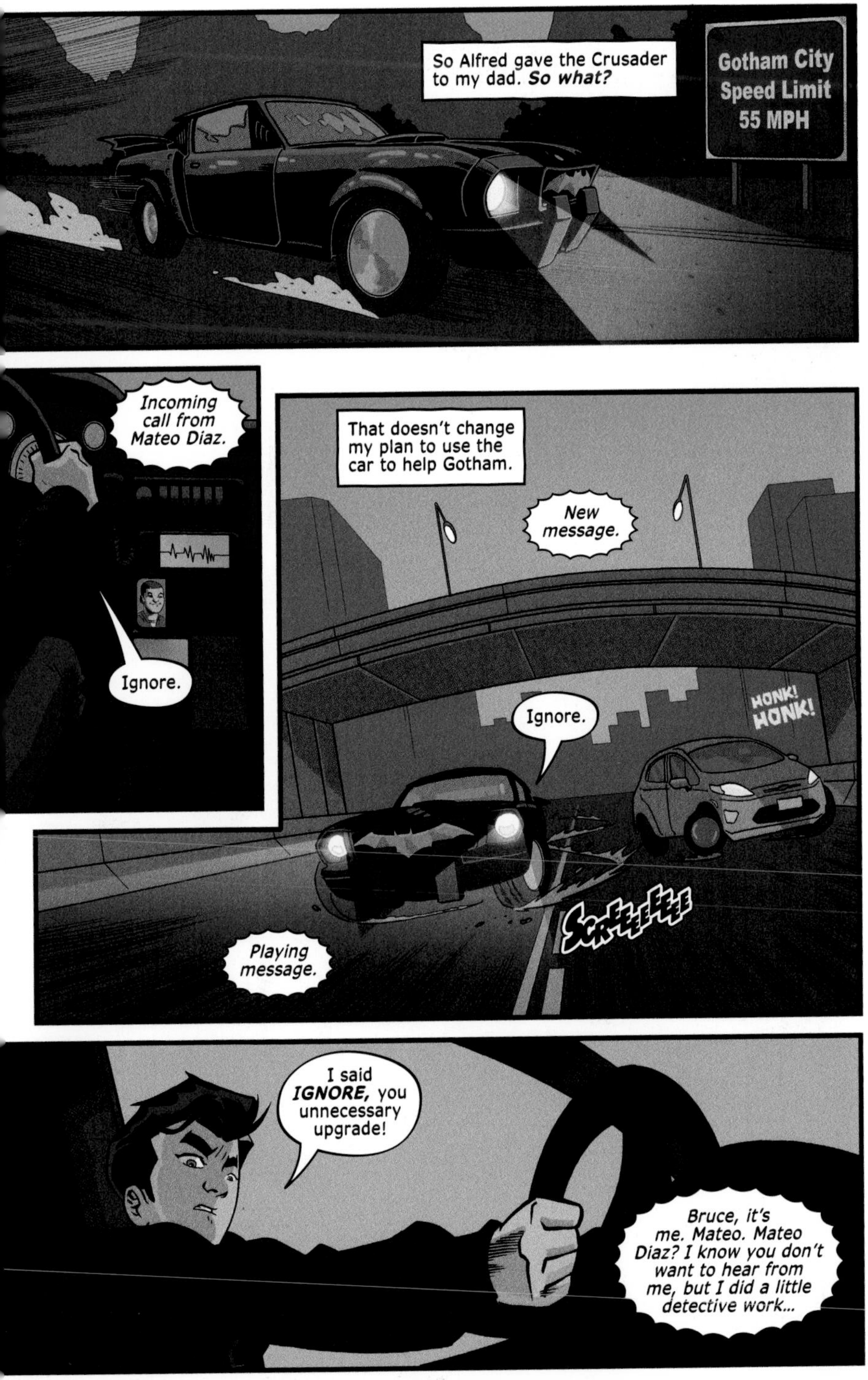

So Alfred gave the Crusader to my dad. *So what?*
Gotham City Speed Limit 55 MPH
Incoming call from Mateo Diaz.
Ignore.
That doesn't change my plan to use the car to help Gotham.
New message.
Ignore.
HONK! HONK!
SCREEEEEEE
Playing message.
I said *IGNORE,* you unnecessary upgrade!
Bruce, it's me. Mateo. Mateo Diaz? I know you don't want to hear from me, but I did a little detective work...

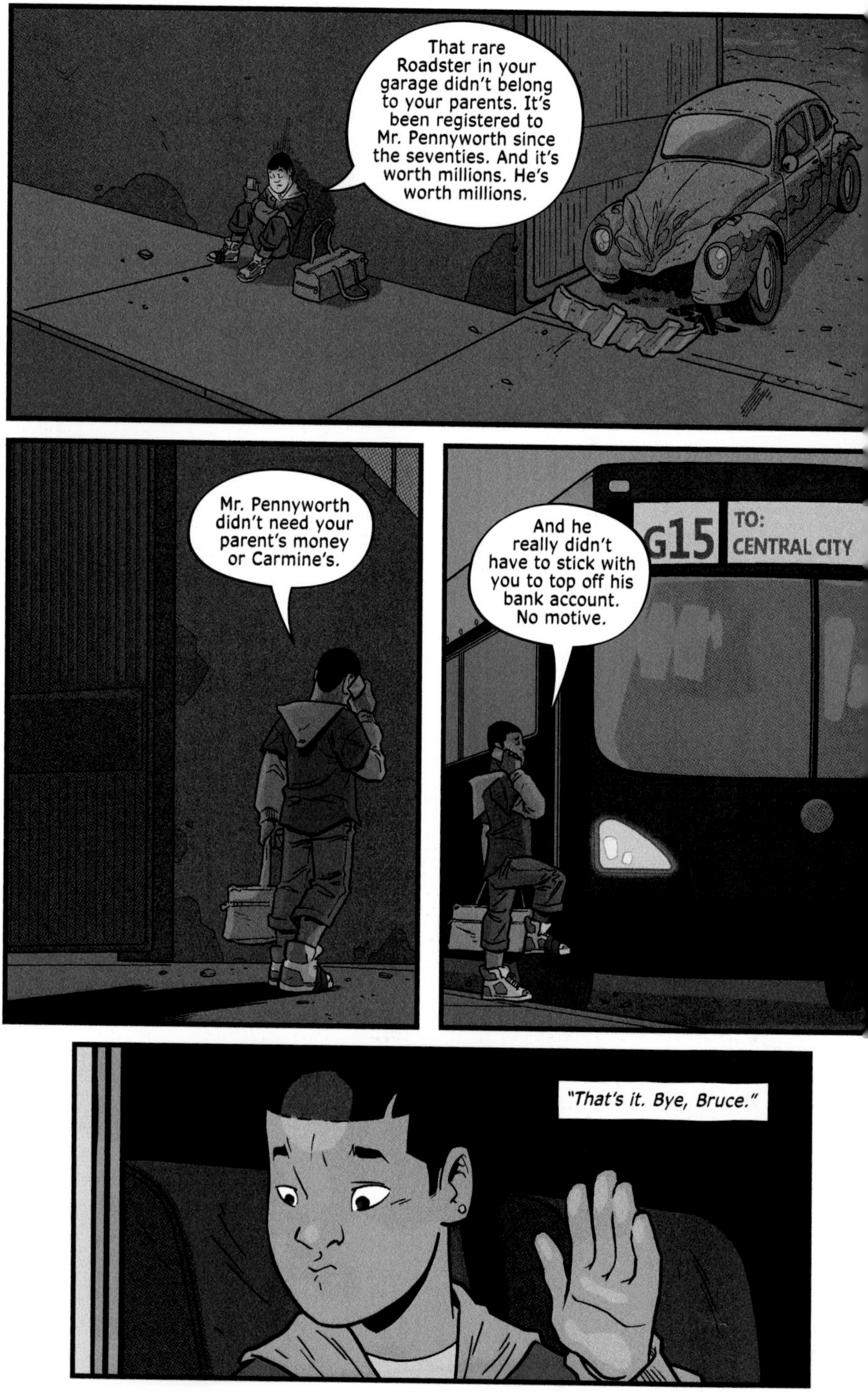
That rare Roadster in your garage didn't belong to your parents. It's been registered to Mr. Pennyworth since the seventies. And it's worth millions. He's worth millions.
Mr. Pennyworth didn't need your parent's money or Carmine's.
G15
TO: CENTRAL CITY
And he really didn't have to stick with you to top off his bank account. No motive.
"That's it. Bye, Bruce."

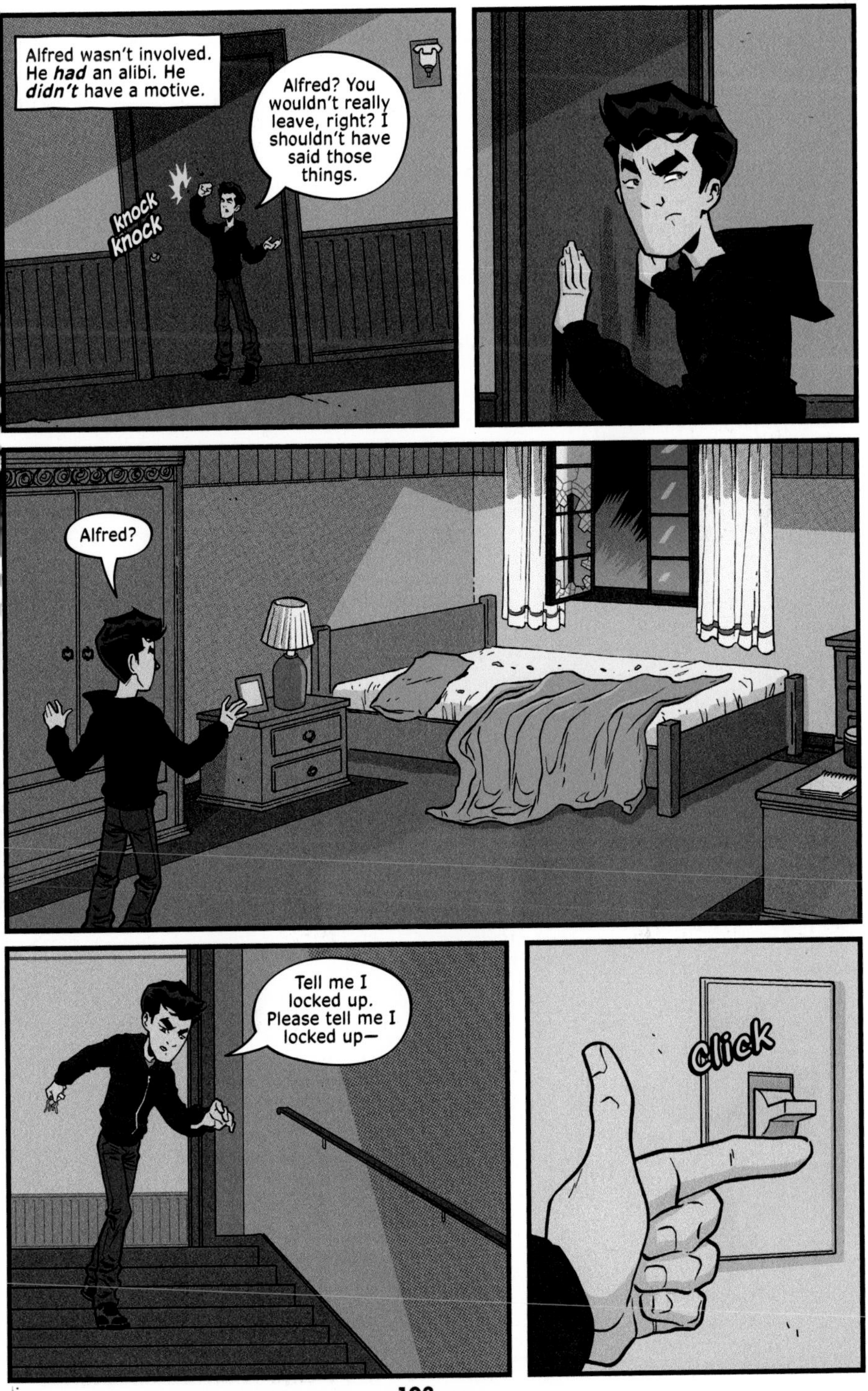

Alfred wasn't involved. He ***had*** an alibi. He ***didn't*** have a motive.
Alfred? You wouldn't really leave, right? I shouldn't have said those things.
knock knock
Alfred?
Tell me I locked up. Please tell me I locked up—
click

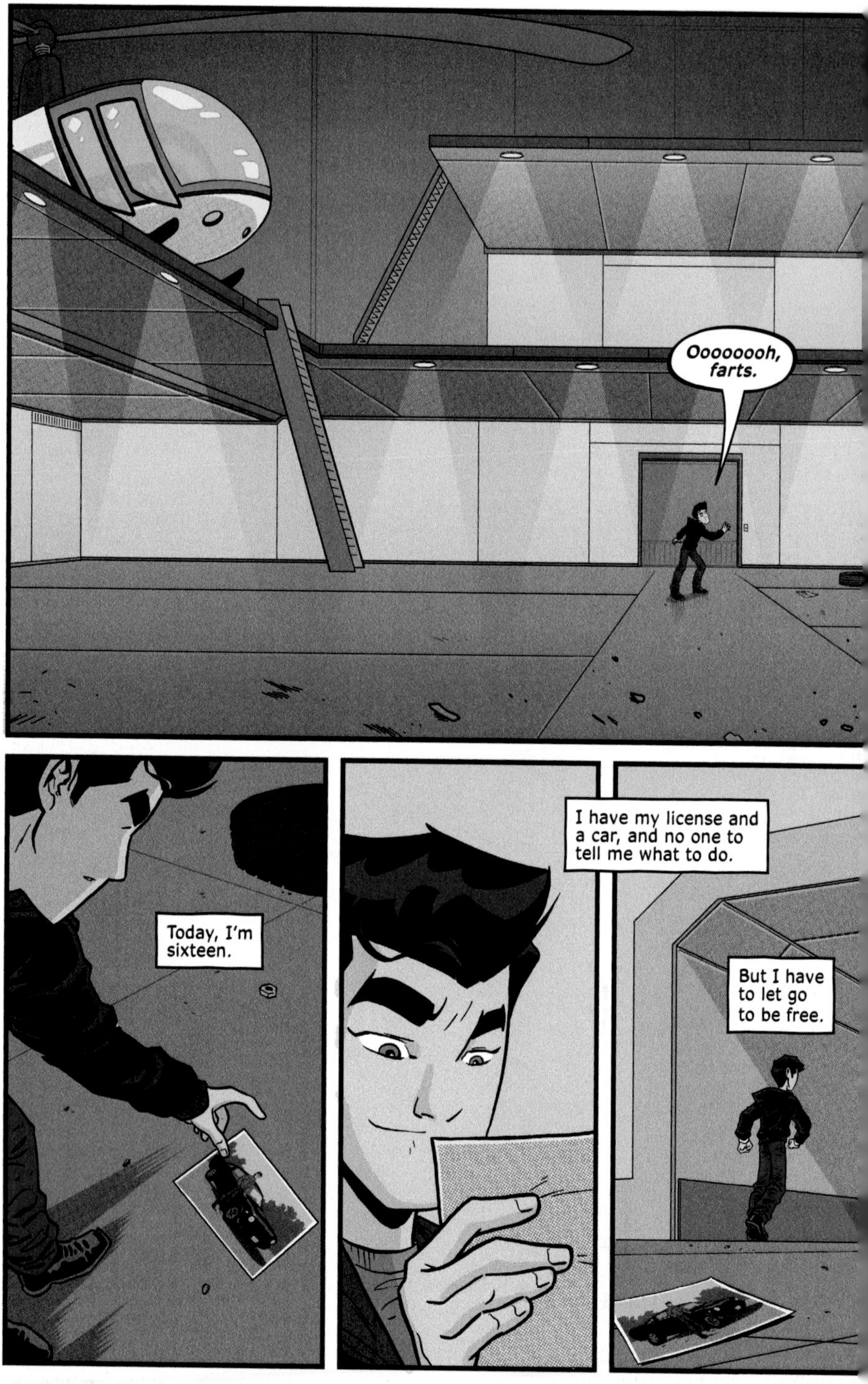
Oooooooh, farts.
Today, I'm sixteen.
I have my license and a car, and no one to tell me what to do.
But I have to let go to be free.

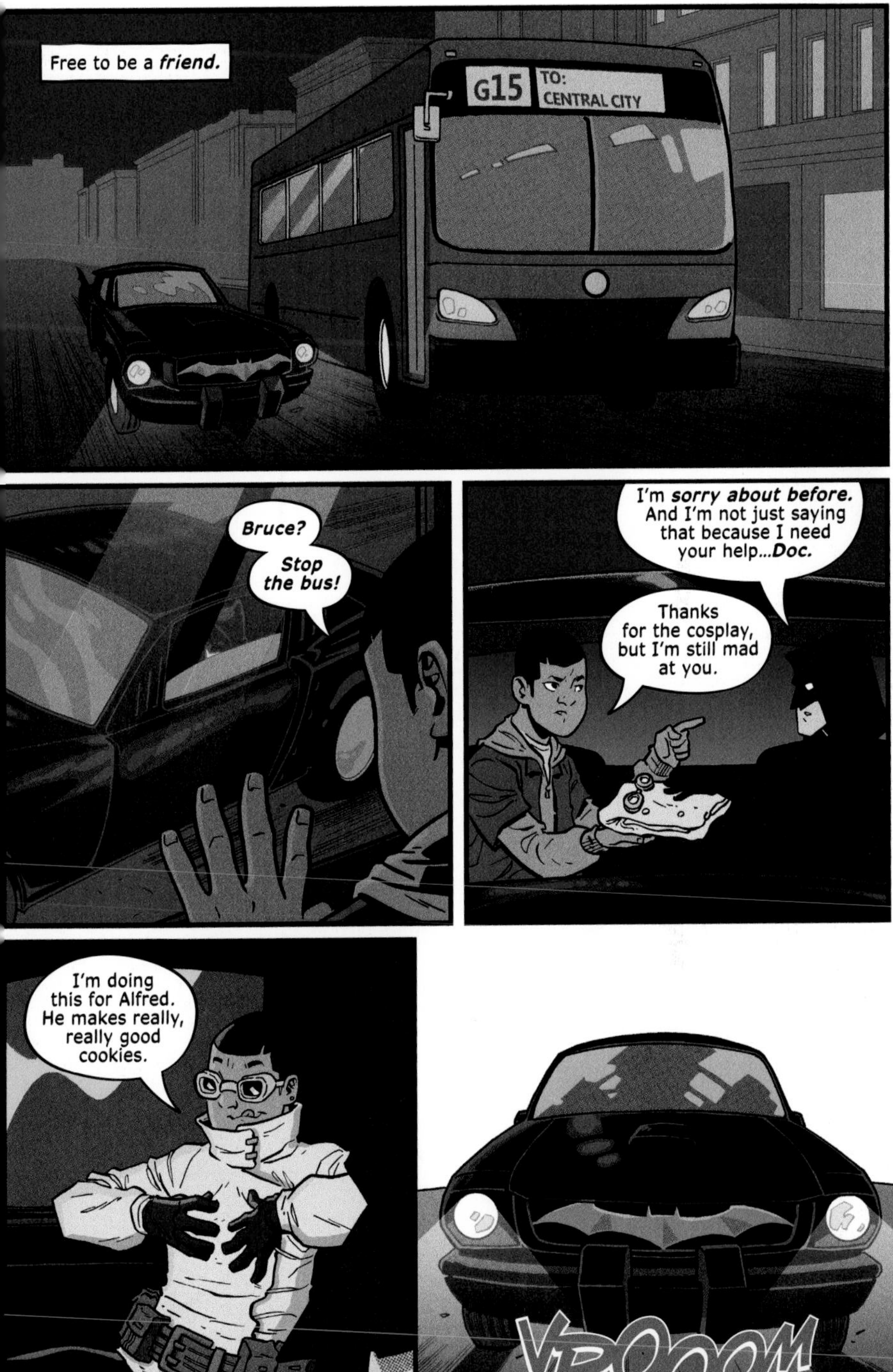
Free to be a *friend.*
G15 TO: CENTRAL CITY
Bruce?
Stop the bus!
I'm *sorry about before.* And I'm not just saying that because I need your help...*Doc.*
Thanks for the cosplay, but I'm still mad at you.
I'm doing this for Alfred. He makes really, really good cookies.
VROOOM

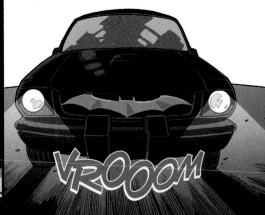

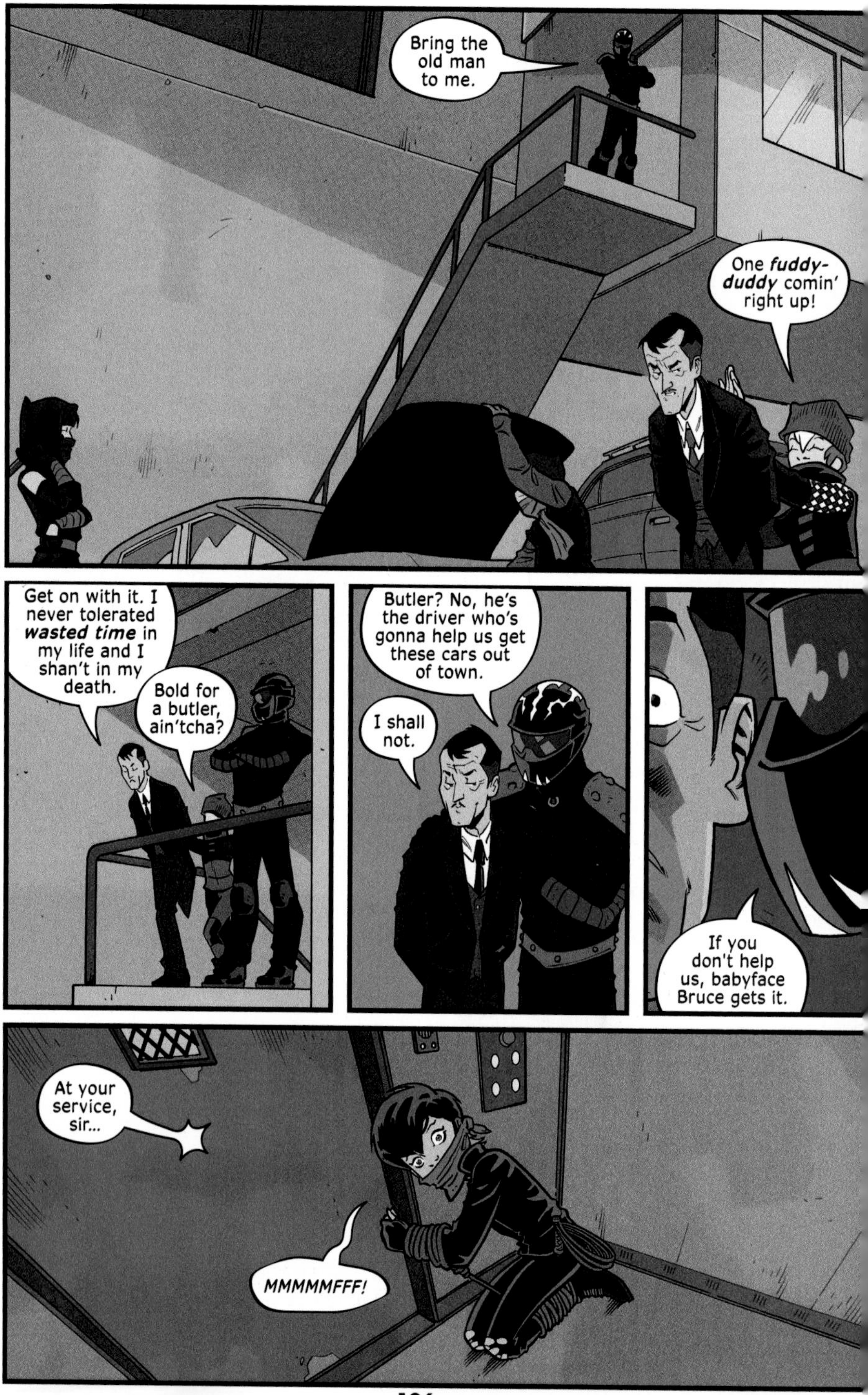
Bring the old man to me.
One *fuddy-duddy* comin' right up!
Get on with it. I never tolerated *wasted time* in my life and I shan't in my death.
Bold for a butler, ain'tcha?
Butler? No, he's the driver who's gonna help us get these cars out of town.
I shall not.
If you don't help us, babyface Bruce gets it.
At your service, sir...
MMMMMFFF!

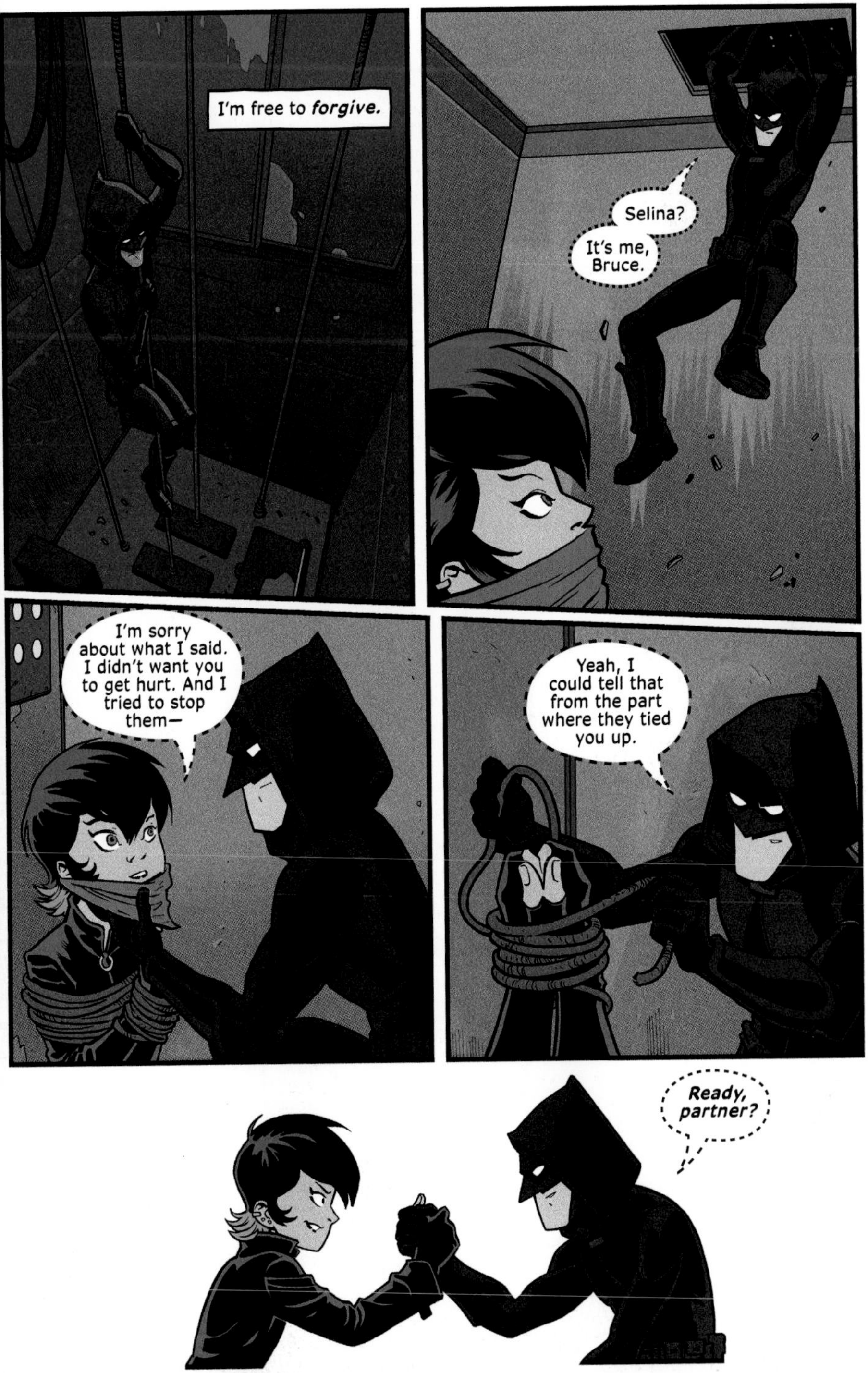
I'm free to *forgive.*
Selina?
It's me, Bruce.
I'm sorry about what I said. I didn't want you to get hurt. And I tried to stop them—
Yeah, I could tell that from the part where they tied you up.
Ready, partner?

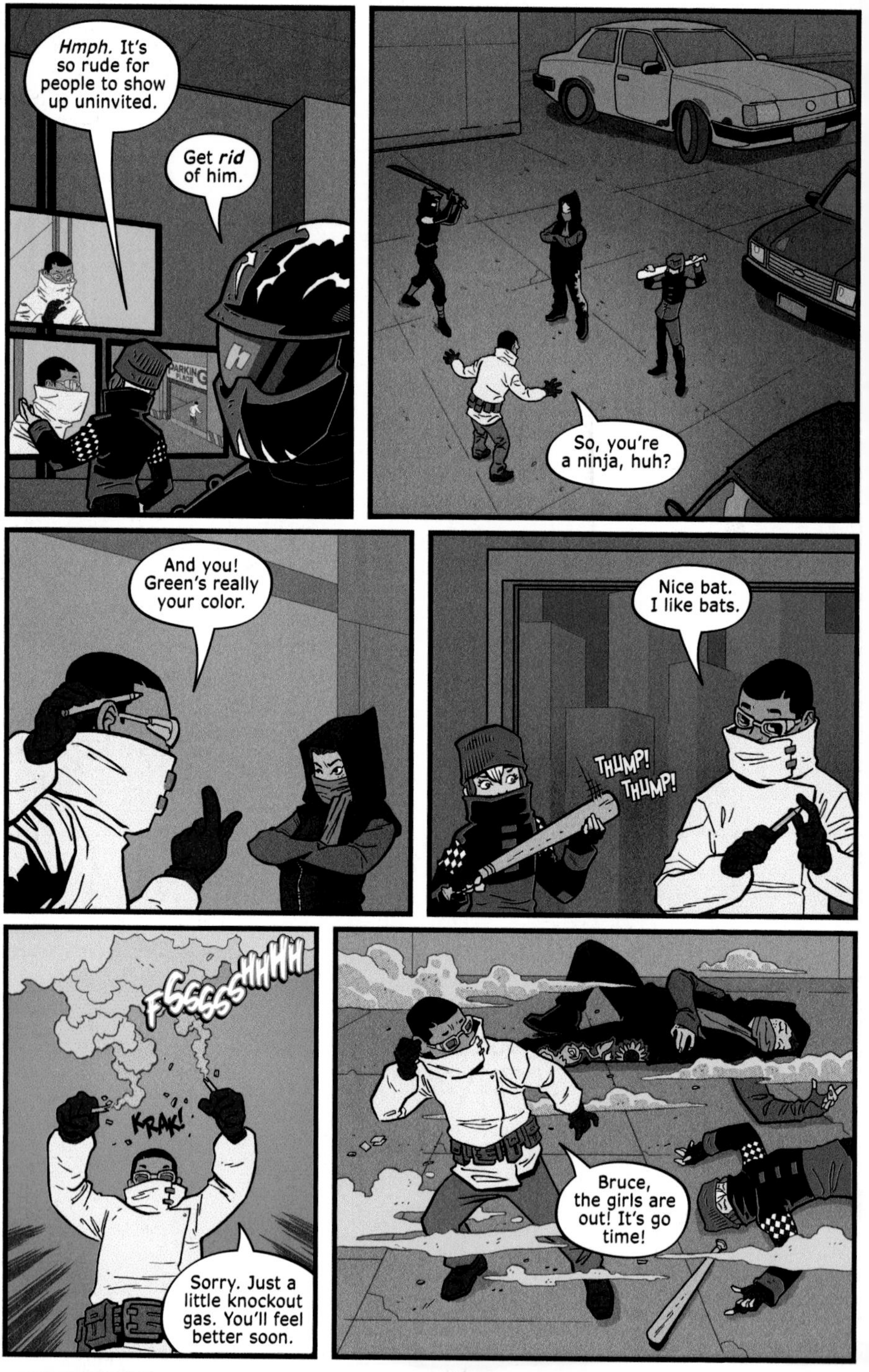
Hmph. It's so rude for people to show up uninvited.
Get *rid* of him.
PARKING PLACE G
So, you're a ninja, huh?
And you! Green's really your color.
Nice bat. I like bats.
THUMP! THUMP!
FSSSSSSHHHHH
KRAK!
Sorry. Just a little knockout gas. You'll feel better soon.
Bruce, the girls are out! It's go time!

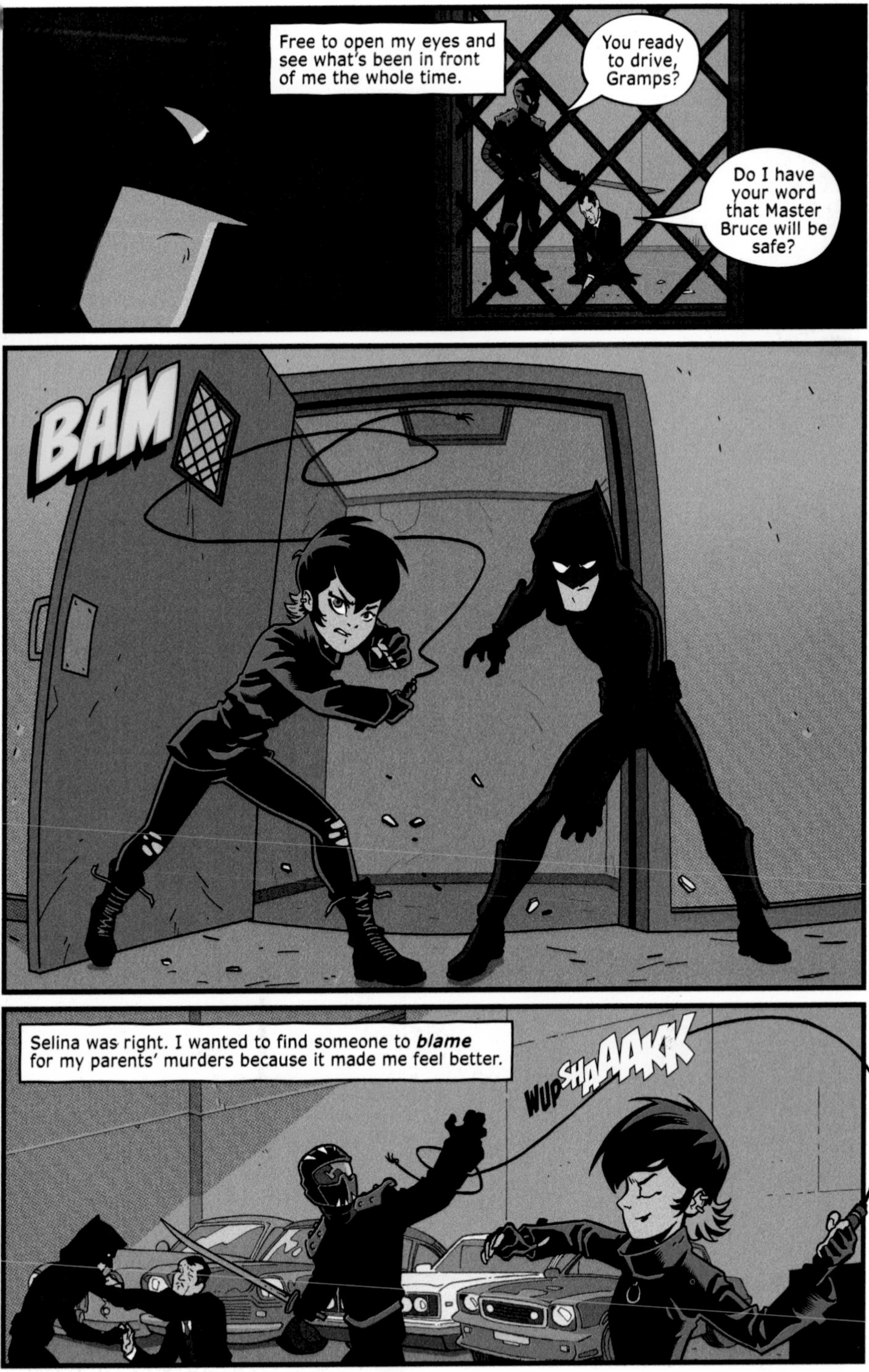
Free to open my eyes and see what's been in front of me the whole time.
You ready to drive, Gramps?
Do I have your word that Master Bruce will be safe?
BAM
Selina was right. I wanted to find someone to *blame* for my parents' murders because it made me feel better.
WUPSHAAAKK

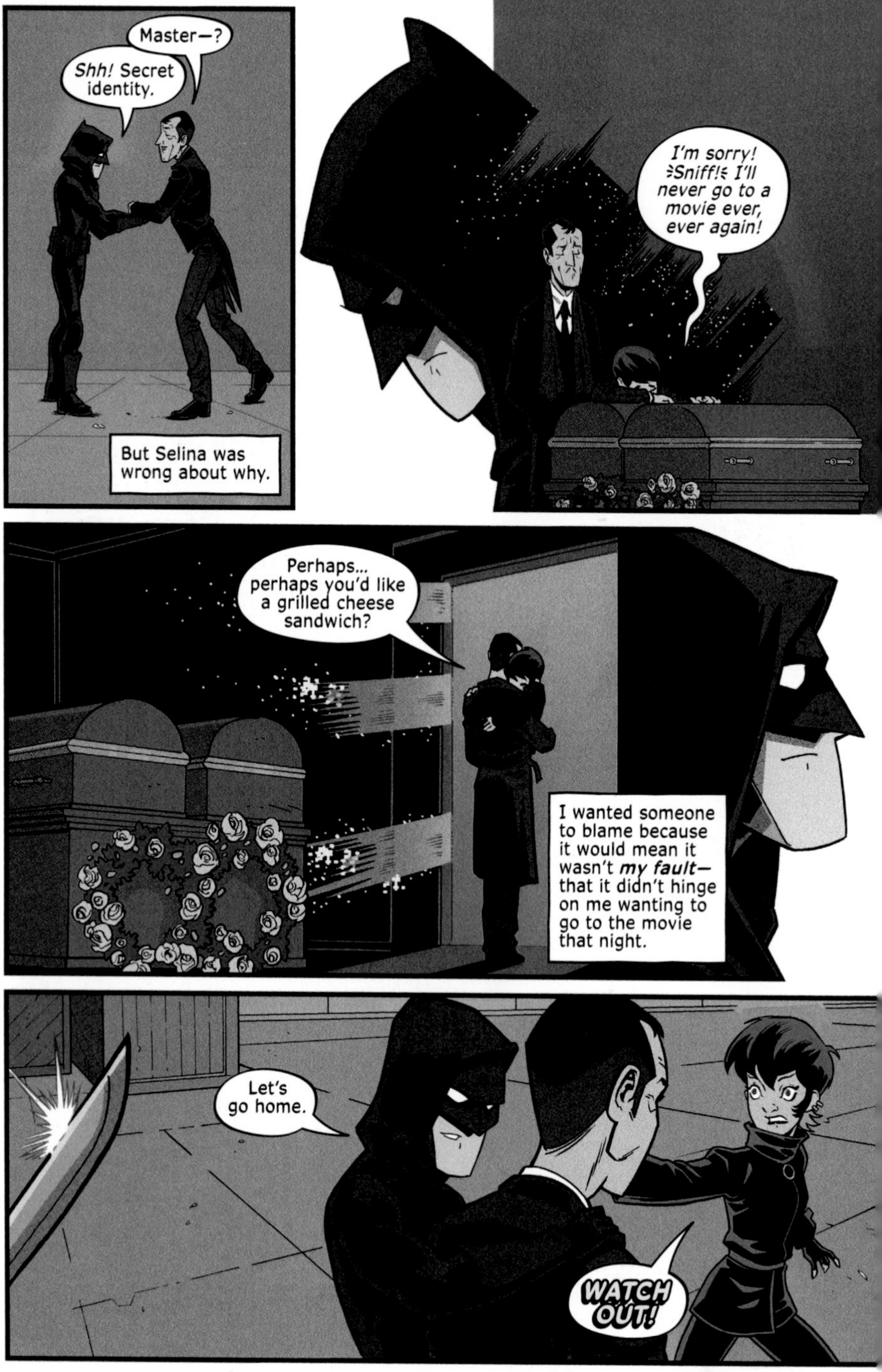
Master—?
Shh! Secret identity.
But Selina was wrong about why.
I'm sorry! Sniff! I'll never go to a movie ever, ever again!
Perhaps... perhaps you'd like a grilled cheese sandwich?
I wanted someone to blame because it would mean it wasn't my fault— that it didn't hinge on me wanting to go to the movie that night.
Let's go home.
WATCH OUT!

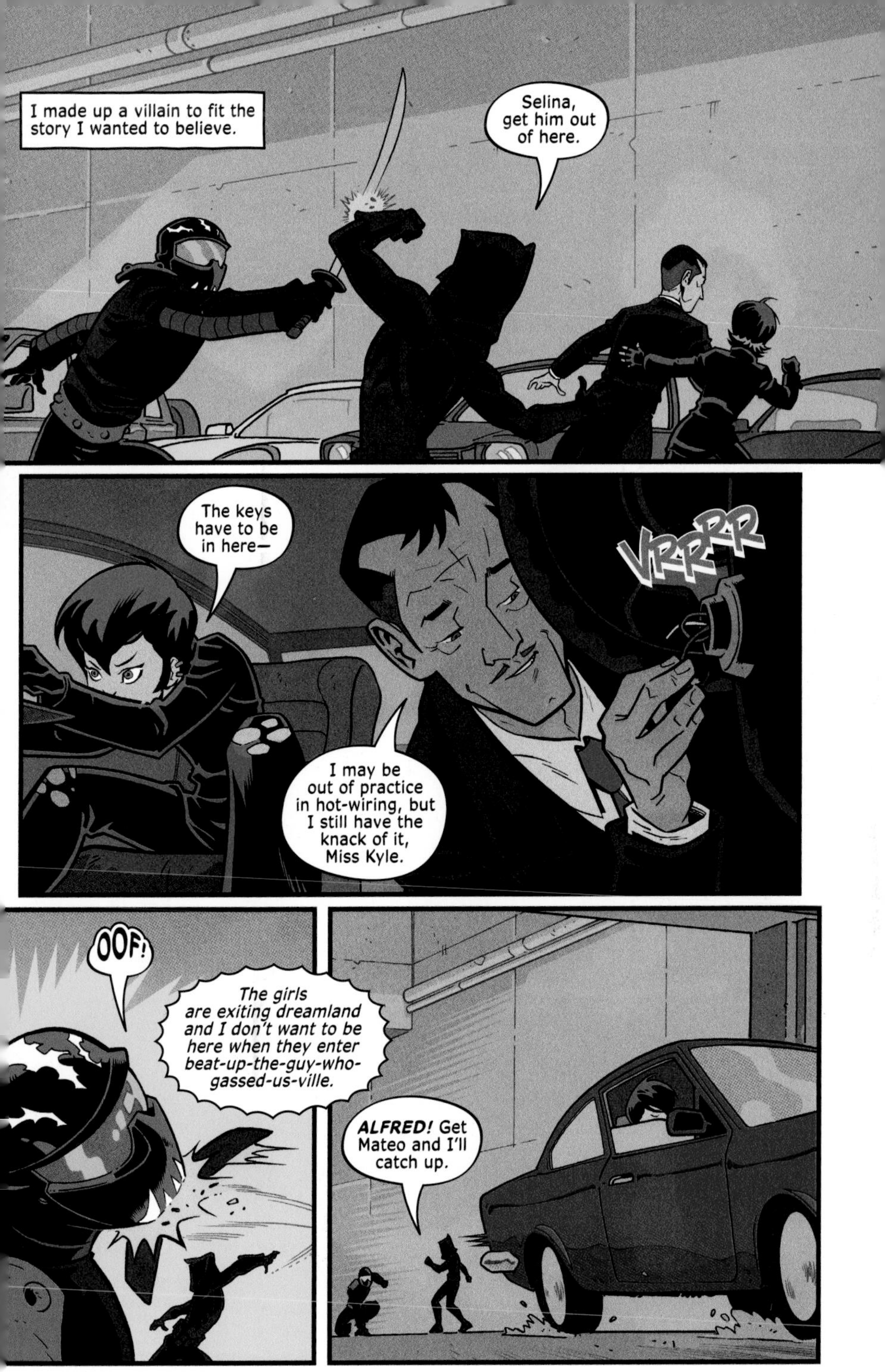
I made up a villain to fit the story I wanted to believe.
Selina, get him out of here.
The keys have to be in here—
VRRRR
I may be out of practice in hot-wiring, but I still have the knack of it, Miss Kyle.
OOF!
The girls are exiting dreamland and I don't want to be here when they enter beat-up-the-guy-who-gassed-us-ville.
ALFRED! Get Mateo and I'll catch up.

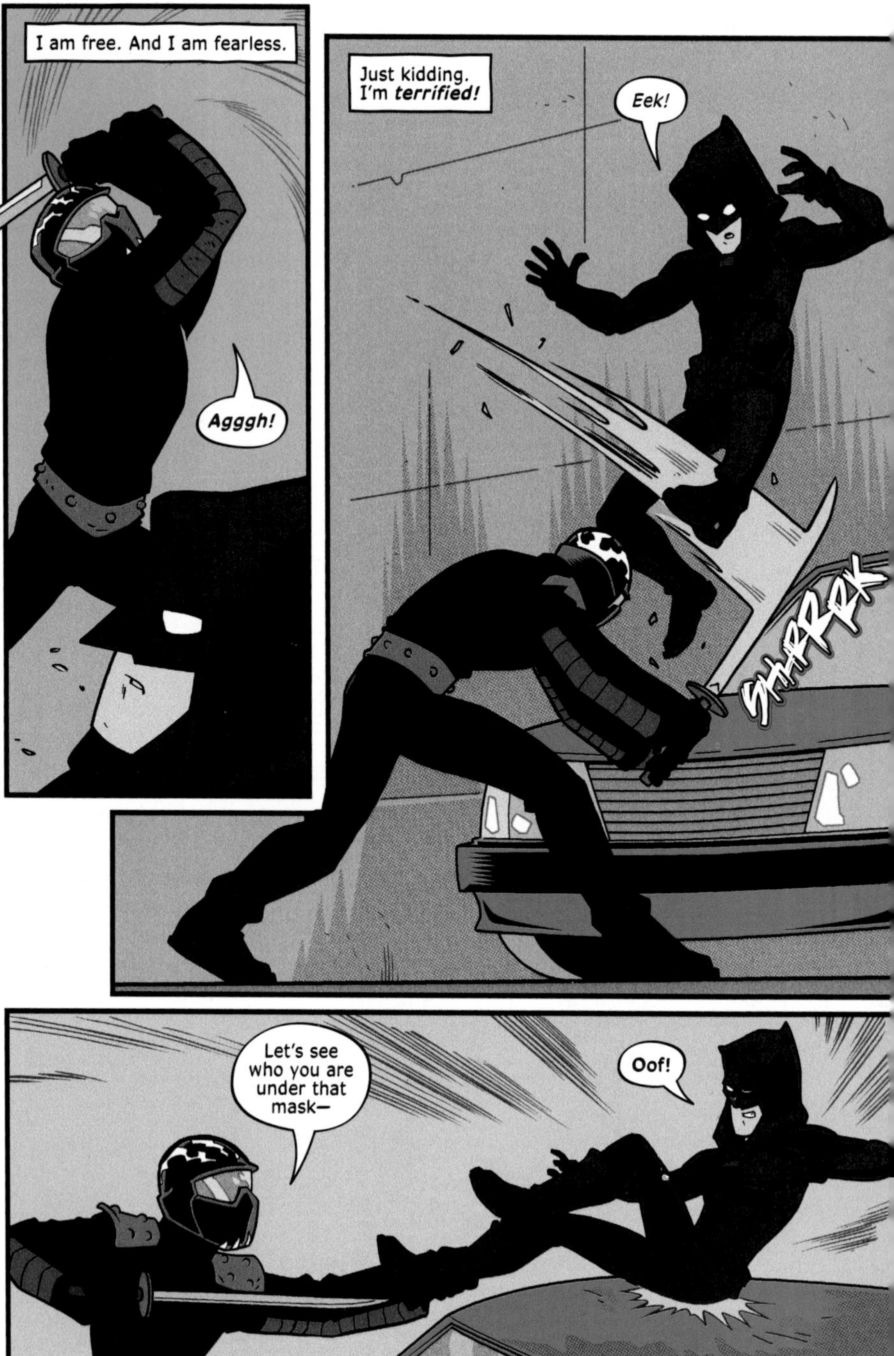
I am free. And I am fearless.
Agggh!
Just kidding. I'm *terrified!*
Eek!
SHHRRK
Let's see who you are under that mask—
Oof!

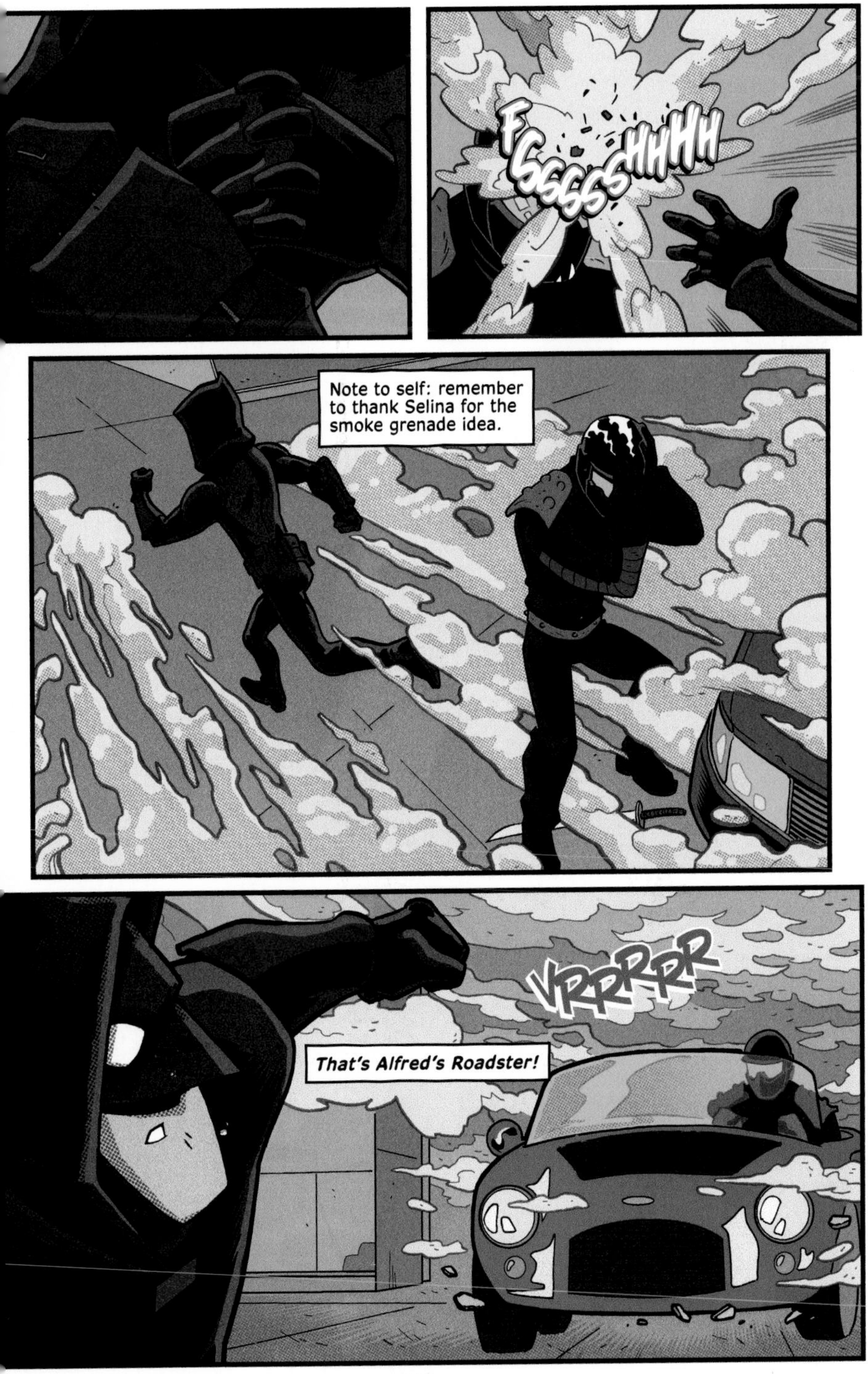
FSSSSSSHHHHH
Note to self: remember to thank Selina for the smoke grenade idea.
VRRRRR
That's Alfred's Roadster!

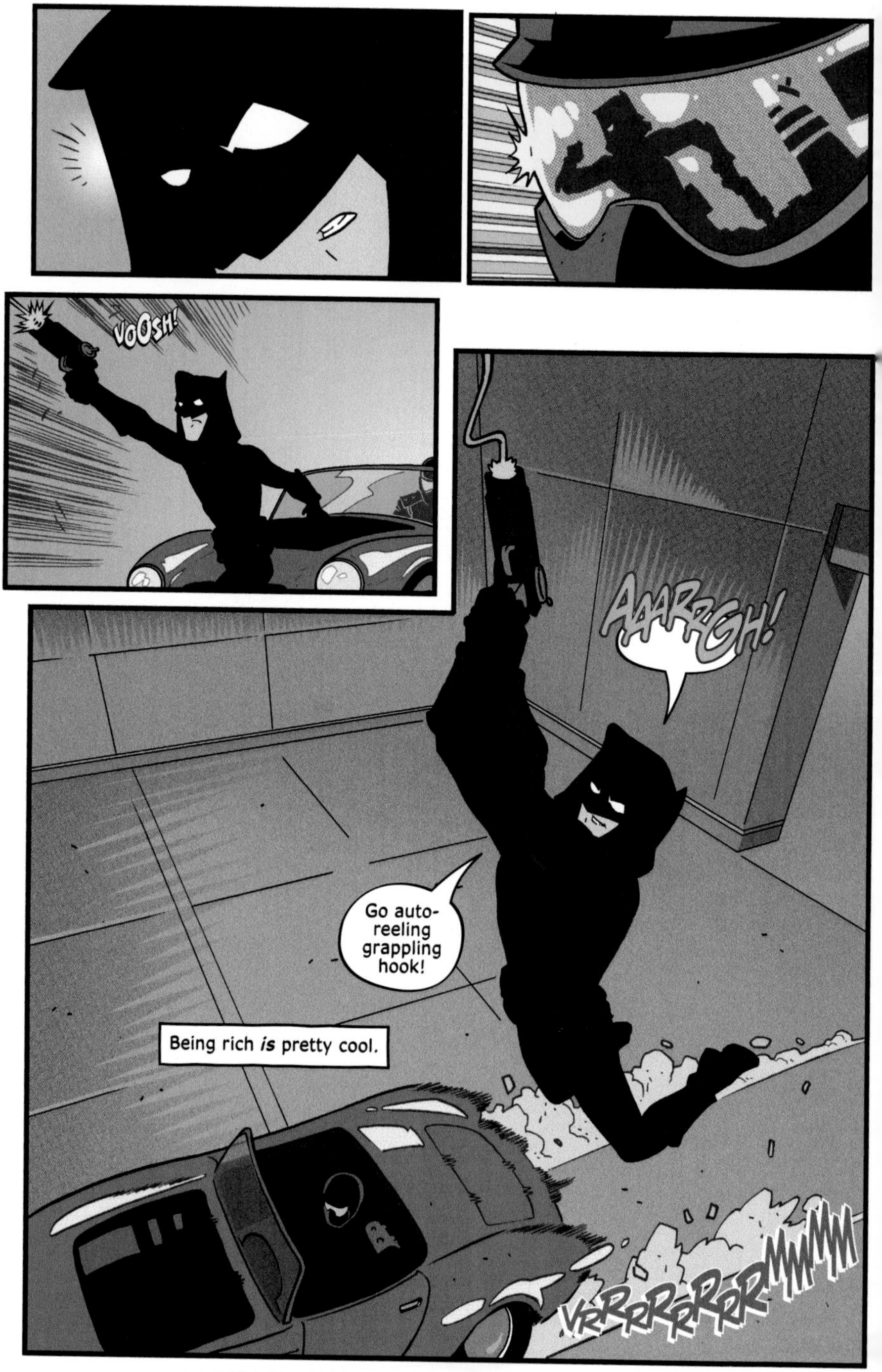
VOOSH!
AAARRGH!
Go auto-reeling grappling hook!
Being rich *is* pretty cool.
VRRRRRRRRRMMMMM

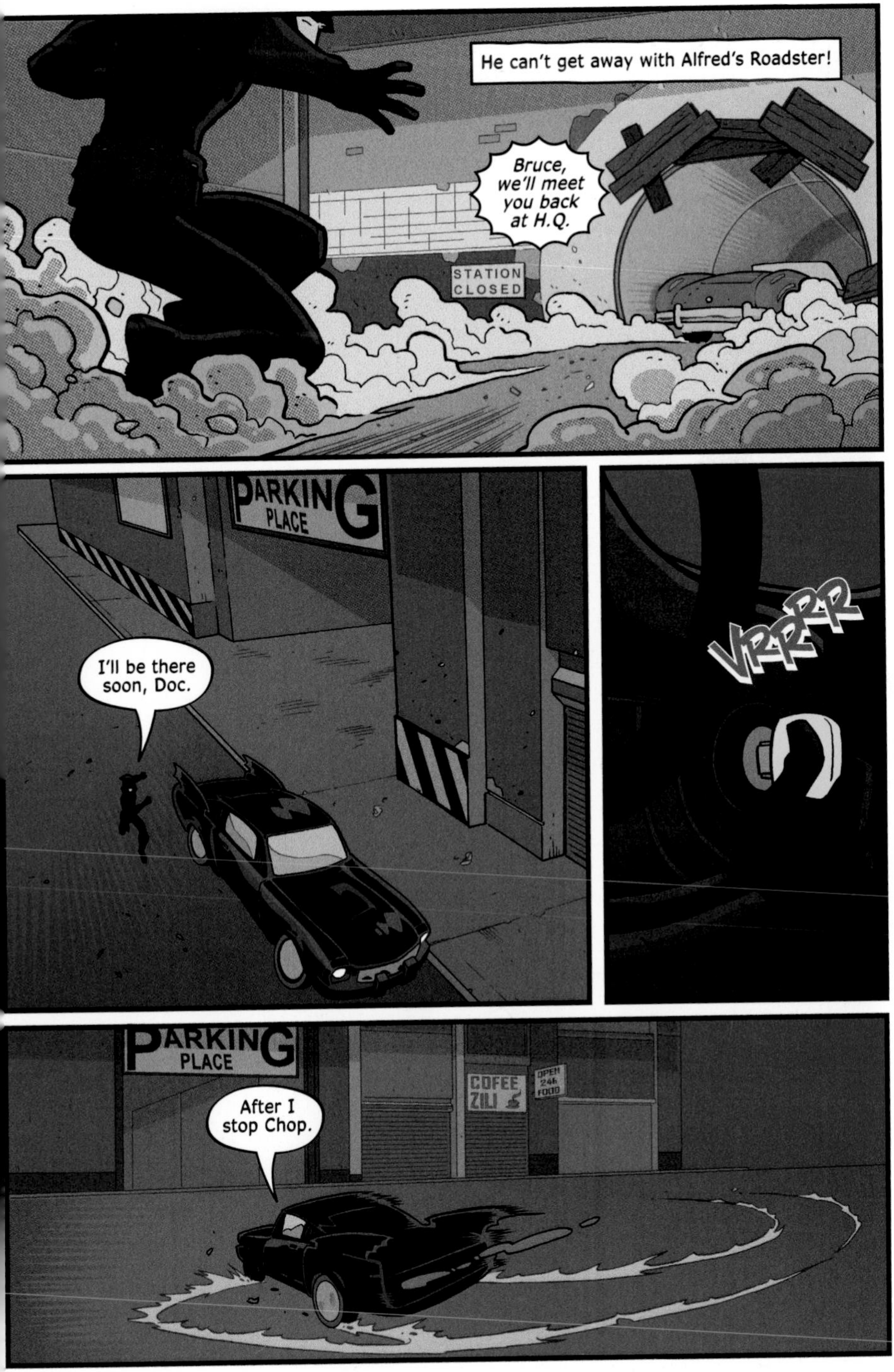
He can't get away with Alfred's Roadster!
Bruce, we'll meet you back at H.Q.
STATION CLOSED
PARKING PLACE
I'll be there soon, Doc.
VRRRR
PARKING PLACE
COFEE ZILI
OPEN 24h FOOD
After I stop Chop.

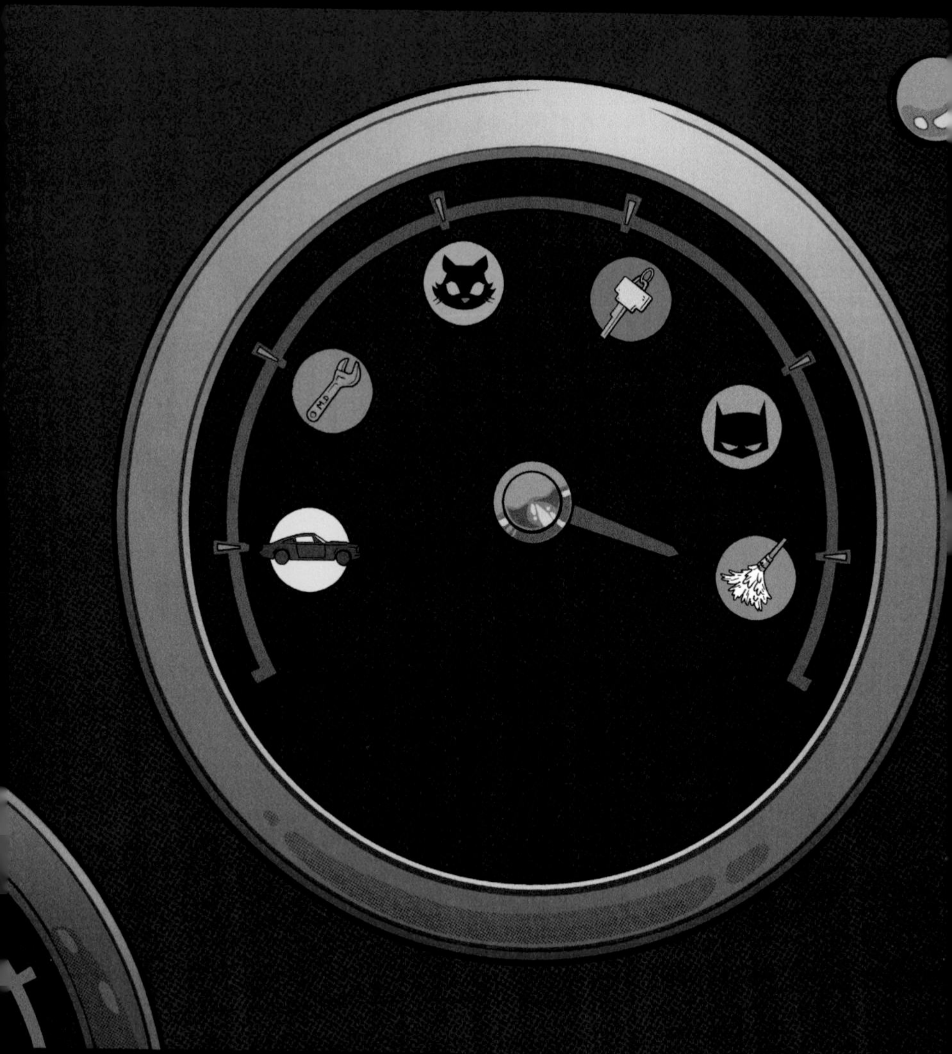

FULL THROTTLE

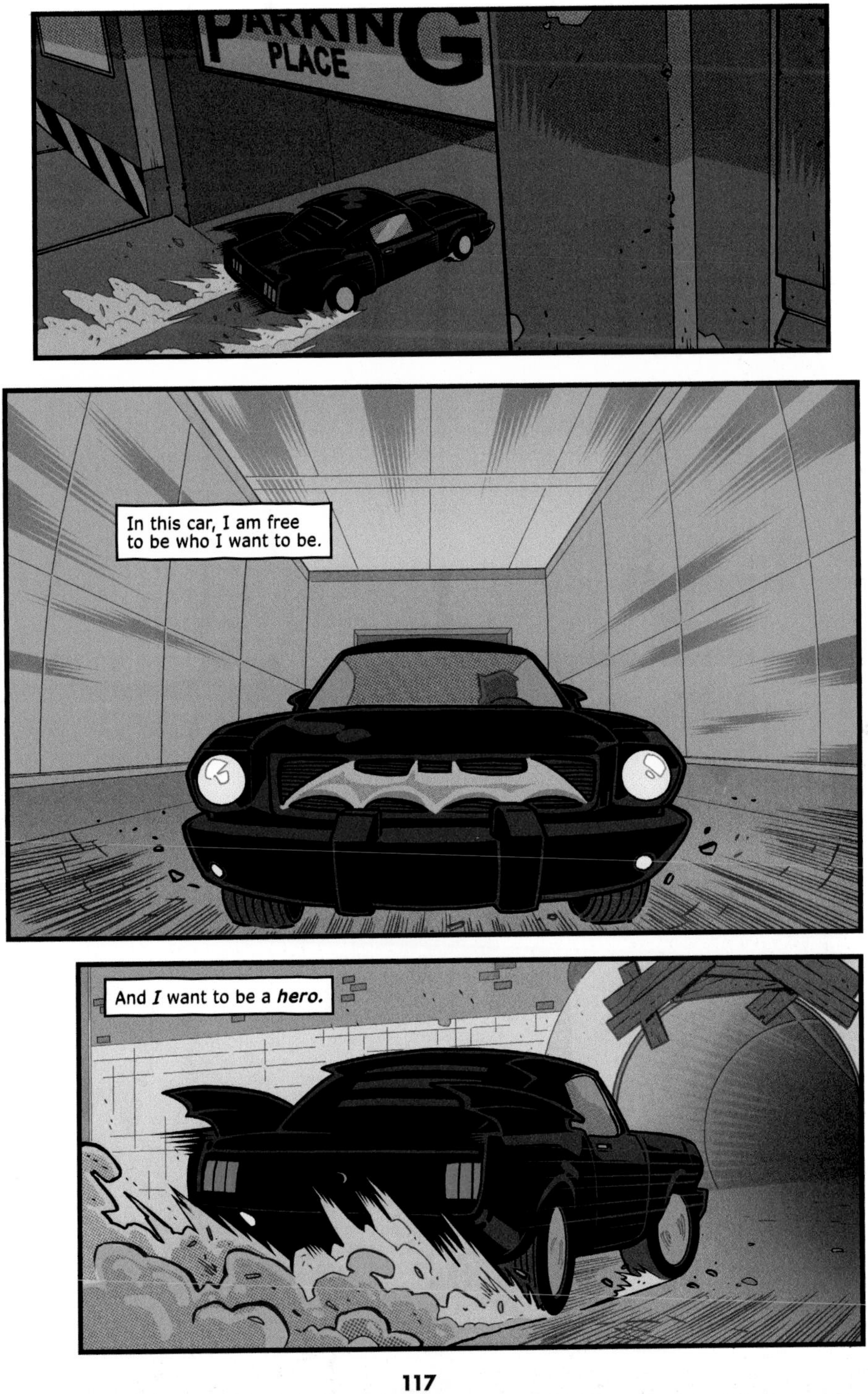
PARKING
PLACE
In this car, I am free to be who I want to be.
And *I* want to be a ***hero.***

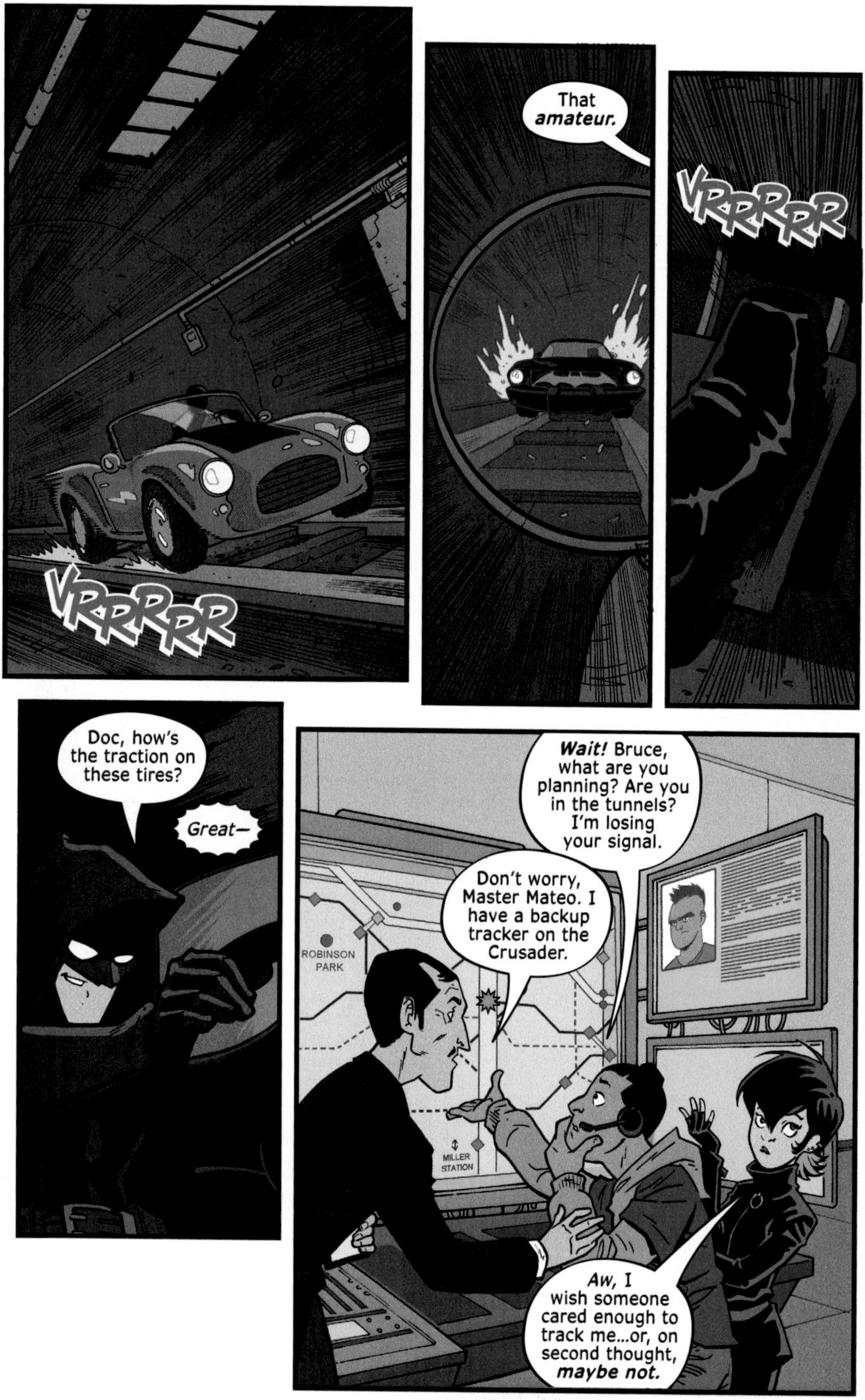
VRRRRR
That amateur.
VRRRRR
Doc, how's the traction on these tires?
Great—
Wait! Bruce, what are you planning? Are you in the tunnels? I'm losing your signal.
Don't worry, Master Mateo. I have a backup tracker on the Crusader.
ROBINSON PARK
MILLER STATION
Aw, I wish someone cared enough to track me...or, on second thought, maybe not.

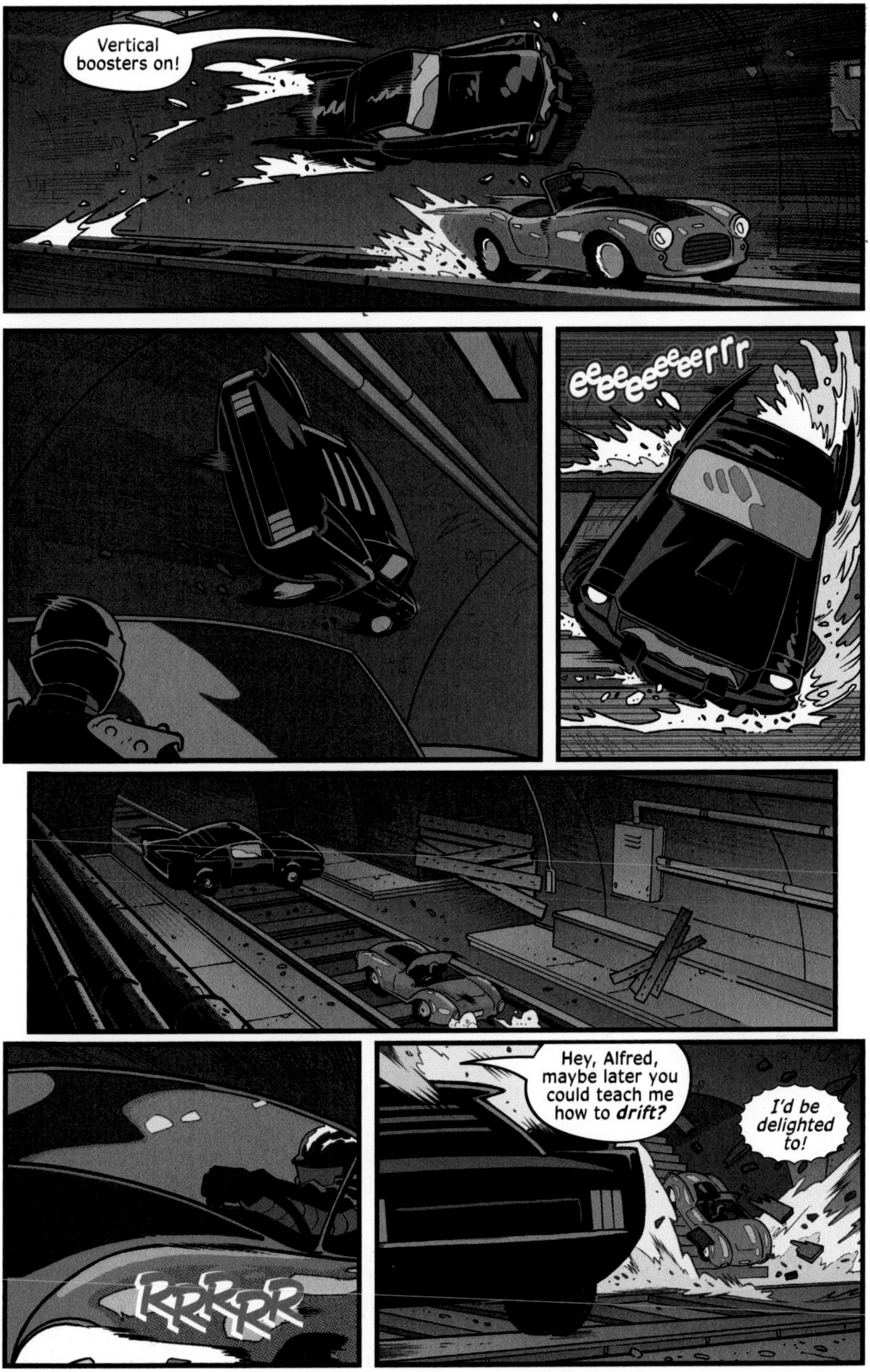
Vertical boosters on!
eeeeeeeeerrr
RRRRR
Hey, Alfred, maybe later you could teach me how to *drift?*
I'd be delighted to!

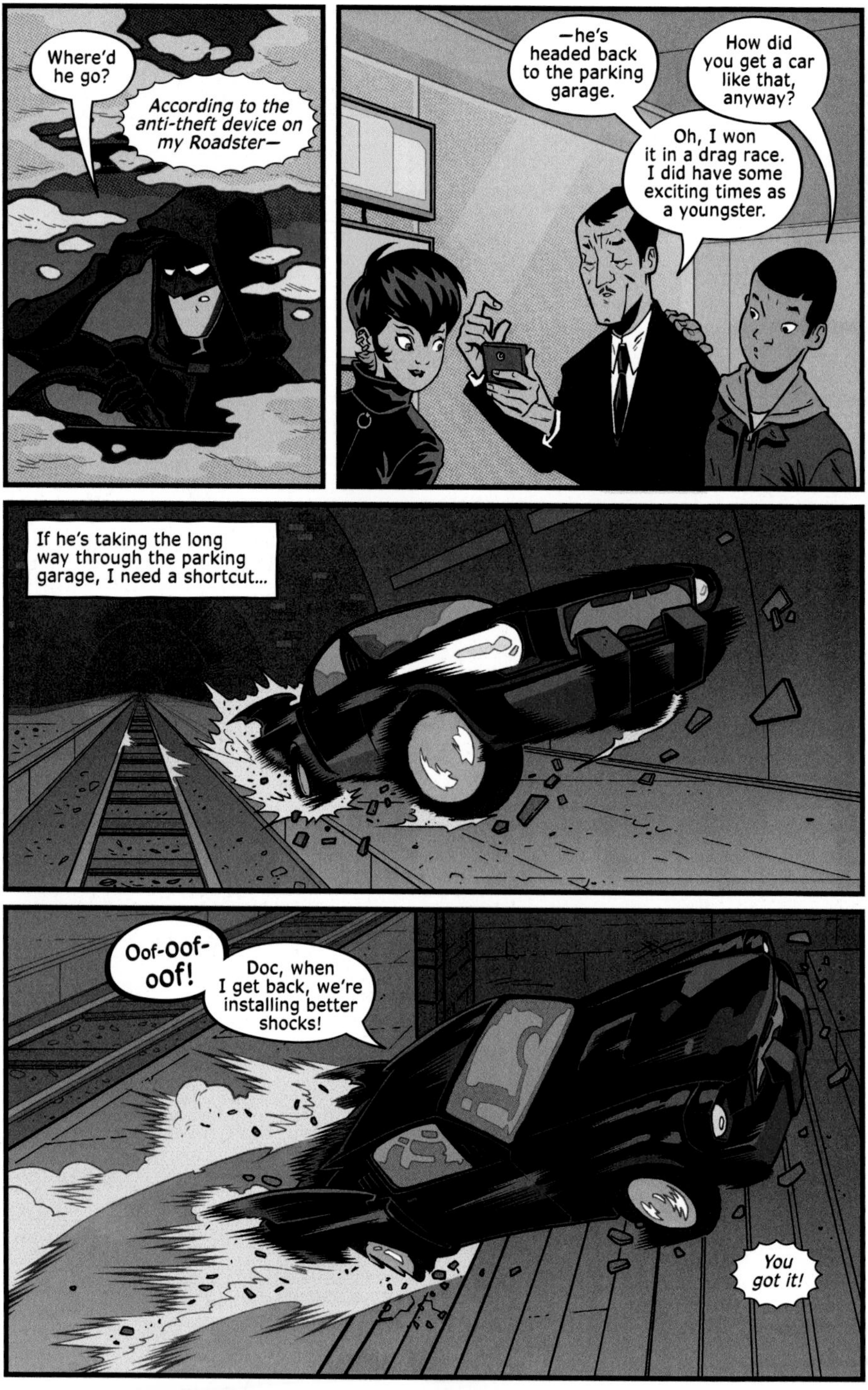
Where'd he go?
According to the anti-theft device on my Roadster—
—he's headed back to the parking garage.
How did you get a car like that, anyway?
Oh, I won it in a drag race. I did have some exciting times as a youngster.
If he's taking the long way through the parking garage, I need a shortcut...
Oof-oof-oof!
Doc, when I get back, we're installing better shocks!
You got it!

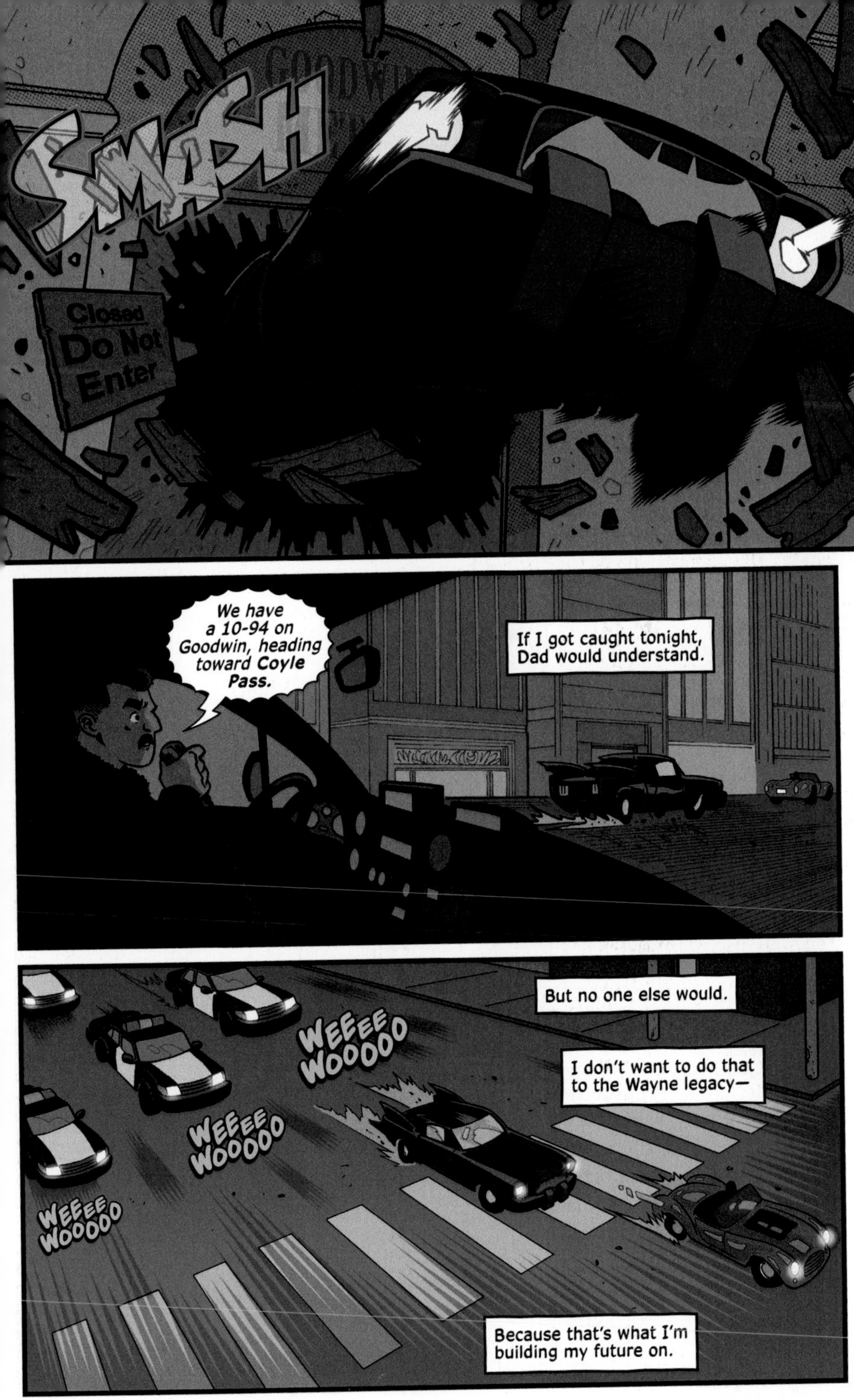
SMASH
Closed
Do Not Enter
We have a 10-94 on Goodwin, heading toward Coyle Pass.
If I got caught tonight, Dad would understand.
But no one else would.
WEEEE WOOOOO
I don't want to do that to the Wayne legacy—
WEEEE WOOOOO
WEEEE WOOOOO
Because that's what I'm building my future on.

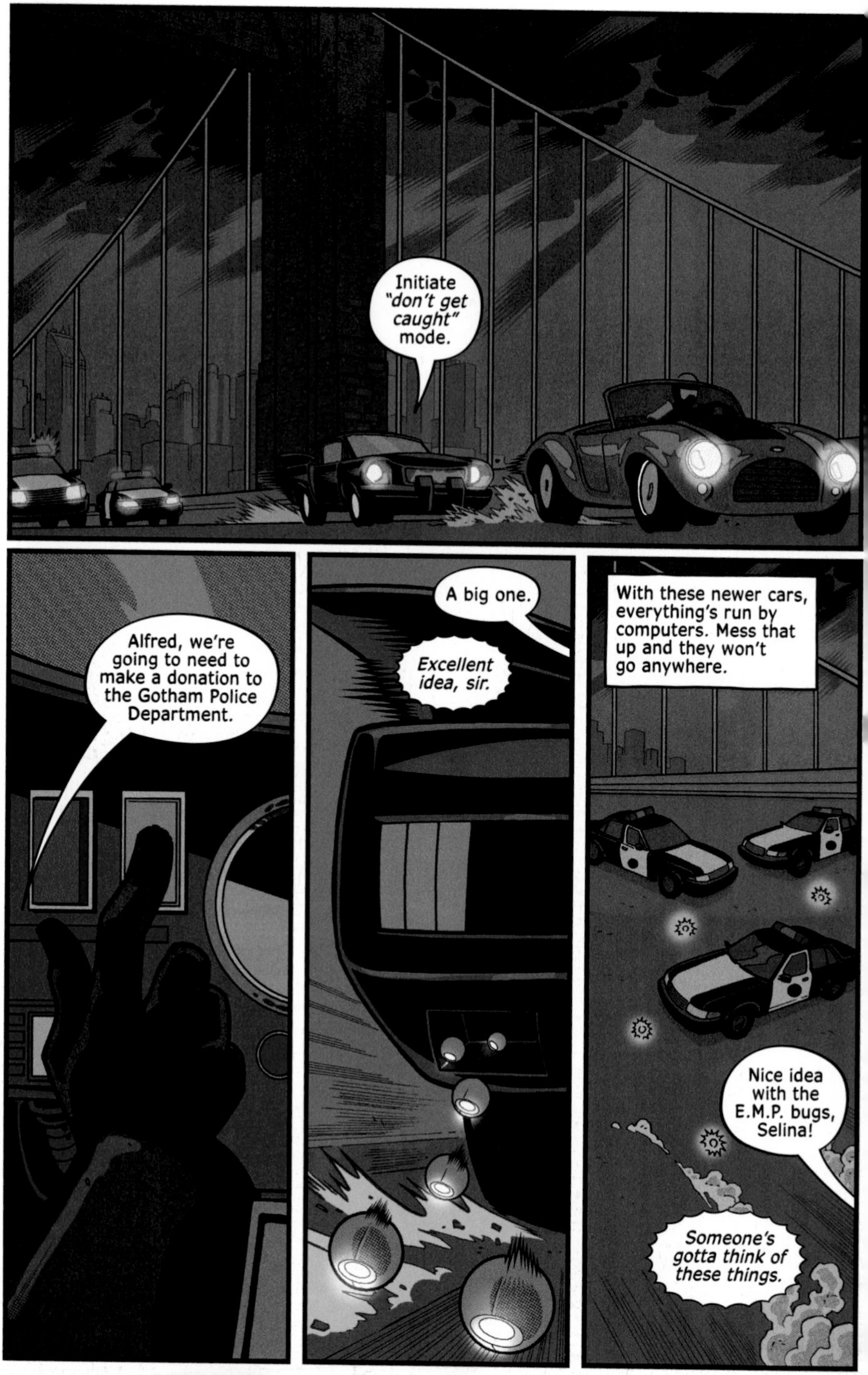
Initiate "don't get caught" mode.
Alfred, we're going to need to make a donation to the Gotham Police Department.
A big one.
Excellent idea, sir.
With these newer cars, everything's run by computers. Mess that up and they won't go anywhere.
Nice idea with the E.M.P. bugs, Selina!
Someone's gotta think of these things.

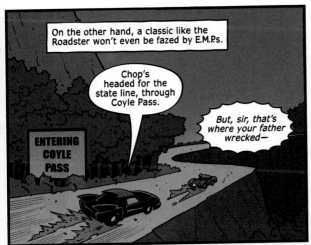

On the other hand, a classic like the Roadster won't even be fazed by E.M.P.s.

Chop's headed for the state line, through Coyle Pass.

But, sir, that's where your father wrecked—

ENTERING COYLE PASS

Good thing I'm *not* my dad then.

VOOSH!

Let's see how well you tow, Chop.

THKK

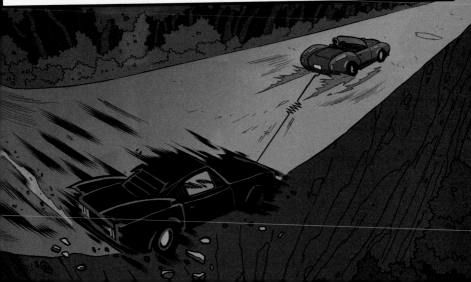

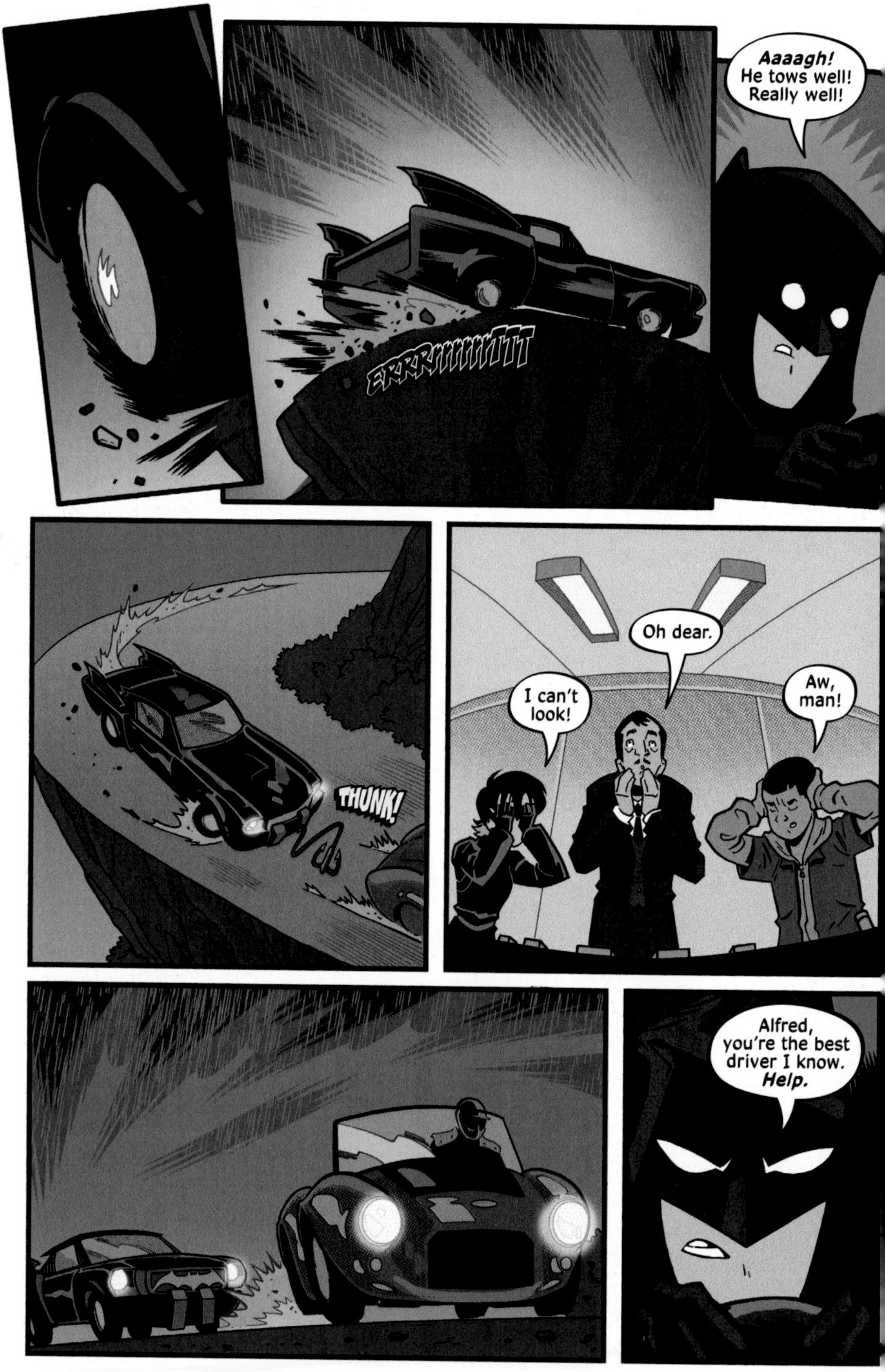
ERRRrrrrrrrTTT
Aaaagh! He tows well! Really well!
THUNK!
I can't look!
Oh dear.
Aw, man!
Alfred, you're the best driver I know. ***Help.***

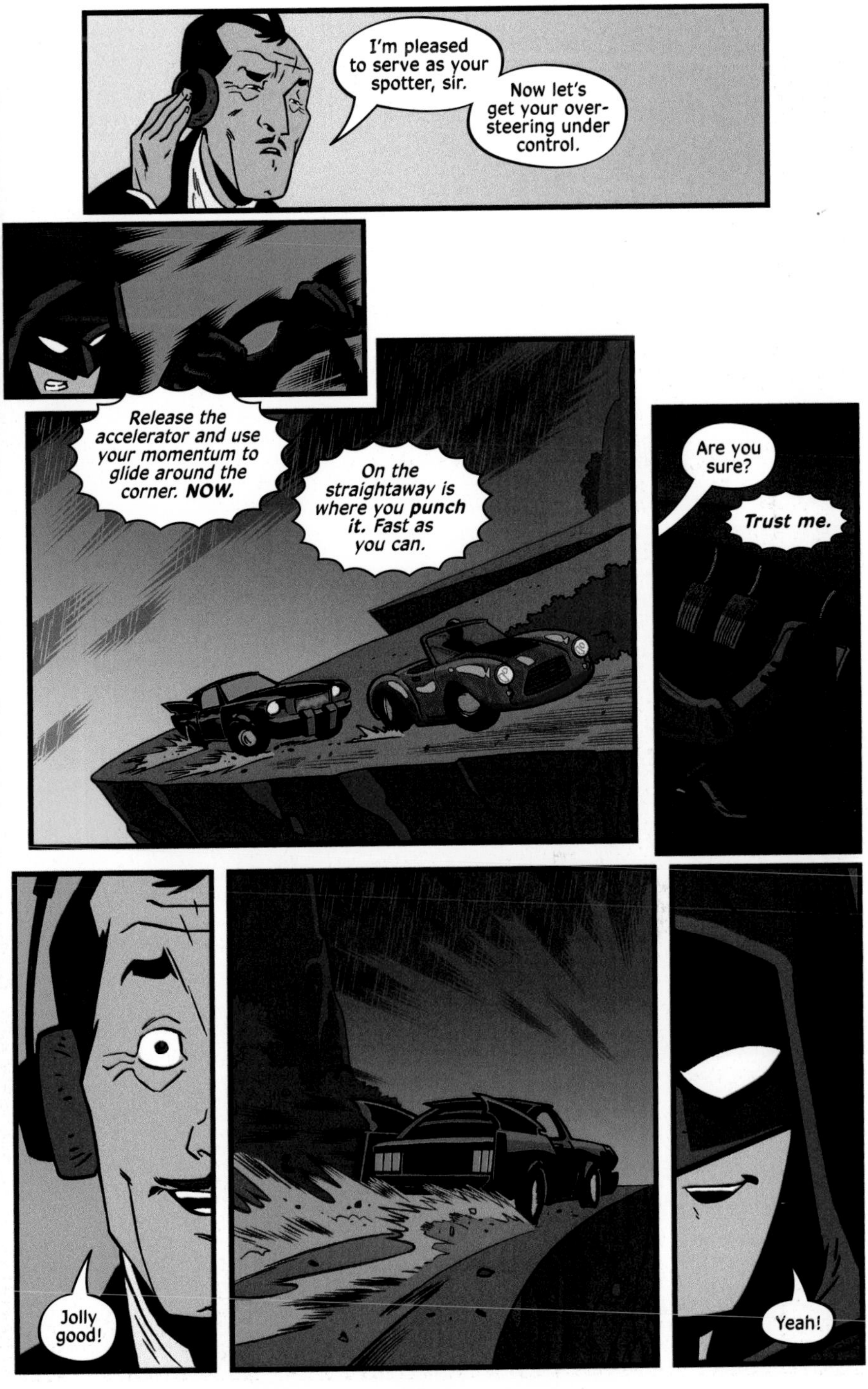
I'm pleased to serve as your spotter, sir.
Now let's get your over-steering under control.
Release the accelerator and use your momentum to glide around the corner. **NOW.**
On the straightaway is where you **punch it.** Fast as you can.
Are you sure?
Trust me.
Jolly good!
Yeah!

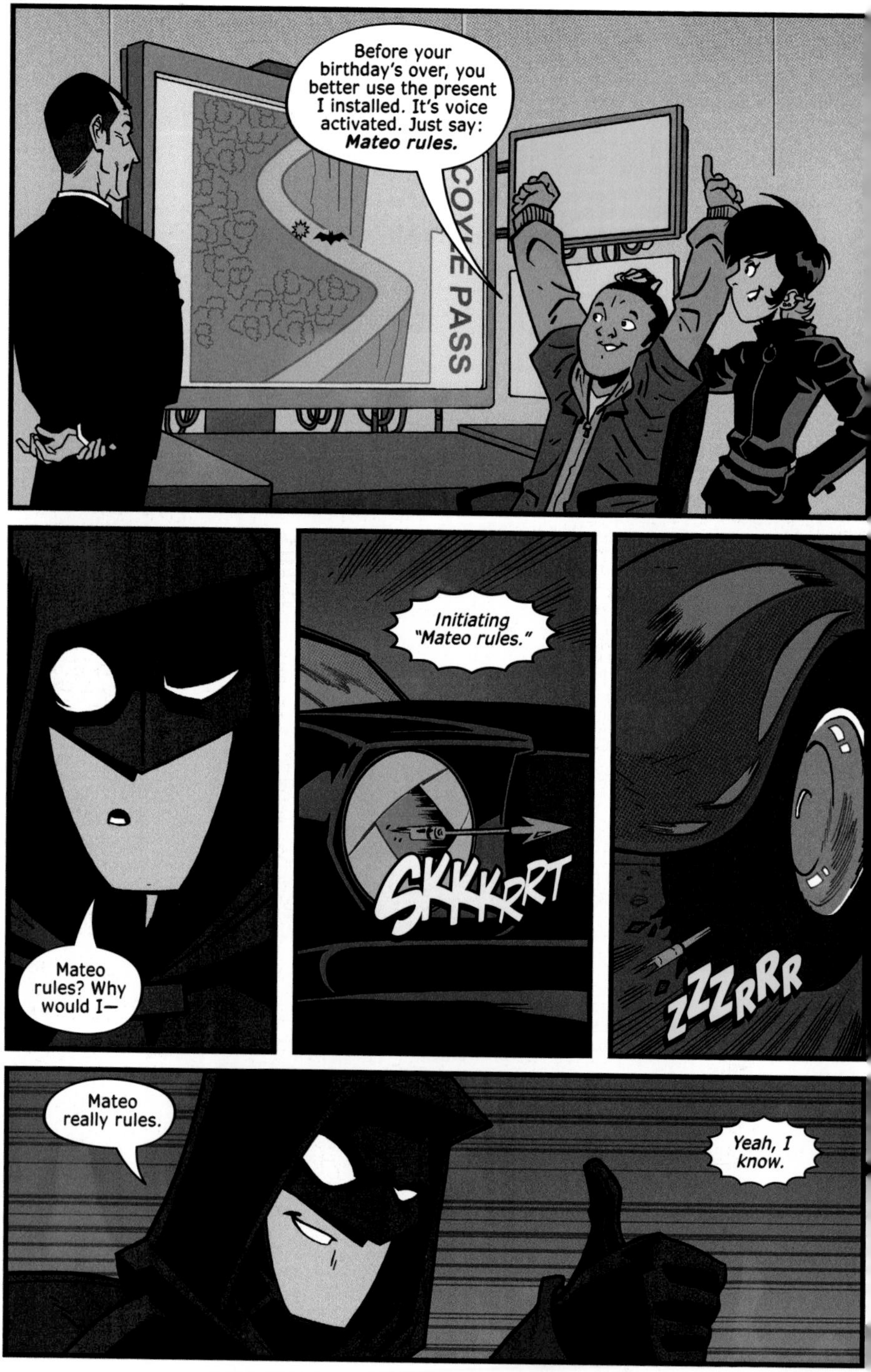
Before your birthday's over, you better use the present I installed. It's voice activated. Just say: *Mateo rules.*
COYOTE PASS
Mateo rules? Why would I—
Initiating "Mateo rules."
SKKKRRT
ZZZRRR
Mateo really rules.
Yeah, I know.

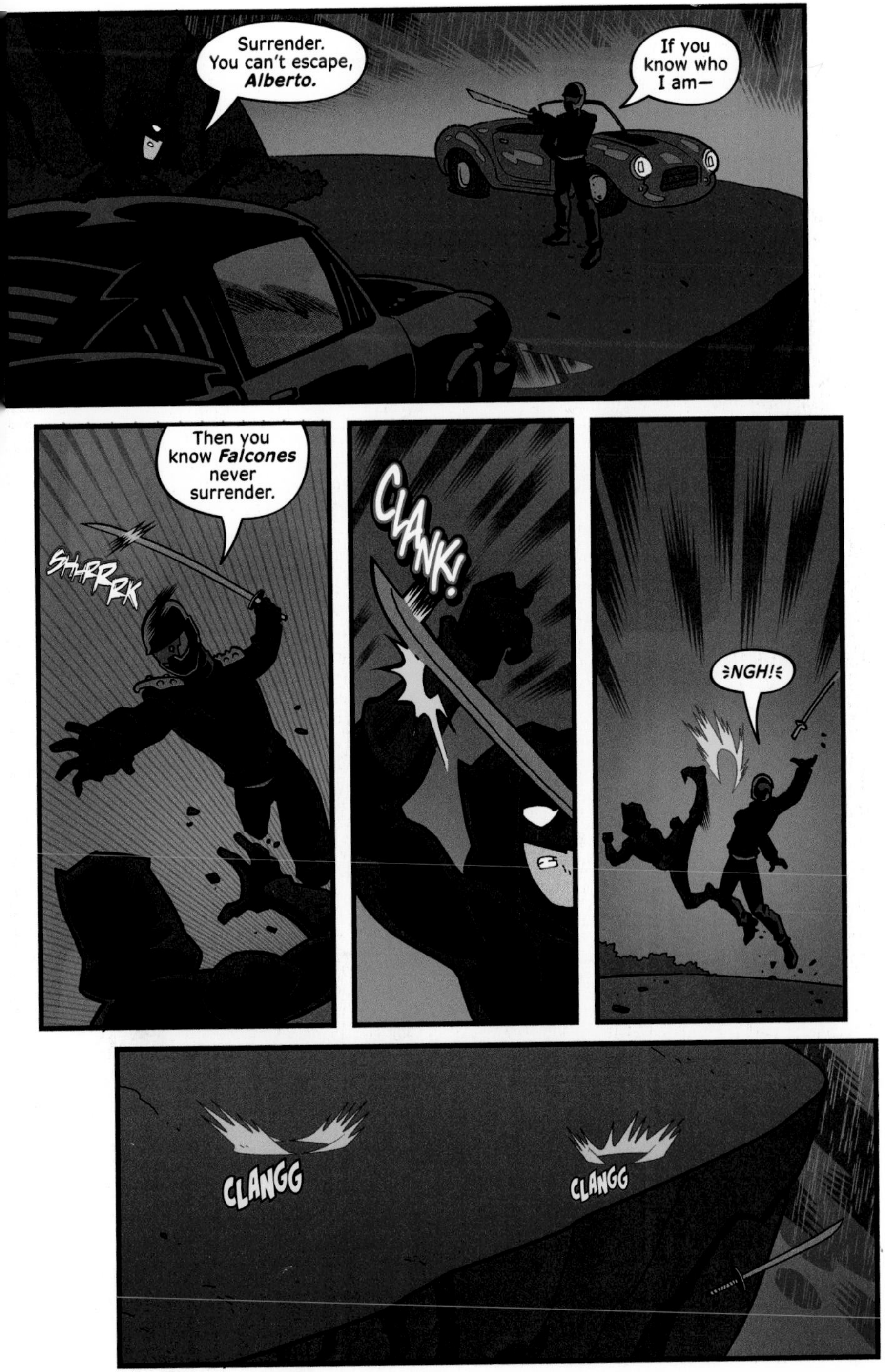
Surrender. You can't escape, *Alberto.*
If you know who I am—
Then you know *Falcones* never surrender.
SHHRRRK
CLANK!
NGH!
CLANGG
CLANGG

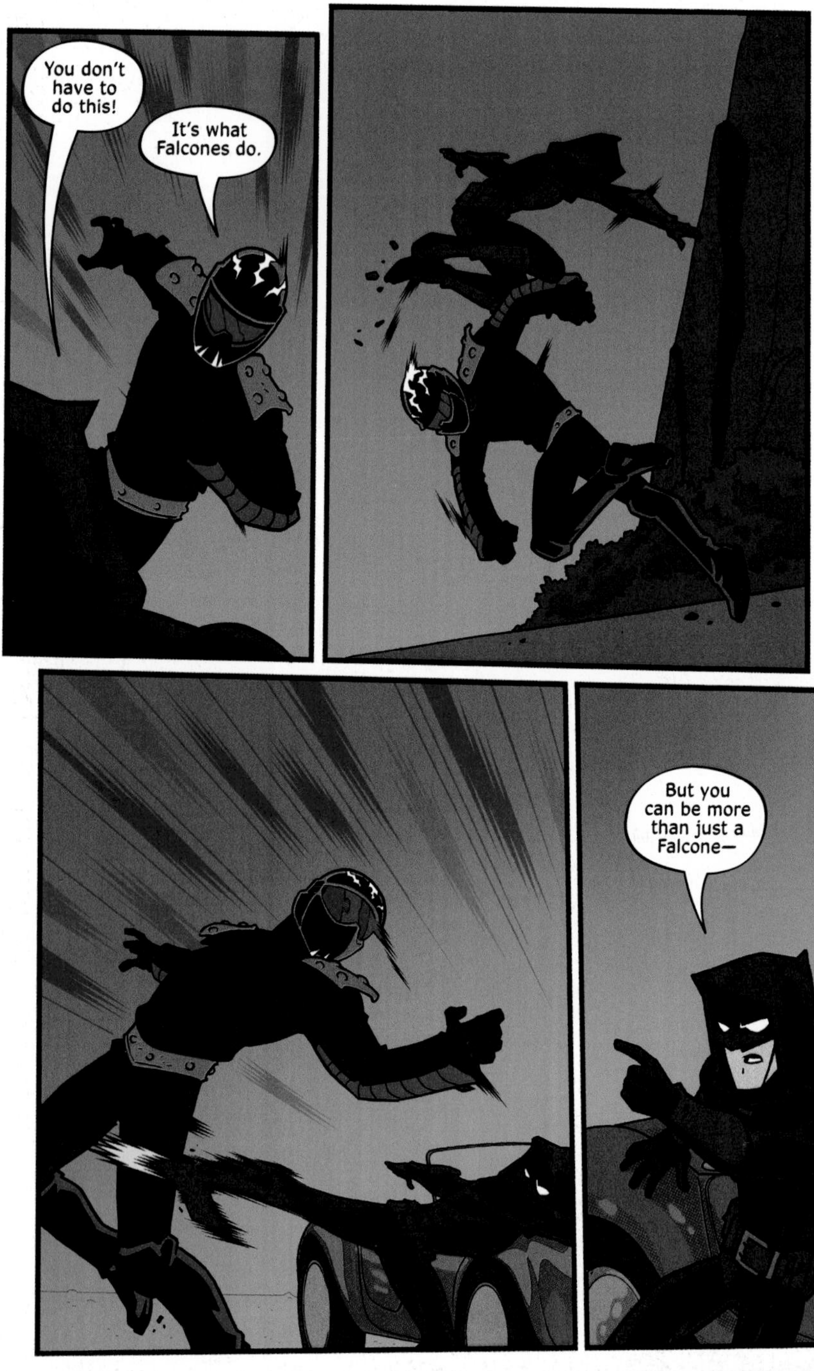
You don't have to do this!
It's what Falcones do.
But you can be more than just a Falcone—

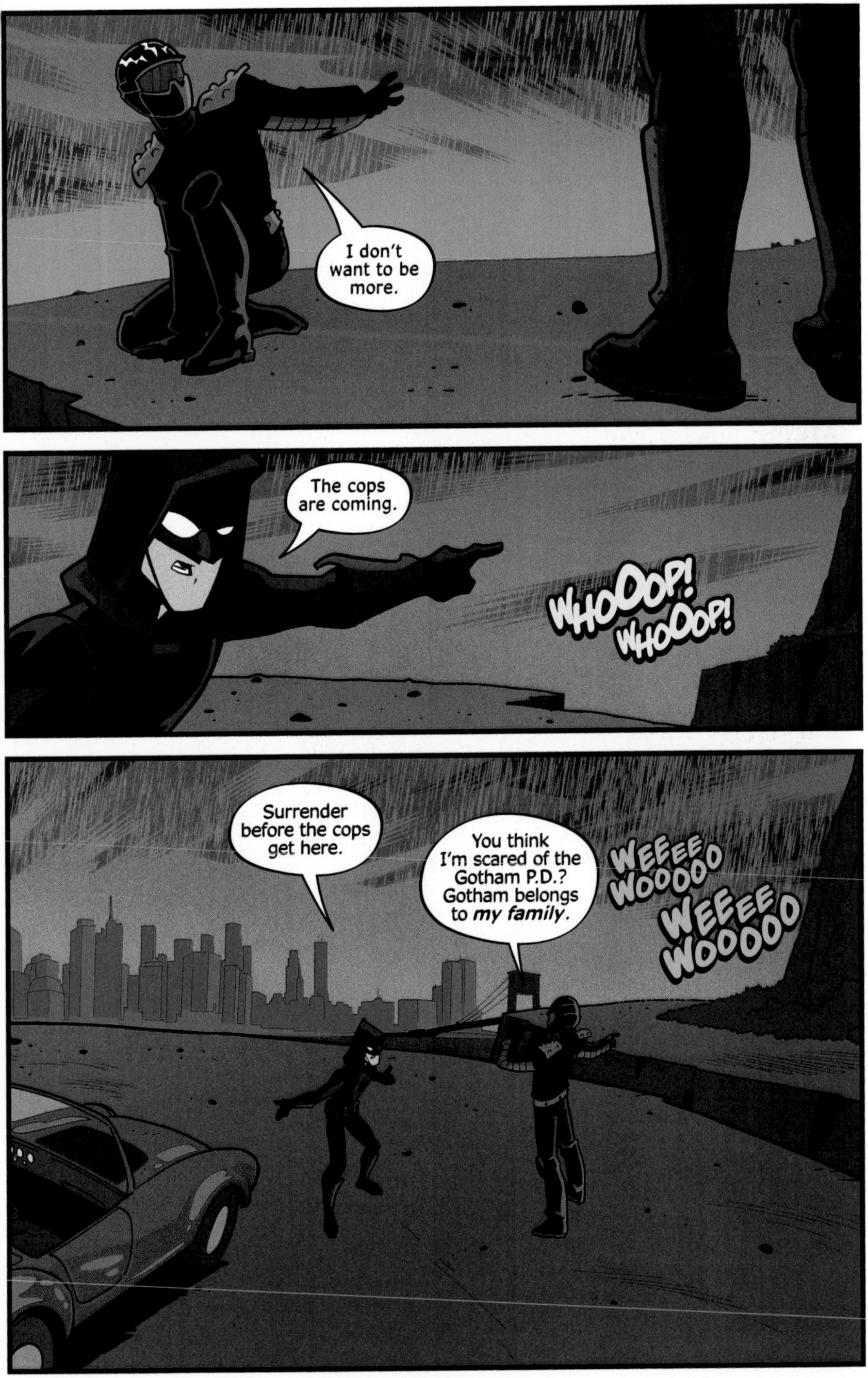
I don't want to be more.
The cops are coming.
WHOOOP! WHOOOP!
Surrender before the cops get here.
You think I'm scared of the Gotham P.D.? Gotham belongs to *my family*.
WEEEE WOOOOO WEEEE WOOOOO

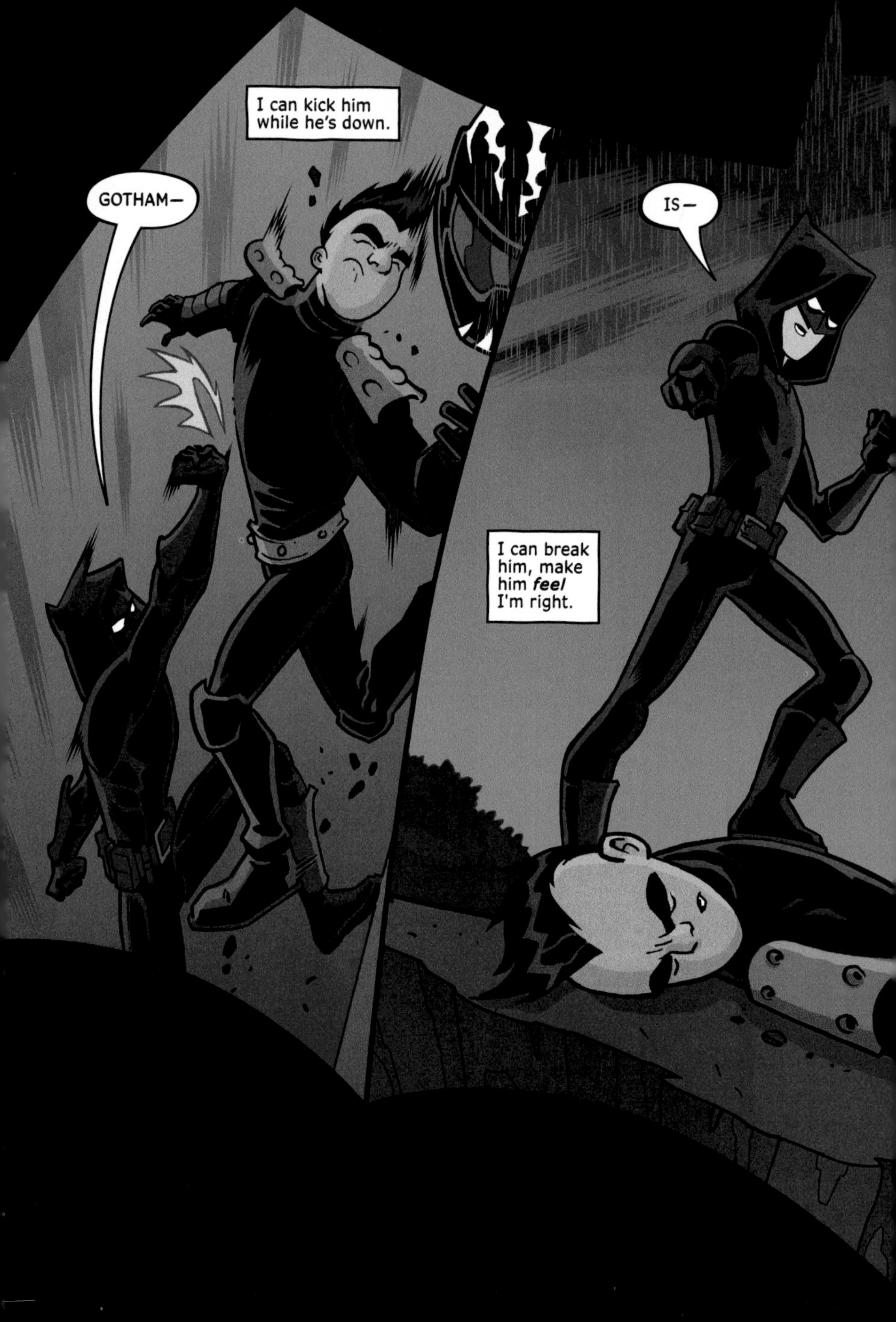
I can kick him while he's down.
GOTHAM—
IS—
I can break him, make him *feel* I'm right.

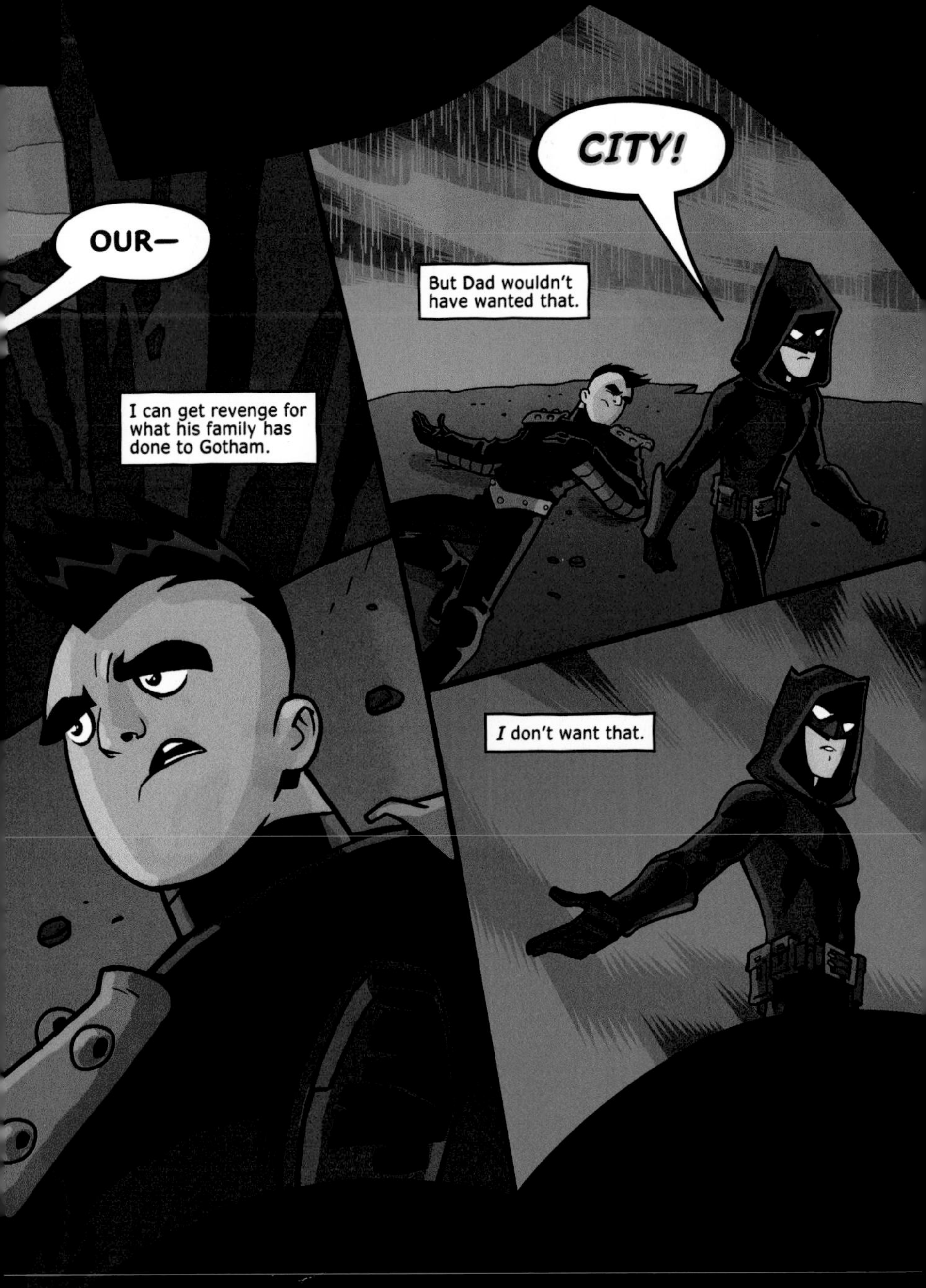
OUR—
I can get revenge for what his family has done to Gotham.
CITY!
But Dad wouldn't have wanted that.
I don't want that.

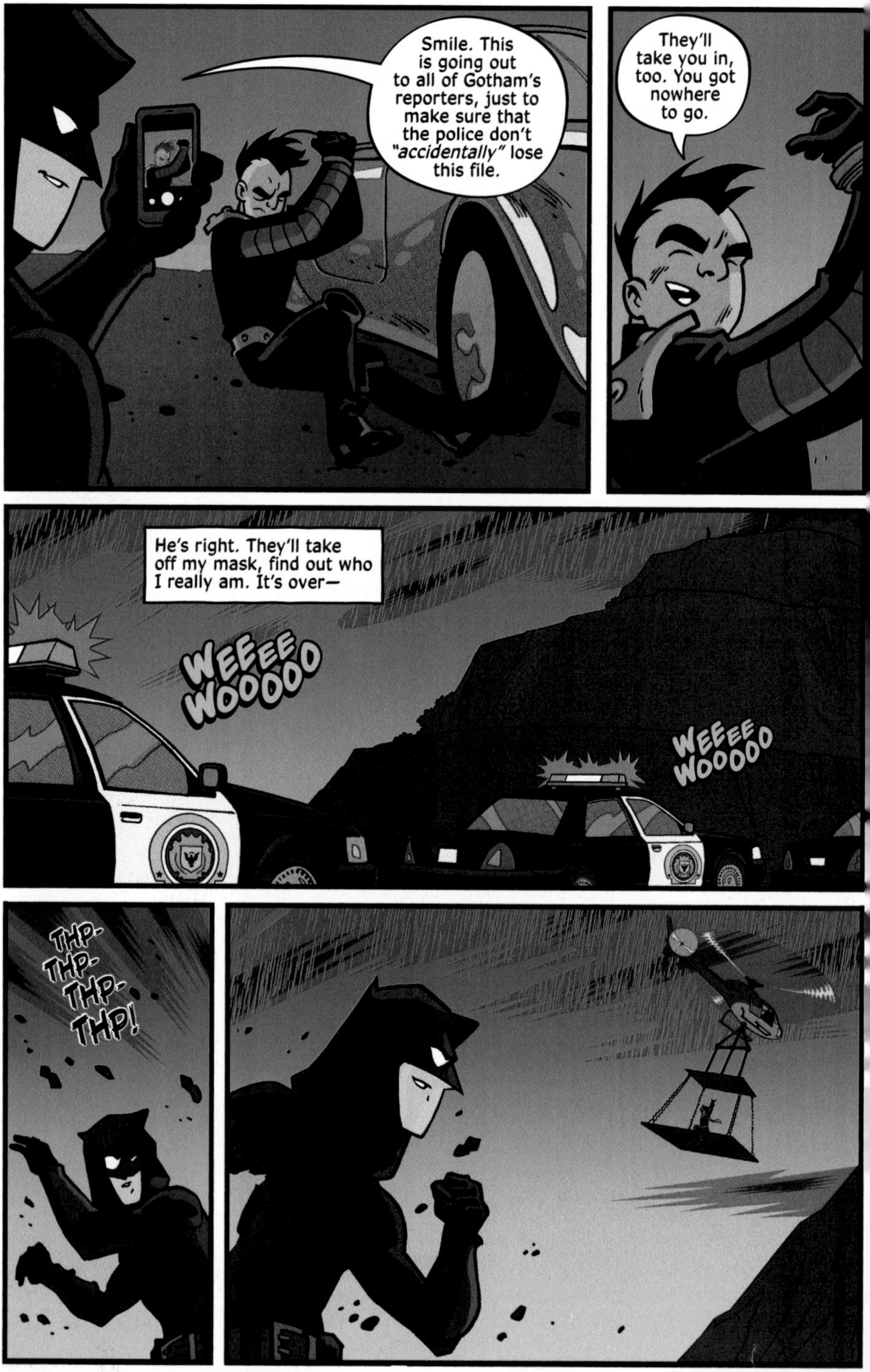
Smile. This is going out to all of Gotham's reporters, just to make sure that the police don't *"accidentally"* lose this file.
They'll take you in, too. You got nowhere to go.
He's right. They'll take off my mask, find out who I really am. It's over—
WEEEEE WOOOOO
WEEEEE WOOOOO
THP-THP-THP-THP!

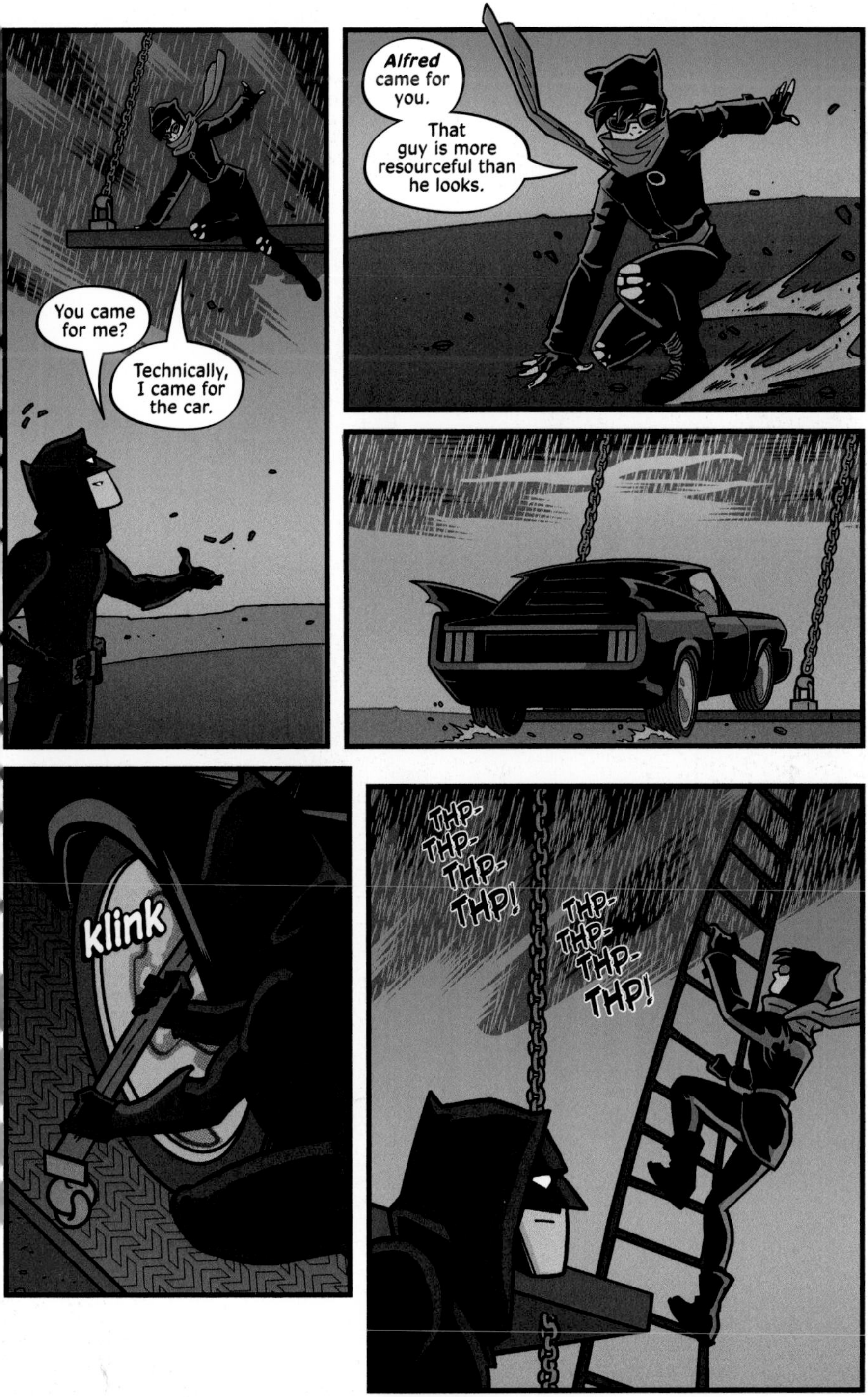

You came for me?
Technically, I came for the car.
Alfred came for you.
That guy is more resourceful than he looks.
klink
THP-THP-THP-THP!
THP-THP-THP-THP!

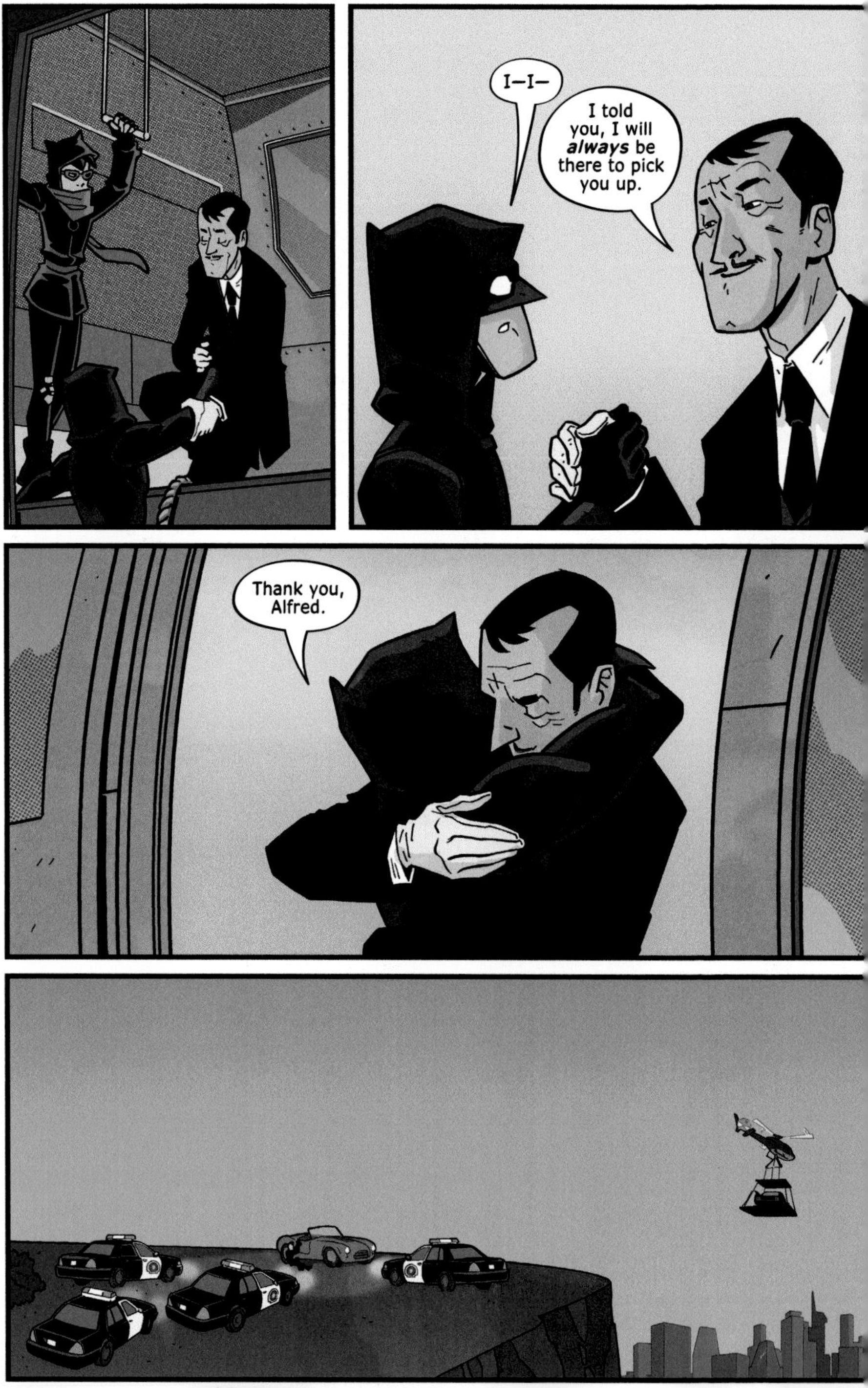
I—I—
I told you, I will *always* be there to pick you up.
Thank you, Alfred.

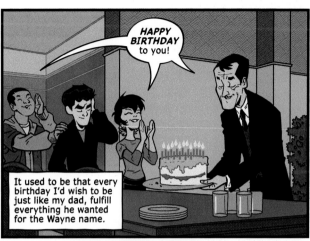

HAPPY BIRTHDAY to you!

It used to be that every birthday I'd wish to be just like my dad, fulfill everything he wanted for the Wayne name.

Master Mateo, while your uncle is uncooperative, you are welcome to stay with us.

Yeah!

I got you something.

For the last eight birthdays, I'd wish to solve my parents' murders, prove it was something more—

From Falcone's files. They amped up security since last time, but the Cat always lands on her feet.

The Falcones had nothing to do with the murder. For once, the Falcones are *innocent*.

But your *legacy* can't meet your *destiny* when you're holding onto the past.

So, who's the next suspect? What do we do now?

I let it go.

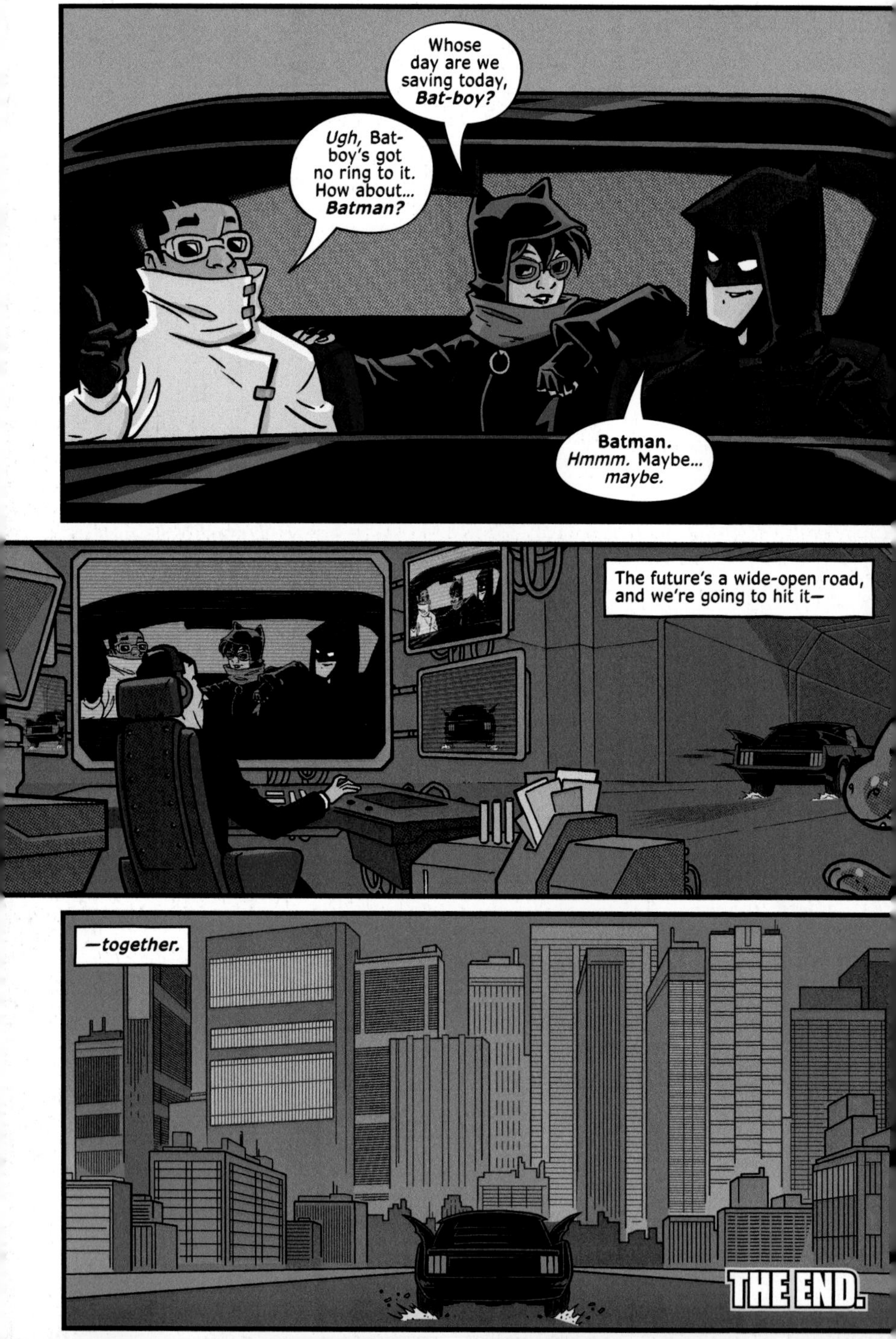
Whose day are we saving today, *Bat-boy?*
Ugh, Bat-boy's got no ring to it. How about... *Batman?*
Batman. *Hmmm.* Maybe... *maybe.*
The future's a wide-open road, and we're going to hit it—
—together.
THE END.

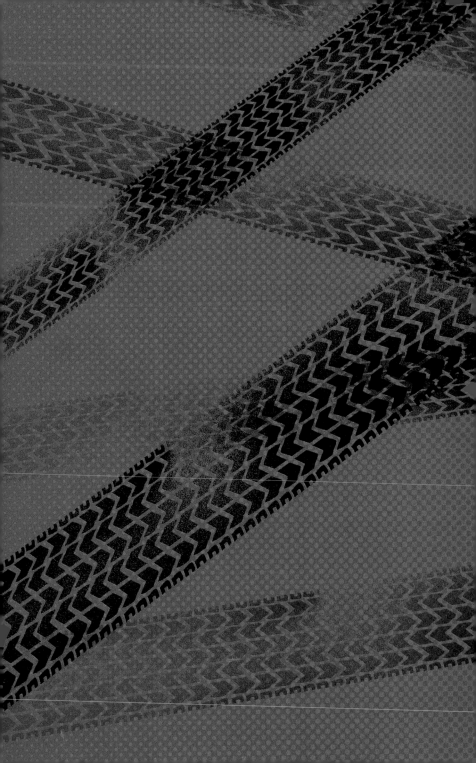

Shea Fontana

Shea Fontana is a writer for film, television, and graphic novels. Her credits include *DC Super Hero Girls* animated shorts, TV specials, movies, and graphic novels, as well as *Strawberry Shortcake, Polly Pocket, Doc McStuffins, The 7D, Whisker Haven Tales with the Palace Pets*, two *Disney on Ice* shows, and the feature film *Crowning Jules*. She has also written for top comics titles including *Justice League* and *Wonder Woman*. She lives in sunny Los Angeles where she enjoys hiking, aerial dance, and snuggling her puppies.

Marcelo DiChiara

Brazilian comics artist Marcelo DiChiara began his
career doing illustrations for French publisher Semic.
In the United States, he has worked for Image
Comics and Marvel Comics on *Iron Man and Power
Pack*, *Marvel Adventures: Super Heroes*, and *Marvel
Super Hero Squad*. Since 2014, he has worked
for DC Comics as an artist on *Smallville*, *DC
Comics Bombshells*, *DC Super Hero Girls*, and
Teen Titans Go!

WITH THE HELP OF YOUR FRIENDS, FAILURE IS NOT AN OPTION.

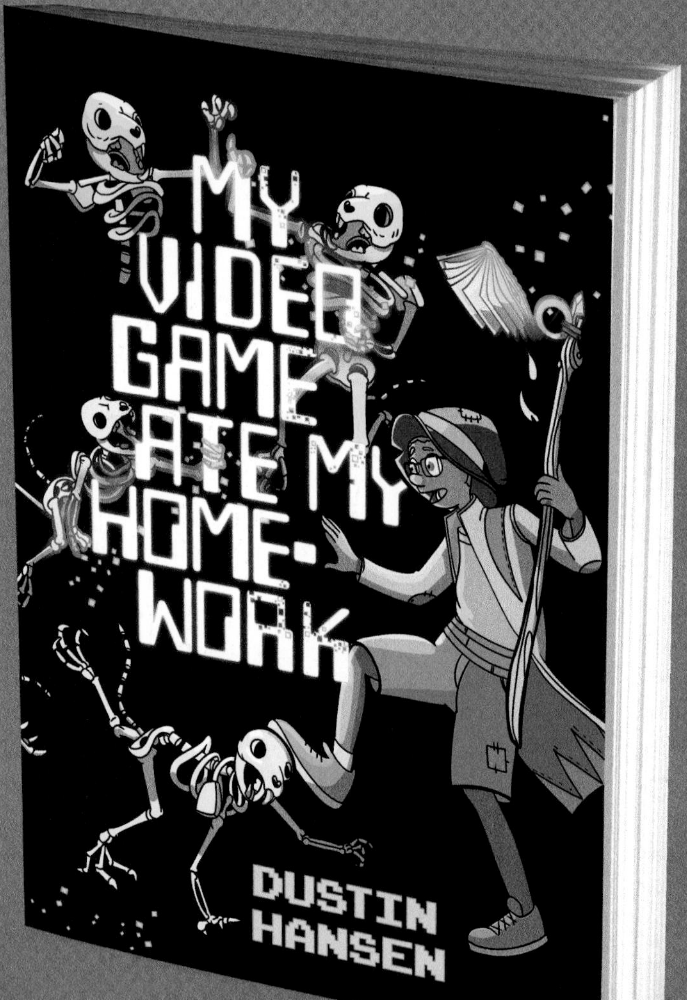
MY VIDEO GAME ATE MY HOME-WORK
DUSTIN HANSEN

When Dewey Jenkins's science project gets sucked
into a new state-of-the-art virtual reality video game console,
he and his friends must journey into the video game to get it back!

The following pages are a sneak peek of *My Video Game Ate My Homework*,
written and illustrated by Dustin Hansen!

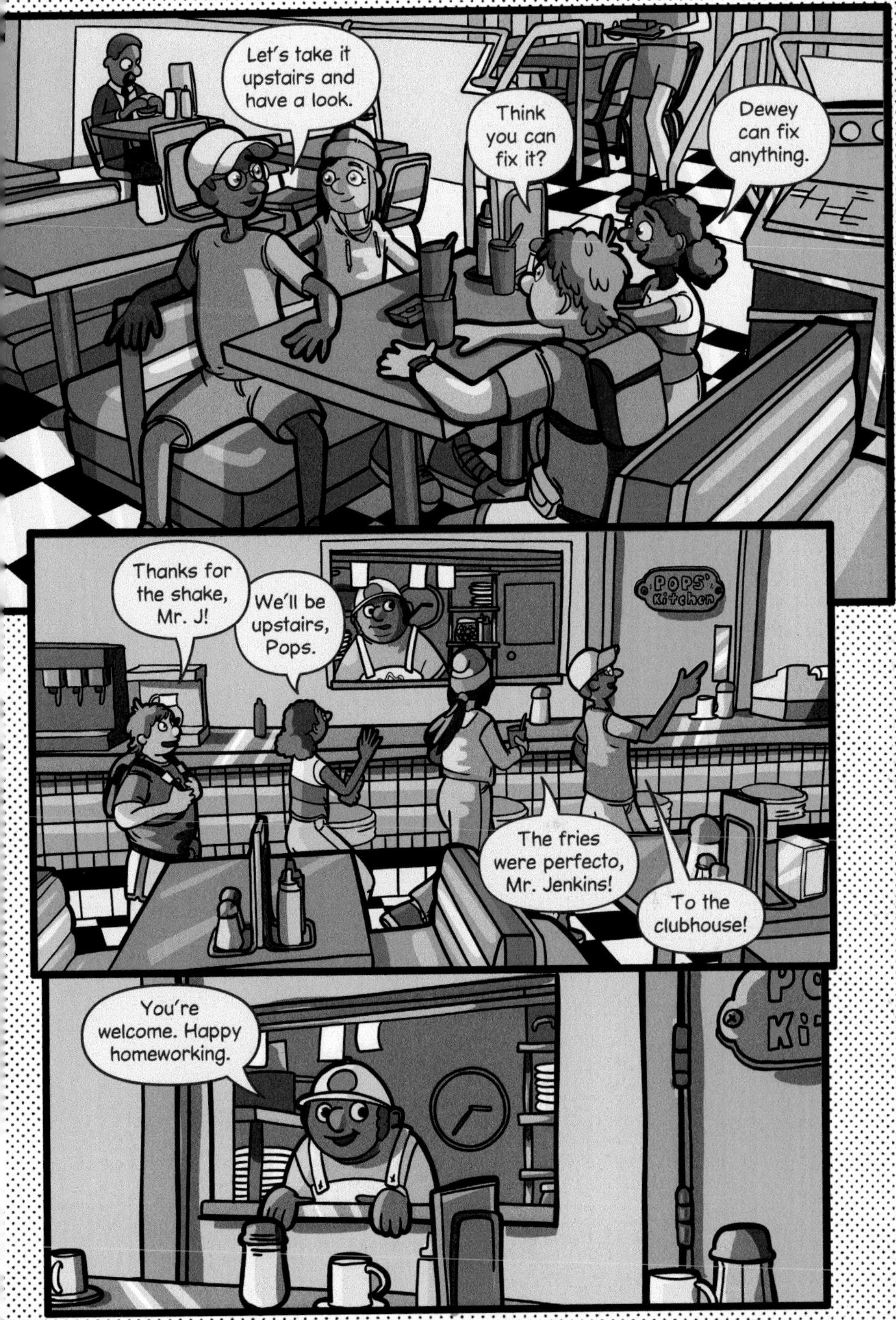
Let's take it upstairs and have a look.
Think you can fix it?
Dewey can fix anything.
Thanks for the shake, Mr. J!
We'll be upstairs, Pops.
POPS' Kitchen
The fries were perfecto, Mr. Jenkins!
To the clubhouse!
You're welcome. Happy homeworking.

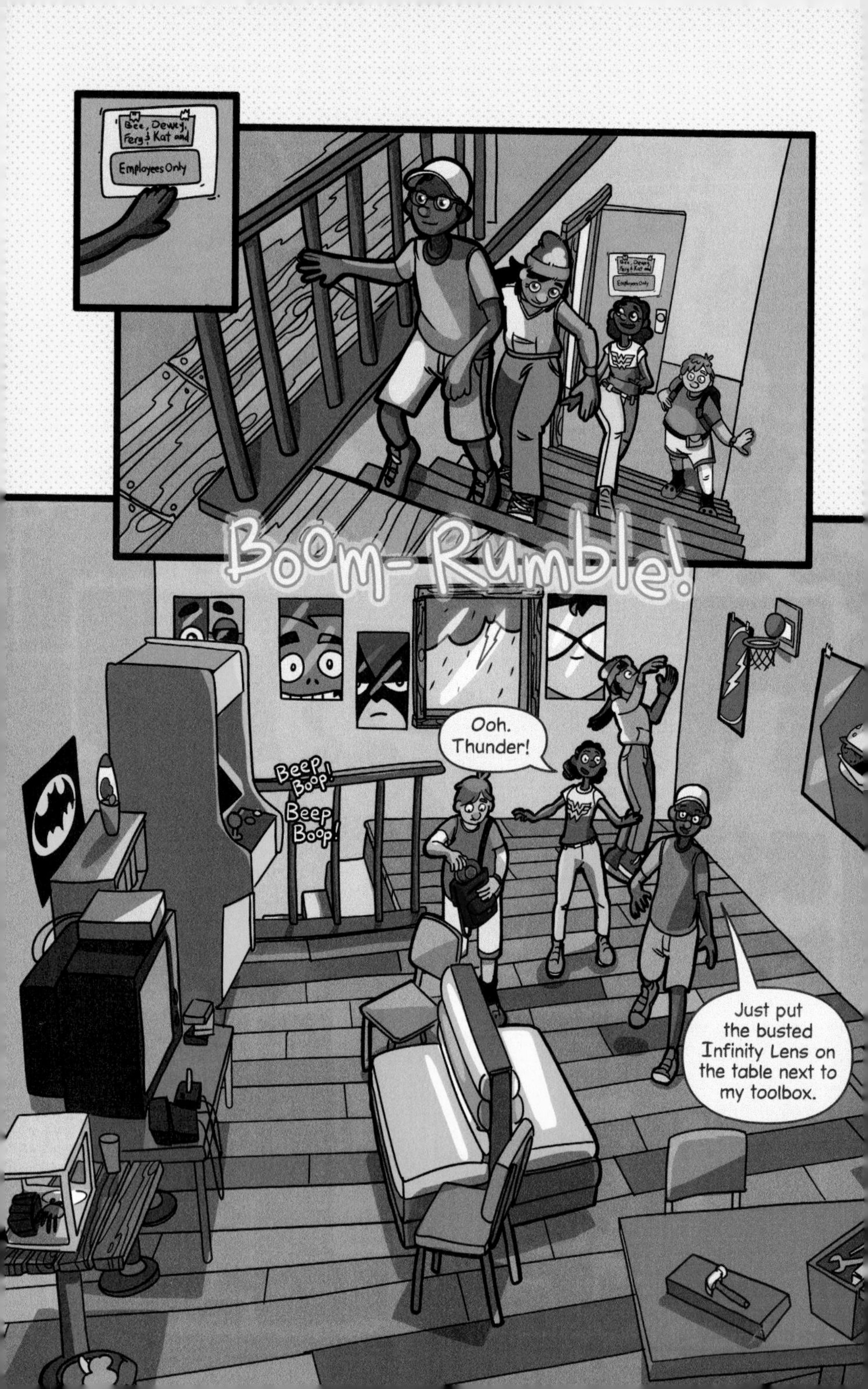
Bee, Dewey, Ferg & Kat and
Employees Only
Boom-Rumble!
Ooh. Thunder!
Beep Boop!
Beep Boop!
Just put the busted Infinity Lens on the table next to my toolbox.

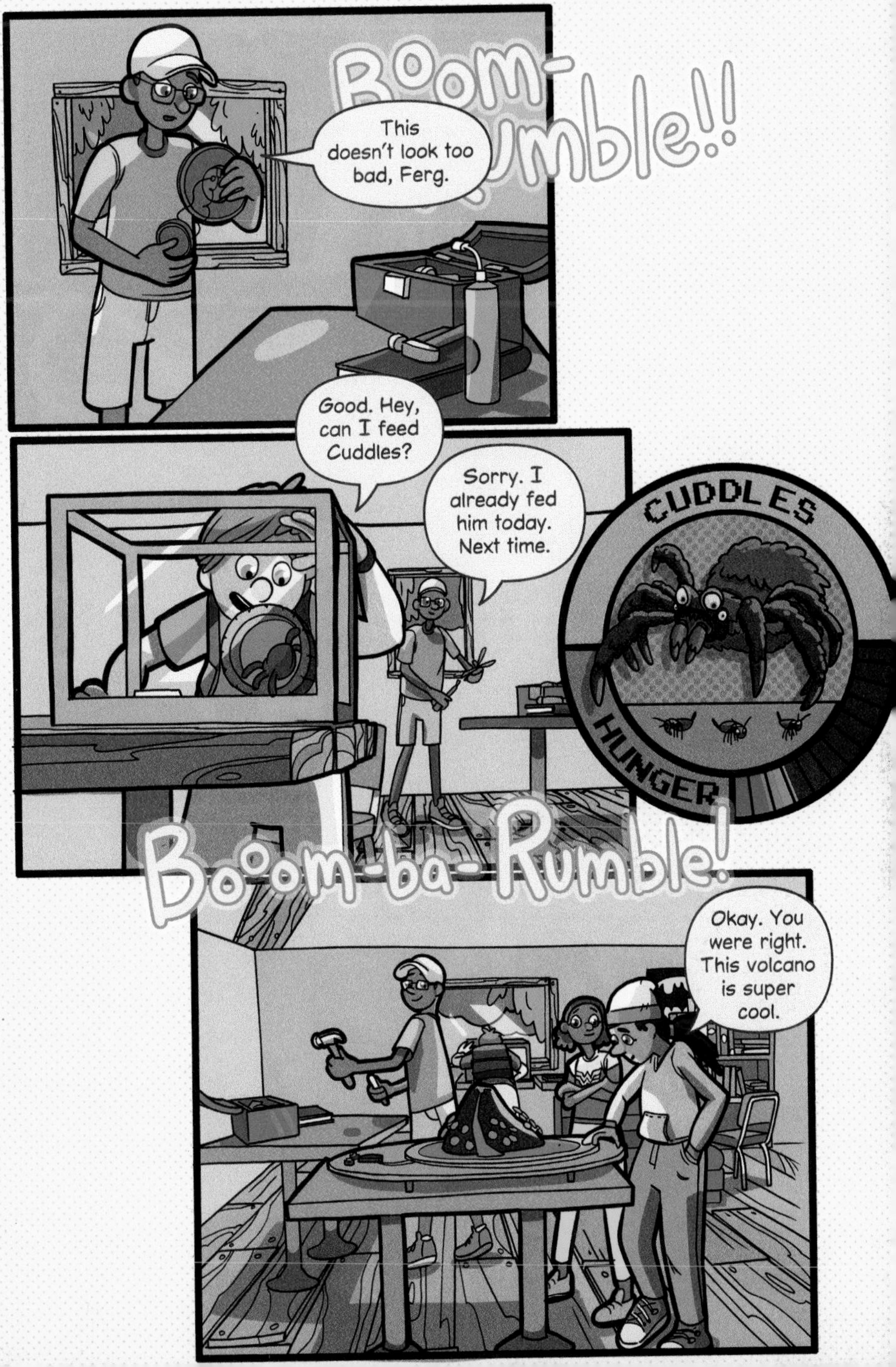
Boom-Rumble!!
This doesn't look too bad, Ferg.
Good. Hey, can I feed Cuddles?
Sorry. I already fed him today. Next time.
CUDDLES
HUNGER
Booom-ba-Rumble!
Okay. You were right. This volcano is super cool.

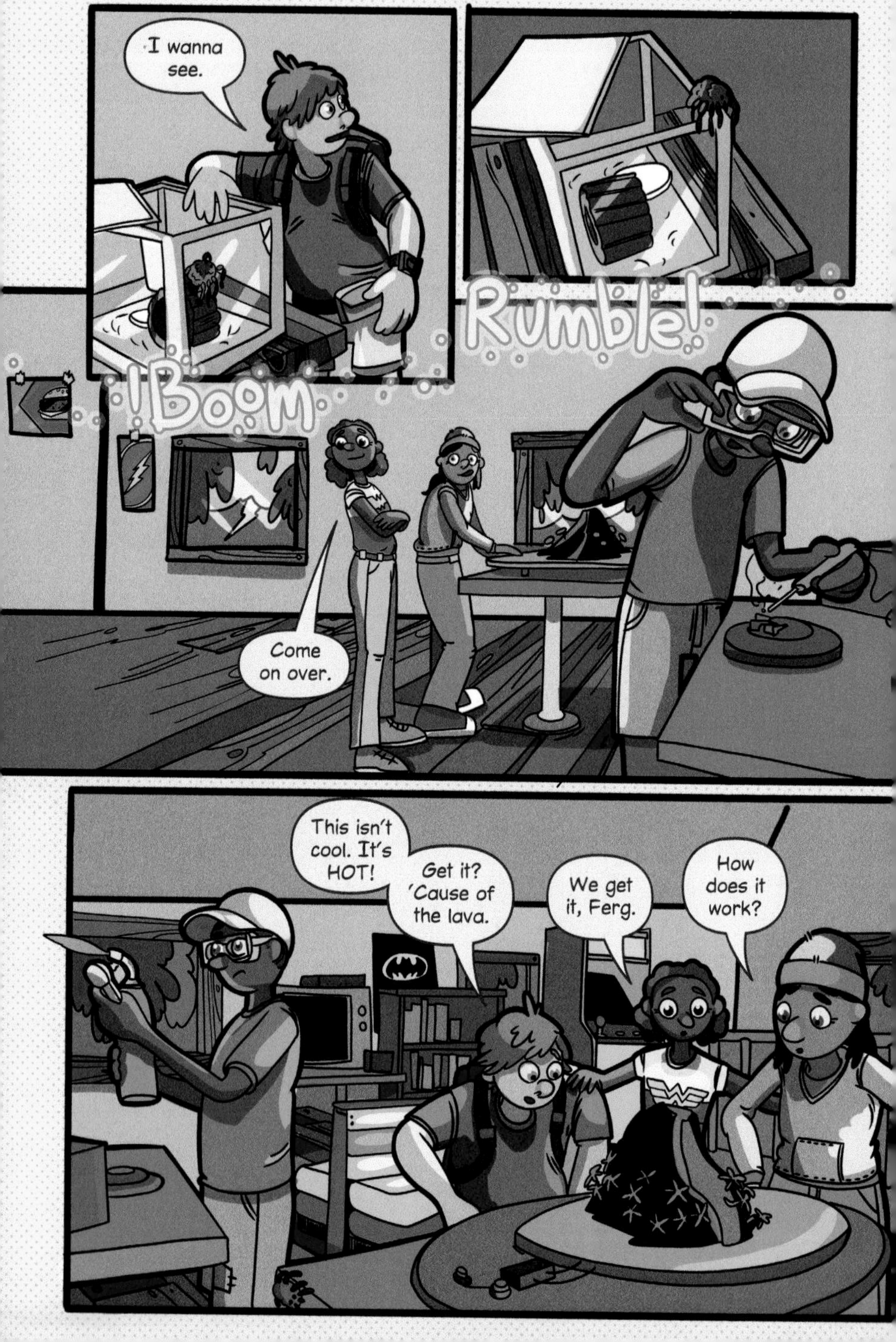
I wanna see.
Rumble!
Boom!
Come on over.
This isn't cool. It's HOT!
Get it? 'Cause of the lava.
We get it, Ferg.
How does it work?

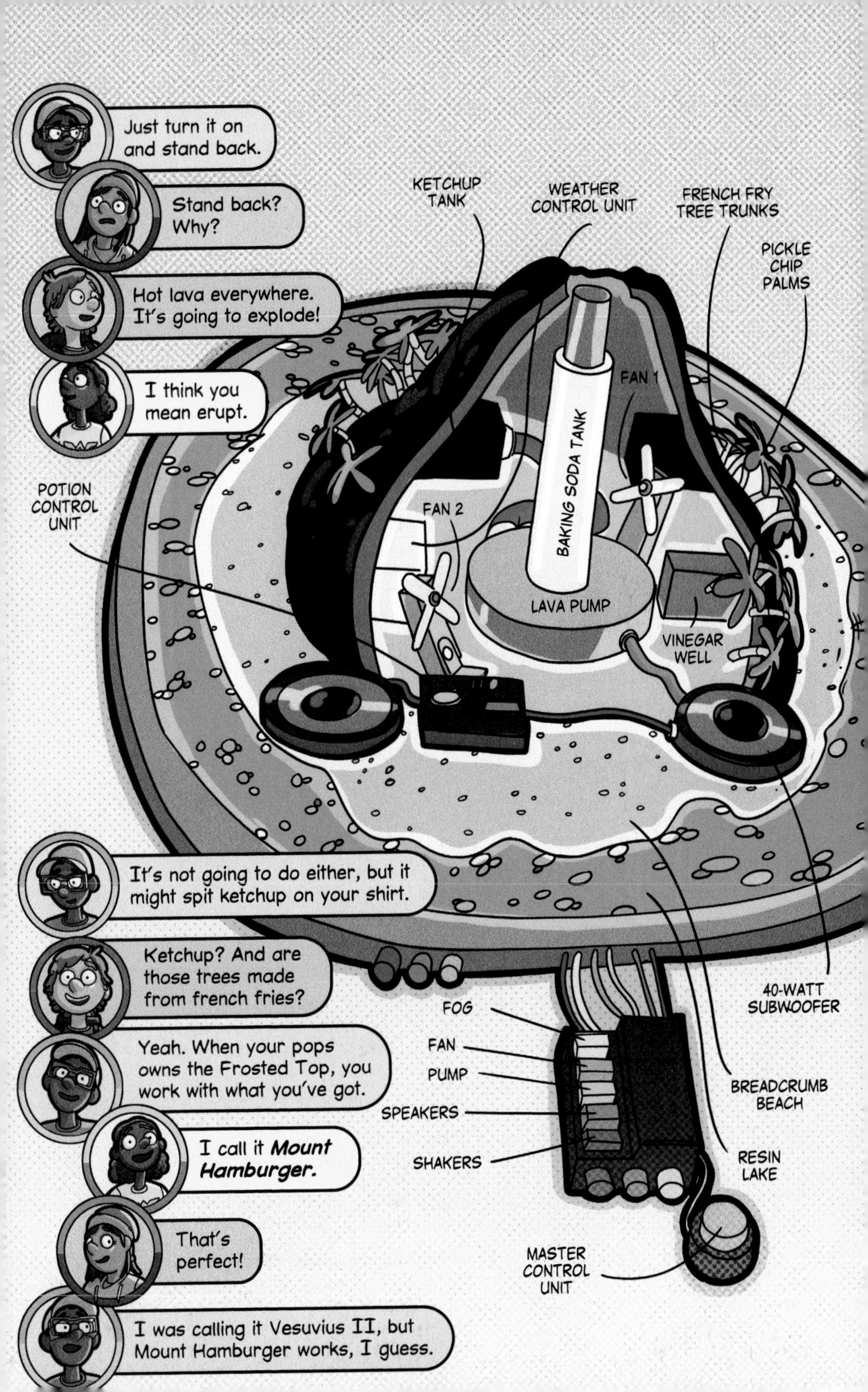
Just turn it on and stand back.
Stand back? Why?
Hot lava everywhere. It's going to explode!
I think you mean erupt.
KETCHUP TANK
WEATHER CONTROL UNIT
FRENCH FRY TREE TRUNKS
PICKLE CHIP PALMS
FAN 1
BAKING SODA TANK
FAN 2
POTION CONTROL UNIT
LAVA PUMP
VINEGAR WELL
It's not going to do either, but it might spit ketchup on your shirt.
Ketchup? And are those trees made from french fries?
Yeah. When your pops owns the Frosted Top, you work with what you've got.
I call it **Mount Hamburger.**
That's perfect!
I was calling it Vesuvius II, but Mount Hamburger works, I guess.
FOG
FAN
PUMP
SPEAKERS
SHAKERS
40-WATT SUBWOOFER
BREADCRUMB BEACH
RESIN LAKE
MASTER CONTROL UNIT

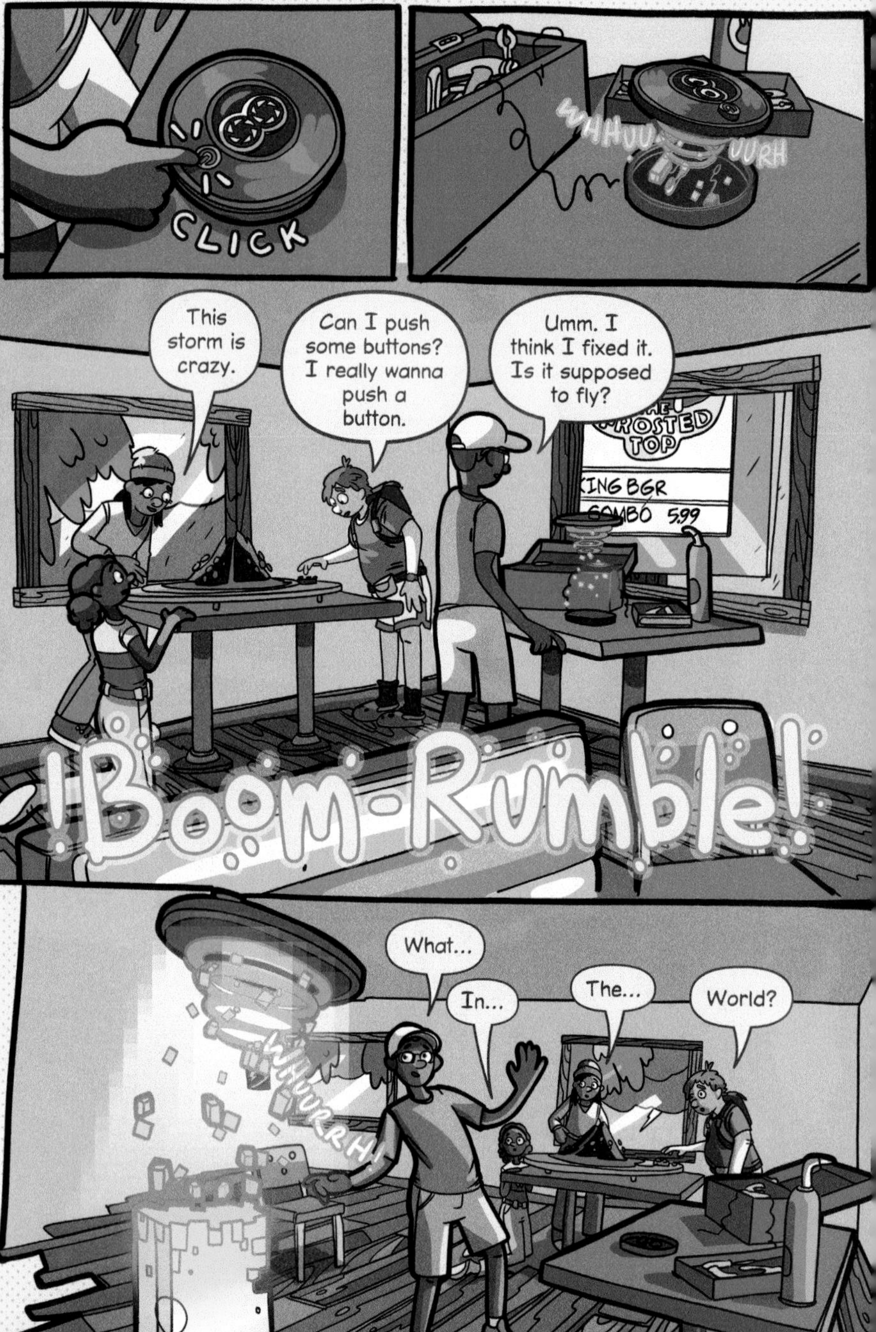
CLICK
WHHUU URRH
This storm is crazy.
Can I push some buttons? I really wanna push a button.
Umm. I think I fixed it. Is it supposed to fly?
THE FROSTED TOP
KING BGR
COMBO 5.99
!Boom-Rumble!
What...
In...
The...
World?
WHHURRH!

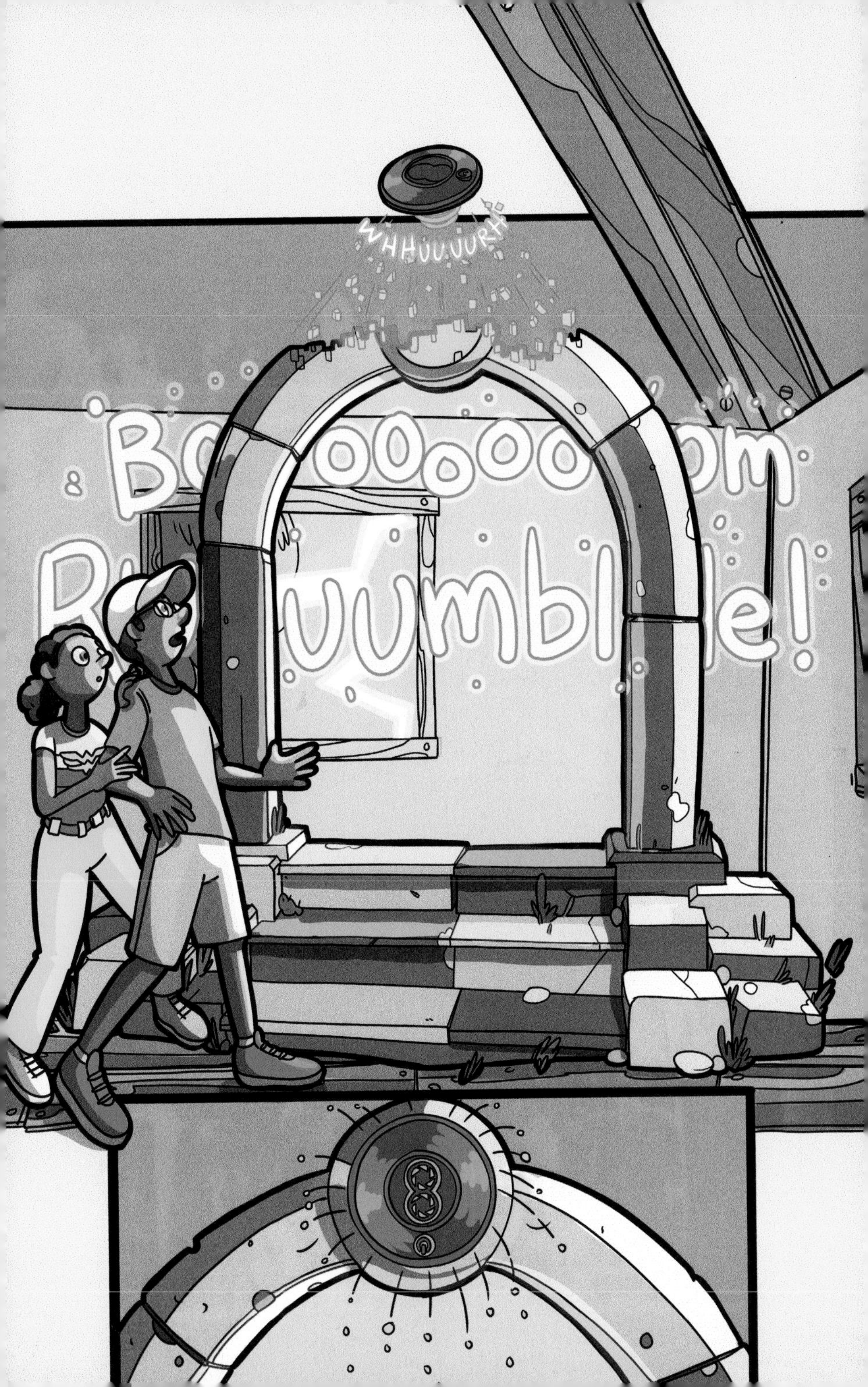
WHHUUUURH

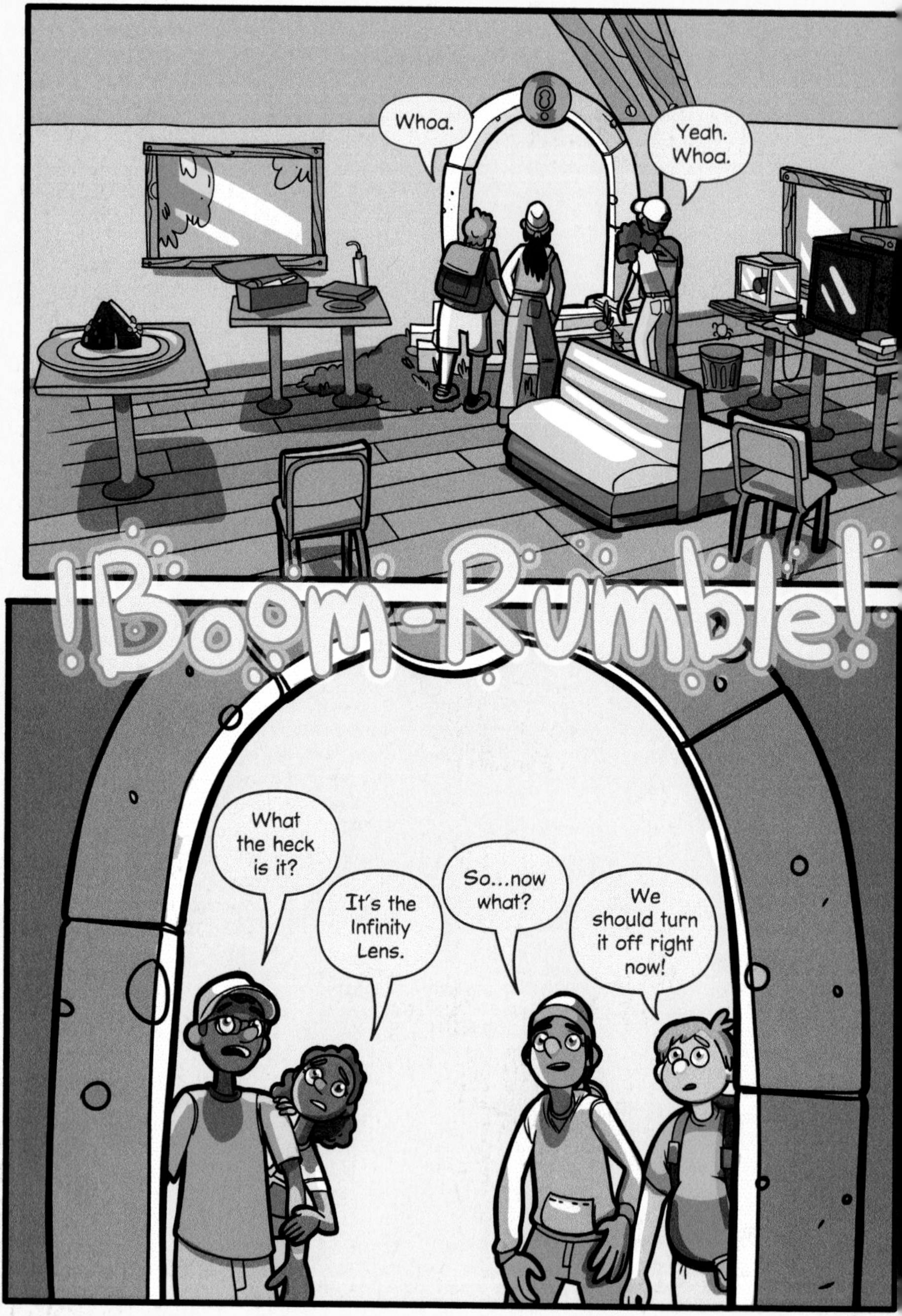
Whoa.
Yeah. Whoa.
!Boom-Rumble!
What the heck is it?
It's the Infinity Lens.
So...now what?
We should turn it off right now!

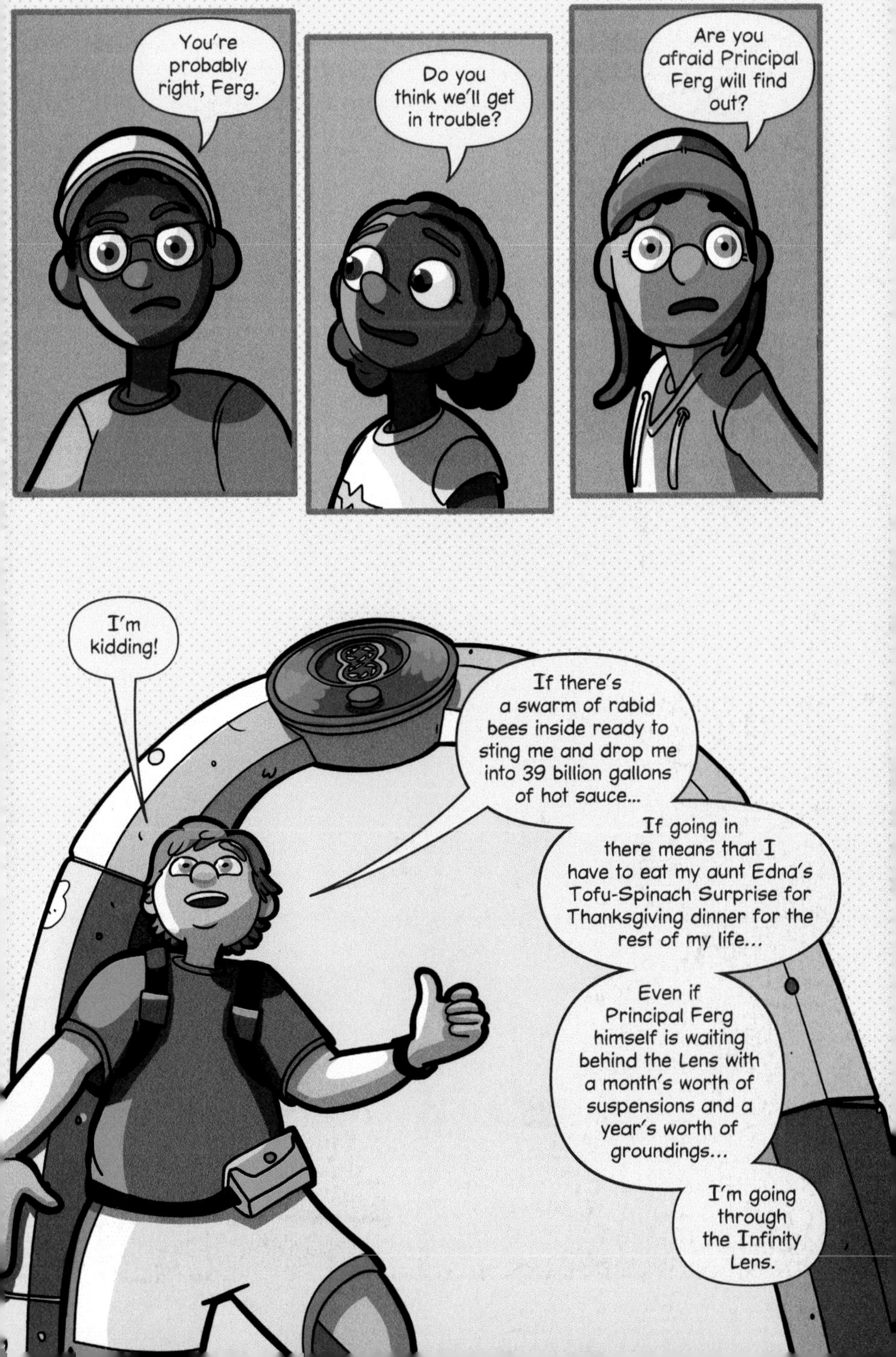
You're probably right, Ferg.
Do you think we'll get in trouble?
Are you afraid Principal Ferg will find out?
I'm kidding!
If there's a swarm of rabid bees inside ready to sting me and drop me into 39 billion gallons of hot sauce...
If going in there means that I have to eat my aunt Edna's Tofu-Spinach Surprise for Thanksgiving dinner for the rest of my life...
Even if Principal Ferg himself is waiting behind the Lens with a month's worth of suspensions and a year's worth of groundings...
I'm going through the Infinity Lens.

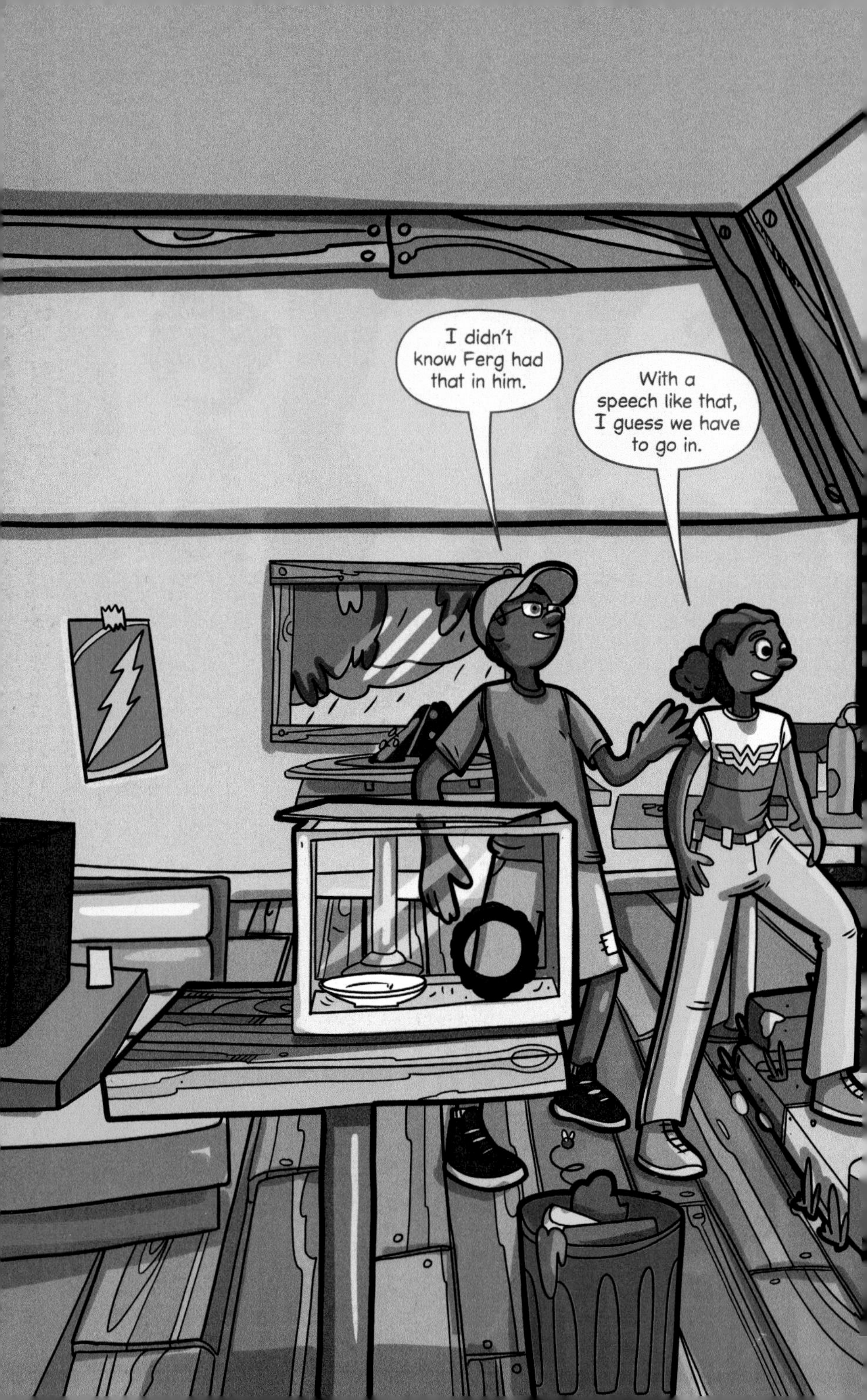
I didn't know Ferg had that in him.
With a speech like that, I guess we have to go in.